Dear Reader,

The tales of ancient Greek mythology are timeless—
filled with epic battles, heroic figures, and memorable
monsters, it's no surprise these stories continue to capture
hearts. Unfortunately, these stories are also littered with
gods abusing their powers, women being victimized, and
male heroes receiving all the glory.

One of the reasons I was so captivated by Claire
Andrews's debut novel is that she's reimagined the
character of Daphne—a victim in her original myth—as
a fierce warrior, a self-sufficient heroine who can hold her
own against the gods. *Daughter of Sparta* is a fast-paced,
action-driven adventure that sees Daphne traversing
the mythological stories we've come to know and love,
performing the heroic deeds that are traditionally credited
to men.

I knew *Daughter of Sparta* was something special
from page one and I'm thrilled to have it on the list at
JIMMY Patterson Books. I can't wait for you all to fall in
love with it, too.

James Patterson
Founder
JIMMY Patterson Books

DAUGHTER OF SPARTA

CLAIRE M. ANDREWS

JIMMY PATTERSON BOOKS
LITTLE, BROWN AND COMPANY
New York Boston London

JIMMY Patterson Books / Little, Brown and Company
Hachette Book Group
1290 Avenue of the Americas, New York, NY 10104
JimmyPatterson.org

First Edition: June 2021

JIMMY Patterson Books is an imprint of Little, Brown and Company, a division of Hachette Book Group, Inc. The Little, Brown name and logo are trademarks of Hachette Book Group, Inc. The JIMMY Patterson Books® name and logo are trademarks of JBP Business, LLC.

The publisher is not responsible for websites (or their content) that are not owned by the publisher.

Library of Congress Cataloging-in-Publication Data
Names: Andrews, Claire M., author.
Title: Daughter of Sparta / Claire M. Andrews.
Description: First edition. | New York : Little, Brown and Company, 2021. | "Jimmy Patterson books." | Audience: Ages 14 & up. | Summary: Guided by the handsome Apollo, Daphne journeys across ancient Greece to recover nine mysterious items stolen from Mount Olympus before the gods lose their powers and throw the mortal world into chaos in this reinterpretation of the Greek myth.
Identifiers: LCCN 2021008994 | ISBN 9780316540070 (hardcover) | ISBN 9780316540100 (ebook)
Subjects: CYAC: Quests (Expeditions)—Fiction. | Mythology, Greek—Fiction. | Ability—Fiction. | Apollo (Deity)—Fiction.
Classification: LCC PZ7.1.A53274 Dau 2021 | DDC [Fic]—dc23
LC record available at https://lccn.loc.gov/2021008994

ISBNs: 978-0-316-54007-0 (hardcover), 978-0-316-54010-0 (ebook)

Printed in the United States of America

LSC-C

Printing 2, 2021

FOR MY MUM,
WHO RAISED THE STRONGEST GIRLS

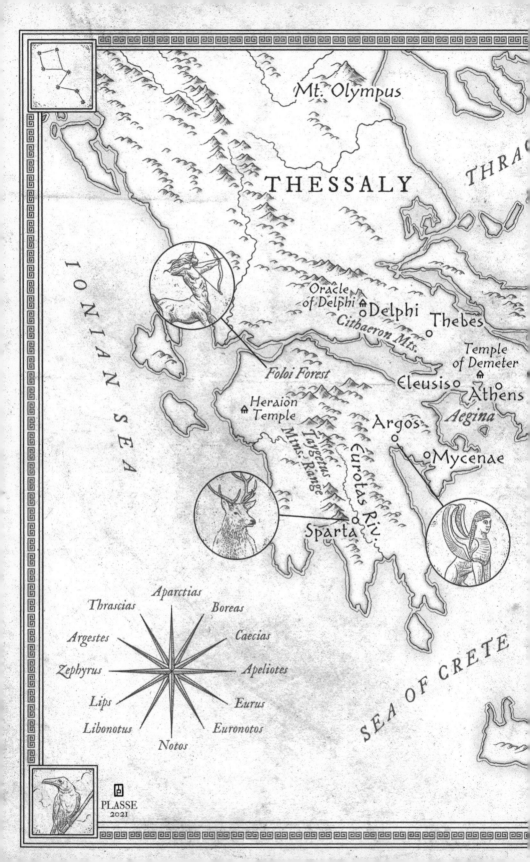

Mt. Olympus

THESSALY

THRAC

IONIAN SEA

Oracle
of Delphi ⌂ Delphi
Cithaeron Mts.

Thebes

Temple
of Demeter
⌂
Eleusis ○ Athens

Foloi Forest

Aegina

Heraion
Temple ⌂

Argos

Mycenae

Taygetus
Mtns. Range

Eurotas Riv.

Sparta

SEA OF CRETE

Aparctias

Thrascias   Boreas

Argestes   Caecias

Zephyrus   Apeliotes

Lips   Eurus

Libonotus   Euronotos

Notos

PLASSE
2021

CHAPTER
I

The sun begins its descent beyond the Taygetus mountains, filling the sky with a golden glow as the honor of my family balances upon my shoulders.

Lykou's challenge hangs in the air. The usual cheers of *Carneia* have dulled to mere whispers, the crowd surrounding us waiting for my response.

Lykou flashes me a crooked grin and accepts the *dory,* a whole three meters of bone-shattering wood and metal that Paidonomos Leonidas hands him. His challenge isn't malicious, but rather a test. We've always jested about who would win in a single-combat duel.

Alkaios stands among the crowd. My oldest brother gives me a small shake of his head, lips pressed together in a narrow line. To fight would bare for all that I know much more than I should. As a *Mothakes* woman—not born of Sparta—I should be granted little but an eternity of servitude, but as the adopted daughter of an *ephor* I have more liberty—though not too much.

To reject Lykou's challenge, though, would be much more than my ego could tolerate.

"Fools," I mutter as both my brother and Lykou, like every other man here, underestimate my determination. Underestimate my desire to win.

This is *Carneia,* and so no better time to prove to Sparta and the gods all I have to offer.

Servants move from pyre to pyre around the makeshift arena that separates us with blazing torches. In the suffocating heat of early summer, my skin is slick with sweat and reflects like amber in the blossoming firelight. I accept the *dory* Paidonomos Leonidas, the great general, passes me and give it a twirl, a delicious ache rippling up my arm. Fury flickers across Alkaios's dark features.

Lykou doesn't give me a chance to make the first move. He leaps across the arena and strikes his *dory* wide. Even a glancing blow will end the duel and declare the victor. I barely roll from his reach in time, shoulder hitting the dirt hard enough to steal the breath from my lungs. Before he can attack again, I swipe for his legs.

He rolls beneath my swing. I scramble to my feet. He stabs toward my chest and I stumble back from his reach. My next swing is wide and a chuckle escapes Lykou.

I bite back the urge to hiss, baring my teeth. My knees tremble slightly, my leg muscles aching from my morning exercises as my untamable hair obscures my glare. I don't take the time to shake the sweat that threatens to drip into my eyes, never turning from my opponent.

Lykou tosses his *dory* neatly to his left hand, jabbing at the space between my arm and hip without so much as a stumble. I barely avoid the attack, my body protesting as I roll painfully across the rocks and dirt, then return to my fighting stance. The sharpened iron spearhead glints as it stabs the air where I just stood.

Show-off. The ass is right-handed.

Never taking my eyes from him, I switch my own *dory* to my left hand, ripped calluses protesting. I fight a grimace as a jolt of pain lances up my left arm with the simple movement. My shoulder aches, a bruise the size of a pomegranate already blossoming. Lykou dances around me, favoring his right leg slightly, knee inflamed from rolling beneath my swing.

The cheers around us are deafening and the acrid tang of smoke singes my nose. Lykou's soldier brethren hoot from the sidelines, their enthusiastic feet stomping dust into the air around us. Even King Menelaus watches from a dais on the sidelines in grim silence as his beautiful wife, Queen Helen, leans forward and clasps her hands over her heart.

Carneia, the annual festival to honor and celebrate the gifts of Apollo, has only just begun; Lykou and I are the night's first entertainment. Dancing, food, and revelry beckons from beyond our arena, but all are ignored.

A spar between a man and a woman hasn't gone on this long in an age, and never between a *Mothakes* and a true Spartan.

I feel naked in front of the jeering crowd, their taunts cutting through my clothes more clearly than any knife could. Though many Spartans, men and women alike, duel naked, I wear a poppy-colored chiton, wrapped tight across my chest and cut so short it dances high on my thighs. From my left wrist a single bronze bangle pinches my skin and shines in the firelight. DIODORUS, my adoptive family name, is etched on the bangle, the only token of my status that I'll allow on my body. Anything more on my person might slow me down.

Lykou still grins. He wears a pitch-black chiton, baring much of his muscled chest, the woolen fabric clinging to his sweaty skin. I can't wait to wipe that ridiculous smile from his face. I parry his next strike, spinning and slashing high so that he has to dive to avoid my spear. The enthusiastic cries from the audience soar around me, deafening now.

I force myself to focus on the muscled intensity of his legs. With an exaggerated grimace of pain, I slump my bruised shoulder ever so slightly, offering an easy target. Lykou leaps forward and takes the bait just as I knew he would, lunging for my injured shoulder.

Idiot.

I twist and swing to meet him as he jumps right into my reach. He shouts in alarm and tries to pull back in midair, but my *dory* has already grazed his side, tearing what little he has of a chiton in a strike of victory.

Both men and women in the crowd groan. Lykou chucks his *dory* to the ground in a flurry of dust, defeat coloring his typically assured movements. I don't dare reach out to clap him on the back or ease the sting of his loss, though. Alkaios has disappeared and I will undoubtedly get a scolding later. Still atop his wooden dais, Menelaus regards me with stern, dark eyes before nodding to his counselors. I have no idea what the nod means, but it is enough to know that my *anax,* my liege, witnessed my victory.

My initial joy from victory plummets, the heated glares and scorn from the audience scalding. I refuse to let their bile affect me; in a society where strength is everything, I can't afford to be seen as anything less than the men I fight alongside and against. Being born a *Mothakes,* an outsider, is only a weapon they can use against me if I let it be so.

Chin held high, I toss my *dory* into the dirt beside Lykou's before marching toward the sidelines.

Paidonomos Leonidas catches my arm. He nods to the waiting king and queen. "Don't forget your place, *Mothakes.*"

He doesn't need to say anything else, that even the adopted daughter of a politician can only rise so high. With teeth clenched, I turn and kneel before Menelaus. My cheeks are burning, but not from the exertion of the duel. Leonidas didn't insist on Lykou bowing.

He stops me again as I'm leaving. "That was good work out there, Daphne Diodorus. Even your brothers could learn a thing or two from you." The words are high praise coming from a *paidonomos*, though salted as he continues, "Your movements are reckless, unthinking. You must learn to not only read others' movements, but your own."

I open my mouth to point out that Lykou could use the same advice, but he cuts me off.

"Before you bother to turn my words onto Lykou, I have told him, your brothers, and all Spartan soldiers the same thing." Leonidas crosses his heavily muscled arms. "I say this to prepare you. Sparta hasn't gone unchallenged for over a hundred years because our monarchs are great peacekeepers. We've maintained our seat of power through the might of our army, the strongest Greece has ever known."

This, the whole world knows. No army in known history has ever surpassed the wealth of power, strength, and strategy that Sparta possesses. Only fool kings with more wealth than wisdom have challenged us in the past couple centuries, and all have been sent back to their measly thrones with their tails between their legs and a fraction of their army remaining... if our kings were feeling benevolent.

"I fear our time of easy battles has come to an end." Leonidas turns to watch the next match. The queen's brother, Pollux, is sweeping the floor with one of Lykou's friends. True Spartans, strength runs deep in Queen Helen's family. "The drought has left our people with ire. The kings of Greece grow restless, their people hungry, and the gods bored. A reckoning awaits beyond the horizon."

My palms itch. Before I can ask what he means, he claps me on the back and walks to the king's dais. I cut through the crowd, the excitement in the air intoxicating enough to push Leonidas's words to the recesses of my mind. I won't let an old man's paranoia ruin my victory, not when the night is still young and brimming with all of the possibilities that *Carneia* has to offer.

I don't make it far before Lykou calls after me. "Daphne."

He shoves his way toward me. Despite his loss, he wears my victory like a banner, reaching me with a broad smile. I grow uncomfortably aware, the closer he gets, of the many, *many* reasons why Lykou sets the majority of hearts in Sparta aflutter.

"Your chiton has seen better days." Returning the smile with a furious blush, I point to the torn cloth and struggle to keep my eyes from wandering across the broad expanse of his chest. "Or are you attempting to start a new fashion trend?"

Lykou drops into a mock bow. "A beautiful woman just couldn't keep herself from trying to rip it off of me."

"Oh." I finger the hem of my chiton, my hands refusing to still. "She must have been sorely provoked."

He laughs. "I guess you could call a duel challenge a provocation."

"Alkaios will never let me hear the end of it, I'm sure." I shake my head.

"I think you quite thoroughly demonstrated tonight exactly why the Spartan army needs women like you." Lykou rubs the back of his neck. "Even if it cost me my dignity."

"Of course they should, but the *paidonomos* would never allow it. A woman can learn to wield a weapon, but gods forbid she ever wield one on a battlefield."

"Regardless"—he reaches out to brush a strand of hair from my face, stirring a traitorous flutter deep in my stomach—"you fought beautifully out there."

My gaze trails the line of his bicep, my mouth suddenly dry. Maybe I could let myself enjoy Lykou's plush lips, find out what it feels like to run my fingers through those dark curls...I give my head an abrupt shake. I will not let myself be tied down to any man. Not while the title *Mothakes* still hangs over me.

I open my mouth to respond, but one of Lykou's friends comes up and tugs on his arm. "Time to prepare for the race."

Carneia reaches its zenith with an *agon*. Five unmarried men are chosen by Sparta's five *ephors* to chase a deer. If it is caught, the year will be a superb one for our harvests and army. And if not...disaster awaits. It is best that the deer is caught. To succeed and bring the favor of Apollo is of particular import this year, with Helen and Menelaus leaving soon to meet with the mad king of Crete.

This year, thanks to our father, my brother Pyrrhus has the honor of being chosen for the *agon*.

Lykou flashes me an apologetic smile, dipping his head so that his charcoal locks fall before his eyes. "Can I count on you to be there when they crown me?"

My mouth pops open with a ready rejection, as it always has when Lykou crosses that line. His eager, dark eyes, warm like smoldering coal, stop me, though. Perhaps I won't be so harsh, just this once.

"Of course I'll be there when you win." His smile could light up the night as surely as the moon. "But don't tell my brother, or he'll disown me for not placing all my bets on *his* victory."

Beaming, Lykou allows himself to be pulled away and I turn to the task of finding the brother in question.

It isn't difficult to find him. Pyrrhus's fiery curls stand out like a beacon among the raven tresses of our Spartan kin. I dodge elbows and overfull cups of wine to reach him. Silently slipping up behind him, I tug the hair at the nape of his neck. "Ready for the Chase, Pyr?"

"I've been ready." Turning, my brother gives an infectious grin.

"Imagine the honor and prestige our family will receive when I win. They won't dare to taunt us anymore."

"Don't get too far ahead of yourself. The gods do not—"

"—take kindly to mortals who presume to possess greatness above their station." Pyrrhus's imitation of Alkaios is perfect, standing with a rigid back and up-thrust chin to mock our scrupulous older brother.

"Careful," I say, stealing a sip of his wine. "Any more sass and the gods will think you don't mean it."

"Damn the gods, Daph." I choke and he takes his *kylix* back. "Why should we offer homage to the gods that brought us to this forsaken place?"

I knock the wine from his hand and hiss, "Are you mad?" I look around to make sure no one overheard, but the revelers are too deep into their own cups to give us even a passing glance. "The *anax* could have your tongue for such sacrilege. Alkaios would have your head."

"Alkaios hates the gods as much as I do." Pyrrhus cocks his head, dark smile deepening the dimple on his left cheek. "And you do, too. Or in your constant striving for acceptance did you forget that the gods are to blame for our current social status?"

Pyrrhus and Alkaios lost much more than I did the night I was born. I never knew our parents. My brothers lost a mother and father that they loved and admired, and had been brought to Sparta, far from the home they'd grown up in.

I don't tell him that his words strike dead on the mark. Crossing my arms over my chest, instead I say, "If this is your way of trying to get out of the Chase, I—"

"I'm afraid of nothing." He waggles his eyebrows. "Besides, Alkaios would hunt down the deer himself if he thought I wasn't capable. Honor over family and all that."

"That's not fair." I thump his arm. "Alkaios isn't here to defend himself."

"He means well, though I could do without the sanctimonious delivery. It's sometimes hard to tell if Alkaios is training to be a soldier or a priest. Now I must find more wine." Pyrrhus presses a small kiss on my cheek and winks as he vanishes into the crowd. My happiness dims the moment he leaves.

Moving through the crowd, I spy my handmaid Ligeia, Alkaios and his wife, and my adoptive parents mingling among the celebrating Spartans. Dipping in the opposite direction, I escape their certain scolding and disapproval. Alkaios has no doubt told them about my duel before the king and queen.

Shedding the shackles of dignity and decorum demanded by Sparta and the honor of my family, I throw myself into the raucous crowd. I dance for hours, spinning and dipping to the beat of a thousand drums. While I sit out a dance, licking the grease of roast lamb from my fingers, the bellow of a horn calls the people of Sparta together for the start of the *agon*. With Selene's crescent moon hanging low in the sky, the crowd flows from rows of canopied tents to the dark fields outside the city. All of Sparta has waited an entire year for this event, the most important tradition in Sparta, and never has it been more important than now.

King Menelaus and Queen Helen wait patiently on the banks of the Eurotas river, illuminated by the light of an enormous bonfire that sends sparks and the smell of burning pine into the night sky. I move with the impatient crowd, thousands of Spartans waiting on the city's edge for our king's command. My heart thunders with heady anticipation.

Four young Spartiates, the light of the bonfire gleaming off their stripped, oiled bodies, march onto the field and face Menelaus, bowing low to the earth.

My stomach plummets to the soles of my feet as I fail to spy the fiery curls of my brother.

Where is Pyrrhus?

CHAPTER
2

Searching the crowd for Pyrrhus, my gaze locks on Alkaios several yards away. His jaw is clenched, brow furrowed, and hands bunched in tight fists.

Pyrrhus's absence tarnishes our family's honor. If he doesn't run, our lives will be forfeit to the gods as a message and warning to others.

My heart thunders in my chest and ears, a hollow pulsing louder even than the festival drums. My breath hitches with the growing restlessness of the crowd, their impatient, demanding gazes turning from the line of runners to Alkaios and me. Soon they will be calling for our blood. This is exactly what they expect of *Mothakes* like me and my brothers. Our father took a chance choosing Pyrrhus, and now my brother is about to sacrifice the honor of our family.

I shoot Alkaios another desperate glance, but all he spares me is a single curt nod, dark eyes unreadable from such a distance. If Pyrrhus won't run, then another youth in our family must race. But Alkaios is married, and past the age of consideration.

The burden of carrying Sparta's fortune falls entirely on me.

Damn Pyrrhus. May Nemesis find him and shrivel his manhood.

Straightening my shoulders, I step forward.

"No woman should run," a man shouts, while another jeers, "A *Mothakes* should have never been chosen!"

"The gods will punish us for this blasphemy," a woman yells. "She brings dishonor to Sparta. Stop her."

"Mothakes! Mothakes! Mothakes!"

Outsider. Outsider. Outsider.

That's all I will ever be to these people. Though free, my worth as a *Mothakes* is little more than a slave. My brothers and I can aspire to only what wealth a marriage may bring us; my brothers will have no careers further than service to the army, despite being the adopted children of an *ephor*. Pyrrhus's place in this race could have changed that, possibly earned his freedom from the ill-begotten title hanging above all of our heads.

I shake my head, clearing the tears that threaten to spill from my eyes. It sears my soul to know that our adoptive parents are somewhere in this raucous crowd, watching helplessly as our family's future hangs by the threads of the Fates and the king's grace.

The heckling recedes as I approach the line of runners, bowing swiftly to the king and queen. They make no protest, only nodding in my direction with grim acceptance. It is unprecedented for a woman to run, but they will do whatever is necessary to secure Sparta's future.

The other runners focus on the monarchs. Even Lykou, standing to my left, ignores me, his chin high and eyes on Menelaus. The queen's other brother, Castor, stands to my right with rigid spine and shoulders, and beside him are two sons of Sparta's most prominent politicians. They sway on their feet with vacant expressions, having tasted far too much of the festival's wine. Would Dionysus be proud of their ill-timed consumption of his favorite beverage?

Kneeling, I peer at the king through my curtain of hair, but instead meet Helen's dark eyes. She gives me a look of both pride and something harder to decipher—jealousy, perhaps? I have no idea why. She is far more lovely, wealthy, and powerful than I will ever be.

But then I remember Helen before she married Menelaus. Running in the fields, the fastest woman Sparta had ever seen, with the promise of the famous Spartan daughter Atalanta.

I drop my gaze to the ground, shoving aside thoughts of the queen as Menelaus's voice cuts through the din of unruly Spartans.

"The rules are simple." He stands so all his subjects can see. "These five youths will ensure the gratitude of Apollo by retrieving for Sparta the offering of his twin sister, Artemis."

Led by a servant, a deer is paraded before us, straining against its captor and not yet resigned to its fate. Around its neck is a garland of laurel branches decked with flowers. A moment's pity for the deer catches in my throat as the whites of its eyes shine in the firelight.

"Retrieve the garland before dawn. Should the deer escape and the dawn of the goddess Eos rise before the garland is returned to me, the crops of Sparta will wither and die. The Eurotas will run dry. The men of our army will fall to plague and death. The drought this spring already tests the strength of Sparta. May your victory bring the rain our crops so dearly need."

He turns to a young oracle, dressed in a red *peplos*, with eyes like a starless night. She steps forward and says, for all of Sparta to hear, "With this race, we not only ask for Apollo's divine favor, but must also give him our strength. You have no doubt heard of the restlessness growing beyond Sparta. The kingdoms swallowed whole by the earth, armies with nothing to eat but sand and bronze, and children of the *Mesogeios* sacrificed each year to beasts lurking beneath cities.

"These ills," she says, waving an arm to the Taygetus mountains and lands beyond, "will reach us, just as they have reached even the gods from the heights of Olympus. Zeus no longer brings us rain and so our crops wither. Hera blesses us less and less with sons to replenish our armies. The lands to the west rumble from Poseidon's ire, and Athena has not blessed our battles to the east. Their powers abandon them and soon we will suffer the consequences."

Impossible. A murmur ripples through the crowd. The gods are untouchable, beyond the reach of our plights. It's unheard of, that anything existed that could so much as tickle their skin.

"Stand, Apollo's chosen," the king commands, raising his arms.

We rush to do his bidding, and servants move forward to paint our bodies red and gold, the Spartan colors of blood and wealth.

"You must not interfere with your fellow runners. You each run for the glory of Sparta. If any of you hinders another champion, the action will be treated as treason and you will be banished." Our king's voice is as cold and unforgiving as an iron blade as he looks each of us in the eye. "The weight of Sparta's future rests on your shoulders."

Menelaus gestures to a pair of servants, and they bring forward a giant cushion covered in a silk sheet. I gasp as the sheet falls away, and there, gleaming in the firelight, is the most perfect *dory* I've ever seen. "Should you be successful, the rewards will be abundant."

The spear is delicately carved with dark vines and laurel leaves, with a cherrywood handle, topped with a leaf-shaped iron spearhead and golden butt-spike. Though not the length of a typical *dory*, barely cresting my own height, the moonlight-colored spear before me has been bought at great cost from the southern continent.

My nails dig into my palms. Spartans are not dazzled by beautiful weapons, but this is no small gift. This is a gift worthy of a hunter whose true prize is the fortune of Sparta. I won't win this race for a mere spear. I will win this race for Sparta's future and mine.

"Runners to their positions." Menelaus raises his right arm high.

I nearly trip over myself as I rush to line up with the other runners. My feet dance with impatience as the deer is led ten paces in front of our line.

"May the wings of Hermes be beneath your feet."

Menelaus's arm falls and I bolt from the line.

CHAPTER 3

I fly straight for the Taygetus forest, dashing across the ground in impossible lengths. Castor and Lykou flank me, their long legs pushing them harder and farther with each leap. The other two runners fall behind us, drunk on the night's wine and unprepared for the competition.

All the better.

I have more to lose than all of them, and more to win. *Carneia* is the province of men, and I am an unwelcome challenger.

My breath escapes my lips in a shrill whistle. I'm already halfway across the field and quickly approaching the forest's edge. The festival food, once delicious, sits uneasily in my stomach. My lungs and muscles, already weary from the festival's delights and trials, scream in protest as I push my body to its limits.

For Sparta. For my family. For my honor.

Lykou pulls ahead while Castor still matches my pace. He soon overtakes me and I focus on his and Lykou's backs as they surge ahead. The line of cypress trees looms before us, marking the Taygetus forest.

The dark tree line beckons me like a friend. Having spent most of my days and nights hunting in Taygetus's depths, I know the forest better than my competitors. But I must reach it first.

A fallen tree marks the end of the field. I leap over it, my momentum pitching me ahead of Lykou and Castor. The thicket swallows me. I leave the firelight behind and hurtle into the darkness beyond.

A hiss escapes me when branches rip into my arms. Lykou's and Castor's footsteps falter as they crash and flounder in the impenetrable darkness but I surge forward, undaunted. This is my domain and sanctuary. I know this forest better than anyone else in Sparta. Sprinting forward, my ears guide my flight.

Calf muscles straining against the steady incline of the forest floor, I continue my chase. The tree line gives way to a rock face that forms a barrier between the foothills and the mountains.

As though the gods guide me, a shaft of moonlight illuminates the deer's bounding white tail to my right. I follow, dodging branches and leaping felled trees, my eyes locked on the fleeing deer. I dip my chase closer to the rock face, ready to slam into the deer's muscled body. I'm never given the opportunity.

It darts away and my outstretched hands graze its side. My feet slide on the loose soil as I change direction, following the deer back into the trees. It dives through the saplings and I curse on a ragged breath.

Pounding footsteps signal Lykou and Castor pressing closer. I follow the deer, too late to register the unfamiliar path before I burst into a secluded glen.

Standing a few feet away, the deer watches me with eyes far too intelligent for a woodland beast. It's a knowing stare. As if he was not the hunted, but the hunter. Then my attention focuses on the shaft of pure moonlight behind it.

In the middle of the glen stands a beautiful young woman, the deer's garland clutched in her fist.

"I've been waiting a long time to meet you, Daphne," says Artemis, goddess of the hunt.

CHAPTER
4

When I was still young enough to laugh and play without feeling self-conscious for it, Ligeia would tuck me into bed, wrapping me in warm furs and wise words. She spun tales like a spider, each word another thread ensnaring me in a web of dreams and legends, of fate and adventures.

While I stared in wide-eyed disbelief, she would tell me of the days when the most fearsome creatures prowled the world, of gryphons and the Erinyes, sirens and krakens. Mostly, though, she would tell me about the gods, their misadventures and lovers, legends fraught with misdeeds and heroism. And always with the cautionary tale of the mortals who became entangled in Olympian games. My favorite were the tales of Artemis, the virgin huntress.

Of her control over animals and the forest, the army of nymphs at her beck and call, and of the promise she drew from Zeus, the most powerful of all the gods: that she would never have to marry.

When I was not yet five years old, Ligeia caught me in the washroom with a basin full of watered clay and mud trying to dye the wheat color from my hair to be dark like the lush curls of Artemis. She slapped my muddy hands away before my adoptive mother could faint over her urchin daughter; as her gentle, callused hands washed clay from my curls, Ligeia told me that Artemis would have been disappointed in me.

"Artemis cares not for trivial things. She cares not one whit about fashion, fine hair, or the rules of mortals. She cares only for the freedom of women and the creatures of the forest."

Those words echoing in my mind, I take in the sight of the goddess standing before me in the middle of the glen. It is a vast, open area—a beautiful paradise. I mentally kick myself for never having found it before.

A small pool reflects the face of the moon, anemone flowers blossom from the earth, and prickly cedar trees arch high into the cloudless sky. Bathed silver in the moonlight, the trees stand sentry around the glen like alert soldiers protecting their queen. Reflecting on Ligeia's stories of tree nymphs and their steadfast loyalty to Artemis, they very well might be soldiers.

"If you're finished gaping like a fool, I have words of portent that need to be shared," Artemis says.

I turn from the strange glen to the goddess watching me with the fate of my people dangling from her hand and immediately fall to my knees in a low bow. Adrenaline from the race still shudders through me, my breath ragged. I should press my nose to the earth in reverence, but my gaze is drawn to her otherworldly beauty. Despite her thousand years or more, Artemis's physical appearance is a reflection of her immortality. She looks just as I always imagined. Only a year or so my senior and in the prime of life, but also bearing the cold arrogance of an Olympian. The frostiness of her gaze is the most surprising. I had always assumed that Artemis would be the most forgiving Olympian when it came to her female subjects.

With a knowing smile, slightly tilted with cruelty, she dangles the garland from a single finger. I know better than to try and take it, because in her other hand Artemis twirls a long, golden arrow.

"You may stand," she says with another spin of the arrow. This time the cold metal sings a hand's breadth from my face. "If you want the garland, Daphne, come and get it."

"You led me here." Not a question, and I can hardly believe my forwardness, but she must have a reason for summoning me. The gods always have reasons for the games they play.

"A dying god is a dangerous god."

The gods also often answer in half-truths and riddles.

I hate riddles.

"I would think that all gods are dangerous to a lowly mortal like me," I say, standing but giving her a reverential dip of my chin.

"Lowly mortal? Do you really think I'd ask just *anyone* for help?" Artemis cocks her head to the side, studying me.

I open my mouth to ask her what she means but she flicks the garland and asks, "Is this really all you want? If you so desire, I can give you anything you ask, things far more valuable than a grubby string of flowers and leaves." She raises it between us, daring me to take it.

"What else could I possibly want?" There are many things I want, but Artemis doesn't have to know that.

Her brows rise. "There's nothing you would ask of a goddess? I could grant you wealth, power, fortune, and grace." She smiles, lips cocked to the side. "I could make you and your brothers true Spartans. Your people will forget that the title of *Mothakes* ever hung about your shoulders."

To truly belong. My breath catches. I have no doubt that she could bequeath such a wish, and I'm instantly compelled to fall to my knees again and to beg her to fulfill my deepest desire. But I resist.

Barely.

"Olympus always demands a price," I whisper. "What is it?"

Artemis releases a long breath. "My powers—my family's powers—are dwindling. Olympus is at its weakest, the love and worship of men long since waning. Soon, I will die, my family will die, and all the gifts that we've bestowed upon men will wash away like dust across the stones under a heavy rain."

I inhale sharply, sucking my lower lip between my teeth. The oracle said that the gods were weakened, but I could have never imagined this.

She turns toward the trees and continues, "I need your courage... and your unswerving loyalty."

A dark shape emerges from the line of trees, nudged into the clearing by the sharp antlers of a stag.

"Daphne." Pyrrhus falls to his knees as he emerges in the moonlight, and I gasp. His face is a mess of blood and bruises, his clothes torn.

"Please," he begs, kissing Artemis's sandaled feet. "Not my sister, she would never betray your trust. Please don't hurt her. Punish me." He becomes incoherent, sobbing with his face pressed into the ground.

"What did you do, Pyrrhus?" He can't even look at me. I turn to Artemis, aghast. "What did he do?"

"He *spied* on me." Her hair begins to rise about her shoulders like an angry storm cloud. The trees around the glen roll and thrash in an unseen wind. In the distance, terrified forest creatures screech. "Not just once, but twice. Like the foolish mortal he is, he came here tonight to spy on me again."

"Leave my sister alone. I'll do anything. I'll never do it again."

Pyrrhus's pleas become frantic. He tries to paw at Artemis, clinging to her pale leg. I've never seen my brother so humbled and pathetic. Artemis shakes him away, her lips curled back with disgust.

"Please," I say, ready to throw myself to the ground beside Pyrrhus and beg as well. "Tell me what I need to do for you to spare him your wrath."

"I need you." Artemis points to me but still glares at the whimpering Pyrrhus. "But I don't need him."

No warning or dramatic fanfare precedes the transformation. One second Pyrrhus is crumpled on his hands and knees at Artemis's feet, and then, in the blink of an eye, a stag stands before me.

"Pyr!" I scream, rushing toward the auburn stag—my brother.

He bucks as if to shake off his unnatural form. Artemis watches in resigned silence. I attempt to grab his bright-red fur. He throws me off, flailing and snorting. I duck out of the way, narrowly avoiding his deadly horns, and cry out as his bucking sends me rolling across the grass.

"Pyrrhus? It's me. You must calm down." I try to get close to him again, to grab hold of his fur for only a moment, but he shoulders me aside. I crash into the pool, the wind escaping my chest in a painful rush.

"I don't think your brother likes his new form much." Artemis laughs, the sound like a chill autumn rain. "With each passing moment a fragment of his humanity disappears, starting with his memories."

My hands bunch at my sides, and it takes every ounce of control to keep from swinging at her flawless face. An unwise mortal is a dead mortal. "Name your price for my brother's life."

"You must leave Sparta behind."

Become a traitor and bring dishonor to my family. My stomach somersaults. "Anything but that."

Circling me with long, swishing steps, Artemis spins the golden arrow through her graceful fingers. Thoughts of my family are shoved aside as she angles the arrow under my nose. Power emanates from the weapon in waves of heat and wafts of smoke. "This was a gift from my Uncle Hephaestus on the eve of his wedding to Aphrodite, a most intriguing sort of party favor. I'm curious to see how well it works."

Before I can even flinch, Artemis spins, slicing the arrow's tip above my now rapidly beating heart. The arrow, longer than my arm and sharper than humanly possible, slices deep across my skin. I cry out involuntarily as searing heat envelopes my chest and spreads to my limbs, holding me immobilized for only a moment before Artemis steps away. My blood drips from the weapon.

It's a warning. Should I test her patience any further, my blood won't be the only thing on that arrow.

Artemis steps close and picks every leaf and twig from my wild curls. She ignores the righteous anger shaking my frame with each long, steadying breath.

"I'll return your brother to his true form," Artemis continues, her voice a warm whisper against my ear as she pulls a sodden leaf from my hair. "But only if you help my family. Something very dear to my father has been stolen. I don't know who stole it, or how, but without it, the powers of Olympus will fail. Without our gifts, the crops of Sparta will wither and die, men will grow weak, and the armies of Greece will be overtaken by powers you could never hope to understand. I need you to seek answers that evade my family. There is only one that could know where what was stolen has been hidden away, and who stole them, but he will answer to none from Olympus."

Artemis looks me up and down. "He will only speak to one brave, foolish, or desperate enough to seek him out."

Pyrrhus now munches on flowers, and seeing him in a body other than his own fills me with rage. Artemis took him from me, the gods took my mother from me, and now they want to take Sparta from me. Her family killed my mother—my true mother—before I ever had the chance to know her.

My emotions must be written all over my face. The arrow slashes out again, faster than any mortal could react, ripping across the belly of my chiton and driving into my stomach.

"Do not make the assumption that I don't feel for you and your family's plight. That I don't know how your mother died, what happened to bring you to Sparta in the first place," Artemis hisses. I gasp as she slams the arrow deeper into my abdomen. "This is but an assurance that you won't betray me or my family."

My blood begins to pour, blending with the crimson dye of my clothes as a searing white flame bursts across my midriff. Artemis rips away the arrow and I stagger backward to the pool's edge, my hands flying to my navel to stopper the bleeding. They come back dry. Gasping again, I touch my stomach, searching for the source of the pain.

Across my midriff is a solid gold line shimmering in the moonlight. It's firm to the touch; I gingerly trace a trembling finger across it. Under my questing hands, the gold blossoms and slithers, branching across my skin, ever moving like a gilded snake.

"What did you do?" My voice is barely more than a whisper, trembling like my hands.

"You wear my mark," Artemis says, lifting the arrow again between us. I involuntarily take a step back, now ankle deep in the pool of water. She steps forward, herding me deeper until the water laps hungrily at my hips.

"The Midas Curse will envelop you, enslave you, and bind you to me. The gold can spread to your toes, molding you into a tool that I might wield as I so choose. Mock me, and the gold will crawl to your neck, choking off any insolent words before they can be uttered. Dare to betray me or my family, and the gold will wrap around your heart, snuffing the life from your veins."

Her words echo between us. I can feel, as keenly as the touch of fingers, the gold twisting across my skin, a permanent threat should I forget the gods that control me.

She smiles wickedly. "Remember, a dying god is a dangerous god."

"You already said that," I say, my face hot with fury.

This goddess has stolen my family's chance for honor, my brother, and has now branded me like a slave. What respect for Artemis I once felt is now replaced with bitter loathing. But for my brother's life—and my country—I will play her games.

"What do you want me to do?"

The Curse stops inching across my skin, waiting above my breast for her command. None comes.

Instead, she says, "Help us and you get your brother back. Find where the Olympian powers have been hidden away, and I will remove the curse from your body. Should Olympus fall, the gold traversing your body will consume you and there will be nobody left to save your poor brother."

Her finger slides treacherously under my clothes and between my breasts, hovering over the band of gold now pooled above my heart. The curse's incessant movements are a tickle across my skin, an unforgiving reminder of the goddess's control.

If I die, Pyrrhus will be next, and no afterlife in the Underworld would prevent the pain I would feel if I were to cause his demise. Spending all night arguing with Artemis won't win me my brother's freedom. Only my cooperation will.

Artemis continues, "The people of Sparta anxiously await news of the Chase. Go claim the prize of *Carneia*. Nobody can know about the dying power of Olympus, or my task for you." After tossing the garland into the water beside me, Artemis drifts away, closer to the tangle of trees enclosing us. "My brother will wait for you outside the city, as an escort and protector. Before you argue with me about needing protection, know that he will attend you whether you like it or need it. Apollo has long been the focus of our father's ire, and this journey will pave the way to peace between them."

She turns to leave, our meeting over, my fated part in her quest assured. Pyrrhus follows the goddess without resistance.

"What about my brother?" I ask. "Is he to be set free and hunted like an animal?"

"You have until the harvest moon, young Daphne, to fulfill your obligation to me. Until then, your brother will be safe," she says, her moonlit figure quickly fading. Her last words are a whisper on the wind as she disappears among the dark trees. "After that day, I make no promises as to his fate."

The sudden silence of Artemis's departure settles around me, and I reflect again on Ligeia's stories. She always said that the gods are just and cruel, beloved and feared. Their life's work is maintaining that balance held over mortals.

Fear for my brother's life—for *my* life balanced on the golden curse—shudders through me in time to the erratic pulsing of my heart, and I realize the gods also fear us.

The gods are just and cruel, beloved and feared. Ligeia insists that the gods are so merciless because they love us, that they only want us to better ourselves. I believe it's because the gods are envious of us. They will never understand the beauty of watching the day pass and knowing that it could perhaps be your last. They will never experience the bitter taste of fear as it floods your senses, or the sometimes bittersweet ache of pain.

They also fear us because they understand that whipped backs will always heal, and eventually they will no longer bow.

CHAPTER 5

My soul is weary when I emerge from the Taygetus forest. A deafening roar heralds my appearance. The people of Sparta scream and crow my name, the garland hanging from my fist. The race feels like a distant memory, the garland heavy but not as heavy as the fate of Sparta and my brother weighing upon my shoulders.

My ragged chiton hangs on my body, ruined by blood, sweat, and mud. The gold curse spins atop my breast, both my body and heart aching. But I don't give a thought to my haggard appearance as I stride across the field.

I have only until the harvest moon. That amount of time, though months for me, must be a blink for Artemis. I can only imagine her, sitting on a throne of oak, picking at her nails with an arrowhead and biding her time. She will likely shoot Pyrrhus for my failure. Or serve him up to Alkaios.

Whichever she deems more poetic.

The rumble of the crowd grows as I walk closer, reminding me of the task at hand.

I raise my fist to the night sky, displaying the garland.

Sparta has her precious victory, another bountiful season assured.

My triumph apparent, the crowd cheers and surges forward in a wave. Many hands reach out to touch my arms and shoulders as I move through the crowd, gaze locked on my king.

Menelaus shifts uneasily in his throne. His hands grip the arms of his seat, eyes unreadable as I march forward. He could be regretting his decision to let me—a *Mothakes* woman, no less—take part in the Chase. My heart races.

Alkaios shoulders his way through the crowd, and then moves to walk behind me. I appreciate his silent support.

By the time I reach the royal platform, the cheering dies; everyone waits on a held breath for Menelaus to announce my victory. With tight lips, he nods and takes the remains of the garland, his knuckles white as he clenches the leaves. Around me, the crowd erupts with cheers and shouts. Helen presents me with the *dory*.

She grips my hand tight enough to make my bones ache. "Your triumph will be a glorious light to see us through the coming darkness."

Winning the race doesn't feel glorious. The meeting with Artemis reverberates through my mind like storm-tossed waves, thoughts of Pyrrhus churning inside me and twisting my gut; the curse hardens my skin and creeps dangerously close to my heart, a painful reminder that I cannot enjoy my victory.

Another bountiful year assured, Helen and Menelaus start the procession back to the palace while *Carneia* resumes. I slip through the crowd, careful not to draw too much attention. The celebration provides the perfect cover to steal away from Sparta.

Alkaios presses close. He will follow me home if I let him. He will stop me from leaving Sparta and tell me it would bring dishonor on our adoptive family. And, in the same breath, he would say he is proud of me. Too logical, too noble, Alkaios would never understand that I am not choosing to leave of my own volition, but instead because of the divine will of Olympus. I can't let him follow, and I can't let myself enjoy his pride in me.

Just as I pass the first line of houses, he manages to catch me, his firm hand latching tight around my wrist. "Wait, Daphne. Let me congratulate you first before you run off to your friends."

My heart stutters. I can feel Artemis's eyes upon me, in the gold latched firmly to my body. I wait helplessly for her to smite Alkaios and punish him for keeping me from immediately obeying her commands.

But she does nothing, and with a soft exhale I let him hold my hand longer than I should, enjoying this rare moment of intimacy. "I don't think I can remember a time when you were ever proud of me."

"Now is not the time to pity yourself." Alkaios's voice is as sharp-edged as a dagger. The voice of a brother forced to play the role of father. "It doesn't suit you."

Heat creeps into my cheeks and I clench my teeth. I should have known that he would never feel anything but contempt for me.

"Jealous?" I yank from his grip harder than I must, my words carefully measured barbs that stab my own heart as well. "Maybe if you had won the race all those years ago, you could have brought honor to our family, as I have. Are you ashamed that I am now more Spartan than you ever could be?"

His lips curl back to bare his teeth. "You are no Spartan. You think winning this race will make you one? We are still *Mothakes*, and nothing will ever change that. No matter how much you, Pyrrhus, Ligeia, and even those imposters parading around pretending to be our parents insist that we belong, we *never* will. Because they're not our parents, not truly, and you're the reason my real mother is dead."

The vehemence with which he believes those words, those stabbing, painful words, shakes Alkaios's frame with every breath, his dark-brown eyes burning into the gray of my own.

That's all I'll ever be to him. Not a sister, but instead a murderer. Pyrrhus blames the gods for our mother's death. Alkaios blames me.

I spin to leave, but Alkaios catches my wrist again, his grip like an iron manacle. "Wait. Where is Pyr?"

"I don't know." I jerk from his grasp and tear the bronze bangle from my wrist, flinging it to the ground at his feet—a reminder that we will never belong. "Good luck finding him. Maybe if you pray to Artemis she'll give you a hint. Pyrrhus is quite the unruly animal."

He bends to collect my bracelet, and I take the opportunity to lose him in the crowd, flitting among the unruly masses like a passing shadow.

I break from the last of the revelers as the goddess Eos paints the sky with the colors of dawn, bathing the city lavender and gold. The echoes of the festival are distant rumbles by the time I arrive home and sprint across the jade-tiled courtyard to my room.

With everything I pass, regret swells in my heart. There's no time to murmur farewells to the familiar things I may never see again. My first bow, a jaguar carved from oak, the flowers left by Lykou yesterday scattered across my floor. The cloak I arrived in Sparta with, wrapped around my tiny frame as Pyrrhus carried me over the threshold of our parents' home in the crook of his arm.

I was far too young at the time to remember our arrival myself, not yet two months old. Pyrrhus has shared much of the day with me, eventually succumbing to my relentless questions about our life before Sparta. He told me of the early snows that swept after their feet, and Alkaios's obstinate refusal to cry, though apparently his face remained pinched nonetheless. He also told me of how he held me every step of the way, the months-long journey to Sparta from the coastal village of my birth. And of the surprise parting my Spartan parents' lips as they looked over us crowding their doorstep.

They were hesitant at first, Pyrrhus said, bitterness lacing his words. It was unbecoming among Sparta's political elite to take in strays. But Ligeia, wearing the red cloak of an oracle, spoke but five words and they immediately swept us inside.

"These are the gods' chosen."

What a fool I was to think it was a simple bluff on Ligeia's part to get us a home. In a way it was. I'm not the gods' chosen. I'm nothing more than a god's pawn.

I shove the memory aside. A soldier's precision guides my movements as I gather the essential belongings for the task ahead of me. One cloak, my fighting leathers, a few durable chitons and a *himation* made for traveling, a *kalyptra* veil necessary for women in the less enlightened corners of Greece, a single sword, and a leather waterskin. I throw all in a worn sack, hoisting it over my shoulders and strapping my new *dory* across my back.

Moving toward the door, I notice the comb resting on my furs. Smooth, unblemished ivory, inlaid with gold filigree and set with emeralds from all the way across the Aegean in Troy. My adoptive father gave it to me only this morning, a token to celebrate what he and his wife hoped to be my last *Carneia* as an unmarried woman.

I stride from my room and toss the lavish comb in the center courtyard for them to find. It bounces and clatters across the floor. Hopefully, they will think I have run away because of the gift, fleeing from any potential marriages, and that I'm ungrateful for all they have done. It would be best that way, to ensure nobody tries to chase me down.

All that they've done for me, all that I've worked for, to make myself equal in the eyes of Sparta, is now laid waste. I choke back a small sob.

Immersed in my thoughts, I fail to notice the smell of sandalwood heralding my handmaid's appearance. Framed in a halo of burgeoning sunlight, Ligeia stands in the doorway.

In one long glance, she takes in my torn clothes and sack. Her weathered and wrinkled face pulls tight in a sad smile. Before I can muster any plausible excuse, she glides forward with arms extended and I fold into her embrace. The fear of never seeing Ligeia again weighs heavy on my heart. I should have paid closer attention to her stories, appreciated her wisdom, and valued her love.

"I knew from the moment I first saw you that the gods would take you from us someday." Holding me at arm's length, she fixes one eye on me, the other unfocused and cloudy. I don't bother to ask how she knows of my dealings with the gods. She always knows.

"Make some excuse for my disappearance," I beg, words tumbling from my mouth in a rush. "They mustn't know where I'm going. *I* don't even know where I'm going. And they can never think that Pyr is a deserter."

Ligeia nods, leading me across the courtyard with a hand on my elbow. She bends and scoops up the comb before tucking it into the folds of her dress. "Thought your parents might think you ran away? Pah." She waves a hand in the air. "They are not fools. You have gone to the Oracle of Delphi to give thanks for your mighty victory tonight, I think. And while you are away, you will need to hunt for food." She hands me my daggers from the wall along with my other hunting gear. "But you will need other provisions."

While I wait in the deserted kitchen, she packs a small bag with dried figs, flatbread, and jerky before disappearing into an adjoining room and returning with a small leather bag that jingles suspiciously.

I know its contents without looking. "It's your savings. I can't."

Ligeia smiles wistfully and drops the small bag into the larger. "Once you get a chance, hide as many coins as you can. A few in your quiver, your sheath, and carry the rest on your body. Maybe even in that unruly hair of yours. The roads grow more dangerous with each day, especially outside the reach of Sparta. Be wary of treacherous Athenians. Better yet, trust no one."

She envelops me in a warm hug and pulls away to press something small and cold into my hand. A necklace, delicate and beautiful in its simplicity. Suspended from a thin silver chain is a small crow, wings unfurled, and made of white gold.

"A gift I have saved for many years now. Your mother's before that day." Ligeia slips the necklace around my neck, her hands resting on my shoulders. "You look so much like her and share so much of her fire and grace."

"My true mother?" I finger the cold metal as it sits between my breasts, the only piece of a forgotten past.

"Yes. She wanted you to have it. It seems she knew her fate." Ligeia's breath catches as her fingers travel over the path of gold that decorates my skin. "The Midas Curse. Oh, my wild *kataigída*."

I spin around, covering the gold as much as I can beneath my palm. "How do you know about the Curse?"

She rests a finger beneath her clouded eye. "This sees much more than you would guess. It saw the fate of your mother, and the fates of many mothers before her. I can see the twisted paths of the gods and the tricks they play."

I want to press for more, but she says, "That is a story for another day. Now you must leave."

Afraid she will see my fear or hear it in my voice, I nod once and press a kiss to Ligeia's cheek. Straightening my back, I cross the courtyard to the stables. Bridling a horse in darkness is always a challenge, but once completed, I ride out onto the streets of Sparta.

At the gates out of town, though, I turn around for one last look at the city I've come to love. Bonfires still blaze in the distance, and drums rumble beyond the houses lining the fields. Looming in the center is the *gymnasion* where I spent a decade learning the *dory*, horseback riding, and parrying a dagger. The theater echoes with the last of the night's revelers, and the palace and the Temple of Artemis cast twin shadows on the horizon.

I once paid fealty to the goddess in that altar. Almost offered up my life in service to her, too. Lykou, as he had many times before, professed his undying affection for me, but that time had been different. His gaze was ardent, his yearning for me as undeniable as the setting of the sun. I knew it was only a matter of time before his words turned to questions I couldn't answer.

So I climbed the hill to Artemis's Temple, crossed the white marble threshold, and bent the knee before her statue. The promise of my eternal service hung on my lips, though. If I turned to the life of priesthood, I would have to give up the *dory*, the sword, and all that comes with blood and battle. I would have to give up my goal of becoming a Spartan.

Had I said those words, would my position be any different now? Only the gods could say.

CHAPTER 6

Artemis's promised Olympian escort waits for me on the other side of the gates.

Apollo sits astride a fine chestnut stallion, and with the rising sun behind him, his face is cast in deep shadows. I ride closer, his features becoming clearer, and my stomach flips despite myself.

"Like two sides of the same coin, Artemis and Apollo are twins. One and the same, unable to live in a world without the other. Artemis is the moon, a cold, healing light, whereas the beauty of Apollo's sun is unforgiving and unyielding."

Ligeia's words fly to the forefront of my memory. Like his sister, Apollo has the body and face of a youth, only a year or two my senior, and otherworldly beauty. His fair skin is impossibly smooth, reminiscent of the sneering nobles that hide in their houses while their inferiors labor under the burning sun. He's unarmed save for a glimmering golden bow hanging across his back. A coward's weapon in the eyes of a Spartan. The thought feeds my growing distaste for the Olympians, and I grasp at it desperately, for how else can I keep company with a god?

Apollo surveys me from under thick lashes with blue eyes that rival the Aegean on a clear day. A smile pulls at the corner of his mouth.

"Daphne." He says my name like a caress.

"The god of sunlight and prophecy relentlessly pursued men and women, like his father, even to their deaths."

I nod by way of greeting. "Escort."

I turn toward the road ahead to regain my composure. Hopefully Apollo doesn't share his sister's penchant for curses.

"Where are we going?" I ask, clenching the reins to still my trembling hands.

"Mount Kazbek. An old friend lives there and he has the answers we seek."

I cannot fight the groan escaping my lips. "That is at least a month's journey from here."

"Don't worry about that," Apollo says with an airy wave. "We'll arrive at Mount Kazbek much sooner than you expect."

"An Olympian perk, I presume?"

"The first of many I can offer you." He leans across the space between us, balancing on his stallion so his face is only inches from mine.

"I will not be seduced by you, or any other god." I turn forward again, snapping my horse's reins.

Perhaps I should be more tactful around the gods that control the very world. But my patience was nonexistent to begin with, and Artemis's manipulation has soured whatever reverence I would have had. Besides, I have no desire to join the list of Apollo's doomed conquests.

A gentle pressure at the base of my spine makes me spin on my horse and Apollo's hand snaps back too fast for me to slap.

"What were you doing?" I demand, pawing my back to make sure he didn't press a burr into my clothes. But all that's there is the Midas Curse. The golden band slithers along my skin, encircling my waist twice over like a snake entrapping its prey.

Apollo is unruffled, his eyes as wide and innocent as a child's. "I wanted to see the Midas Curse."

"Ask your sister to show you," I say, clucking to my horse and urging it to the far side of the road—and away from him. "Maybe she'll give you a taste of that arrow if you're polite enough."

Undaunted, Apollo follows, riding alongside me once more. Heat flushes my cheeks when I notice his gaze trailing my neck. "I'm jealous Heph gave it to Artemis and not me. Gold is obviously my color." He threads large fingers through his burnished bronze curls. I don't even dignify him with a response. I doubt he could be any more pompous.

"Only joking. Red suits me much better."

Apparently, he can.

I huff. "Can you please stop talking?"

Apollo arches an eyebrow. "I cannot abide silence. It bores me."

It takes all my patience to keep from shoving his arrogant ass to the ground. Would Artemis rescind her promise of protection for my brother if I did? Would she command the Midas Curse to kill me over such a small slight? The hardened gold inches up my spine as if reading my treacherous thoughts, but I'm still sorely tempted to find out.

I change tactics. "Wouldn't you prefer to stay with your sister in your fancy palace atop Mount Olympus? Wouldn't Athena or Hermes be much more suited for this task?"

Apollo pretends to gag. "You wouldn't last a day with either of them. Athena would find every opportunity to nag you. And Hermes would have stolen your dress with a snap of his fingers and made you ride naked for a month."

"So I should be grateful that you didn't steal my dress before you put your hands on me?" I give him a sharp glare and tug down the hem of my chiton as far as it will go.

Apollo guides his stallion closer to mine, his unnatural warmth sending a small shiver over my skin. "Precisely."

Before I can retort or shove him away, Apollo leans back with a self-satisfied smile, his knee jostling mine before he rides ahead. Anyone willing to be friends with him must be either a monster or insane.

My horse plods on and on, and it takes all my strength to keep my tired and aching body astride. The trees rise high on either side of the road in impassive walls of deep green.

What an unremarkable start.

Late in the day, my hair rises on the back of my neck and arms. I scour the road behind us, but find nothing peculiar. Not even dust above the road to mark the passage of our own travel. The road has been devoid of any travelers for hours other than a tinker who tried to sell me useless laurel wreaths. The two days after *Carneia* are days of recovery from the festivities, so nobody should be leaving the city anytime soon.

"What can I expect to find at Mount Kazbek? What kind of *friend* awaits us?" I ask to fill the deepening silence. "An angry gryphon perched on the cliffs to swoop and swallow me whole? A band of Amazons that I must fight or become their slave? The Typhon, ready to skewer me with a single glance?"

Apollo turns away for the first time in hours, clenching his reins. "He's more of a *former* friend of the family."

My horse whinnies irritably as I jerk on the reins. "You mean to tell me we're traveling all the way to Mount Kazbek with no guarantee we'll get answers from this *friend*? What did you do? Steal his wife? Never mind, don't answer that. I already know that I won't like the answer."

Unmoved, Apollo leans back on his horse. "I don't think he ever had a wife, and if he did, Father never bothered to introduce us. Probably for the best."

Because you would likely seduce and leave her for dead, I don't say aloud.

The sun begins its descent, quickly plunging beyond the forest. Its last rays reflect off Apollo's bronze hair. I scrutinize his hands: smooth, graceful, and obviously unworked.

"Why you?" I ask. Apollo jerks forward at my question. "Why do *you* have to come with me and not one of your more useful brethren?"

He doesn't meet my gaze, running his fingers through the dark mane of his stallion.

"I must earn my father's favor...and forgiveness," Apollo finally says. I can't help but notice the pale bone peeking beneath the skin of his knuckles as he clenches a fist.

The prospect of embarrassing him further only makes me smile wider. "What did you do to earn Zeus's ire? Defile his throne? Seduce his lover? Set fire to his favorite kingdom half a century ago?" Cynicism seeps into my voice, and I do little to mask it.

My taunts stir not even a glimmer of ire. He searches my face before turning his focus to my mother's necklace. "That's a curious trinket," he says, though without a hint of warmth. "I despise crows."

I tuck the necklace under my chiton and away from his prying gaze. "Curious how?"

"I knew the owner of the necklace many years ago."

"You knew my mother?"

He cocks an eyebrow. "That necklace has been around much longer than your mother."

"Then whose was it before it passed to her?"

"Nobody you should ever hope to meet." Apollo faces the road, dismissing me.

He's determined to kill me with curiosity. Silence stretches between us once again, broken only by the steady plop of hooves. I pass the time by going over Paidonomos Leonidas's lessons in my head, filing through the different blocks and return strikes a soldier would employ while under attack from more than three armed assailants. But my mind keeps spinning back to Sparta and that fateful meeting with Artemis.

The sun god's attention snaps back, not directed at me but to the road behind us. His brows furrow together in a frown.

"We should make camp," he says, and, without another word, guides his stallion into the dark of the surrounding forest.

Shadows reach long, dark arms across the circle of our makeshift camp. The sparks of our small fire dance high into the sky then spiral downward into the glowing coals. Watching them, I nibble on a string of dried meat, though I have no appetite. Apollo brandishes a *kylix* of wine that seems to have materialized out of thin air. He takes a deep swallow, face masked in shadow.

Setting aside the meat, I pick up my new *dory* and balance it in my palms. Despite its short length, the balance and make are decent, good enough to skewer someone who wishes me harm.

"What will you name your prize?" Apollo asks, *kylix* sloshing as he uses it to point at the weapon.

"Naming weapons is for fools."

Apollo blinks. "That's the most absurd thing I've ever heard. You mortals have been naming weapons for centuries. What would an assailant fear more, a puny little stick like that, or a spear named something like Praxidikai, the Exactor of Justice."

I open my mouth to snap a retort, but nothing comes out. Loathe as I am to admit it, that name is rather ingenious. Would the Moirai look upon me favorably if I named my weapon in honor of one?

"You like that." Apollo looks at me askance, grinning crookedly. "Are you going to defend my honor with the mighty Praxidikai if we're attacked by brigands in the night, darling?"

Clutching the *dory*—Praxidikai—to my chest, I lay back on my bedroll with a heavy sigh. "There are no thieves this close to Sparta. The army regularly patrols these woods and rids them of any vermin that threaten trade. Besides"—I thumb the edge of the spearhead—"I'm at least armed. How is a golden bow without any arrows of use?" I point to the golden weapon at his side, shimmering despite the black of the night.

Despite my distaste for the weapon of cowards, I must admit that the bow is exceptionally beautiful, inlaid with ivory and carved with the *meander* from point to point. A design at once plain and unordinary, the *meander* represents the eternal flow of life, a collection of lines that turn in on themselves, very much like the currents of a river, and is only meant to be worn by royalty.

For the price of that bow, I could buy a palace.

"This was given to me by my mother, Leto." Apollo grabs the bow, rolling it in his palm. He points to the moon staring down at us, full and overwhelming. "My sister has its twin, though she can only use it when the moon has faded to the merest crescent of silver." I glance to the moon, hoping to see some hint of Artemis in its silver face, but nothing stares back at me. He continues, "Only one with Olympus in their veins could even hope to draw back the string of either."

"You failed to answer my question." I flip onto my back. "How is it supposed to defend us?"

"You needn't worry about that." Apollo flicks a nonexistent piece of dirt from his chiton. "Not when my sister's nymphs and dryads watch over us."

"Olympian gifts are fading, or so your sister says." A sharp edge leaches into my voice. "What will happen to us when her minions no longer feel the need to obey her commands?"

"You're much smarter than you let on with your brutish act."

"I'm self-sufficient, not a brute. I am a trained soldier of Sparta and I—"

"You're not a soldier," Apollo interrupts, his eyes lit with the barest hint of mockery. "You're a *Mothakes,* and a woman who can never ascend to the status of Spartiate. Besides, if you don't fear mercenaries, thieves, or brigands, then you should be terrified of other denizens of the dark. There are far crueler things that prowl the darkness than criminals."

I sniff. "Spartans don't have time to contemplate the mysteries of the world."

"Says the girl who still begs for bedtime stories from her precious Ligeia. You needn't worry your lovely head over such things, little *kataigída.*" Surprise at the family nickname stirs in my chest, but I don't have the chance to ask how he knows it. Apollo sets his wine jug down with an exaggerated sigh. "For now, the only thing we have to worry about are spies."

He snaps his fingers. A heavy crash echoes through the trees and I leap to my feet. Apollo strides into the forest. A short scuffle breaks the silence before he saunters back to the fire. The spy marches in front of him.

"Lykou?" I gasp.

My friend's cheeks are flushed as Apollo thrusts him toward the fire. I gently tuck one of his dark curls behind an ear, revealing a bruise blossoming on his temple, as well as the deep cut splitting his lower lip.

"I noticed this one tracking us around midday," Apollo says, nostrils flared and jaw clenched. He circles Lykou, cutting a sharp glance from his head to his toes. "I could smell his mortality as keenly as manure in a stable. Friend of yours?"

"My definition of friend?" I snap, taking Lykou's hands. "Or yours?"

I turn over his palm, examining a gash. He must have fallen hard when Apollo caught him spying on us. While I consider whether the cut needs to be cleaned and bound, my gaze catches on his wrist.

Dead flowers and torn leaves hang from a cord around his wrist. The garland from *Carneia*.

"What are you doing, Daphne?" he asks, dark eyes beseeching. "Why did you leave Sparta?"

Apollo answers for me. "You are not in a position to be asking questions."

How did Lykou even know I left? I drop his hand. My jaw clenches, throat tightening around a withheld curse. For whatever foolish reason, now that Lykou has followed us, he, too, has become a pawn in the gods' games. Another person I must protect. I want to urge him to run before Apollo unleashes his ire. But, like an ache in my bones, I know it's too late.

Lykou has unwittingly entangled his fate with the dark games of Olympus.

"I thought you were deserting Sparta," he explains, ducking his head. "And I wanted to come with you...then I saw you with *him*, and I had to know who he is...what..."

Nonplussed, I shake my head. There's no way that he would desert his family, his people, and all of Sparta because I'd had the audacity to flirt with him. I shove him away. "You're a fool. Return to Sparta before they brand you as a deserter." I try to infuse a wealth of anger and contempt into my voice to mask my fear. Maybe I can save Lykou, get him to leave, before Apollo has the chance to bend him to his will.

Lykou turns to glare at his captor. "What do you hold over her?"

"Her brother's life, the lives of everyone she loves, Sparta, everyone in Greece." Apollo ticks off each on his fingers, then points a long index finger at Lykou. "And now *you*."

I blanch. My throat clenches so tight that I have to force the words from my throat. "Just let him go. He won't say a word."

"He's human, of course he'll tell." Apollo tuts with mock disappointment. "But I can change that. Lykou, you said? How fitting."

I cry out, realizing Apollo's plan for my friend far too late. His transformation is different from Pyrrhus's. He falls to the ground, thrashing and roaring. He claws at his head, back, legs, and neck, skin rippling and contorting in the firelight. A ringing builds in my ears as his body turns in on itself, then snaps back, shifting from human to wolf.

My mouth opens and closes, heart thundering in my ears. Dumbstruck and horrified, I run trembling fingers through the coarse, black fur along Lykou's back. He whines, eyes beseeching mine, begging me to fix this. Because I let this happen. Again. I let the gods steal another person from my life.

Behind me, Apollo chuckles. Lykou snarls, baring long fangs.

"What is it with Olympians and their obsession with turning mortals into animals?" My voice rises with each word, and by the end I'm screaming.

"There." Apollo points at my face. I swat his finger away, wanting to shove it down his throat. "There's the fire inside you."

"Oh, you want fire?"

My fist meets Apollo's chin with a solid crack. He spins, crumpling to his knees.

Impulsive? Yes.

Gratifying? Yes.

Insane? Sadly, also yes.

Lykou's eyes are wide, his fur on end. The Midas Curse stirs around my throat, ready to snuff the life from my veins.

With one thoughtless swoop of my fist, I've damned my life, my brother's life, and that of my friend, to Tartarus.

Apollo climbs to his feet and brushes the dirt off his chest and knees with slow, deliberate movements. He doesn't look my way for what feels like an age. I'm ready to kneel and beg, if not for *my* life, then at least for those of my brother and Lykou.

Apollo faces me. His grin is slick and dangerous like a sidewinding viper. I drop, hands pressed to the ground.

"Forgive me, I did not think…" I begin, but falter.

He saunters forward until his knee rests against my head. I bite my lip, watching him through my lashes, and he bids me to rise, pulling me up with a firm finger under my chin. Apollo's gaze rests on the crow between my breasts before assessing my face.

"I like your fire," he says, voice low and husky. The Midas Curse moves on to drape itself across my shoulders. "But know that when you play with fire, the flames are not forgiving."

I stagger from his grasp, mouth open. "Are you going to punish me?"

Apollo scoffs, collecting his *kylix*. He gestures to my bedroll, indicating for me to take a seat, which I do without hesitation. Lykou paces behind me, fangs bared at the Olympian. Apollo ignores him and watches me across the flames. I fidget under his intense gaze, my fingers reaching for the hem of my chiton, bedroll, water jerkin, anything to distract me from his unyielding scrutiny.

"I will not punish you, but neither will I return your *friend* to his true form." I open my mouth to protest, but he cuts me off by raising a hand, palm facing me. Pale calluses I had not noticed before glimmer in the firelight. "Not, at least, until our quest is at its end. He must earn his freedom for himself."

Lykou snarls again. His basalt fur ripples in the firelight, the muscles of a Spartan warrior tensed and ready to spring.

Apollo's back straightens. "Don't be a fool. I could have done much worse. I could have transformed you into a snail and crushed you beneath my heel."

Lykou's snarls abruptly stop. With a resigned growl, he plops onto the bedroll and glares at Apollo over his paws. I run a hand along his fur, soothing his furious trembling.

"We can't be constantly at each other's throats if we expect to survive this journey, Daphne." Apollo looks upward, to the earliest stars puncturing the darkening sky. "Artemis chose you for a reason, so I suggest you don't make her look like a fool by killing us all."

I itch to ask if he knows Artemis's reason for choosing me, but some deep part inside of me also loaths to. I don't want to owe anything to Apollo, least of all answers.

He meets my gaze levelly. "I am your ally, not your enemy."

I want to argue with him, tell him that I wouldn't ordinarily ally myself with someone who transforms my friends and family into wild beasts. But Apollo, loath as I am to admit it, will probably be the only one standing between me and the Underworld throughout this quest. I bite my tongue and allow the god a curt nod.

"Good. Now get some rest. The journey is long and our time is short." Apollo lies back, gazing at the stars with the *kylix* resting on his chest.

Following his lead, I lean back on my bedroll with my *himation* bunched up into a makeshift pillow, having neither the energy nor the will to fight with him further. I surrender to the god Hypnos, letting him draw me into a fitful sleep.

Nightmares plague me, my worst fears brought to life by my dreaming mind.

I dream of Pyrrhus, wandering the forest in deer form, stalked by an ever-encroaching hunter's gait. The hunter steps from the trees, arrow aimed. A beam of iridescent sunlight reflects off his pale skin to reveal Alkaios's stern face. Ignorant of our brother's transformation, Alkaios lets the arrow sing.

I jerk awake just as the arrow finds its mark in Pyrrhus's heart.

CHAPTER
7

On and on we ride, our path taking us beyond the boundaries of the world I know, farther than the reaches of Greece, to the Caucasus Mountains. A journey that should have taken months takes us only days. Each night, Apollo leads us off the roads into the forest for our camp and I'm haunted by nightmares, and each morning as we leave the trees, we step onto a path entirely new. Leagues of land are swept past under my slumbering body, and after only seven days we arrive at the foothills of Mount Kazbek.

I stare up at its breathtaking height, my throat suddenly dry. The mountain juts from the earth like a titan's thumb, bereft of trees to mask the expanse of snow and gray rock face, a stark contrast to the lush red and green mountains of Sparta.

Without a word, Apollo leads our horses on, climbing steadily upward into the foothills. I struggle not to be daunted by Kazbek's sheer height and the icy breeze descending from its snowy peak. I pull my cloak close, wrapping my arms around my chest; my fingers rest on the Midas Curse. Each day the curse spreads, reaching long, spindly golden tendrils from my abdomen to my breast, reminding me that I'm now an instrument of Artemis's will and power.

Lykou trots alongside my horse. He's followed us, whining with every step. Though I pity him, there is nothing I can do. Attempts to convince Apollo to change him back have elicited only smirks or silence, both equally enraging. My latest request results in the god launching into a randy tune about wolves and maidens that makes me grind my teeth.

When Apollo finally calls our horses to a halt at the mountain's base, I would prefer another week of his singing. Its menacing rock face and jagged peaks loom before us. An unknown specter lurks from the highest peak, biding its time, waiting for my arrival. The fact that the Olympian is unmoved about who awaits us fills me with greater alarm.

I allow myself only a heartbeat of fear before leaping from my horse, gathering my weapons and satchel.

Spartans don't fear death. Death fears them.

A tic forms at Apollo's temple, his jaw clenched, as he brings his horse beside mine. Since reaching the Caucasus Mountain range, Apollo has fallen unusually silent, only throwing an occasional glance my way. He dismounts, his clean, white chiton flaring to reveal corded, muscular legs. I force myself to look away, picking at my own disgusting clothes. Once a beautiful crimson, my chiton is now the color of clay and stiff with dirt and sweat.

"Going unarmed?" I ask, noticing that he's left the golden bow behind with his horse.

"Worried about me? How touching." Apollo's gaze rests on me briefly before refocusing on the mountain. "Weapons are useless to us here."

I turn to Lykou, kneeling and running a hand through his dark, dense fur. He rumbles in response, predicting what I'm going to say. "I need you to stay with the horses. Keep them to the shadows."

Lykou snarls, ears back. A firm no.

I angle my head, searching his dark eyes. It pains me that nothing remains of his once handsome face other than those eyes. "Please, Lykou. This isn't the kind of terrain for a wolf. And we'll need the horses for the return journey, so you have to stay and make sure they're safe."

He huffs on my face, yips once and then snaps at the horses' hooves, herding them toward a small grove. At least the shade will provide him a respite from the unrelenting sun.

"You may go first," Apollo says from beside me. I can feel his gaze on my face.

"After you, *aeráki*." I flash him my sweetest smile.

The treeless slopes of Mount Kazbek are rough and unforgiving. Knee-high shrubs bite my skin, rough stones threatening to rip through my only pair of sandals. Trying not to think about how far I have left to trek, I focus on putting one foot in front of the other and block out everything but the sound of my heavy breathing. Though my endurance is high from years of tutelage in Sparta, the many sleepless, nightmare-addled nights have left me drained.

The narrow footpath rises sharply then vanishes around the rocky outcroppings. My instincts guide me as Helios shepherds the sun high above us, scorching my shoulders and leaving me drenched with sweat. I press close to the rock, dragging myself over ledge after ledge, treading carefully along crumbling precipices.

"Just think of nice thoughts, mortal, to get yourself through this trek. Like cold water, crispy lamb..."

"And punching you in the face again."

"To each their own."

"Sorry," I say between gritted teeth. "Civility is hard when the god holding my life hostage presses on my heels."

"Then let's move on to more polite conversation." Apollo quickens his pace to walk alongside me. "Where did you get that necklace?"

I almost can't hear him over the sound of my own heavy breathing. "What? Oh, I already told you. It was my mother's."

"Yeah, but where did *she* get it?"

"How would I know?" I snap, walking faster. "The gods stole her from me before I even took my first breath."

"And you're not curious as to where she got it?"

"Of course I'm curious." I swipe the back of my hand across my sweaty forehead. Apollo doesn't have even a drop of sweat on him.

"We could take a break if you like," Apollo says, indicating to a boulder for me to sit.

"I'm not tired, truly." I shake my head. I'm not lying when I say, "Just overwarm."

"Curious." Apollo's lips purse, his eyes taking on a knowing glimmer. "This pace would kill a lesser man."

"Well I'm no *lesser man*." I continue up the mountain, the muscles in my calves and thighs straining against the sharp incline. The burn feels good though, reminding me that I'm still alive. "The training in Sparta has prepared me for worse toils than this."

"Have you never noticed how much faster you are than your peers?" Apollo easily keeps pace. His hand brushes mine and I snap it away. "How much stronger you are than most of the men, even?"

I halt, the air leaving my chest in a huge rush. "What are you implying?"

Apollo stops, too. His face is inches from mine, gaze again on the crow at the hollow of my neck. "Do you really believe that you beat Prince Castor and Lykou to the forest simply because you trained harder than them? The prince is a born and bred athlete, his family a legacy of wrestlers and runners, despite their royal status. Lykou is the swiftest in his age group and had been training for *Carneia* for years."

My nostrils flare. "I knew the forest better than either of them."

"You beat them both to the forest, and you would be a fool to believe that it was simply because you're faster." He steps even closer. His warm breath brushes my cheek as he plucks the crow from my chest and holds it between our faces. "But you're no fool. Consider where this necklace came from, and why your mother would bequeath it to you and not one of your brothers. That she gave it to your precious Ligeia on the eve of her death, which you blame on the gods. That all your life, you have persevered above the odds in races and fights, against men twice your size and skill. Do you really think that you can credit all that to how hard you train?"

"Yes." I jerk the necklace from his grasp and take a step back. "Because I grew up with the odds towering high against me. I saw those odds, and I strove to best them. I saw the men with, as you say, twice my size and skill, and I worked four times as hard as them. I owe nothing to the gods, least of all the victories I paid blood, sweat, and tears for."

Apollo inclines his head. "Your mother wasn't nearly as stubborn as you."

I blink, mouth popping open. He leaves me oscillating between surprise and fury, clenching my jaw so tight my teeth threaten to shatter, and resumes the long climb. It is a long moment before I have my temper reined in enough to follow without shoving him off the face of the mountain.

When we reach a narrow outcropping only just large enough for the two of us, the air escapes my lips in a shrill whistle. An impossible expanse of rock face stretches into the cloudless sky. I struggle to find my footing, the stone rough and scalding beneath the midday sun. Apollo scales the surface easily, immune to the laws of nature that are the bane of mortals like me.

He reaches down from the top of the wall. "Take my hand."

"I'd rather eat stone."

He shrugs. "You just might."

Ignoring his offered hand, I leap, and immediately regret my pig-headedness when my body meets stone with bone-jarring impact. My hands just barely manage to grasp the rock ledge.

I make the mistake of glancing down to find footing, and my stomach somersaults. The earth falls away beneath the platform and I dangle in midair. I hadn't realized how high we'd climbed, or just how far from safety we've pushed ourselves. If luck was with me, a fall might land me on the platform below. As panic seizes me, I send up a prayer to the goddess Tyche for luck and press close to the rock, clenching my eyes shut.

"Find your footing, Daphne."

I can barely hear Apollo over the thundering of my heart.

"You've got to open your eyes," he commands. I look up to see him watching me from the ledge, the corners of his mouth drawn down in concern. "Find your footing and climb. Don't think about what is beneath you, only how far you have left to go."

I force my eyes open and look up. There, just beyond my right hand, is another small crevice. I grab at it eagerly, then find another, and again before I drag my body over the ledge. I recover the shreds of my dignity amid gasps for breath.

Apollo regards me with a smug "should have accepted my help" smirk.

"I don't need your help," I say, refusing to meet his gaze further.

"Then your stubbornness will kill us both."

I look up and immediately regret it. His smile has fallen. Fury colors the god's cheeks a dark red, his eyes lit with the fires of Tartarus. Hugging my knees to my chest, I will the blush creeping inexorably up my neck to disappear.

"It's one thing to sacrifice your own neck," Apollo continues, each word like the lash of a whip, "but it's another to sacrifice this entire mission because you're too proud to accept my help. This isn't just about getting your brother back; it's about saving my home. If the loss of either of those things doesn't inspire you to ask for help when you need it, then Artemis chose the wrong person."

I leap to my feet. "She did not."

He leans close, his face a scant few inches from my own. "Prove it."

At the next outcropping, when he offers assistance again, I choose safety over pride for the first time in my life.

When we finally crest the top, I want to rest, savor the victory of climbing the peak. The wind whips around me, making my hair slice against my cheeks and shoulders. Snow covers the ground, and I blink away tears as the sun's golden rays reflect off the white surface. I raise a hand to shade my eyes and freeze.

A man, spread-eagled between twin stone columns, hangs limp from his chained wrists before us. When he lifts his head and sees us, he manages a tight smile.

I never enjoyed Ligeia's stories of Prometheus's plight and his cruel punishment—though Alkaios loved them. She shared his story to warn me of the cruel realities of this world and the crueler punishments of the gods.

He is not at all how I imagined him, barely surpassing my own height, his black hair dense with silver strands. Under the slashes and scars, and despite centuries of malnourishment and neglect, his well-muscled and toned body holds firm in the wind. Deep-brown eyes that convey a universe of knowledge pierce me, holding me paralyzed.

"So, Zeus has sent a child to barter with me." Prometheus slumps against one of the pillars and the chains rattle in protest. I look to Apollo for guidance, for a clue as to what to say, but he remains tight-lipped.

"Believe me," Prometheus says, nodding toward Apollo. "*He* has nothing left to offer me."

I step forward, but Apollo tries to pull me back, his hand scalding against my wind-chafed skin. Jerking free with a simmering glare, I march toward Prometheus. The closer I get, the harder the wind blows. My necklace seems to thrum with each step.

I offer my water jerkin and the titan nods his acceptance. He gulps the water eagerly, moaning as I pour it into his mouth. After drinking his fill, he coughs, heaving against the chains before sagging into them. I reach into my bag to pull out a piece of flatbread.

Prometheus shakes his head. "Mortal food cannot sate my hunger, but I thank you for the gesture." His gaze drops to my mother's necklace and a knowing smile spreads across his lips. "It's not every day that a *kataigída* appears on your mountaintop seeking answers."

"Can you tell me what was stolen from Zeus?" I ask, grasping at my necklace. Despite the brisk air, it's warm to the touch. "And where Apollo can find it?"

Apollo inches closer, hoping to hear. Prometheus's gaze focuses on him, smile vanishing. Something akin to fear flashes in his eyes.

I turn and press a hand against his chest. "Go back to Lykou and the horses. Prometheus will tell me nothing with you here."

"Giving me orders, mortal?" His words, though callous, are lilted and teasing. But the wariness with which he watches Prometheus leaves me to believe that perhaps Ligeia didn't have the whole story.

"We need answers," I grind out, teeth clenched to keep from chattering. "You brought me here to get them."

With the sun at his back, his features are unreadable but his anxiety is evident in the tight set of his shoulders. Finally, he strides away, muttering under his breath as he vanishes from view.

"He's infuriating. I can see why you didn't want to talk to him." I return my attention to Prometheus.

"Pride is one of the god of prophecy's many vices. It undoubtedly irks him to be ordered about by a disgraced titan and a young woman of seemingly little consequence."

"Seemingly?"

Prometheus chuckles dryly and ignores my question. "The Moirai toy with him. Being the son of Zeus is a heavy burden to carry."

"Must be horrible to have the world handed to you on a golden platter," I say, bitterness lacing my words. Before Prometheus can lecture me further, I come to the point. "What payment will you demand for the answers to my questions? Your freedom, perhaps?" I finger the chains above his raw wrists.

Despite the centuries atop this lonely crag, the metal is unblemished from the elements. The divine work of Hephaestus, no doubt.

Prometheus shakes his head. "If only that was yours to give." At my look of uncertainty, he elaborates, "Only Zeus can grant me that gift. Believe me, I've had friends that tried. Mot made an attempt at the height of his power, and was swiftly imprisoned."

I jerk my hand from the chains. "Who is Mot?"

Prometheus's lips split and bead with blood as he flashes a small smile, gaze traveling past me. "The world is much larger than Greece."

Titans must share the gods' penchant for riddles. "So, what can I offer you?"

"A promise."

Immediately wary, Ligeia's warnings echo in the back of my mind.

"Never make a deal with a god. A simple promise can result in a lifetime of servitude."

As if reading my mind, Prometheus's smile widens. "Your nursemaid has taught you well. Share with me some of your water—these ancient lungs have long since dried into husks and each word feels like a stabbing dagger in my throat."

After draining the skin, the titan sighs, a grimace replacing his smile. "I will not ask you for your life, or your future, or even the lives of your loved ones. I request that you promise to complete a task for me."

My hands tighten on the empty waterskin. A promise, though it be today or many years from now, can be just as damning.

He sighs again. "You don't trust me. That's fair, considering your recent experiences with Zeus's children. If you are unsuccessful, the Midas Curse will snuff the life from your veins before the summer is over. Lykou and Pyrrhus will never be returned to their human forms. Apollo, fickle as the summer wind, may ensnare your heart, willingly or not, and leave you in ruins. The paths of the gods are not lightly tread. See for yourself my own misfortune."

His words quickly stir a maelstrom of fear within me, be they prophecy or warning. I try not to let my feelings show, hardening my face and straightening my shoulders. Echoing what Alkaios has ingrained in me since the day I took my first, shaky steps, I say, "A true Spartan will not be weighed down or destroyed by that which could—"

"But you're no Spartan," Prometheus cuts me off, eyes sharp and cold like flint. "Sparta may be your home, but you are no Spartan."

His words cut to the bone. I've strived my entire life to be Spartan, to leave behind the *Mothakes* title hanging over my head. "Then what am I?"

"You will have to learn and accept that for yourself. And now the true purpose of your journey." Prometheus stretches his neck, his head straining from side to side. "Nine precious items have been stolen from Olympus and must be returned. Each day of their absence from Olympus, the magic, the power of all Olympians is unbound. These *pieces*," Prometheus makes a noise of distaste, "refine the power of Olympus so that it can be captured by the gods. Without them...it is volatile. It can be captured and harnessed by anyone, be they mortal, titan, or god."

"Anyone could capture this power?"

He nods. "They must be returned before that can happen. Even a single one of them missing has disastrous consequences. One was spirited away nearly a thousand years ago and entire kingdoms fell to ruin."

My throat tightens and I swallow back the dry taste of fear. "Who stole them?"

Prometheus looks back to where Apollo disappeared over the ledge. "A traitor among the Olympians."

"And what are these nine pieces?"

"My compassion toward Zeus's plight extends only so far. Besides, he and Apollo know very well what was stolen." Prometheus shrugs his shoulders, making the chains rattle. "But I can share with you four clear visions. Clues. Come closer, Daphne, for the winds have ears, and I don't wish them to carry this knowledge to anyone other than you."

I lean as close as I dare and his dry, hot breath tickles my cheek. I suppress a shiver.

Prometheus tilts his head, studying my face. "Place a finger upon my brow. You will see what has and what will be. My divine curse is knowledge."

"Curse?" My hand hesitates above his inclined head. "Not gift?"

"The powers of Olympus are no gift." He shakes his head before leaning toward me again. "Go on."

My trembling fingers press against his cool, pale forehead.

My life and a thousand others whip before my eyes, there and gone in a blink. And then they return, upended and awash with blue and gray. Gone again, then returned and completely new.

This is what is means to have the power of knowledge. This is the world through Prometheus's eyes.

He sees all that has been, will be, and could be. He sees the turns we will all take, the twists in life, and how our lives are shaped not by fate but the choices we make.

I'm no longer on the lonely mountain. Daubed walls surround me, rattling beneath a howling wind. A fire struggles in one corner of the cottage and in another corner a woman sits on a bed of dry grass and rough sheets. Agony rips through her body, wave after endless wave of painful contractions as the winds howl and rage outside. She grips the sheets below her with trembling hands.

It's not meant to be born, mutters a man in the vision. He's passing the length of the cottage and cursing under his breath. *It will be hideous,* he says, *a monster. It will spell disaster for the people of Greece, will incite wars and leave behind a river of blood.*

The door slams open, an oracle—Ligeia, I recognize the frizzy halo of hair above her head—strides to the screaming woman. I gasp as Alkaios, so small and innocent, runs inside the cottage and young Pyrrhus, his hair a bonfire of bright-red curls, cries in the corner, clutching a ragged quilt to his chest. His shimmering hair is a rat's nest I long to fix, the soot on his cheeks begging me to wipe his face.

The woman, whose blond hair and narrow chin match my own, gives one last scream. A baby forces her way into this world, kicking. The man disregards both oracle and newborn as he rushes to the shuddering woman, wiping a shaking hand across her sweat-sheened forehead.

Pyrrhus collects the child from the midwife, and I realize belatedly that it's me, my head already bedecked in a crown of flaxen curls. Pyrrhus presses his forehead to mine and a warm ache fills my chest. Seeing Pyrrhus hold me close like that, the man's face falls from despair to fury.

"Leave," he hisses, spittle flying from his mouth. Dropping the now lifeless hand of my mother, he leaps to his feet and points at me in Pyr's arms. "And take that creature far away from here."

"No, Papa." Alkaios grabs at his father's knees. "She's our sister. You can't send her away."

"She's not your sister." He considers my brother, now wrapped around his leg. The flame flickers in the hearth, illuminating the myriad emotions flitting across the man's face. Grief, fury, and finally resignation. He kicks Alkaios away, lips curling back to reveal his teeth. "She's a curse. The spawn of gods only know who. An Olympian begat.

"And your mother a whore." He points to his motionless wife again, then Pyrrhus, and then finally Alkaios. "How do I know that you are not all cursed godspawn?"

Ligeia steps close, wrapping an arm around Pyr's shoulders. "Speak gently. The gods hear every word and they do not easily forgive."

"Damn the gods," the man rages. "What more can they do to me? They have nothing left to smite me with. They have taken my wife and given me the spawn of Tartarus as a daughter. They can curse me all they want, for no curse nor weapon can wound me any longer." He points a long finger at me. "Especially not that monster."

"No, Papa," Alkaios says. His lips tremble as tears stream down his sooty cheeks. "I'm your son."

His father spares him not even a single glance. "Take the bastards away. Far from here. If I ever see them again, I will be branded for filicide."

He slams the cottage door open. The rain comes pouring in as he departs, leaving us huddled together against the fire.

Tugged away, I slide from one vision to the next as if guided by the gentle flow of a creek. Numbness envelops me. There is no surprise, despite Prometheus's revelations.

"To free the power of Olympus, three have been traded to the *anax* of Crete as playthings for his unruly son," Prometheus says, standing beside me and bereft of the chains that have burdened him for half a millennium.

I'm in what I imagine to be a cave, dark and dank, the stone floor littered with bones. Before me stands a tall cage, and inside huddle three figures, their features obscured by shadows. A rumble echoes behind me and I spin around, a ruined sword in my hand. Nothing emerges from the darkness, but at my feet sits a bull's mask. Its horns drip with blood.

I stumble backward and collide with something hard. I recoil but when I turn around it's a sandstone wall, the ground beneath me bloodstained. Howls pierce the air around me, before being abruptly drowned out by a symphony of hooves.

Prometheus raises a fist and sand pours between his clenched fingers. "Three more have been given to the plague of Thebes as a sacrifice so that the power may never return. Their only salvation lies behind doors opened through a test of wit and words. Do not despair of hope. They will wait for you."

Suddenly, there's water lapping at my feet, shimmering black and green and blue. Across the water, a man waits for me. He wears a midnight *peplos,* and his hair is gilded by moonlight. I don't need Prometheus to tell me that he is Hades and before me is the River Styx.

"A sacrifice will reveal two at the limits of Okeanos, meant to sow dissent, their fates bound to the river of the dead. And the last, the most celebrated, joins Tantalus, demanding body and soul."

Shadows lick the edges of each vision and the air reeks of magic, the smell as tangible as a field of lavender. The river swells, and from the depths steps Apollo. His hair is longer, bronze curls brushing his elbows, and a golden circlet rests on his brow. He grabs me by the wrists and jerks me to his chest. His skin is scalding to the touch. Rage burns in his eyes.

But he reaches up and brushes curls from my eyes, his touch nothing but tender. "My lovely Koronis. What did I ever do to deserve such a betrayal?"

His words are nonsensical, fingers tightening with every breath I take. A lyre plays from somewhere beyond us.

"Why would you betray me, my love?" Apollo asks, ignoring the noises of pain escaping me as his fingers dig deep enough to bruise.

The lyre's melody grows louder, building in a crescendo around us. Apollo opens his mouth to say more. A white crow cuts him off, flying into the god's face. Ivory feathers fill the air between us. Apollo roars and I rip free, stumbling backward.

The bird turns on me, attacking my face. With every beat of its white wings, another image appears, each more confusing than the next. I see the garden of the Hesperides, the tree's golden apples rotting and falling to the ground. There's a large *pyxis,* taller even than I, standing alone in a darkened tomb. The vase is carved but I can't get close enough to read the inscriptions before I'm ripped away once more.

It's all too much. None of it makes any sense. The roar of crashing waves, a strangled howl, and thunder of hooves. I fall to my knees and cradle my head. My eyes are clenched shut, crows screaming from the skies as arrows rain around me. It rises, all together, into a single long screech.

A hand rests gently on my trembling shoulder, and all the noise comes to an abrupt stop. My eyes flicker open. Prometheus pulls me to my feet and when he releases my hand, I stagger onto the lonely crag, the chains reappearing around his wrists.

I struggle for breath. My ears still ring. "What does it all mean?"

"It will all make sense when the time comes." He stretches, grimacing when the skin of his wrists tears beneath the manacles.

"And Apollo alone must find all of those…things?" My hair whips painfully around my face, the wind picking up as though spurred by my growing trepidation. "Alone?"

He assesses me again, gaze raking me from head to toe. "Would you have it otherwise?"

"What if Apollo is the traitor?" I ask, my hands clenched at my sides, so tight my nails dig into my palms. "He has always enjoyed dangerous games, messing with mortals' lives. What if he's the one who took the pieces of power in the first place? I can't trust him with this knowledge."

Prometheus merely gazes up at me, eyes unreadable.

"I need to do this," I say, more to myself than the titan. "I need to find these pieces and return them to Olympus." *Even if it means Pyrrhus will remain a deer,* I don't add. Guilt eats at me like a sickness.

"You are a small part of this world, one in a million souls, each as strong and determined and brilliant as you. What makes you think you're up to this task?"

"Because I have to be. This is what I have been training for my entire life. This is about more than saving my brother. Even if I returned to Artemis with the answers she sought, what use would they be if the power of Olympus falls into the wrong hands? Sparta could be destroyed by a single thought."

The titan smiles crookedly, as though his question was a test and I passed.

I may still be a pawn, a weapon wielded by the gods, but Prometheus has given me a gift. In his visions, he has planted hope inside me. Hope that I can be the one to see this journey to its end and the pieces safely returned to Olympus.

Past the edge of the Caucasus Mountains, Greece stretches wide and open and full of greater possibilities than I've ever known in Sparta. I will cross the shimmering blue sea, brave the vast golden deserts, and pick my way through the red mountains. Miles and miles of jagged and smooth, dangerous and unmapped terrain stretch before me, an endless expanse of land and sea.

My descent of Mount Kazbek is arduous and time consuming; I have difficulty climbing back down the steep rock faces without dropping to my death. A voice in my mind urges me to go faster, to take more risks descending, reminding me that my time is short, but I ignore it.

Instead, it takes me many hours to ease down the cliffs, clinging for dear life to any handhold I can find. It isn't until the final rays of daylight leave the sky when I finally spill down the last stretch of trail in a flurry of rocks and dust. Apollo and Lykou leap to their feet.

"What did Prometheus say?" Apollo demands, ignoring the new assortment of bruises and scrapes from my fall. "Where do I go next?"

Lykou yips at my heels, likely demanding the same. I ignore them both, pulling myself astride my horse and taking up the reins.

My horse is already trotting down the road as Apollo yells out. "Where are you going?"

"To the sea," I yell over my shoulder. "We're going to the sea."

His stallion thunders after me, but I don't turn around. Kicking my heels into the sides of my horse, I'm soon galloping down the road, Lykou racing at my side.

I cannot, will not, tell them any more than that. Prometheus entrusted those clues to me, and me alone.

There is a traitor among the Olympians, and it could be Apollo.

CHAPTER
8

The forest is alive. Dryad eyes follow my every movement, lingering on my weapons, and trailing my steps. The birdsong dwindles as the night deepens around us, but I swear the dryads linger in the shadows.

I first noticed their presence one morning before Mount Kazbek, when I found my belongings moved from by my head to the foot of my bedroll. Though I initially suspected Apollo or Lykou, the splayed footprints around the camp betrayed them.

From the corner of my eye, the trees would reach toward me before snapping back the moment I turned my head. Their breathing, sometimes soft, sometimes heavy like the panting of a hungry dog, lingers in my dreams.

Lykou is off sniffing the forest for any signs of bandits or mercenaries that could do us harm, leaving me much too alone with Apollo. The fire is dying, and the shadows claw hungrily toward me. I shift uneasily from their reach. "How much longer until we can leave these forests behind?"

"You know," Apollo says, his long legs stretched before him, "this journey might progress more quickly if you told me exactly where we're going."

"I'm comfortable with the pace," I lie, anything but comfortable. Thoughts of the rapidly impending harvest moon make the falsehood go sour in my mouth. My recurring nightmares of Pyrrhus's death only add to my discomfort. I wonder how much longer Artemis will keep my brother safe. I shift on my bedroll with a wary glance to the trees.

"Or," Apollo says, swirling a *kylix* of wine beneath his nose, "you could just go home. Tell me where I must go and you can return to your precious Sparta. I promise not to judge you too harshly for it, little *kataigída*."

I clench my teeth. "I can't turn my back on this mission, not when I know the true cost."

Apollo scoffs into his wine, my words not fooling him. "The self-importance of mortals never ceases to amaze me."

I've told him nothing more than that we're heading for the coast, information he takes begrudgingly. He wants more, which I am reluctant to give him.

As if reading my thoughts, Apollo adds, "Remember on Mount Kazbek when we discussed the importance of trust between us?"

"Of course I remember," I say quickly. After Prometheus's visions, I trust Apollo about as far as I can throw him.

"Really?" He turns to me, taking a careful sip of wine. "Because your behavior says otherwise."

I swallow my waiting retort. "So give me a reason to. You tell me that I cannot trust Ligeia's stories. Tell me your side, then."

Apollo considers me a long moment before leaning back on his elbows. "What do you know of the kingdom of Pherae?"

"Nothing beyond their prince being one of Anassa Helen's many suitors."

He nods to himself as though expecting as much. "Eumelus. Well, Eumelus's father was a great friend of mine. Admetus."

"You have friends?"

"Your skepticism is scathing." Apollo sets aside his wine, drawing a finger through the dirt. "Anax Admetus is one of my closest companions. I spent a decade in Pherae, living as a sheepherder, and we got quite close."

"Ah, yes," I say, a smile tugging at my lips. "Ligeia told me this one. You had been exiled from Olympus for killing someone. Again."

Apollo's lips press in a firm line. "Do you want me to continue or not?"

I wave a hand across the space between us.

"Where were we?" His gaze turns to the stars above. "Ah, yes. Admetus. I've loved few as much as I loved that man, but he did not return my love. Instead, he yearned for the Princess Alcestis. It was through my divine intervention that he secured her hand in marriage."

His drawing in the dirt has become a face, narrow paned with high cheekbones and knowing eyes.

"Am I supposed to applaud you for helping out a friend who spurned your advances, as opposed to burning his entire kingdom to the ground?"

"No, you're to understand that not all of my stories end in bloodshed and betrayal." Something akin to hurt flickers in his eyes.

"Well, I guess someday we'll hear what the ballads say of *this* misadventure." I sniff. He can get my trust when he's earned it. "So... where are we?"

"Perhaps a league or so from Maroneia, with only a day more of traveling from there to the coast." He leans back, a jug of wine resting on his chest. "There's a pool, not a mile from here if you follow the constellation of Auriga." He points to the sky, tracing the five-star pattern of his own chariot. "Naiades frequent the pool, though they are friends of Artemis and mean us no ill will. They will protect us this night."

I cock an eyebrow. "Do you always pick places for our camp in such a way? Places easiest for Artemis's minions to protect?"

Apollo chuckles. "Careful what you call my sister's friends. You might offend them and then I'll have to do all the work protecting us."

"Gods forbid you do any work and actually dirty your hands."

The hiss of suffocating flames spins me around on my blanket. Apollo pours the remaining water from my jerkin into the hissing coals.

"You. Arrogant. Brat." My voice rises to a piteous screech. "It took me ages to get that fire going."

"I do more than you could imagine." Apollo stands, glaring down at me. "If it wasn't for my gifts, we wouldn't even have Prometheus's clues by now."

I leap to my feet. "And for all I know, we could be in this mess *because of you*. I have no idea what was stolen from Olympus, or who took it." I march around the fire and jab a finger into his chest. "You pompous, self-important ass! You need me much more than I need you, and until I know why, I don't owe you a damned thing, least of all Prometheus's clues."

"You need me more than you think." Even in the dim light of the dying fire, I can see the fury in his eyes dimming to a simmering rage.

"You've already said that." I raise my chin. "And you've done very little to prove it thus far."

Apollo's face is a mere hand's breadth from my own. "Sparta has bred the arrogance of a thousand warriors in you. Put your blade where your mouth is and prove your mettle."

A blade appears in his hand. Longer than the reach of my Spartan sword, the black metal glimmers with an unnatural light. I step back when he swings it above his head, movements elegant and precise.

I draw my own sword. Apollo lunges before I can take up a stance. I raise mine just in time, metal singing into the dark night as they collide. The world seems to still as we join in a deadly dance.

Apollo tests me with feint after feint. His legs bend. He leaps within the reach of my sword, swinging a fist toward my midriff. I slap his hand away and spin. He chuckles, easily avoiding my retaliating swing.

"Didn't your *paidonomos* teach you to how to mask your face?" Apollo asks. "I can read your every move before you even make it, little *kataigída*."

"Why wear a mask when in battle I will wear a helmet?" My breath curls in the air between us. Though I am loath to admit it, my breathing is already heavy. The incessant toll of the journey is wearing me down.

"You're not in a battle now, so what's your excuse?" He tests me again, dropping low and swinging a leg. I leap, barely avoiding getting knocked to the ground. I can't leave him any more openings.

And I can't stop from looking for his. My eyes follow his legs, waiting for him to lunge. He feints again, right arm jabbing at my shoulder. I take the opening he leaves me, lunging forward. I throw an elbow into his chest. He coughs, eyes going wide as he clutches at his ribs.

Before I can savor my small victory, Apollo's ankle hooks around mine.

I fall, tucking in my elbows to roll away before he can try anything else. I'm back on my feet in a second, face burning and hissing through my teeth like a wildcat. Fury thrums through my veins like molten iron. I will fillet that smug bastard.

My sword is a living extension of my arm, jabbing again and again. Too fast, too assured are his movements, leaving no room for error or miscalculation. He dodges each assault, a grin slicked across his face.

"You're looking in all the wrong places." He dodges my swing again, moving to the other side of the fire.

The fire bursts back to life, flames reaching high and wide into the sky. I yelp, the blaze blinding. The flames are low again in an instant.

Arms encircle my waist. A blade presses against my throat.

Apollo chuckles, his warm breath tickling the hair at the base of my neck. "You're too easily distracted by the little things." As if to emphasize his words, his fingers trip up my side, traveling from my hip to my hair. Each touch is a dying ember upon my skin. "The fire was not nearly as much a danger to you as this blade."

He rests the cool metal on my collarbone. "What would you do if someone held you like so?" The hand in my hair drops to my hip, gripping tight enough to make me gasp.

"I would make them regret ever laying hands on me." Before Apollo can react, I lock a hand around the wrist holding the sword. My head knocks back, cracking into his chin. Now it's Apollo's turn to yelp, but I'm not finished yet. I twist his wrist until he drops the blade. My other arm elbows him in the gut. Both hands release me and I twist free, racing for the other side of the fire.

Lykou leaps into the clearing, snarling.

"Stop, Lykou," I say, willing all the command of a *paidonomos* into my voice. "I've got this."

I cannot control the exultant smile spreading across my face. Apollo's features are impossible to read, eyes dark like onyx in the dim firelight. Dark ichor, the blood of Olympus, beads at the corner of his mouth. His eyes never leave me as he stoops, reaching for his sword.

And then abandons it, leaping across the flames and catching me across the middle. We tumble to the ground in a flurry of limbs. My sword soars into the night. Air escapes my lungs in a great gasp. Before I can catch my breath, Apollo is on his knees, hands pinning my arms to my sides.

I buck, but Apollo's immovable. A strangled screech pierces my lips. Lykou rushes forward but I shake my head.

"I can deal with this," I insist, twisting my arms in an effort to loosen his grip. "Get off of me, Apollo."

"Make me." He grinds my wrists into the earth, my bones groaning beneath his weight.

"You've got to try harder than that," he says. "Take me by surprise. You said you had trained to best men bigger and more skilled than you, so prove it."

"Just get off of me. You've made your point. You caught me by surprise and won." The words taste sour in my mouth, all wrong like rotten fruit.

He lets go of one of my wrists, hand moving up to brush the hair veiling my face. "If you hadn't been so focused on the little details, you could have bested me." He tucks a curl behind my ear. "If you had trust in your own abilities, not doubted yourself, you would have won this fight. Better learn quickly, or go back to Sparta with your tail between your legs. Greece will chew you up and spit out your bones before summer's end."

Apollo shoves away, climbing to his feet. The pity lacing his features sends a new wave of disgust through me. But not with him.

With me.

"Sparta gave you the tools to become a great warrior." He collects my sword from the dirt, handing it to me hilt-first. "Don't be afraid to use them."

Before I can reply, Apollo turns and walks into the woods, disappearing among the dark trees.

Before the encounter with Artemis, my nights were sound. Now they're restless. I toss and turn on my bedroll, the night an endless fight between sleep and wakefulness despite the weariness enveloping me. My brothers, my people, and my future, an endless cycle of disappointed faces stirs me from sleep, but one haunts my dreams.

"You think the gods will return your brother to you, relinquish their hold over you? You're a fool."

Framed in a cloud of dark hair, a small, pale face appears each night, a specter watching me with ruby eyes. Her nails, outstretched like claws, dig into the shoulders of my brothers and drag across their throats. Her face is unfamiliar to me, but her taunts echo my fears.

"Did you never listen to Ligeia? Do you not know the troubles that come with playing the games of the gods? You are just another puppet to them."

A sharp crack at the edge of our camp jerks me from my dreams. Ruby eyes vanish as my own snap open. I leap to my feet, brandishing my dagger. Lykou sleeps on the edge of my bedroll, his paws twitching in a deep slumber chase. I creep past him to press past the line of trees.

A cackle in the shadows spins me around, dagger ready and poised to slice open any assailant. A swish to my right turns me back around, but I find nothing again, and I spin in a small circle, focused on the surrounding forest.

In the darkness, my imagination breeds the denizens of nightmares, creatures with long, silver fangs and eyes that burn with the fires of Tartarus. I swivel, slashing at their imaginary clawing arms, hacking at the shadows as if it were their encroaching forms. With each step, I move farther away from the safety of the camp.

I should have never trusted Artemis's minions to watch over the camp. We should have set up a watch duty and taken turns sleeping, or even picked a more secure place to rest. I curse Apollo under my breath for leaving Lykou and me alone. In the same breath, I curse his sister, too. And then all of damn Olympus just for good measure.

All around me a soft rumble grows, making the hairs on my neck prickle. Another crack like the snapping of a branch. A shriek pierces the darkness and I flinch.

That face, the specter from my nightmares, appears from the shadows. I stumble away, tripping over a log and falling hard to the earth. Her crimson eyes are the only features visible in the dark, burning like embers as they draw nearer. I clench my dagger, retreating— desperate to escape.

Her claws dig into my arms, dragging me to my feet. She holds me immobile, her gaze leaching my courage and sucking it straight from my soul. Wrenching from her grasp, I slash my dagger across her pale throat.

Warm blood seeps down her chest and stains her white chiton. She staggers forward, pale hands swinging wildly for my face. She falls forward—harder, leaner, taller than I imagined. A scream bursts from my chest as her lips press to my neck. The handle of my dagger is slick with her blood, but I find my grip and plunge the dagger forward. She chokes, cackle cutting off with a gurgled screech as my dagger finds its home in her heart.

"Daphne," she says, jerking backward. The moon filters down between the trees, reflecting the blood spilling from her mouth, a river of black that hisses as it falls to the earth. "What have you done?"

A cloud passes, veiling the moon as branches thrash around me.

We're shrouded in darkness. I leap backward as the woman collapses at my feet, the trees unfurling above me to reveal the crescent moon. A beam of ivory moonlight alights upon my assailant.

My dagger drops to the earth.

Apollo is spread-eagle across the ground, a river of red pooling beneath his tangled curls.

"Daphne," he says again, the woman's voice fading from the air, replaced with his deep timbre. He reaches out to me, gaze beseeching, before his hand falls to his side and a last breath rattles from his chest.

CHAPTER 9

I drop to my knees. Apollo lays lifeless upon the earth, chest still and eyes closed. My hands, sticky with still-warm ichor, flutter helplessly above his curls, above the raw crevice tearing his neck, the fissure atop his heart from my dagger.

"No, no, no, no!" My voice is somewhere between a screech and wail. My fingers tremble as they pat along his body, pressing his throat together. "This can't be happening."

The Midas Curse suddenly leaps along my skin from my breast to my throat, a golden noose tightening with every erratic heartbeat. My gasps escape my notice at first, so focused am I on bringing a god back from death. The Curse begins to tighten, suffocating me.

"Please, Artemis," I rasp, praying that she can hear me. I can do nothing as Artemis uses the curse to squeeze the life from my veins, retribution for the brother she's lost. "Please. Let me try to save him."

Her golden noose recedes, pooling above my breast—a chance.

I leap to my feet, ignoring the raw ache permeating my throat. I drag Apollo's arm over my shoulders, struggling with his weight, and search the sky for the five stars he pointed out. The constellation gleams, each star flashing as though to guide my way, the chariot to save us both.

Without hesitation, I move in the opposite direction, Apollo's feet dragging behind us as I try to find our camp. I can feel the barest of pulses in his arm, his ichor dripping down my shoulder, staining us both crimson. I can't have run more than a mile from camp, but in an unfamiliar forest, weighed down by his body, in the deep of night, the return journey could take hours.

I will every ounce of my strength into hauling Apollo through the forest. Cackles still echo in the shadows, the beasts of my imagination still run rampant through the trees. But desperation shoves my anxiety aside as the forest parts to reveal a clearing.

Lykou leaps to his paws when I crash through the trees. Leaving Apollo, I run to his bedroll and rip through his belongings. He carries nothing more than the golden bow and the *kylix* of wine. Tossing aside the bow, I grab the *kylix* and make a silent prayer to Dionysus. "Hopefully there's more to this Olympian wine."

Lykou is sniffing Apollo and mewling when I bring the jug back to the god's body; I shove him aside. The jug is miraculously full.

"Please, this must work." I pour the wine over Apollo's face. "Work, damn Olympus, work!"

Apollo remains still, the wine pouring uselessly from the corners of his mouth. I slap his face, beat his chest, and scream, but my efforts are useless. His eyes remain shut. His chest bleeds.

It isn't until stars and dark spots begin to fill my vision that I realize my time is up. My life is being squeezed inexorably from my body by the gold collar around my neck.

I claw at the Midas Curse, digging my nails into the flesh around the gold band. It squeezes tighter and tighter, my nails doing nothing to stop its constricting. I fall to my back, flaxen curls splayed in the growing pool of Apollo's Olympian blood. Lykou howls, clawing at Apollo's lifeless body. My vision fades to a single light, the moon a diamond captured in onyx gauze, as my eyes slide shut.

CHAPTER 10

Warm hands shake me awake hard enough to rattle my teeth. A cough and groan force through my cracked lips. I pry my eyelids open to find Apollo staring down at me.

The stab wound above his heart is completely gone; there's not even a scar across his throat to mark the passage of my knife. His skin still glistens with dark ichor and wine, his once pristine chiton stained burgundy in the moonlight.

He cups my cheek with one hand, an arm wrapped around my shoulders to hold me to his chest. He is warm, warmer than I ever thought possible, and I fight the urge to curl into his heat and hide my face.

"I'm sorry," I croak, my throat still raw. It would have likely ached for weeks if Apollo had not moved his hand from my cheek, tripping his fingers down the length of my tender throat to my collarbone where the Midas Curse now curls. The pain recedes instantly. "How are you alive? I saw you die. I didn't know it was you. The night played tricks upon my mind."

Apollo is silent for a moment, considering my face. "I almost did die. It is lucky you thought to pray to Dionysus. He must have imbued the wine with the last of his gifts. And lucky that you did not think to use my bow." He waves to the glittering weapon resting against his bedroll. "Though the circumstances may have been dire, I would not have wanted to waste its single arrow with my own life."

"What do you mean?" The fog hasn't yet cleared from my mind. I struggle to process what his words mean. One of Ligeia's stories stirs in the recesses of my memory. "Your arrow...can bring back the dead?"

He nods, thumb rubbing the back of my neck as he cradles my head. "But only once. My sister's bow can take a life, but mine grants it. They were given to us to protect our mother from Hera's wrath, to be wielded only by heirs of Olympus, but Hera has long since set aside her insecurities.

"Tell me what you saw that drove you to try to kill me," he says.

Against my better judgment, I tell him everything. I, more than everyone, have the right to distrust the gods. But, just this once, Apollo has earned my honesty with his life, felled by my careless knife. He listens as I describe my dreams, the nightmares that have plagued me since leaving Sparta, the woman haunting my sleep, and how she tricked me into the forest. Tricked me into taking his life.

Once I finish, I disentangle myself from his arms and climb to my feet, reaching a hand out to a nearby tree for balance. Apollo steadies me, capturing my elbow in a warm hand.

"We are lucky that Olympian gifts are still so strong, otherwise I'd be lost to Hades's realm. My immortality was the first of my gifts to leave me, and it won't be the last," he says, his words halting and rough.

Ice grips my stomach. "If you're mortal, how much longer until all your gifts are also gone?"

"With the powers stolen from Olympus, all gifts will ebb like the tide. With each return, the current will grow stronger, quicker, but also fade that much more quickly." Apollo's hands reach back and forth across the space between us, slow, then fast. He glances to the moon. "Soon, the magic will recede too far for the return of a few to suffice. By my best guess, we have only two more full moons before the effects of their disappearance is irreversible."

My heart thunders in my chest. That's not enough time.

"This face, though"—he waves to the forest—"what more can you tell me about it? To say Olympus has many enemies is an understatement, but I might know who this woman is."

"I..." I wrack my memory for any details, any discerning clues. "She had eyes the color of spilled blood. Her hair hovered above her shoulders like an angry cloud, dark like a storm and her skin was pale, so pale I could see black veins beneath its thin surface."

"Only a god could have that much power," Apollo says after a moment of consideration, threading large fingers through his bloody curls. "Nobody on Olympus meets that description, but that means nothing. There has been a divide among Olympians for many centuries that started with Prometheus's punishment, and she could be among the dissenters. Many do not agree with my father. They felt that his treatment of the titans when he ascended the Olympian throne was too cruel, that we were alienating ourselves. They also feel that we have no right to judge when we use our powers often with selfish intent."

"And you don't agree with them?"

His face is stone, hard with razor-sharp edges. "No."

An uncomfortable silence stretches between us. Sleep calls to me, begging for my return, but the thought of dreams, giving that woman another opportunity to torment me, makes me ill. If Lykou had been my victim, and not Apollo, he wouldn't have been so lucky. The thought sends shivers along my spine.

"What if I could ease your nightmares?" He looks up at me, blue eyes reflecting like silver coins in the moonlight. "I can help you sleep."

"Do your Olympian perks extend to sleeping curses?"

"They could," Apollo says, shrugging a shoulder. "But I have something better in mind, and you could use a bath anyway. You reek, *kataigída*."

With a gentle hand in the small of my back, Apollo leads me through the dark forest. The trees and waist-high bushes part to reveal a large pool, fed by five gentle streams. Moonlight fills the clearing with ivory light and illuminates the dancing figures in the water.

Bathing in the moon's reflection are four naiades.

With their stunning white hair, ethereal pale-blue skin, and the simple, smooth curves of their bodies, they are water embodied. I'm drawn to them as if pulled by the current of a river. Even their coy smiles reflect the hidden dangers of a rough current or an ocean riptide. I should never underestimate these creatures. Silently, I step back farther into the shadows, ready to flee, but my back brushes against Apollo's warm chest.

As if they can hear the rapid beating of my heart, they turn to us, their beautiful faces lit with welcoming smiles instead of fury. Apollo, my hand in his, urges me forward.

"They are the companions of Artemis, and the kin of Poseidon. Their song will pass you between dreams and the day. You no longer need to fear the terrors of sleep," Apollo whispers, his lips brushing my ear. "I will see you in the morning, Daphne."

The protectors of water begin to sing, a choir of hypnotic notes flowing through my veins. I should fight this song, my mind screams, but their voices are so beautiful, their words so soothing.

"Sister of the sea," they croon. "Clear the shadows from your memory. Let the water cleanse you, refine you. Let the spring refresh and fortify you."

My fear abandons me as I fall to my back, floating in the water and buoyed by their melody.

"The darkness has no power over the sea. Teach the shadows to witness the ocean and flee."

Their hands untangle my hair and massage my scalp, the mud and grime floating free of my curls to dissipate in the water around me; my chiton slips from my frame as I let them massage and draw me into a blissful sense of security. The water is a cool balm on my weary body, shrouding my pains and easing my nerves.

"Embrace the water, and fear not. The *anax* of the *Mesogeios* has plans for you."

I drift into my first night of dreamless sleep in many days as if drawn by the undeniable pull of a tide.

Their song still floats through my mind when I open my eyes again. Early morning mist hangs heavy over the ground, broken by the light of the rousing sun as Helios begins his ascent into the sky. I blink back the light threatening to blind me.

I'm safe, albeit naked, and lying across my bedroll. Beads of water on my arms pluck light from the stirring sun, my hair completely untangled and the softest it has been in years. I climb to my feet with a pleased sigh, the knots in my back and legs gone. I feel truly rested for the first time since leaving Sparta.

"I sent Lykou away to hunt us some breakfast." Apollo's silky timbre startles me from my self-examination. He watches me from across the cold remains of our campfire, eyes fixed to mine instead of exploring my naked form. In his hands are my clothes. "Maybe he can make himself useful for once and catch us a rabbit or something."

Apollo's clothes are likewise clean, his dark bronze hair no longer matted with ichor—the god's blood that I spilled. He climbs to his feet and turns to leave. It isn't until I make a small noise of protest that he glances down at the dress in his hands. He sighs heavily before tossing it to me.

I cradle the chiton, the fabric slipping through my fingers like a stream. Pressing the dress to my face, I revel in its delicious cleanliness. With a firm shake of my head, I clear the lingering melodies from my mind and find my voice. "Thank you."

Apollo's face is unreadable. "You're welcome."

Cheeks burning, I throw the dress on. My fingers toy with the fraying hem, my eyes looking anywhere but at him.

"I meant what I said before. Nobody would judge you harshly for returning to Sparta. There are darker forces at work than the trivial machinations of mortals. This is the province of gods."

My voice is raspy when I find it again. "This isn't just the gods' fight, though. Whatever happened on Mount Olympus, whatever was stolen and by whomever, affects all of us, mortals, titans, gods. I couldn't wake each morning in Sparta knowing I had turned my back on this, wondering if you were successful in returning them, fearing the setting of the sun each day and wondering if it may be the last.

"You've said so yourself, that I am more than a mere mortal, and as much as I'd like to deny it, I'm not returning home until I get answers." I meet his gaze and hold it, knocking my chin high. "I have Prometheus's clues. Without them you have no hope of returning the pieces of power to Olympus."

He exhales softly, eyes dancing with a wicked light. "Then will you tell me where we're going?"

The words stay on my tongue. I should tell him, do more to express my gratitude for this gift. He's earned a bit of trust, bought it with his life.

"Thank you for easing my nightmares," I repeat.

"You already said that." He turns to leave.

"No, wait." I catch one of his hands in my own, sending a flood of warmth up my arm when our skin meets. "We are journeying to Crete. Prometheus told me that there are nine things we must find, and that three of them were given to the *anax* of Crete and his son. I don't know much more, honestly. He showed me a dark cave, and a mask dripping with blood."

Apollo's tan blanches, his hand suddenly cold. "Is that all he had to share with you?"

"No," I say, throwing back my shoulders and tugging my hand away. I need to keep the location of the other pieces close to my chest, or else I might as well just return home.

"Very well." His jaw clenches, and he turns to leave, only walking a few steps before hesitating at the edge of camp. His back is to me as he stiffly says, "Thank you for your honesty."

He leaves me alone with my thoughts. The camp is still. Even the horses are silent as I braid my hair to distract my thoughts. I push away the memory of Apollo's hand in mine and his disappointment as he left.

As much as Alkaios, Apollo, and even Prometheus say otherwise, I am a Spartan. Sparta has forged me into a weapon, and weapons care not for feelings and tears.

CHAPTER
II

Pyrrhus's hands travel the length of the *dory*, a gift from our adoptive father, before pointing to the spearhead. "Most enemies will focus on this little bastard. Sure, it's sharper than Ligeia's tongue and meaner than Ares, but the bottom is the real weapon here."

I lean forward, my young eyes wide. I'm not yet eight, and Pyrrhus's twelfth birthday has just passed. He's started training with the *paidonomos* and already thinks he knows everything.

We're sitting in the courtyard, perched on the edge of a cushioned *kline*. His hair is even longer than mine, vibrant red curls falling before his eyes because he refuses to let Ligeia cut them.

He slaps the butt of the *dory*. "This can crush an enemy's skull with enough force. It can crack a kneecap or a rib and give you enough momentum to sweep the legs out from underneath your enemy."

My eyes grow impossibly wider at the possibilities. Alkaios, his hair and clothes as immaculate as ever, looks over Pyrrhus's shoulder and sniffs. "The bronze would just crack if you tried to hit some-one's head with it. You'd be better off attacking with little jabs of the spearhead."

"It would still hurt," Pyrrhus snaps. "Go away. This is *my* lesson!"

"Why not a sword?" I mimic the swing of a sword, albeit poorly, and nearly fall from my chair. "Or a bow? Can't I just shoot an enemy before they even reach me?"

Both Alkaios and Pyrrhus sneer, and the elder says, "The coward's weapon? You would forfeit our family's honor because you were too afraid to face an enemy?"

"I'm not afraid," I protest.

"Careful what you say around these Spartans," Alkaios says, frowning. "They will always look for a weakness in us. Give them no reason to think you're a coward."

"I'm no coward." I cross my small arms over my chest, pouting.

"We know, darling Daphne." Pyrrhus claps me on the shoulder. "But these Spartans have the right end of it. Never trust a man who prefers the bow to the blade. Paidonomos Leonidas says that a man willing to spill the blood of someone else but not his own has no honor."

"And a man without honor," Alkaios says, "is nobody you can trust."

I'm stirred from the memory by Lykou licking my palm. Grimacing, I snatch my hand away. "What?"

"You were drooling on his fur." Apollo drops some bread and figs on my bedroll. "If you've finished dreaming about me, we've got to find a ship to take us to Crete before they all sail away with the south-ern winds. We'll be hard-pressed to find any sailors willing to travel to the island so close to the Reaping, but I'm sure there's a trader somewhere in this blasted place."

We'd made camp on the outskirts of Maroneia, resolving to find passage in the morning. Despite the lack of nightmares, my sleep is still uneasy, plagued by thoughts of home and my brothers. I must have fallen back asleep on my bedroll after Apollo woke me up.

I rub the sleep from my eyes. "The Reaping?"

"I always forget how closed off from the rest of Greece you Spartans are." Apollo shakes his head. "Each year, the port cities of Greece are required to sacrifice eight children to Crete or suffer the wrath of Anax Minos's navy."

Apollo doesn't exaggerate. Sparta is very much closed off from the rest of Greece. Unchallenged in war for more than a hundred years, and trade primarily limited to Troy, Mysia, and Mycenae, we have little use or patience for foreign dramas. Though that didn't stop me from pestering Ligeia with questions about the rest of Greece.

I'd heard stories about the Reaping, but assumed they were only rumors. "Crete couldn't withstand all of Greece."

Apollo leads our horses from the trees and I follow, Lykou loping at my heels. "Perhaps. But they are backed by the wrath of the goddess Pasiphae. She is a favorite of Poseidon, was once the *anassa* of Crete and is the mother of all Minos's children. Using the might of his Navy, the Reaping acts as a sort of tax, so to speak. The lives of eight children, or the entire naval battalions of kingdoms will burn. All kingdoms that have resisted so far have fallen. Akontisma, Neapolis, Miletus, Aegina, and Hyleessa, just to name a few." Apollo ticks each name off his long fingers. "All have either been obliterated beyond recognition or are completely under Minos's control. Though the Reaping secures Crete's power over the Aegean, it is actually the design of Pasiphae to ease the insatiable hunger of her most terrible child, the Minotaur."

A chill sweeps through me. Reclusive Sparta may be, but even I have heard whispers of the Minotaur, a half human beast said to tower from the height of three men and carry the strength of more than a dozen. They say his skin is made of iron and his gaze can turn the fiercest of men into stone.

"If Minos is married to the goddess Pasiphae, won't she know we are coming? Why would she hide the pieces of Olympian power in Crete when her own power is tied to them?" I ask.

"Remember when I said before that Olympus is divided?" We pass the first line of houses in Maroneia, and though the city is still waking, Apollo lowers his voice. "Pasiphae and her siblings were of the side that looked upon my father's actions less favorably. No gods have stepped within the walls of Knossos since Pasiphae and Minos began their reign, and she hasn't returned to Olympus in more than a century. But she has been estranged from her husband for many years and is said to spend her years in exile among the Cyclades. It's also said that her son's temper has grown even more unruly since her departure."

"Meaning Minos has no idea that we are bound for his shores?"

"Doubtful. If he knows the importance of the stolen powers currently in his possession, he must also know that Zeus will seek retribution. He will be expecting an attack from Olympus."

A sickly dread sweeps over me. In Sparta, we're trained for the battlefield and prepared for the agonies of war, not duplicity. How can I expect to catch King Minos unawares when he's already expecting me—and when I have all the cunning of a headless bird?

Bedraggled ships line the harbor, preparing to catch the eastern winds as Apollo predicted. Most dismiss us outright, unwilling to also take a wolf aboard.

"The Anemoi have been fickle as of late," one sailor says to another as we pass, of the wind gods, as they strip their nets. He flings the half-eaten remains of his breakfast, dried fish, into the harbor with a sound of disgust. "And all the food tastes like ash and salt. I have half a mind to just stay ashore."

His companion laughs. "Well, the captain always says that you'd make a better goat-herder than a sailor."

While Apollo continues the search for a ship bound for Crete, I sell our horses. It's doubtful we'll find a ship willing to take us three and the horses, and we can use the spare money, but it still hurts to part with my horse from Sparta. She'd been in my father's stables for ten years, and I remember the many times I'd ridden her alongside my brothers.

"Take care of her," I say, an ache forming at the base of my throat. When the trader leads the horses away, I turn to Lykou. "Let's go find some food."

I'm inhaling a handful of pomegranate seeds and feta—and suffocating any feelings—when a woman marches up to me. Lykou only gives her a cursory sniff, more interested in my food, and snarls when I shove the last piece in my mouth.

She can't be more than a year older than I, but her skin and face are already twice as scarred. Her skin is dark brown, her long hair in an ebony braid that hangs over a single, scarred shoulder. Muscles ripple in her arms and legs with every step toward us, her dark eyes locked on my own. Despite the sweltering early summer heat, leather armor sheaths her torso, and a crimson *chlamys* fans behind her.

A mercenary.

I recall the sword at my hip, Praxidikai hanging across my back, and the daggers hidden under my chiton. Her movements are casual, too casual, when she stops in front of me. She rests a hand on her *rhomphaia*'s hilt.

"I heard your companion asking around the harbor for a ship to Crete," she says by way of greeting. Her voice is warm and sweeter than her appearance belies, like honey.

"YESH," I say, around a mouthful of feta. Blushing, I quickly swallow the tart cheese. "Yes, yes we are. Do you know of one?"

Lykou, forgetting the food, is now giving the woman a thorough once-over. His eyes narrow as he looks her up and down, but he's not snarling or baring his teeth, so he must not find anything untoward on her person.

She ignores the wolf and points to the east. "At the far end of the harbor, a captain is readying his ship for departure. Crete's port city, Heraklion, is one of his stops. Your friend is heading in the opposite direction, so I thought I should pass the information along to you."

She turns to leave and is almost gone before I finally remember my manners. "Wait," I call out to her. "Thank you … what is your name?"

The woman turns around to face me, her eyes flicking to each of my weapons. I swear she notices the hidden daggers. "You can tell the captain that Lyta sent you."

When she disappears around the corner, I turn to Lykou. "Think we can trust her? She didn't smell like a god or anything, did she?"

Lykou tries to lick the last remnants of feta from my fingers. I snatch my hand away and he snorts, turning and trotting in the direction of Apollo.

"Just because I didn't give you any of my food isn't a good enough reason to send me after a mercenary that could probably kill me," I yell after him.

He doesn't turn back.

I look up and notice an elderly woman watching me from the doorway of a house. Right, I probably look like a madwoman, talking to a massive wolf, no less. With a grimace in the woman's direction, I say, "Sorry, my dog's got a mind of his own."

The woman's eyes turn sharp, assessing, and a slow smile spreads her pinched lips. "Do the gods really deserve your help, child?"

I swivel to face her fully. "Excuse me?"

Her eyes are dark in her pale, lined face. "Why should the gods be given their powers back when all they do is torment the lives of mortals with them?"

"Because," I start, unsure really of how to react to the woman's bold questions, "...because they're the gods and that's the order of things."

She steps so close I can smell the lavender she must use for her laundry or hair. Her eyes, so close to my own, are almost the color of spilled blood at night, but that must be a trick of the light.

Her smile broadens at my obvious discomfort, revealing a row of rotten teeth.

I swallow, my throat suddenly dry.

"Haven't the gods taken enough from you? Do you really believe that Apollo knows nothing about your mother's death?" She pats my cheek. The smell of lavender is overwhelming, stinging my eyes. They begin to water, my vision wavering. "Maybe it is time for mortals to decide their own fates. You do not need to suffer the whims of the gods any longer, Daphne."

The overwhelming lavender aroma suddenly dissipates, but I'm still gaping when I can open my eyes again. The woman has disappeared.

I find Apollo ogling a jewelry stall. He presses his fingers into his chin, leaning over a golden necklace dotted with pearls and rubies.

"Contrary to your opinion, red really isn't your color," I say, walking up behind him. "And shouldn't you be finding us a ship to Crete?"

"Any color is my color. Besides, it's for you, so you can throw that ghastly crow necklace into the sea." He steps close and trails a finger over the crow at the hollow of my throat. His thumb brushes my neck, sending shivers down my spine. "You needn't worry about my time management, *kataigída*. I secured our passage."

"How is that possible? Lyta said you were walking in the opposite direction."

"Lyta?" He fixes me with a pointed stare. "Daphne. I'm a god. You don't think I managed to walk from one end of port to the other while you were stuffing your face full of food?"

Blushing brighter than the rubies on the table, I shove Apollo away. "Oh, go to the crows. Shouldn't we be boarding soon before the winds turn?"

Apollo considers the clouds lingering above us. "The captain said that we might fare better should we leave in the afternoon, and I quite agree. Poseidon and the Anemoi have been bickering lately, though their moods usually settle later in the day, in the mortal realm at least."

Ligeia told me stories of the Anemoi—the four winds—and their fickle natures.

"Does time pass differently on Olympus?"

"I haven't the slightest." Apollo gives the jeweler a gold coin but doesn't buy anything. He continues down the docks with a leisurely stroll.

"Don't we need that money?" I ask once the stall is far enough away.

He inclines his head. "Not as much as that vendor. He has ten mouths to feed back home."

He haggles at the next stall over the price of pomegranates and is shooed away, but not before I see him surreptitiously drop a couple coins in the merchant's bag when their back is turned.

Smiling, I exchange a few coppers for the pomegranates—much

cheaper than the vendor offered to sell them to Apollo—and hold one out in front of him, not bothering to hide the smugness pulling up the corners of my mouth.

"I warmed him up for you." He accepts the fruit with a puffed-out chest. "That or he was blinded by your beauty." He breaks the pomegranate open with a single hand and I watch, enraptured as he drops a handful of seeds in his mouth. Despite myself, my eyes linger on his lips. I jerk away when he reaches out to brush the curls from my face. Something I can't name flickers in his eyes before a small smile dances on his lips. "You might not be so blind, either."

CHAPTER 12

The ship cuts through the waves of the Aegean, the wind brisk but not threatening, blessing us with a quick journey. I ignore the sea breeze pulling my curls from my careful braid, focused on the woven *petteia* board spread before me. Worn carved pieces litter the checkered print, though not enough of my own remain.

My thumb travels over my mother's necklace, lips pursed as I consider my next move. Strategy has never been my greatest strength—nor patience. My hand travels from the necklace to hover above the king, his dark rosewood face mocking my indecision.

Lykou lounges at my feet, watching the sailors with distrusting eyes. He releases a low growl as a familiar, warm presence steps close behind me. Apollo leans over my shoulder and I roll my eyes.

"To the left, my *kataigída*. Your king can protect himself," he whispers, pressing closer, warm hips brushing my shoulders. There's a traitorous flutter in my stomach. His lips graze my ear as he continues, "I love when you roll your eyes. Such an endearing, mature habit you've picked up among mortals."

I resist the urge to roll my eyes again. Begrudgingly, I move my king to the board's edge. It's a shrewd move, but I'll never admit that to him. My king can't be jumped there, and my other pawns can protect the back edge of the board.

Sitting on an upturned crate, Lyta stares at her own king with a perplexed frown. The first on the ship to approach me, she showed little care for my territorial companions by pressing her sack of *petteia* pieces into my chest and demanding I play a few rounds. Now, after only two weeks at sea, I've already played at least half a hundred games with this woman.

Lyta glances up, revealing a disarming smile. "I can find no other move. You've won this game."

I return the smile in full. "Don't give up so easily. You haven't lost yet."

She shrugs, still smiling as she waves to my *petteia* pieces on the right side of the board. "I could chase your pawns over here and possibly win a few small victories, but your pawns would capture my king before I have any opportunity to move to your edge of the board." She waves to the other side. "And I have no chance of sneaking by your left flank."

A gust whips my curls into my face, stinging my eyes and sticking to my lips. Brusquely, I shove my hair back behind an ear, only for them to be set free again by the grasping wind. Fingers tickle the back of my neck, gently brushing my hair back and tucking the errant strands behind my ears, where they stay—for the first time in my life—without a single attempt at escape. I don't have to look to know it is Apollo's doing. When he brushes past me afterward, I reward him with a rare, grateful smile.

I sneak a glance at him, striding across the ship like a king, and rub the back of my neck. He joins the rowers, grunting and straining along with the crew, his energy and strength endless. The wind licks up spray from the waves, drenching his chiton and making him laugh. Warmth tinges my cheeks at the sound, a smile threatening to part my lips. It is the most human I've seen the god yet.

I push my queen forward a space, ignoring him. "Good strategy is a matter of perspective. One is only as strong as the other is weak."

Lyta's dark brows narrow, moving her own queen after my bait. "How do you mean?"

"A well-matched army may battle for years, even decades, numbers diminished by foolish actions, battles won by wise men." I knock my pawns from the board, one by one, Lyta's queen slicing through their ranks. "But even the most powerful army can fall from a single misstep." My remaining pawns move into formation, springing the trap I've laid for her queen.

"What a natural military commander you are." Lyta leans across the board, her long, ebony braid falling over a shoulder as she flicks her cornered queen to the deck. A pale scar splits her left eyebrow as she cocks it.

While Lyta and even the sailors aboard this vessel have readily welcomed me because I am not above laboring, the people of Crete are likely to be far less accommodating. Grecian law demands women wear the demure *kalyptra* veil outside the house, and most women outside of Sparta won't know the difference between a sword and a dagger. I already miss the freedoms and liberties of my home, and I have no doubt that a veil will feel suffocating.

"Do you bother with a *kalyptra*?" I ask, waving to the sword at her hip. "Or does being a mercenary mean you don't have to wear one?"

Lyta barks a laugh. "A mercenary? I'm no mercenary."

"Then why the sword?" I point to the *rhomphaia* ever present on her hip, the blade curved like a crescent moon.

"I could ask the same of you," Lyta says. She taps the board, peering at my own sword. "Are *you* a mercenary?"

"Would you believe me if I said yes?"

Another short laugh. "No. You're far too young and educated."

I could say the same for her. Curiosity itches at the back of my mind, as persistent as the scratching of mice in a pantry. Our rapport these two weeks has been much of the same. A bit of pulling and prodding from me, with Lyta unrelenting, and vice versa.

A crew member bellows from the prow, declaring land within sight, distracting me from my thoughts.

"Thank Poseidon. The gods have blessed us. It is rare that to be gifted with such an uneventful journey," Lyta says.

"Done a lot of sailing before, have you?"

My poor attempt at prying only elicits a shrug in response. She untangles her long legs from beneath her and moves to the railing. The cliffs of Crete shine from miles away, a mere sliver on the horizon.

My heart thrums with excitement at the prospect of exploring somewhere new. Zeus's birthplace, Mount Ida, rises above the golden foothills and cliffs, begging us to come closer and explore its hidden depths. Pyrrhus would envy where I stand right now. He's spoken endlessly of a desire to travel, to see the world beyond Sparta. Maybe someday I'll return with him to explore the caves and find the hidden treasures of Crete. Thinking of Pyrrhus fills me with a sudden sadness.

I catch my lower lip between my teeth and turn from the island, picking at the paint on the ship's railing. Best to focus on the task at hand. There's no point planning for the future when I might die this very day.

Lyta's garnet chlamys billows in the breeze, knocking over the pieces of our game. I collect the strewn pieces and toss them into a small bag that Lyta accepts with a grateful smile. A shimmer beneath the cloak catches my attention. Decorated with the gold lines of the *meander,* her chiton's hem flaps erratically in the sea breeze.

Lyta doesn't seem to notice my scrutiny, her dark gaze locked on the coastline. "Are you finally going to share with me your business on Crete? It's rare for a Spartan woman—or any woman, for that matter—to journey to the islands, and with such a dashing companion, no less."

It takes a moment for me to recall his fake name. "Apollodorus is far less dashing when you've been traveling with him for nearly a month." I wave dismissively in his direction. Lykou snorts in agreement.

"Well that seems to have insignificant effect on how he sees you." Lyta's nose scrunches and her eyes shimmer with amusement. "He can hardly keep his eyes off you."

I snort. "He doesn't care half as much for me as he does for himself."

"You know"—she leans over, shoulder brushing my own—"I'd be more inclined to believe you if you told me his true name."

I'd avoided talking about Apollo as much as possible. Though it would have been easy to fabricate a fake persona for Apollo, it is far easier to just hardly acknowledge him and treat him as a begrudging ally. But the bait of Apollo's identity might be enough for Lyta to share hers.

I cough and look away, as though uncomfortable with the trajectory of our conversation. "So, what brings you to Crete? Can you not at least share with me a clue?"

Lyta bites at the bait. "A clue for a clue?"

I nod, schooling my face into a blank mask.

"My sister sent me." Lyta hesitates before saying more, taking a deep breath. "To find something stolen from our family." She shakes her head, frowning as she contemplates the horizon. "But all I will find on this damned island are more false leads. My sister leads me down an endless, winding path."

Before I can press further, she nudges me with an elbow. "And *your* business in Crete?"

I purse my lips, weighing my answer, but I cannot hesitate too long for fear of angering Lyta. I search her face for any reason not to trust her and find none. Her dark eyes, though imploring, are also inviting.

Finally, I say, "Like you, I'm hoping to find something stolen and return it. I have a bit more faith in finding said object, but the returning of them...it will be dangerous." I wish I could trust her with more. Perhaps she could help me understand Prometheus's clues.

"Then it's good that you know how to use that sword on your hip." Lyta leans backward, resting her elbows on the railing, and assesses me. "Or so I assume."

"Just as well as you, I'm sure," I say.

Lyta barks a laugh, grinning. "I have no doubt, my friend, that I could have you unarmed and on your ass in less than three moves. I've fought, and even killed, Spartans before." Her tone is suddenly placating as she continues, "I've no doubt that you're a fantastic fighter, but every warrior needs to learn that there will always be somebody better."

An itch to challenge her words stirs inside me, to prove to her my skills. "I could surprise you, Princess."

"Princess?" Recognition dawns on her face; a chill sweeps over me. I've stepped too far over that invisible line between us. Lyta takes a step back, lips tight as she tucks the hem of her chiton—and any hint of the *meander*—out of sight. "I recognize I've made a mistake by being so forward with you."

With a sharp nod, Lyta spins on her heels, marching below deck with a rigid back and filling me with an aching emptiness. Watching her leave, regret pulls me taut like a bowstring, begging me to go after her and apologize for my boldness.

"Trouble in Elysium? I thought that you had learned your lesson when it comes to challenges of prowess." Apollo comes up behind me again, his breath tickling the curls on the back of my neck. "Such a shame to watch mortals let their egos ruin friendships."

I allow him to see the full glory of another exaggerated eye roll, before turning again to the sea. "You are hardly the person to lecture me about my ego."

No retort is forthcoming. We stand, side by side, watching in comfortable silence as the waves slap the belly of the ship. My eyes trace the swell, the myriad colors and foam that spread across the surface. Dark forms stir the water before diving again below the reach of my gaze. I can still sense them, though, and they don't feel entirely human.

"You can see them, can't you?" Apollo's eyes bore into me, bluer even than the sea, filling me with his uncanny warmth.

"No," I admit, inclining my head. "But I can feel them. Are they dolphins?"

"They're Nereids." Apollo's gaze turns from me to trace invisible figures beneath the surf. "They've been monitoring our journey for the last three days."

"Does that mean Poseidon watches over us?"

"No, my uncle is not among them."

I blink. "I thought they always accompanied him."

"They usually do, but"—he turns to me again with a mocking smile—"like calls to like, little *kataigída*. They are following *you*."

I scoff, but there's a tug deep within me, drawing me to the figures watching from the deep.

"This journey, your insistence on helping me reclaim Olympus's power, it isn't just about saving my family." Apollo drags a finger on the railing beside me, knuckles brushing the arm I rest upon it. Heat flares beneath my skin from the simple touch. "Prometheus showed you something about yourself, about your family, didn't he? Questions you're hoping to find answers to." His finger drifts up my arm and across my collarbone, resting on the chain of my necklace. "You won't find them on Crete."

I slap his hand away and ignore the look of hurt he throws me. "Maybe I'm hoping that you'll stop speaking in riddles and just tell me."

"There's nothing about your history that I could tell you that you don't already know and must accept for yourself." With an incline of his head, he leaves me.

I don't see Lyta again before we disembark in Crete. Apollo seemed overly pleased to inform me that she leaped from the ship the moment we docked and didn't spare a single glance back in our direction. Remembering my incessant pestering fills me with shame.

Before disembarking, I wrap my face and hair beneath my *kalyptra*, donning an ankle-length chiton. I try to lead the way, but Apollo pulls me aside.

"What?" I demand, tugging my sleeve from his grasp.

"Best to let me walk ahead," he says. "Here in Crete you are my wife and must behave accordingly."

"I am not and will behave in no such way," I say, practically spitting the words in my vehemence.

Apollo clenches his teeth. "You must. Crete is not a forgiving place, and freedom a foreign concept where women are concerned. An unescorted woman may be thrown into a prison cell if she draws the wrong attention."

A moment of tense silence stretches between us, my good sense and pride warring for the space of a dozen heartbeats.

After another dozen, I begrudgingly incline my head and Apollo takes the lead, though I still glare daggers into the base of his spine.

Sandstone buildings line the harbor, their thatched roofs crumbling; the crowded port city reeks of salt and brine. Locals fling their waste from high windows, and vendors shove their wares in my face, haggling prices and bickering among one another.

We need to find new horses and replenish our supplies. Knossos is at least a day's ride inland, and I want to be out of this crowded city before the sun sets.

A stall in the far north corner of the bustling agora boasts the swiftest horses from the southern continent. I check a pair of horses, peeling back their lips to examine their teeth before running a hand down each of their legs. I can find nothing wrong with them.

"How much for this pair?" I ask, waving to the horses.

The merchant says nothing, only looking at me as though I've sprouted snakes for hair.

Apollo hooks an arm around my waist. "Forgive my wife. We're newly wed and I've yet to use a firm hand with her." He presses a kiss to my cheek, whispering, "Let me do the talking from here. Cretans aren't accustomed to women who are so...audacious."

"I'm sure Cretan women have plenty of brass." I raise a hand between us and rest it on Apollo's cheek. His eyes widen infinitesimally as I lean forward and whisper against his lips, "If the men here ever released them from their shackles."

I seal my words with a soft kiss, the barest brush of my lips on the corner of his mouth. Apollo gapes slightly when I turn to face the merchant and give the man a reverential incline of my head.

Apollo has arguably less luck bartering than I would, though, and the exchange soon escalates to an argument of a more personal nature.

"Did your mother give birth to these horses?" he demands, face flushed. "Is that why they are so expensive?"

"And what do you know of the price of labor?" The merchant stabs a meaty finger into Apollo's collarbone hard enough to make the god stumble backward. "You don't know a day of hard work. Just another rich lord's son."

I'm thoroughly impressed with the merchant's gall and want to applaud.

While Apollo haggles, I explore the labyrinthine sprawl of canvas stalls in the city center. Pressing close to my side, Lykou surveys the crowd with sharp, too-human eyes; many people give me a wide berth, clearly terrified of my fierce companion.

I'm admiring a set of nautical-themed tapestries when a familiar face moves past my periphery. I spin around, watching a helmeted Spartan soldier march in my direction, his gait eerily familiar. Just when my eyes alight on a bronze bangle around his wrist, Lykou jerks on the hem of my cloak. Wanting to put as much distance between me and the Spartan, I let my friend drag me across the agora. We follow the chorus of singing metal, drawn to a blacksmith's stall tucked into the side of a sandstone building.

Swords hang from the front of the stall, a wider variety than I've ever seen. Compared to the shorter Spartan swords, some extend longer than my legs, and some even curve like a crescent moon, handles decorated with stars of gold amid lapis lazuli marble. Decorated swords seem trivial. I pass over these with a disdainful scrunch of my nose, my unwavering curiosity drawing me toward the long swords like a moth to a flame.

The idea of extending my reach with a long blade intrigues me.

Still, I prefer the maneuverability and compact nature of the Spartan sword hidden beneath my cloak. Lykou pants, tongue lolling and snout reaching up to sniff the blades.

"Get your mutt away from my wares." The blacksmith storms out of the smoky depths of his stall. "I won't have him damaging the fine metals with his mongrel teeth."

The blacksmith shoves his beefy body between us and the swords. Glaring, I take a step back. Lykou bares his teeth.

"If your metals are so flimsy that a dog's mouth can damage them, maybe you should consider another profession," I say, fury flushing my cheeks.

The blacksmith sputters. Other customers suppress laughter behind their hands. "And what would a woman know of it? Get back to your husband before I call the guard over to kill your wild animal."

Lykou snarls and the blacksmith snatches the nearest blade, brandishing it before him. "Another noise and I'll slit your throat, beast." The blacksmith's arm quivers and sweat beads on his brow.

A low growl fills the space between him and Lykou. A ripple of fear dances down my spine.

"Let's go, Lykou." I tug on the wolf's scruff, but he doesn't budge. There's something in his dark eyes, something I've never seen in my friend before. A glimmer of the wolf nature more than just the animal mask he is forced to wear.

Lykou snaps again, another snarl ripping through the air. Chaos breaks loose.

The blacksmith swings for Lykou's throat just as the wolf leaps into the air. I don't have time to second-guess myself before leaping between them. I grab the blacksmith's wrist and clamp my other hand around Lykou's muzzle. His fangs barely miss my fingers.

I slam the blacksmith's wrist into the brick wall. He yelps, dropping the sword and swinging his other fist at my face. I duck and the black-smith's meaty fist soars above my head. I swipe the blacksmith's legs out from under him in the next breath.

A roar pierces the air. The blacksmith's apprentice charges toward us. He towers over me, nearly as broad as he is tall with arms the size of my thighs. He flings a hammer at my head, and I duck just in time to hear it sing past. A fist follows in quick succession, much quicker than should be possible for someone of his size.

I catch his fist a heartbeat before it can pummel my gut. Using the fool's own momentum, I swing his arm over my shoulder. I ram it down farther than an arm is meant to go, until I hear that satisfying pop and the apprentice's squeal of pain.

"Big men don't bend," Alkaios once told me. *"Big men break."*

I grab both blacksmith and apprentice by their fingers, bending them backward until they're on the precipice of such a break. Both men howl in agony.

The blacksmith, likely used to broken fingers, makes a foolish attempt to punch me. I double my efforts, pressing backward on both of their fingers. Once both men are on the ground, I slam my knee into the blacksmith's face, knocking him unconscious instantly.

"Care to make the same mistake?" I ask the apprentice with a grim smile, giving his fingers an extra squeeze.

The apprentice shakes his head, bottom lip trembling.

"Pity." I drop his hand, and the apprentice gasps in relief. I yank Lykou back by the scruff of his neck and into the gathered crowd.

Ignoring the gaping stares, I give Lykou a rough shake and demand, "What was that about?" I throw a wary glance over my shoulder. "Hopefully that *suagroi* doesn't send the guard after us. They will kill you on the spot."

Lykou only rumbles in response, refusing to meet my eyes. Dipping into a shadowed corner of the agora and away from curious eyes, I drop to a knee in front of my friend.

"Have you lost your senses?" I jerk his muzzle toward me so that he cannot avoid my eyes. Is that rage still simmering in his gaze, or does something more feral linger there? He jerks from my grasp. "I already draw too much attention with a giant wolf by my side, let alone a rabid one."

Lykou bares his teeth at me. I flick his nose, making him yelp.

"Keep that up and you'll never return to your human form." That catches his attention, his eyes snapping back to meet my own. "This mission isn't about you. It's not even about me or Pyrrhus. It is about Olympus and the failing power of the gods. You'll never return to your human form if Apollo loses his powers."

Cupping his face between my hands, I press my brow to his. "Don't lose your humanity. I need you, Lykou. Don't abandon me, too."

He gives my face a conciliatory lick. I giggle slightly when his tongue tickles the underside of my chin. He rubs his face against mine, blowing warm breath across it. My stomach gives a rumble as though in response.

Standing, I look down at him. "Now that you've come to your senses, shall we treat ourselves to some food?"

We peruse the food stalls lined up along a far quarter of the agora, Lykou pressed close to my hip and my stomach rumbling loud enough to wake the dead. I splurge on a purchase of flatbread stuffed with spices, lamb, and feta. Forget insufferable gods—feta cheese is the only thing a woman needs in life.

Drool dripping from Lykou's mouth, he devours half with a single snap of his fangs. We meander through the stalls, munching happily, when the lilting sound of a lyre pierces the din of human commotion around me. The melody is chipper and bright, begging my feet to dance to its song. I stand on my toes to peer over heads for the source of the beautiful music. Lykou whines, trailing behind me.

"Can you not hear it?" I ask, peering through a pair of stalls.

Lykou rumbles, pressing his snout into my thigh. He's ready to abandon the crowds of Heraklion.

I make him search every nook and cranny of the city center with me, my frustration building each step of the way. My search draws me closer to the harbor. Not watching where I'm going, I don't see the coil of rope at my feet and fall face-first into the chest of a passing man. "Oh, I am so sorry."

His hands grip my hips. He's my age, skin not yet lined from the passage of time, hair long and dark, and skin pale. A boy not used to working beneath the sun. "No apologies necessary. It's not often that a beautiful woman falls into my arms."

His dark-gray eyes probe my face with galling familiarity. "What lovely eyes you have," he says, catching my chin between his thumb and forefinger to force my face up to meet his. He's also used to getting whatever he wants, obviously. I resist the impulse to bite his fingers. "It's so rare to meet another who shares the same color as I. Has anyone ever told you what a special color it is?"

"There are other things more important than eye color," I say, jerking my chin from his grasp. "Manners, for example."

"Forgive me, my lady." His grin widens slowly. Before I can pull away, he tucks a curl beneath my veil. "I wanted to assure myself that the blacksmith didn't injure you in any way."

My mouth pops open. "You saw that?"

"I'm afraid half of Heraklion saw that unfortunate incident," he says with a small wink.

"My apologies." I'm yanked from the man's grasp. Apollo shoves me behind him. "It must concern the gods to see my wife so easily ensnared by another man."

"I'm sure the gods have more pressing concerns this moment," the stranger says, undeterred by the warning in Apollo's face. I wonder if he would be so bold if he knew that my "husband" is a son of Zeus.

I step around the insufferable god and bow my head. "Thank you, sir. My *husband* does not mean to be rude."

With a wink in Apollo's direction, the stranger takes my hand and lays a kiss upon its back. "There is no harm in being overprotective, my lady."

"I beg to differ."

With a small chuckle, the stranger saunters into the crowd.

"Well, that was odd," I remark, turning to Apollo. The god glares at the young man's back weaving in and out of the crowd. "What's wrong?"

"He's trouble."

I scoff. "How can you say that when you don't even know him?"

"One of those Olympian perks." Apollo turns to the horses, tightening their bridles. He slaps a set of reins into my hand. "That crook of a horse-seller would have charged me an arm and my firstborn child if I let him, but I managed to persuade him to part with his two best horses. Threatening the future of his own unborn offspring seemed to have the desired effect."

I cross my arms over my chest, though a smile pulls at the corners of my mouth. "That seems brash. What made him take your threats seriously?"

"I have my ways," he says with a lopsided shrug.

"I'm sure you do. Those Olympian perks and all." I adjust my veil and grimace when a sharp pain jolts my heel. Resting a hand on Apollo's shoulder for balance, I lift my foot. A pebble pokes through the sole of my sandal. "Any chance those perks extend to clothes mending? My shoes are worn down."

My sandal is immediately mended, the pebble vanishing. I wiggle my toes and joy buoys me. My sandals are now the most comfortable they've been in years.

"That's handy," I say with a bright smile. "Thank you."

He inclines his head. "It's the least I could do, considering you're helping save my family and all that."

"And don't you forget it." I laugh and his smile matches mine.

The song pierces the din of the crowd like the trill of a bird. I peer over Apollo's shoulder as the lyre teases me once again, melody drifting above the crowd like a flock of songbirds.

Apollo follows my gaze, frowning. "What are you searching for?"

I sigh and let my arms fall to my sides. "The musician. His music is beautiful, but I can't find him anywhere."

"Music?" Apollo scans the crowd. "I hear only the petty squabbles of mortals and the grunts of animals."

"That could be your subconscious," I say with a chuckle. Lykou snorts.

The music rings loud and clear through the din, a hypnotic, dizzying melody compared to the human chaos surrounding us. Suddenly light-headed, I spin around as the music comes at me from every direction.

The concern that furrowed Apollo's brows vanishes. With one hand, he tugs on the reins of the horses and with the other he shoves me from the agora. "We leave. Now."

I want to slap his hand away, but the alarm filling his eyes keeps my protests at bay. Could it be the woman from the shadows?

The music chases us as we rush from the agora. Emerging onto an open street, Apollo wordlessly tugs me into the closest alleyway. We break into a sprint, Lykou loping alongside us, ignoring the curious gawking of the people we pass, crossing crowded streets and dashing around corners, dragging along our poor, confused horses.

We reach an abandoned alleyway and Apollo jerks me to a halt. I shoot him a withering glare, yanking my hand from his grasp.

"Do you still hear the music?" He searches the alley, flipping over crates and checking burlap sacks.

I tilt my head from side to side, straining to hear the music, but its notes have been lost in our flight. "No."

Apollo slumps against the side of a building. Sweat beads his brow, his cheeks flushed. "That was close."

I nudge the god with a toe—resisting kicking him outright. "What is going on?"

He opens his mouth, then pauses. The color drains slowly from his face.

"I'm sorry, my dear," an unfamiliar voice says. "I'm afraid Apollo was trying to hide from me."

CHAPTER 13

Like the Midas Curse spinning atop my breast, intricately painted roosters and snakes quarrel and play up and down the young man's broadly muscled chest and neck, inked in midnight blue to match his loose-hanging chiton.

Lykou snarls a warning and our horses whinny nervously behind us. The stranger's hand shoots out, yanking the *kalyptra* from my head and strands of my hair with it.

I try to snatch the veil back, but it vanishes with a snap of his fingers. He tucks away the strands of my hair in the folds of his chiton and waggles his eyebrows at me. A rooster on his brow fights for balance, wings unfurled and flapping wildly.

My gaze narrows, but I rub my head and take a step back. Gratifying as it would be to knock him onto his back, a handful of my hair isn't worth gaining another enemy.

"Hermes," Apollo hisses, hands curling into fists.

It's then I notice they share the same azure eyes, but where there's an intense heat within Apollo's, Hermes's sparkle with mischief and perhaps a hint of dark malice. As Apollo is the intense heat of the midday sun, Hermes reminds me of shifting shadows, impossible to hold.

A shiver runs up my spine. Hermes, trickster and foil to many of Apollo's schemes. They have a rivalry that often results in destruction.

"The god of heralds and thieves is twice as likely to give with one hand while stealing with the other. An alliance with Hermes could either help or hinder, depending on how useful he deems you to be."

"Aren't you going to introduce us?" He uses the tip of the short, golden staff to jab his brother's chest. A snake at the hollow of Hermes's throat hisses and spits at Apollo. He tips his head to the side, black curls catching the light when his eyes rest on the crow necklace. "She looks exactly like her. Where did you find this wonder, Apollo?"

Apollo takes my wrist, holding me close to his side; my pride bridles at the possessive gesture, but common sense stays my tongue. Maybe if Hermes turns me into a laurel tree, Apollo might be nice enough to turn me back.

"Why are you here?" Apollo's voice is rough, his shoulders tight.

"Still lacking in your manners." Hermes wags a finger at his brother, but his gaze rests on me.

"Oh, so he's always been this tiresome?" I ask with a breathy, forced laugh. "Apollo is much more of a hindrance than helpful. If he's needed on Olympus, please feel free to take him with you when you go."

"I like this one." Hermes walks slowly around me. He winks at Apollo. "She's definitely your type."

"*Apollo* is Apollo's type," I mutter.

"And I'm sure he's even tried to seduce his own reflection." Hermes leans forward conspiratorially. "Between you and me, he'd have more luck with his reflection than even a fish."

"I'm sure he's tried, though."

"Oh, undoubtedly." Hermes points his golden staff at me and I'm tempted to swat it away. "Brother, will you not share your new pet with me? I like the ones that bite."

Despite my indignation, I recognize the staff from Ligeia's teachings. Scarcely the length of my arm and made of pure gold, the top is adorned with two long, unfurled wings that glint in the sunlight, while the length is wrapped with intertwined silver snakes. It is the *kerykeion*—and Hermes could use it to smite me with a single swing.

Apollo crosses his arms and looks down on his brother, face unyielding. "I will ask one more time, Hermes. What are you doing here?"

"Hades informed Father of your quick emergence, and disappearance, in the Underworld, and sent me to assess your health. It seems, with our powers upended, you are no better than a demigod." I detect a hint of revulsion lacing Hermes's words. With a dramatic sigh, he points the *kerykeion* in my direction with a look of mock solemnity. "Are you *still* not going to introduce us? This is the one who stole your life, is it not?"

What reason could Apollo have for not wanting to share even my name? Noting the rigidity of my companion's shoulders, I cross my arms. The stories of Hermes's fickle nature must not be too far from the truth.

"Why are you here?" Apollo repeats, biting out each word.

"You know why. Obviously, you're asking for the mortal's benefit." Hermes waves a dismissive hand in my direction. But the movement is slightly forced. His curiosity must be eating at him. "You didn't really think Father would let you go on your little adventure without checking in on you from time to time."

When Hermes turns his shrewd gaze back to me, my palms itch. "Now won't you please *finally* introduce me to your lovely traveling companion? I'm perishing of curiosity."

"Daphne of Sparta." I ignore the choking noise Apollo makes and put a hand over my heart, then gesture to my lupine companion. "And this is Lykou. Apollo decided to turn him into a wolf."

"Because he was *spying* on us," Apollo says between gritted teeth.

Hermes grins. "I've heard of you, though not as a Spartan. The *Mothakes* that caught the stag. You've earned quite a reputation for yourself back in Sparta—an outsider who seduces men and encourages them to become deserters."

My cheeks flare. I open my mouth, ready to snarl an indignant reply, but Hermes continues. "And how fares the mysterious Ligeia? She was acting as your handmaid, was she not? She was quite the cunning little minx back in her prime. Eluded even the cleverest Olympians."

Before I can ask for more, and if Hermes is referring to himself, Apollo steps forward and cuts me off.

"What news from Olympus?" He asks, tan face earnest.

With a wide yawn, Hermes rests his chin on the *kerykeion*. "Things are as expected. Hera has imprisoned herself to convince our family that she doesn't have anything to do with the theft. Aphrodite has fled with Eros to Troy, so that she and her son might live in comfort should her gifts fail her. Ares is taking out his anger on some poor eastern country, and Athena has locked herself in the Library of Alexandria to search for answers."

"So we're divided at a time when we should all be united," Apollo says with a mirthless laugh. "And my sister?"

"She stays in her forests." Hermes kicks a pebble down the alleyway. "Artemis hardly spent any time on Olympus before everything went into calamity. Why start now?"

I blurt, "And your powers? I mean, the powers of all Olympians. Are they faltering? Are you too no better than a demigod?"

Hermes stops twirling the *kerykeion*, pressing his lips together in a firm line.

Apollo throws me a stern look before pulling Hermes aside. I hear very little of what's said between them, other than talk of games and Apollo being an ass. My curiosity is further piqued when Hermes points to me and says something about the white crow, but then Apollo mutters something about Hermes's mother. Just when I think a physical scuffle is about to break out, Hermes flashes his brother a withering glare.

There's obviously no lost love between these siblings.

Hermes turns back to me, white teeth glittering amid a wide smile so boyish I could almost forget the viper lurking beneath. "I have a gift for your lovely traveling companion."

From midair, he pulls a small set of *auloi*. Carved from a light wood I don't recognize and inset with blue etchings that match the animals on his skin, Hermes drops the music pipes in my palm.

"They are much more durable than they seem," he assures me. "They're made from the shell of the largest turtle in the world."

My fingers trace one of the etchings, a blue rooster framed by myriad intertwined snakes. The power in them thrums against my palm, emphasizing his words. "What are they for?"

Hermes barks a laugh, as if the answer is obvious. "To summon me. When you've found what's been stolen, I will take them back to Olympus."

"We don't need your help," Apollo grinds out between clenched teeth.

"Nine," I say.

Hermes and Apollo exchange surprised glances. Even Lykou's nose jerks sharply in my direction.

I continue, "Nine things have been stolen, and unless you want to haul all nine across Greece all summer, Apollo, I think we should accept his help."

"Maybe you can learn a thing or two from her." Hermes flashes Apollo a close-lipped smile before giving me a conspiratorial wink. "It's the hair. He's blinded by his own good looks and loses all of his sense."

Despite myself, I smile. "Or the dimples. You could get lost in those."

Apollo waves his arms. "Go home. Tell Zeus what you need to, but nothing else. He doesn't need to know my whereabouts."

Hermes rolls his eyes before turning to me. "I hope to see you soon, Daphne."

The *kalyptra* is suddenly on my head again, and with a curt nod to his brother, the messenger vanishes.

"You should not have accepted his gift," Apollo mutters, turning back to the horses.

"Why should I trust you and not him?"

"You should know better, Daphne, than to trust any of the gods." He turns and leaves to prepare our horses.

Lykou brushes against my hips. Whining, he sniffs me worriedly. Reaching a shaking hand against the wall, I cradle the *auloi* against my breast, once light, now heavier than shackles.

CHAPTER

14

A bird sings overhead, whistling an obnoxious tune so like Apollo's it could have only picked it up from the god. How and when, only the Fates can guess.

We set up camp, far from the road and prying eyes, beneath the boughs of an olive tree the maddening bird has decided to call home. I open my mouth to ask Apollo if we can move camp, but he grimaces. "Save your petulance for another day, my *kataigída*. This is the perfect place to plan my next move."

"Quit reading my thoughts," I snap, throwing my bedroll into the dirt. "I've had enough of Olympians doing whatever they please with me."

"I can't read your thoughts." Apollo pops an olive into his mouth. "It isn't my fault that you wear your emotions for everyone to see. Not a very Spartan habit. But, then again, you're not a true Spartan so what does it matter?"

"Then what am I?" I ask, hoping futilely for some forthrightness from the god.

He gives me a look that says I should have known better than to expect any answers from him, and continues around a mouthful of olives, "This is the perfect place to plan our next move. Not only have I absorbed that you have all the tact of a puppy, but also all the patience of child. If this venture is to succeed, I need two things from you." He flicks up a pair of fingers. "Patience and trust. We will not succeed without both."

Lykou snarls, pressing closer to my side. He'll likely never trust Apollo.

I rest a hand on the scruff of my friend's neck. "If you want my trust, you have to earn it." Some answers about my heritage would suffice. Maybe.

"And so I will have to resign myself to an eternity in the dungeons of Knossos." Apollo throws his hands in the air.

"Don't be so dramatic. It's unbecoming for an Olympian. And spit out those olives. Your breath is ghastly, even from here."

Apollo mutters in a language I don't recognize. I run my fingers through Lykou's rough fur, considering our options. "I agree that we need a plan, though. As you're the only one of us to step foot inside Knossos before, what do you suggest?"

"Well, let us start from the beginning. I need to find a way into the palace, find the pieces, and then find a way out, all with as little blood lost as possible." He picks up a branch and carves the layout of Knossos in the dirt.

The palace is a massive square atop a hill, with hundreds of rooms surrounding a large central courtyard in a labyrinthine sprawl. "From my years spent in Knossos, prior to Pasiphae and Minos's...shall we say *unsavory* reign, the East Wing was reserved for guests and servants, the West Wing for the *anax* and his family."

Apollo jabs his stick at the courtyard. "This is where Minos plays host and...is said to toy with his guests. The courtyard serves as both banquet hall and audience chamber. In Heraklion, I heard some mortals speak of a banquet tomorrow evening. If I can latch myself on to one of the arriving parties, I can at least get through the gates."

"And, once inside, we'll attend this banquet and search the castle that night?"

"Yes." Apollo grins. "I will dance, dine, and have a merry time until Minos's guests fall upon their furs. Then, when the moon is high, I will steal the pieces from beneath Minos's feet and flee before the old *suagroi* even wakes."

I pause for a moment, letting his words sink in. "From...right beneath them?"

I've heard many stories, from both my brothers and Ligeia, about King Minos's son, the Minotaur.

"Beneath the House of the Double Axe lies a city of the dead and the damned. As a price for Anax Minos's evil deeds, his soul is forfeit, its evil seeping into the earth. Home to a creature so dark and foul that even Hades refuses to explore its depths, all who enter never return to the land of light. There treads a beast whose bloodlust is only sated by the sacrifice of eight noble Greeks each year, and whose wrath can be felt throughout the Aegean."

As if to emphasize Ligeia's words, the earth trembles. Lykou whines beside me and even Apollo balances himself against a tree.

When the shaking stops, he nods slowly. "Yes, beneath them. The only part of Knossos I have yet to see is the city of the damned beneath, and that is the most likely place Minos will think to hide the pieces from Olympus."

"What about me?" I cross my arms over my chest. "You keep just referring to what *you're* going to do. Are you just expecting me to wait here, twiddling my thumbs, while you get the pieces?"

"Well, yes." Apollo massages his temple with the butt of the stick. "If I pretend to be a noble, which won't be difficult, it should be easy for me to attach myself to a larger party or pretend that my name was forgotten on the list of attendees. I might even be able to glamour my way inside, but the more conspicuous the circumstance, the less likely it's going to work."

"But I can help," I say, climbing to my feet.

"You'll only be in my way."

I kick the dirt, ruining his map. "Because I'm not a god, or because there's something you don't want me to see? You only know they're here because of me, because I trusted you enough to share Prometheus's clue with you. If you keep me from going inside Knossos, I won't tell you the other clues."

Apollo merely blinks, unmoved by my outburst. "And you'll be even farther from returning to your brother."

I'm a fool for ever believing that he truly cared about my brother's welfare, not when his own is in question. The gods are nothing if not selfish, it seems. My hands clench and unclench above my hips, itching for a dagger. "I'm going to go find us something to eat. Come on, Lykou."

Fury courses through me, hot as the searing sun. I could do more than get under Apollo's feet. I could defend him, take down at least a dozen soldiers while he steals away the pieces. If he gave me another chance to spar with him, I could probably have him on his ass in seconds. I still have some tricks up my sleeve. But in his eyes, I'm nothing more than a helpless mortal.

I grab a stick and hit any branch within reach. Olives rain around me, but I'm lost to the anger thrumming through my body. Apollo will probably just get himself caught anyway, cocky bastard, and all I can do is sit here kicking at the dirt, waiting for him while he rots in a dungeon.

Temper ever rising, I clench my eyes shut and repeat the words spoken by my adoptive father when Alkaios was young and more tenderhearted, afraid of the shadows that followed him night and day.

"Away to the darkness, cowardly offspring. The Eurotas does not flow even for timorous deer. Our harvest does not grow for chicks that fear leaving the nest. A son afraid of the dark is no son of Sparta at all."

Opening my eyes, my nose immediately crinkles, the stench of olives filling the air. They litter the ground, staining the bottom of my sandals. One squelches between my toes, and despite my disgust, an idea pops into my head.

I look down at Lykou, a grin slowly spreading across my face. "And so into the darkness we will go."

By the next morning, my confidence has drastically waned.

Apollo rises before dawn, bedecked in a red silk *peplos* and a dozen gold rings he plucked out of thin air. Golden vambraces are molded to his muscular forearms, matching his golden breastplate and the bow strapped across his back. Ever the appearance of a wealthy, impossibly handsome nobleman.

I sniff, feigning indifference. "Not bringing any of your arrows? Will the mortals not find it odd for you to travel with an arrowless bow? Gods know it is absolutely baffling to me."

"Any mortal-made arrows shot from this bow are absolutely useless."

"And Hephaestus can't make some for you?" I arch an eyebrow. "Otherwise what's the point of carrying it around?"

"I can only shoot one arrow from this bow, only in a time of great need. My sister's bow has the same conditions…" He trails off, assessing me as I stretch languidly across my bedroll. His eyes narrow with suspicion. "You're asking about my bow to distract me. What are you up to?"

"Nothing," I say, shrugging and tossing my curls over a shoulder. The effect is ruined by the fact that they're a tangled bird's nest on my head. "I'll just be here, twiddling my thumbs. Just like you instructed."

His brows narrow. "Without a fight?"

"Wouldn't want to waste your strength," I say with an added touch of sweetness to my voice. I feign a yawn. "We both know that it's limited."

Apollo opens his mouth to snap a retort but shakes his head. "Whatever you're planning, because I know you are planning *something*, it better not interfere with my plans or ruin this entire mission. Just don't do anything stupid."

I smile. "Likewise."

Once he's gone, I pull out the satchel of olives I've hidden away behind a nearby bush, tuck my hair beneath my *kalyptra*, and follow. Apollo will go in the front gate and I'll sneak in through the servants' entrance. Nobody will question a serving girl bringing a basket of olives for a banquet.

Lykou and I crest a stretch of narrow, steep road, and a shadow rises above us, hiding the sun from view. Unlike the bustling, lively Heraklion, and despite the splashes of blue, red, and gold paint across its balconies and rooftops, the palace is a cold and unwelcoming blight on the horizon. I crane my neck to see the sheer heights of the palace, the House of the Double Axe, and home to the Minotaur.

Twin vultures circle above as we pass the first line of buildings, the beat of their ebony wings ushering us into the cursed city. Arrowheads glint from doorways and roofs, trained on the heads of every passerby. Four are trained on Lykou alone. King Minos's paranoia is evident in the hundred soldiers marching up and down the road, inspecting wares and belongings, their weapons always within reach.

Lykou trots by my side, baring his teeth at anyone who looks at us for too long. I lay a reassuring hand between his pointed ears, whispering from the corner of my mouth, "You're attracting too much attention. Meet me at the servants' gate."

He slows to lope between houses and darts out of sight; I continue my trek to the palace. A line of nobles streams from the gates waiting for entrance. All are surrounded by an entourage of soldiers bearing their kingdom's sigils and mottos. I almost don't notice Sparta's symbol, the red *lambda*, painted across the shields at the rear of the line before it's too late.

I skid to a halt, panic seizing me. Thankfully, the nearest Spartan soldier, the one I thought I saw in the market, doesn't turn to face me. My heart stops as my gaze drops from the raven locks escaping his helm to the bronze bangle peeking from underneath his leather vambraces, DIODORUS etched across its surface. My family name. My bracelet.

"Alkaios," I say, my brother's name passing my lips in a whisper.

He couldn't have possibly heard me, but his back straightens nonetheless, and I imagine confusion flitting across my brother's face beneath that bronze helm. Before he can turn and see me, I dart into the shadows of the nearest building.

My mind is racing as I make my way toward the servant's entrance. If Alkaios and other Spartan soldiers are here, so must Helen and Menelaus. Paidonomos Leonidas told me of their trip to Crete during *Carneia*. The Moirai are just toying with me now. Whatever their reasons for accepting Minos's invitation, Sparta's presence in Knossos will be problematic. Should any of them recognize me, the whole mission will be in jeopardy.

I take a deep, steadying breath. I can't let anything foil this mission. Not when all of Greece is at stake.

Taking a road around the outer wall of Knossos, I press into a line of servants and farmers carrying wares into the palace. Beneath the relentless sun, the line inches forward; soldiers inspect the baskets and bags of each person in line. The wind tugs on my *kalyptra*, snatching it from my head. I yelp, grabbing at my veil floating away, my unruly blond curls tumbling free. The servants around me titter and whisper to one another as I blush, yanking the cursed thing back on my head and securing it under my cloak.

A soldier steps toward me and a trickle of sweat slips down my spine. If he finds my weapons, Minos will have me thrown in a cell for the rest of my life.

The soldier licks his cracked lips, eyeing my face beneath the veil. He reaches into my bag. A cold sensation spools in my gut, my fingers longing for the dagger on my thigh. With bold familiarity, he rifles through it for a long, tense moment, before pulling out a handful of olives. With a curt nod, he tosses one between his yellowed teeth and walks past.

My hands clench and unclench beneath the folds of my cloak. I miss the familiar weight of Praxidikai, now hidden in an olive tree with much of our belongings outside the city, but at least my daggers and sword are hidden beneath the folds of my chiton. Not even the most skilled soldier could spot them—a trick Pyrrhus shared with me.

I finally pass through the gate and into the crowded kitchens. Leaving the bag of olives on a counter, I press into the crowd. The room teems with more activity than a beehive, making it easy to flit from shadow to shadow until I'm in the servants' corridor. I move along, following the servants rushing from one chore to the next. Wetness presses into the back of my hand, making me jump.

"Lykou," I hiss. "You startled me." He licks my fingers before disappearing into the shadows of a nearby room.

I throw a glance over my shoulder. Thankfully, too focused on their tasks, nobody notices as I slip into the room. Lykou leads me through another door to an abandoned hallway.

"If we're caught, don't try to save me," I order him. "They'll only kill you, and if at least one of us completes this mission, maybe Artemis will still set my brother free."

He rumbles in reluctant acquiescence. We walk as quietly and quickly as possible, ducking into another room when a pair of guards turn the corner into our hallway.

I hold my breath as they march our way; Lykou and I press as deep into the shadows as we can. Once they are far enough away, we continue. I keep a hand pressed against the dagger hidden atop my thigh.

"See if you can smell anything like Apollo...or godlike...whatever that is."

Lykou takes this command very seriously, keeping his nose astutely pressed to the ground. My tension mounts with every step we take. I didn't think this far ahead, believing the entrance to the Minotaur's lair would be somewhere on the lowest level of the palace. We hide again as more guards pass. The frequency of patrols grows the deeper into the palace we explore. We turn another corner, narrowly missing a guard on patrol. I step into another room.

And a hand slaps over my arm.

"What have we here?" I'm spun around. Two soldiers assess me, gripping my wrists together. Lykou has vanished into the shadows, thank Tyche. Panic rises in my throat like bile, choking off any protests.

One soldier pulls a dagger from his hip, using the tip to peel back the veil covering my hair. My curls tumble free like a flaxen waterfall.

"I don't recognize this one. Not one of the servants. Not of Crete, either. I'd remember that hair."

I could show them exactly where I'm from.

"Nor one of the slaves." The other guard strips me with his gaze. "Too proud. The *anax* would have broken this one in the moment she passed through the gate."

I dip my chin to my chest, glancing to the nearest guard beneath my lashes. He's the smallest, probably the most insecure. "Please, I'm part of the envoy from Sparta. I brought olives to the kitchens and lost my way to the Spartan quarters."

"Ah, yes. Knossos is a bit of a labyrinth to outsiders." He's easily beguiled. A small smile tugs at his lips. "And those Spartans are terrible at keeping their women bridled. I could help you find their rooms."

He drops my wrists, offering up an arm instead. The other guard shoves it away. "Don't be a fool, Dictys." Taking my wrists again, he roughly spins me around. "The Spartans were told at the gates not to traverse the palace alone. They were commanded to stay in their quarters, and only leave when a guard accompanies them.

"This one"—he tips my chin up—"is a spy."

"Wha-what?" I stammer. "No, please. I should have gone to the kitchens with a guard. Take me back to my rooms and I promise I'll stay there."

"Spartans don't bother bridling their women, as they should," the guard says. "They leave them free to roam. They don't preserve their purity. I heard"—he drags a finger across my chin, and I barely refrain from biting it—"that they let their women ride naked through the streets."

"They even give us daggers and teach us how to use them." I raise my chin. "Care to see?"

The soldiers drag me inexorably up a flight of stairs. "Our *anax* will know what to make of her."

I struggle against the man's grip. He holds firm and gives my arm a painful yank for good measure. I make a silent prayer to the Moirai that the guards don't find the weapons hidden on my person. My mind is in a panic, fluttering like the wings of a bird. I should have listened to Apollo and stayed at the camp. Minos will throw me in a dungeon the moment he sees me. Even worse, when they search me, they are sure to find my weapons, and there will be no prison cell for me. Only a quick death.

I stop struggling and notch my chin high, ready to meet my fate with honor, not tears. They guide me up a shadowed stairwell as my tears dry. We crest a landing, turning right. A crack spins us around.

A short *dory* rolls across the floor, stopping at our feet, and standing down the hall from us is the young man from the Heraklion market. A grimace splits his face, and he drops the rest of the weapons in his arms.

Knives, swords, and arrows crash to his feet. He gives us all a derisive smile. "You're not supposed to be on patrol in this hallway."

The guards drop my arms and whip out their swords.

"Hands against the wall, Athenian," orders Dictys.

"As you wish." With a mocking, reverential dip of his chin, the man raises his arms high, turning and slapping them against the wall. "But if you try to sneak a feel, you'll regret it."

The guards leave me behind to march forward. Their mistake.

I slip the dagger from beneath my sleeve and ram it deep into the nearest guard's back through his flimsy Cretan armor, angled up to pierce beneath his bottom ribs. He collapses and I drop to my knees. I jerk the dagger free. Dictys spins around, shock and anger warring on his face. He swings the sword for my head and I roll beneath his reach. My dagger slices right through the tendons of his ankles. He opens his mouth to scream, but the Athenian slams a blade through the back of his neck.

Dictys falls forward. His blood pools at my feet.

"I see you've lost your sea legs." The Athenian steps gingerly over the bodies, and offers me a hand. "And that we've found ourselves in quite a bind."

CHAPTER

15

I don't bother to conceal my horror. "What have we done?" I whisper.

"Let's get this mess cleaned up and go to my rooms." The man gestures to the bodies. "Explanations can wait."

Lykou emerges from the shadows and follows behind us, jowls pulled back to reveal sharp fangs.

Though explanations truly can't wait, neither can the guards at my feet. "And what do you suggest we do with them?"

"There are hundreds of empty rooms in this palace, even with the sudden influx of royal guests." He cuts a hand through the air. "Pick one and toss the bodies inside."

"I'll do the tossing." I rip a tapestry from the wall and toss it at his chest. "You can clean up the blood."

He grimaces but doesn't argue. Lykou helps me drag both men into a storeroom down the hall.

Grunting, I say, "I'm sure these two could have learned a thing or two from Spartan women that might have saved their lives."

I drop Dictys's body on top of his comrade's in the corner of the room. I pile some boxes around them, throwing a sheet over it all for good measure. When I turn around, the Athenian has trailed us to the storeroom to clean up any blood.

"Just in time," He says, shutting the door behind him. There's a soft patter of footsteps on the other side.

"I hope they don't notice the pile of weapons I hid in the *pithos* out there," he whispers with a grimace.

I hold my breath. Lykou's head tilts in their direction, ears perked, and when he turns to me, I open my mouth to speak.

The Athenian cuts me off, holding a finger in the air between us. "Explanations can still wait until we're somewhere I know we won't be walked in on."

I bite my tongue to keep from arguing with him. He has a point. "Fine. Can I at least know who it is that I'm gambling with my safety?"

The stranger grabs my hand, giving it a tight squeeze; the dozen gold rings adorning his fingers bite into my fingers. One is inlaid with emeralds and an ivory owl. "I am Theseus, heir to the throne of Athens, and you, my friend, will help me claim my kingdom."

I don't trust the Athenian, but I'm willing to play his game.

For the time being.

Theseus guides us around Knossos to his rooms and I take the opportunity to memorize the layout of the palace, planning possible escape routes and marking suspect corridors in the back of my mind. Despite the colorful frescoes decorating every other wall, the airy terraces, and lush gardens around each corner, Knossos exudes an eerie chill that teems with suspicion and fear. The servants are skittish, avoiding my eyes as they slink between corridors. There's no sign of the Spartan entourage, though I have no doubt that the Fates are merely waiting for the opportune time to reveal my presence to Alkaios.

Theseus shares story after story of his exploits, each of them at length and in theatric detail, his voice echoing down the morose halls.

"And the Gorgon's head was enormous, larger than my whole body." Theseus holds his arms wide to elaborate his point. "I knew I would have to sacrifice myself to save the poor women of Lesvos. So I flung the pieces of my broken spear into the Gorgon's eyes. Her screech pierced the air as the Gorgon fell into the sea, slipping off the craggy cliffs."

"Wow," I say, cynicism leaching into my voice. "That's very impressive."

Theseus chuckles. "Spartans are such terrible actors."

"Have you been on Crete long?" I ask, forcing small talk. Other guests of Minos pass us in the corridor, thankfully none of the Spartan variety.

"No, I only arrived two days ago." The smile on Theseus's mouth drops into a grim line for the first time. "The *anax* has been kind enough to invite me to his palace, though I'm not the only noble in attendance. The high kings of Eperus, Massalia, and Cyrene arrived before I did, and I'm sure you saw the Spartan entourage pouring in through the gates this morning."

"Couldn't miss them." The image of the back of Alkaios's head, of him wearing my bracelet, is still vivid. "Rumors of their departure to Crete have been circulating for many months. Any idea why Minos has called some of Greece's greatest leaders to his palace?"

"I haven't the slightest." We pass a colorful fresco, and Theseus drags a hand across the azure and golden tiles, leaving smudge marks in his fingers' wake. "Many more are expected to arrive before the banquet this evening."

"What of Anax Minos's son?" I ask. "Will we get to meet him at the banquet tonight?"

A group of nobles wander past us. Lowering his voice, he says, "The Minotaur? I've yet to meet his infamous bastard. Hopefully he'll make an appearance at the banquet, but in a cage."

When the sun begins to set, filling the corridors with amber light, the prince ushers me to his rooms. The suite Minos has given Theseus is grand, consisting of three bedrooms and a washroom, all divided by sheer gold silk curtains and a terrace overlooking the city. In the center of the rooms is a massive hearth, surrounded by furs white and plush enough to be mistaken for clouds.

Lykou, having trailed us through the palace, assesses the room for any obvious threats, sniffing corners and beneath tables for enemies. He gives me a small nod of assurance, and I share a grateful smile. Having him with me in the palace is an immense comfort.

I turn to Theseus. "No more tales. No more games."

The flames in the hearth flicker and spit as a draft sweeps through the rooms. Theseus's skin glows like amber in the firelight, but his eyes are shaded. "My intentions for the House of the Double Axe are just as false as yours."

"Only a fool would ever think otherwise, but the armful of weapons may have given you away."

When he meets my gaze again, he looks younger than I initially thought, maybe even younger than I. Not a single scar marks his skin, and not even a shadow of a beard brushes his jawline. "Athena has deprived me of my birthright. I can only claim my throne once I've completed six labors, and I have only two more. End Minos's reign of terror by killing the bastard's son, and free the city of Thebes."

Theseus takes a measured step forward, watching my every move as though I am a beast with its leg caught in a trap, ready to lash out. "The assuredness with which you took those guards down, how easily you incapacitated the blacksmith in the Heraklion market. Had I not seen it for myself, I would have never believed a mercenary hid beneath such a delicate visage."

"Nobody has ever called my *visage* delicate before, and nobody ever will again, should they like to keep their limbs intact." I cross my arms. "Though I cannot argue your usefulness in garnering me an invitation to tonight's banquet, you can wait here while we take care of Minos's son for you."

"No." He drops his voice with a vexed glance around. "There is a weapon in the Minotaur's lair, one that I must find. Thebes has been plagued for years by some sort of foul beast that haunts the roads leading in and out of the city. An oracle prophesized that I will find the weapon to vanquish it beneath the city. You will help me kill the bastard son of Minos, and then I will find the weapon."

I thumb the hilt of a dagger, considering Theseus, as Prometheus's words ring in my ears.

The plague of Thebes.

As though fated by the stars, it seems our plans align.

I pass him the dagger handle-first. "Allies then."

Theseus's eyes lock on mine, gray to gray, before he slides the blade across his palm. His blood hisses as it drips into the hearth. "By my honor, by my throne, I promise not to betray you. May every Olympian hear me now—we are allies until my mission is complete."

With little other choice, I nod a wordless acquiescence.

We will attend Minos's banquet, flirting and mingling thieves in the guise of perfect guests. Under the pretense of enjoying the night's revelries, we will search the courtyard for clues and pray to the remaining powers of Olympus that we're not discovered as liars and frauds.

Someday, I will learn to make a decent plan beforehand.

Clothing lies on the silver furs of Theseus's bed. My dress for the banquet is delicate, ruby-red silk that clings to my every curve. The Midas Curse squirrels away to the soles of my feet to avoid the gaze of the servants wrapping the expensive fabric once around my body and draping the end over the back of a single shoulder. A delicate golden corset clings to my waist, matching the golden bangles on my wrists and the diadem holding my curls and a red silk *kalyptra* from my ochre-painted eyes, hair bound in an intricate plait down my back beneath the veil.

"Please, milady," a servant says, so low I can barely hear her. "I thought you might wear the necklace milord Theseus has provided instead." She holds up a gaudy golden chain, large and cumbersome. Too much like the chains of a slave.

With a curt shake of my head I dismiss Theseus's necklace, tucking the white crow between my breasts. I slip a small dagger on my thigh while the servants' backs are turned, and another deep within my braid.

Lykou returns to the room first. His eyes widen when he sees me, mouth dropping open slightly. I blush and avoid his eyes. It is so easy to forget that inside the wolf is a very handsome man who might possibly love me.

When Theseus enters, a slow smile spreads across his face. "Perhaps I should have picked out a less distracting dress. You'll catch everyone's attention wearing that."

Lykou rumbles unhappily when Theseus reaches out, wrapping an arm around my waist.

I step from his grip and run trembling fingers across the gold encasing my ribs, and the Curse now draped across my hips.

Ligeia and my adoptive mother always hoped that I would warm to prettier dresses and *kosmetikos,* and I always brushed aside their wishes. A warrior has no time to spare worrying about dresses, I would say. Now, as Lykou and Theseus both eye me with open admiration, I recognize that there is a different kind of strength in embracing your femininity and the vulnerability that comes with it. Dresses can be a weapon, too, a blade of cloth to turn heads and guide eyes, to influence the decisions of others.

I hold my arm out for Theseus. "Shall we?"

CHAPTER
16

The tail of my silk gown slithers across the floor, trailing my steps. The Midas Curse whorls around my navel, thrumming with my rising heartbeat, dancing in time with each step closer to the banquet hall. With a deep, steadying breath, I step from the passageway and into the central courtyard.

Servants with ash-painted skin descend upon us bearing trays of foods and drinks. A warm breeze stirs the bonfire in the center hearth. Musicians stand in each corner of the courtyard playing a soothing melody in perfect harmony. Hundreds of nobles crowd the banquet hall, mingling and laughing. But, above the laughter and chatter, a dark cloud harangues the guests, read easily in the anxiety pulling each of their faces tight.

King Minos stands atop a high dais made of blackened wood. He wears a bull mask, with large black horns dipped in red paint to resemble blood. Just like the one in Prometheus's vision. I shiver, giving my arms a brusque rub.

A guard presses close to the king and whispers something in his ear. Minos's eyes flick in my direction and I quickly turn back to Theseus, aware of him asking me a question. "Pardon?"

"Intimidating, is he not?" Theseus looks over his shoulder at Minos.

I accept an offered *kylix* of wine from a passing servant. "For lack of a better word."

He nods to a couple across the room. "Isn't that your husband with Princess Ariadne?"

My stomach roils. Apollo leans close to whisper in the young woman's ear as she giggles. His hands rest on her hips. A pale rose *peplos* and *kalyptra* envelopes her petite frame in large, silken folds; her dark curls divided and spilling over her shoulders, waist wrapped twice over with strings of pearls. Many young women surround them both, throwing the princess begrudging glares.

"He has the attention span of a gnat," I say, sipping my wine.

"Is that jealousy I hear?" Theseus teases.

"Only disinterest." I take another drink of wine, this time a gulp large enough to warm my uneasy stomach.

Apollo glances in my direction. Recognition flickers in his gaze, despite my veil, a moment before shock blanches his features. My heart thunders in my chest. I will him to keep his silence.

A heartbeat passes and a knowing smile spreads his lips. He examines me, gaze traveling leisurely from every wayward curl of my hair and down the length of my waist and settling on Theseus's arm wrapped around my hips. My core erupts with heat to match the fire burning behind his eyes. I turn away before my expression can betray anything.

The courtyard opens to the north and south, overlooking a dark, sleepy Crete, while to the east and west narrow passages lead into the palace. Earlier, Theseus guided me primarily around the eastern half of the House of the Double Axe, but the Olympian treasure could be hidden in the western half of the palace.

Theseus downs goblet after goblet of the fruity wine while I sip on mine, wanting to be as lucid as possible for the evening ahead. Turn after turn, we tour the courtyard searching surreptitiously for any signs of the stolen Olympian treasure. I see neither Alkaios nor Spartan royals, but that doesn't mean that they're not here, nor that they haven't noticed *me* yet.

Apollo and Ariadne step in front of us as we take a fourth turn, blocking our path.

"Prince Theseus," Ariadne's voice is tart, like a spring wine. She looks over my dress and hair expertly. "Will you not introduce me to your guest?"

I struggle to remember the name Theseus gave the servants but give up when it escapes me. "Khryseis, your highness." I flash Apollo a warm smile. "And who is your handsome guest?"

"His name is Apollodorus," Apollo answers for the princess, cutting an elegant bow and winking behind the veil of his curls.

I struggle not to laugh, still facing Ariadne. "And have you known...Apollodorus long?"

"Sadly, no." Ariadne arches a dark, delicate eyebrow. "How did you and Theseus meet?"

"Khryseis is an old friend of mine from my travels," Theseus says, adopting my new name easily. His fingers tighten on my hip, pulling me against his side.

Despite me being taller than her, the Cretan princess still manages to look down her pert nose at me. The threat is fairly implied when she says, with a small purse of her lips, "You are both so insufferably coy. If I cannot get any information out of you, my father will." She takes another delicate sip of wine. "By any means necessary."

"He's welcome to try," I say, refusing to be cowed.

Ariadne straightens further, something new, curious, and unreadable alighting behind her eyes.

Apollo turns to me with a sharp cough. "Care to take a turn with me, Lady Khryseis?"

I pout, wearing the Lady Khryseis façade easily. "But I've only begun to know Princess Ariadne."

Apollo looks pointedly at Theseus's arm still draped around my hips, so I make a big show of sighing and begrudgingly accept his arm. "If you insist."

"I think Ariadne and Pyrrhus would be quite smitten with each other," I say conversationally as Apollo leads me away. "He's always been taken with feisty women. Though I doubt Princess Ariadne has any interest in being courted by a deer."

"Perhaps it's for the best." Apollo smiles slightly, lips curving to a single side. I recognize the smile as one of a withheld secret. "Dionysus is absolutely enamored of her and, handsome though your brother may be, he doesn't stand a chance against *my* brother."

Over the rim of my goblet, I follow the movements of Minos's guards, each armed to the teeth and cloaked in quiet hostility. Evenly stationed around the courtyard, they don't appear to be protecting anything or anywhere in particular, but they always have a hand rested on their swords.

A sudden wintry breeze licks about my ankles, sending a shiver up my spine. The chill makes me gasp.

"The northern winds are here? It can't be the harvest season already."

Apollo's face darkens like a storm as he too feels the undeniable bite accompanying the northern breeze. "The failing powers of Olympus have pulled Boreas from his hibernation early."

"What will happen to Sparta's crops?" I grip my chiton to still my hands' trembling.

"The winds and crops are the least of our troubles." With hooded eyes, Apollo gazes over Crete.

Shaking his head, he changes the subject, "I shouldn't have been surprised to see you here. Though I'm grateful you seem to have more tact than your kin. Most Spartans would have barreled their way through the gates with the discretion of a battering ram."

I deliberately fail to mention the two dead guards rotting in a storeroom somewhere in the palace, and take another large gulp of wine.

Apollo, indifferent to my discomfort, continues, "Though not Anax Menelaus and Anassa Helen. I wonder what Minos said to get them to accept his invitation."

His skin is warm where it meets mine, and he drops my arm to instead wrap his own around my waist with a contented sigh, distracting me from the arrival of my brother. All too aware of the hot arm around my waist, I can hardly concentrate on anything else. "How did *you* manage an invitation?" Apollo asks.

"I have my ways."

"I guess I should be grateful that you didn't ruin my plans...yet."

"Any idea where Minos could be hiding your treasure?" I peer into the shadowy passage behind King Minos. Nothing unusual lurks in the dark. "How are we going to sneak it out once we get it? It was a challenge enough to sneak into the palace."

"One thing at a time," Apollo says. How he is always so nonchalant is beyond me. He leads me around the courtyard, nodding to the Spartan monarchy as they finally make their entrance.

Helen is the most beautiful woman here, bedecked in an indigo dress that accentuates her lithe curves and lush, chestnut curls. And, of course, she is flanked by three personal guards—led at the forefront by Alkaios. My knees go weak, panic seizing the breath from my lungs.

"And how are you so calm? I feel as though I'm about to snap like a bowstring strung too tight." I fidget with my dress and roll my shoulders, the stretching of my muscles a welcome ache and distraction.

"Maybe you need more wine. Care for another cup?" Apollo inclines his head to a passing servant bearing a tray of overfull goblets. "A snack, perhaps?"

"Some feta and grapes would be nice," I admit, though my nerves will likely impede any chance of enjoying the food. "If I drink any more wine, I might be sick."

Apollo leaves me for only a moment, and I grace him with a smile as he returns, bearing a plate piled high with fruit and cheese. My stomach rumbles at the sight.

"Thank you, Apollo." I snatch away the plate, stuffing my face so quickly one might confuse me with a chipmunk.

He gapes, eyes wide and sculpted jaw slack. With a furious blush, I pass my plate off to the nearest servant.

"What? Have you never seen a woman eat before?"

Apollo gives a curt shake of his head, the stars disappearing from his eyes. "That was the first time you've ever said my name."

"Really?" My blush deepens further as I realize that he's right. I've kept him at a distance, avoiding the possibility of attachment, acknowledging him only when I absolutely must.

A pair of guards marches past, and Apollo closes the space between us, blocking me from their view. My spine brushes against a cool marble column, a balm against the searing heat radiating from Apollo.

My knees tremble. "You're standing too close. People will notice."

"Let them," he says. I lay a hand against his chest. The heat, the power thrumming under my palm makes my stomach flutter. "Say my name again."

"Apollo." His name passes my lips with a soft sigh.

His gaze is like a tendril of smoke, the arm around my waist the flame, scorching the narrow space between our bodies. My mind and heart do battle, filling me with contempt for the gods that control me and longing for the god that holds me. It is hard to focus on anything else but the arm pressing me close. I look anywhere but his eyes, with the depth and untamable ferocity of oceans.

A red-haired noble passes, downing a goblet of wine. Eyes glazed from her drink, she tosses her ginger curls over a shoulder, their color catching in the torchlight. Pyrrhus's face swarms my vision. The agony in his face as he was transformed into a deer before my very eyes.

By the sister of the god holding me now.

Apollo whispers, "You look lovely tonight, Daphne."

"The ladies of this court think that you look lovely, too." I nod to a pair of whispering noblewomen ogling him from across the court-yard. "There are plenty of other men and women lining up to be your next conquest."

"You think you know me." His face grows severe, shadows glancing off the angular panes of his face. "I am an ocean full of secrets, with a hundred lifetimes of answers. You will never truly know me, no matter how hard you try."

Apollo continues, drawing me even closer, sealing the space between us with smooth deftness. "You only know what your dear Ligeia told you. Let me tell you, Ligeia does not know as much as she believes. Is it fair to judge an individual because of stories alone?"

It takes every reserve of my will to pull away, stepping far enough from his reach.

"Maybe I have judged you unfairly," I allow, wrapping my arms around myself. A cold draft licks my skin once released from Apollo's intoxicating warmth. "But when your sister used my brother as a bargaining chip, she affirmed all those horrible stories Ligeia said about you and your family. The second you changed Lykou into a wolf you created for yourself endless miles of hurdles to jump before you *ever* gain my respect. I don't need Ligeia's stories to judge you. Your actions speak volumes. Oceans."

Apollo staggers a step back. "Daphne, I..."

A sudden beating of a drum from the front of the throne room makes us jump. The crowd parts for the king of Crete. Minos walks with short jerking steps that do little to hide the way he favors his right knee; his dark-gray eyes bore into mine and the pale scars crisscrossing his dark skin jerk with each step, slashing across his entire chest.

Minos pulls away the mask and lets it clatter to the floor, revealing a face unpleasant to look at. His low-sloped brow hoods deep-set eyes, thin lips pulled into a grimace that emphasize his chin so deeply dimpled that you could tuck a coin inside. His hair is shorn so short that the light of the hearth reflects off his scalp when he inclines his head toward us.

Reflected in his eyes are the horrors, the stories shared across Greece of his crimes against humanity. The darkness there unfurls as he looks me over, a reckless, all-consuming obsidian that bespeaks his evil deeds.

I kneel low to the floor, Apollo mimicking my movements beside me. My braid falls over my shoulder, pulling my veil with it and baring the back of my neck. With a single wave of his hand, Minos could bid a guard to slice off my head. My hands tremble and Apollo lays a palm over them, stilling their quivering.

"I don't believe we've ever had the pleasure of being introduced,"

Minos says when I rise to my feet, my hand still locked with Apollo's. Both of his front teeth are chipped, as though he chews on gold for sport. It takes me a moment to realize that he is talking to both me and Apollo, though his steely eyes are fixed only on mine.

A crowd of hushed nobles gathers around us and, to my horror, Helen and Menelaus stand among them. For once, I relish the privacy of my veil. They all watch the exchange between Minos and us with naked curiosity.

"Ariadne!" Minos's voice cuts through the crowd like a rough-edged cleaver. Ariadne rushes to her father with Theseus in tow, her chin raised high enough for a wave of admiration to come over me.

"Yes, Father?" Her lips curl slightly, the faintest suggestion of a sneer. There's obviously no love lost between these two.

"Introduce us." Not a suggestion or request—a command.

Ariadne glances between Apollo and me. "These are the guests Apollodorus and Khryseis."

"Apollodorus and Khryseis." Minos repeats our fake names, rolling them around on his tongue as though savoring a sip of wine.

"Khryseis is an old friend of mine," Theseus hurriedly explains. "She has traveled all this way to visit the Temple of Anemospilia and seek the favor of Zeus."

Minos ignores the Athenian. "You don't have the figure of a noble lady." His gaze strips me. I'm a horse at an auction, and he is a merchant looking for any fault he may barter over. I feel naked in the crowd, assessed and appraised by this cruel king. "You have the musculature of a woman used to hard labor, the scars of a warrior, and the blistering arrogant gaze of a mercenary."

I resist the urge to ask how, exactly, arrogance can blister. "You're mistaken, sir," I say, lacing my words with the dignified venom of a scorned princess, bunching my hands at my hips to hide the calluses dotting my palms that proclaim me for a liar. "I've never held a sword in my life."

My horror grows in a crescendo as, in my periphery, Alkaios comes to stand behind Helen.

Theseus shifts behind me. A whisper grows among the nobles surrounding us, at first as soft as a sea of grass, before growing to a steady hiss.

Minos snaps his fingers in my face, making me jump. "Remove your veil."

No. Anything but that. Alkaios will recognize me. Helen and Menelaus will probably recognize me.

"Wha-what? Why?"

"My liege," Apollo says, stepping before me. "The gods would consider it an affront for a woman to remove her *kalyptra* in public. It is sacrilegious to ask it of the lady."

"The gods do not rule in the House of the Double Axe," Minos says, each word an angry lash of a whip. "*I* do. Now remove the *kalyptra*."

All eyes in the courtyard are locked on me as I reach for the veil. My hands move of their own accord, my heart rammed in my throat, choking the air from my lungs. Helen raises a hand to her mouth. Apollo opens his to argue with Minos again and damn himself to the dungeons of Knossos. I can see Alkaios, even from my periphery, his eyes glued to mine as my fingers slowly grasp the fringe of my veil. The silk begins to slide from my head.

A hand reaches out, laying on top of mine. Ariadne has come to stand beside me, reaching up to straighten my veil before turning to Minos.

"Stop this nonsense, Father," she commands. She has the voice of a queen, imbued with the power of a goddess, as she steps carefully in front of me—blocking me from her father's view. "No need to humiliate the Lady Khryseis before all these nobles and the gods."

My breath catches in my throat for a long, tense moment.

Minos gives a curt nod. Reaching around his daughter and grasping my fingertips, he gives them a quick, wet kiss before disappearing among the throng of nobles.

Too easy. Too quickly did the mad king accept defeat.

Minos isn't done with me yet.

The silence that permeated the courtyard with Minos's attention to us scatters in a flutter of uneasy chatter. The nobles disperse, no longer crowded around me, but Alkaios's eyes still linger on my own. I turn, dismissing him as though he were nothing but another soldier, but not before I recognize the confusion alighting behind his dark eyes, the growing pale of his skin.

The drums start to rumble from the corners of the courtyard, mounting like approaching thunder.

"Servants of Greece, I have called you here to celebrate your freedom." Minos prowls back and forth across the dais like a caged lion. "Freedom from the shackles of the gods."

The gathered nobles shift uncomfortably. The drums slow to the unsettling rhythm of a dirge. I dare to tear my gaze from Minos for a mere second, locking eyes with Theseus. We exchange a wary glance. Ariadne presses close to his side.

"Since their creation of us, we have been at the mercy of their tyrannical rule. They have suppressed, stolen from, and murdered us. I will now free us all from Zeus's lecherous grasp and Hera's spite. We need no longer bow and scrape to their selfish siblings, no more sacrifices of our children to appease their unruly children's whims."

Apollo's jaw is clenched so tight a tic forms at his temple. I reach out and give his hand a gentle squeeze. Only to let him know that I'm still here to help him—and to keep him from making a scene.

"Before you flee in fear, like gutless mutts with your tails between your legs, I command you to stay and bear witness." Minos holds his hands open before him, palms bared and fingers splayed wide. "The gods no longer have power over me. No power over any of us. Because their power rests within us, the people of Greece, and we will no longer bow before their tyranny."

My heartbeat is erratic, so loud Poseidon likely hears it from the depths of the *Mesogeios*. A nervous trickle of sweat beads down my spine. Many audience members inch toward the exits.

"He sounds like a madman," I whisper, giving Apollo's hand another squeeze. "What point is he trying to make? Being so dramatic is foolhardy when Zeus could strike you down at any instant."

Apollo is silent for a moment, eyes locked on the King of Crete, before he says, "The power of Olympus, my family's power, lies with the people of Greece. Until we get those nine pieces back, Olympian powers, their depth, focus, and intent are in calamity. And that could have disastrous consequences for the world."

He leans close, lips brushing my ear. "Imagine if the power to control the skies, the power to command the seas, and even the power to enter your dreams fell into the wrong hands. Imagine if the power to command the armies of the dead was bestowed upon an unwitting human. Imagine if that power fell to a tyrannical king such as Minos. Imagine the wars that would be fought, how many Spartans—your brothers—would give their lives to keep this mad king at bay."

Cold floods through me. My breath grows shallow, and I fight to keep my body from shivering at the implications.

"Minos holds the fate of Olympus in his hands, and, unless we got those pieces of power back, we are powerless to stop him from destroying us." Apollo turns back to Minos, his face pained. "You think we gods play such petty games with our powers, but they are nothing compared to the games *mortals* would play with just a small fraction of them."

I regard Minos with renewed horror as he speaks again, "I know some of you may wonder where this rebellion has risen from. How can I dare to poke the angry gods in the chest and spit at their feet? I have long tired of bowing and scraping to Olympus, holding my throne by the spilled blood of my people."

"I taunt the gods because I've been gifted with a rare treasure. Something that gives me complete power over them." He waves away a pair of guards, and they stride from the room with blank faces. "I have been bestowed a great gift in retribution for the sins committed against him by Olympus."

Screams echo from the passageway behind the dais, and Apollo goes rigid beside me.

Nine things, Prometheus told me. Nine things were stolen from Olympus. But they are not things.

They are women.

Dragged before the stunned audience, three Muses struggle against the guards restraining them. Their clothes are torn, lips split and beaded with ichor. I snap a hand out, and it takes all my strength to keep Apollo from leaping to the dais, his eyes lit with the fires of Tartarus. Minos will pay for this sacrilege, but it cannot be now. Apollo pulls against me, drawn to save and protect these women with every ounce of his Olympian power.

Goddesses of the arts and the source of all knowledge, the Muses are the sacred caretakers of the Hesperides, the source of all the power of Olympus. The Muses are also under the protection of Apollo.

My head spins at the implications. It's not surprise, I realize, but fury that pulls the god taut. His teeth are clenched so tight they might crack. A tic forms at his temple. He knew, all this time, that it was the Muses that had been taken from Olympus. Not just some random pieces of treasure from Zeus's trove. These women, who were supposed to be under his protection.

Fury to match his own overwhelms me, but I can't berate him now. Not while the lives of the Muses balance on a needle's point.

Minos continues, "Three of the Muses, to do with whatever I bloody want."

The nearest Muse tries to cower away as Minos reaches out for her, his fingers hooked like mangled claws. Minos yanks on the Muse's hair as she squirms and whimpers. I'm about to rush the dais myself when suddenly he flings her aside. She stumbles away to huddle with her sisters.

Minos gestures to two more guards, who move to stand behind his throne. Each take hold of an armrest and drag it backward across the floor. A horrible, grating rumble fills the chamber and a gaping abyss opens up on the floor, a blast of cold air sweeping through the audience.

The cheese and wine I scarfed down earlier now threaten to forcibly leave my stomach. The Muses begin to cry anew, their sobs castigating me for my cowardice, for my inability to save them. Apollo's hand begins to sweat in mine.

"This is madness, Minos," Helen exclaims beside me. Menelaus holds her back, but she struggles against his grip. Alkaios and the other solders have their hands on the hilts of their swords. She throws down her *kylix* and it shatters across the floor. "Let these women go before you damn us all to Tartarus."

Minos ignores my queen, his face split in a maniacal grin. "For thirty years, I have sacrificed the children of the *Mesogeios* to my son, at the behest of the gods, thirty years of bloodletting to prove my devotion to them and keep my seat of power. You all came here to implore me to end this bloodshed, to bargain and beg at my feet. May this be the ultimate sacrifice, the last blood spilled to ensure my hold over the *Mesogeios*. Let it be known that Olympus no longer has any power over men."

More of the audience begins to protest, trying in vain to argue with the insane king, while some stand in stunned silence.

A rumble from the pit steals the chatter from the room. Slowly, the rumble grows and the floor begins to shudder, a dull roar beginning to echo around the chamber. The noise chills my soul, and I step closer to Apollo's warmth. Audience members begin to scream, fleeing for the exits; soldiers press from the doorways, blocking their way.

"I would introduce you to my son," Minos quips. "But I didn't invite you here to be his dinner. He has a very careful diet, making sure to only eat at dawn. Better for digestion."

"You're mad," Menelaus bellows, dragging his wife from the crowd.

"Better than a mewling child blindly following powerless gods." Minos turns to the Muses. "Make sure to run fast. He enjoys a good hunt."

And then with a curt nod from their king, the guards shove the screaming Muses into the pit and out of sight.

CHAPTER

17

Olympus no longer holds power over us." Minos's words chase me from the courtyard. "We are no longer playthings of the gods."

Guests bolt for their rooms, shoving past the guards and fleeing the scene of a crime that can damn them to Tartarus. No exceptions, Apollo and I make haste for Theseus's chambers.

"You knew," I accuse once we're safely behind the chamber's door, leveling every ounce my frustration and fury at Apollo. "You knew that we were seeking the Muses. How could you not? How could you not tell me?"

I snatch up my small bag of possessions hidden behind a pillar. The chamber is dark and lit with only a few torches. I tear off my gown without regard as to who might see my naked frame in the firelight, and quickly replace it with my leather Spartan uniform.

"Because, initially, you were only a means to an end," Apollo says, raking a hand through his curls. "Someone to help Artemis and me pry the secrets from Prometheus's mouth."

Lykou growls behind me, low and lethal. The sound trails around us as the god looks quickly between us.

"That's why you wanted to leave me outside of the palace." Rage rushes through me, a tempest drowning all other feelings in its path.

My body trembles, every muscle begging me to beat Apollo senseless. "You and Artemis never intended for me to save all the Muses. You just wanted to use me to get Prometheus to speak."

Apollo's skin blanches. "Daphne, that's not—"

"Well, I have," I yell, cutting him off. I storm over, jabbing a finger into the god's chest. He stumbles and backs away. I follow, until Apollo is backed against the hearth. Sweat beads his hairline. "And I will help you get the damn Muses back. But only to save these women. And all of Greece. After that, all the gods can stay out of my life, *mysterious blood* or not."

And then, my voice low, "It should be you in that labyrinth. Not them."

I lock his gaze with mine, daring him to look away, to betray even the slightest cowardice. Lykou's growl has quieted, until the only sounds in the room are the hiss of the fire and the pounding of my heart.

"Well, Minos seems to have lost touch with reality. We will..." Theseus storms into the room but stops short when he sees Apollo, mouth dropping open. "Am I interrupting something?"

Apollo holds up his hands. "On the contrary, you've arrived at the perfect moment."

Theseus glances uneasily between me and Apollo.

Apollo steps toward him, placing a hand over his heart. "Olympus thanks you for helping Daphne get inside the banquet, but now we need your help getting out of the palace. Athena has commanded you to find a weapon beneath the city of Knossos, and now I command you to help us rescue the Muses."

"How do you know about Athena's labors?" Theseus rounds on me. "What else did you tell him?"

Apollo stands straighter, taking another step so that their chests brush. "I am Apollo, son of Zeus. Heir to the sun, god of music, truth, and prophecy. My sister cursed you, and now I demand your allegiance. Help Daphne kill the Minotaur, and I will help you best Athena's impossible tasks."

The Athenian snaps his mouth shut and wastes no more time. He strips quickly behind a silk curtain and emerges armed to the teeth, a dozen daggers strapped across his leather-plated chest, two axes strapped across his back, and a pair of ancient iron swords swinging from his hips. He's pulled his long, brown hair at the nape of his neck in a leather thong, his face and shoulders painted black with ash. Beside him, I feel naked with only my leather uniform and motley assortment of daggers and single sword.

"Do either of you have any brilliant plans," Theseus says, strapping on a pair of bronze vambraces, "or shall we just lay siege to the throne room and be done with it?"

"As much as I would love to watch you try to storm the throne room," Apollo says, crossing his arms over his chest, "the soldiers of Knossos outnumber us a hundred to one."

Theseus shrugs, the dozen daggers across his chest reflecting in the firelight with the movement. "The guards won't know what hit them. Minos is likely delighting himself in his bedchamber, fanned by slaves as he boasts that his guests are nothing more than frightened livestock."

I turn to the god. "What do you suggest we do, Apollo? Ask him politely if we can have the Muses back and kill his son?"

"I have a plan," Apollo says, a rueful smirk tugging at the corner of lips. He turns to me. "But you're not going to like it."

A sharp voice from the doorway spins us all around. "Even if Apollodorus's plan works, you're unlikely to survive a single hour with my brother."

Framed by the doorway, Ariadne holds the hem of her rose chiton in one hand, the other clenched over her heart. Veil gone, her hair spilled across her shoulders in ebony rivers to match her narrowing dark eyes, she looks us over. Her keen gaze takes in our array of weapons and battle attire.

Theseus steps forward, palms up in a placating gesture. "Let me explain."

Ariadne cuts him off with a withering glance and impatient wave of her hand, before turning to me. "You'll need more than weapons to survive what awaits beneath Knossos."

She strides forward. I raise my chin, prepared for more of her cutting remarks. She stops an arm's length from me. The Cretan princess holds her fist out in front of me, and I let her drop something small and cool in my palm. A small silver medallion, engraved with a hundred letters and symbols that spiral toward the coin's center, hanging from a thin stretch of black cord.

No power emanates from the medallion, no secrets waiting to be spilled. I feel nothing wicked lingering in the black script etched across its surface.

"What is it?" I pass a thumb over the first symbol, a reverse arrowhead inlaid with black paint.

"A Phaistos Disc," Ariadne says with a smug smile quickly replaced by a grimace. "Daedalus helped me design it. I got lost far too many times in the process. My brother's realm beneath Knossos isn't for the faint of heart."

"And what's it for?" I consider giving it back to her. Whatever it is and whatever it can do, Ariadne could still use it to betray us to her father.

She takes the disc from my hands and passes the length of rope over my head. The cool metal bounces against the crow between my breasts. "If these fools can indeed get you past my father's guards, it will help you find the Muses. Follow the symbols I've carved, and it will lead you to his lair."

She turns to leave. I find my voice when she reaches the doorway. "Why help us? Will you not be punished by your father?"

"I can no longer stand by and watch as my father murders innocents to keep his throne." Ariadne raises her chin, her cutting gaze passing over each of us again. "The god Dionysus told me you would come to save Knossos, and that I must help. The Phaistos Disc will guide your passage. I will distract my father as long as possible." She disappears beyond the doorway, leaving us in stunned silence.

Clenching the disc, I turn to Apollo. "Now, about your plan."

Apollo is right. I don't like his plan.

Lykou, Theseus, and I cling to the shadows of Knossos's long hallways, keeping our ears trained for any noise, our eyes peeled for any movements other than our own. Guards patrol the breezeways, but are easily avoided by hiding behind the massive pillars. Lykou slinks in front of us, using his wolf hearing to scout ahead.

When we reach the throne room, I poke my head around a column. Before the pit entrance are two guards with ramrod-straight backs, armed with spears, daggers, and heavy iron swords. Hopefully, Apollo's distraction will be enough. We press against the wall, waiting for the god's signal.

The clap of strutting, sandaled feet echoes down the corridors. Lykou releases a quiet snarl and bares his fangs. I thrust an arm out to press Theseus into the shadows. Rounding a corner with clipped steps, Minos marches down the hall toward us. Theseus tenses beneath my arm, hand inching toward one of his swords. The shadows behind the column provide cover for us, yet the Cretan winks at us with infuriating cockiness as he passes.

Apollo, magically disguised as Minos, strides past our hiding place with that swagger I know all too well.

"And what, exactly, are you doing in here?" the imposter king demands of the two guards. His voice peaks with a roar, spittle flying onto the faces of the stunned guards. "Do you two thickheaded fools think that you are have no need to patrol the palace? That the gods won't seek their vengeance so soon after my sacrifice?"

"Milord, *you* commanded us to protect the entrance to the lair," one guard stutters.

"Are you implying that I forgot my own commands?" Apollo's voice drops to a whisper. The guards exchange unsure glances, knuckles white as they grip their spears. "I pay you to keep my palace safe. Not to ensure that someone else doesn't warm their ass on my throne. Now leave, before I report to your commander that a couple of his *koprophage* soldiers thought themselves important enough to avoid patrol duty by hiding in my throne room."

"But... but, *I* am the commander, your highness."

I cringe, resisting the urge to groan. A long moment of painful silence passes. I debate storming the throne. I'm a split second away from leaping around the corner to take out the unsuspecting guards when Apollo speaks again.

"Not after this disgraceful behavior, you're not." His voice low and lethal, he continues, "I know exactly who you are, and if you and your fellow layabout don't remove yourself from my royal presence this instant, you will both be my son's next meal."

The guards stumble as they race from the room. Apollo-as-Minos stays a moment longer before following. He whistles his typical jaunty tune as he struts past without a glance in our direction, off to keep any other guards from approaching the throne.

"A bit overdramatic," Theseus mutters.

Once Apollo turns the corner, I shove the Athenian forward, almost tripping over Lykou in my haste. Theseus and I grunt, dragging the throne back, while Lykou creeps forward. I cringe when a horrible, grating rumble picks up in its wake.

The dark abyss yawns wide. A gust hits our faces, bringing with it putrid waves of brine and decay. Theseus had the foresight to grab a torch, but it barely pierces the gloom. The shadows fight against its dim light, shifting with each rancid gust of air.

My heart thunders in my chest. I hesitate over the chasm, reaching a foot tentatively past the lip. A stone stairwell descends into the darkness from the opening, extending past my line of sight.

"Be brave," I whisper to myself before beginning my descent into the darkness. "For Pyrrhus."

The silence is deafening beneath the House of the Double Axe.

I force myself to breathe through my nose to maintain some semblance of quiet; my eyes begin to water from the stench of rot and death. Lykou presses against my legs, a reassurance in the darkness. We eventually come to a stone wall covered in decades of gray slime like the pus of a festering wound. It doesn't smell much better, either. Nose wrinkled, I turn to the curved arch in the center of the wall, scored by deep gouges. For several feet, they split the wall like claw marks. Behind me, Theseus pulls free an axe.

We continue through the archway down a long corridor. The passage takes a downward trajectory and I hesitate the barest of moments when we reach black water, calm and unreadable. Taking a deep breath, I step forward. The water floods up to my knees, dispelling any hopes for silent movements. With each splashing step, frustration rises in me and reaches a peak when we reach twin passages.

"Which path?" Theseus asks. Despite the chill, sweat beads his brow.

I snatch the torch from him. The light reveals more clawed furrows along the wall of the left path and I'm about to gamble on the left path, but similar marks gouge the walls to the right.

"The gods have forsaken this place." I clench my sword's hilt, fingers thrumming against the warm metal. "This is a test. If you're to find the weapon to claim your throne, and if I'm to find the Muses, we'll have to use more than brute strength to best this abyss."

"So, what do you suggest?" Theseus tosses his axe between his hands. "I use my infinite wit to make the beast laugh and you tickle it to death?"

"Or"—I hold out the Phaistos Disc for inspection—"we use our heads."

"And headbutt the damn thing?"

Ignoring him is a feat worthy of heroes. I look up; arrowheads are carved into the fanlight above the center stones of the archways. Atop the left, one faces upward, and above the right, the arrowhead is in reverse. Sure enough, the first symbol on the disc, a reverse arrowhead, glints in the firelight.

I surge forward under the right arch. Theseus follows without argument. The path abruptly turns and forks without any logic to it, and the deeper we venture, more such intersections arise in our path. Each time, I follow the symbols carved out by Ariadne.

"It's a labyrinth," Theseus says, pointing out the obvious. "Don't lose that damn disc or there won't be a return journey."

Lykou whines his concurrence.

I sigh through my nose. "Good to know I can always count on you two for a vote of confidence."

We continue to navigate the labyrinth for what feels like hours before the first inkling of hope bubbles in my chest. We are nearing the center of Ariadne's Phaistos Disc, the end of her carefully detailed directions, when my hope is abruptly burst by heart-stopping fear.

A rumble ripples through the darkness toward us, causing my torch to flutter.

"Well at least we know we went the right way," Theseus says. I smack a hand over his mouth to silence him.

We leave the narrow passageways behind, creeping into a wide room littered with boulders and a white marble fountain, one side smashed away, its black water pouring out and down into the labyrinth. Statues of the Olympians dance together in the fountain's remains. Dark water seeps from their eyes and mouths like rivulets of blood. I pass the stone-carved Hermes, startled by the likeness. His alabaster eyes follow me across the room.

A pair of passages on the far side beckon to us, onyx chasms in the charcoal walls. Stepping closer, though, I curse.

Claw marks make the symbols at the top of the archways illegible.

"Damn Tyche. Our fortune has abandoned us." I hold the torch higher, peering into the endless shadows within each archway. No answers forthcoming, I turn to Lykou. His jowls curl back as he sniffs each passageway. "Does your nose have any ideas?"

The stench of Minos's son is equally flagrant from both. Lykou leaps between the two archways, sniffing. He turns to me with a low whine and shake of his head. The growling noise has quieted. I start toward the left on a whim when Lykou's ears suddenly perk and he swivels to face the far side of the room.

A soft, slow splashing of waves against the walls and the infinitesimal rise in the water bristles the hair on the back of my neck. The son of Minos has come to greet us.

I suppress a shiver as its malevolent presence hovers at the edge of my vision. Judging from Theseus's lack of reaction, still studying the carvings, the Athenian hasn't yet noticed the creature. Subtle shifting in the water tells me that the Minotaur paces slowly along the far side of the room, biding its time. Likely deliberating over which one of us would be the most delicious.

I turn, and though the room is too dark for me to track the beast with my eyes, his presence is keenly felt. I drop my gaze down to the water lapping my calves.

And then I feel, as keenly as a hand down my spine, the beast take a step in my direction.

I throw our torch into the water. With a hiss and splash, darkness cloaks us. Theseus begins to protest, but I slap a hand over his mouth and drag him through the left arch.

The loss of our torch forces me to rely upon my instincts and Lykou's nose. I lead Theseus and Lykou through turn after turn, memorizing our route while listening for our monstrous hunter.

Left. Left. Right. Left. Right. Right. Left.

On and on into the darkness we creep.

The growling grows louder and louder. Sometimes it's to our right, sometimes above, and other times ahead of us. At the end of a narrow corridor, we reach a sandstone wall. The growling rumbles from directly behind us.

I let the creature herd us to our death.

"No!" I beat on the stone wall, my voice rising to a screech.

"You led us into a trap!" Though I can hardly see his face in the darkness, I can feel the desperation leaching into Theseus's words.

"Like you would have done any better," I snap.

Theseus beats his fists uselessly against the wall. "Just get us out of this mess before we're nothing but blood and bones."

"It can go ahead and try to kill me." My voice is low, but loud enough for him to hesitate and stop beating the wall. I turn around, holding my sword aloft. "I was trained by the great Paidonomos Leonidas of Sparta, and I will litter the ground with pieces of its body."

Theseus scoffs and resumes searching for an escape. "Your precious Paidonomos Leonidas probably doesn't know a sword from the backside of a horse."

A stone skips across the ground between us. Lykou erupts with a series of feverish snarls. In the darkness, only the whites of his bared teeth are visible. The stench is overwhelming.

He's found us.

The Minotaur rumbles as it stomps forward. My heart jumps to my throat, knees trembling. It towers over us, taller than any man I've ever seen. A mass in the shadows, and though I cannot distinguish its features, I can feel its hungry gaze. Even in the dark, I can see the shadows of horns, the great maw of its mouth, the long, muscled arms hanging at its sides, ending with clawed hands dripping with a black liquid.

Its massive chest heaves. I take a step back and my back brushes against the cold stone wall, a remorseless reminder that I'm trapped.

Lykou is the first to react, his black fur bristling on end and white teeth flashing in the dark. A series of snarls erupt from him and he leaps, snapping at the beast's legs. The Minotaur ignores Lykou, interested in a more filling—human—meal.

It lunges. I leap to the side, narrowly avoiding obsidian claws as they rip through the air. Theseus is not so quick and releases a horrible, anguished yell. His shoulder shreds beneath the Minotaur's reach.

I spin and lash out with my sword. But Spartan steel fails me; the blade barely leaves a mark. Painful reverberations ripple up my arm. The Minotaur rips angry gashes in the wall behind me. Rolling away from outstretched claws, I swipe at the beast's thigh. My blade shatters, the thigh unmarred.

Lykou leaps and catches the beast's arm between his teeth. The

Minotaur only growls in annoyance, shaking the wolf off. I hack at the beast with what's left of my sword and grit my teeth. Metal meets skin as hard and impenetrable as stone, making my arm ache. Theseus attacks from behind. His sword slashes across the Minotaur's calves.

The beast spins around, and before Theseus can jump away, it sends him hurtling backward with a solid kick to the gut. I cry out as he crashes into a wall and crumples to the ground.

The legs of the Minotaur bunch. I hold my ground as it charges. My heart screams at me to run. When the Minotaur is a mere heartbeat from crashing into me, I leap out of the way, rolling across the rock-strewn ground. The beast smashes through the wall behind me. A scream escapes my lips as the ceiling begins to collapse. Debris rains around us and I crawl toward the wall to avoid getting flattened.

I allow myself a sigh of relief as the chaos comes to a standstill. The moon shines down through the ruptured ceiling, painting the labyrinth in ivory light and shades of gray. Lykou nudges me to my knees, whining and pawing at my legs. Coughing dust from my lungs, I crawl through the debris toward Theseus.

"Did your *paidonomos* teach you how to mend a shredded shoulder?" He forces a weak smile, cheek pressed against the dusty ground. "Or the importance of a fine wine in circumstances where you cannot?"

I can't help but snort, despite the imminent danger. I throw his unwounded arm over my shoulder and we stagger to our feet.

A rumble in the darkness snaps our heads toward the broken wall. There's another crash of debris. More rubble falling from the ceiling makes us both duck. When the ground stops shuddering, Theseus grabs my shoulders with rough hands.

"Go." He shoves me away. "I can't run in this sorry state, but you can. Go find the Muses and the weapon to defeat the plague of Thebes. I will distract the Minotaur."

I can't afford to hesitate. The rumble grows into a roar that rips the air from my lungs. It stomps toward us, making the ground tremble.

I collect my sword from the rocks before looking Theseus in the eye. "I will bring you the finest wine in all of Greece," I promise. "And you will get your throne, *symmachos*."

With regret clutching my heart, I leave him. Lykou lopes beside me and shame trails my pounding footsteps as we plunge deeper into the labyrinth.

CHAPTER 18

The roar of the Minotaur merges with Theseus's shouts, following us through the labyrinth. Ariadne's disc and Lykou's feral senses guide us. We dash around corner after corner. My blood pounds in my veins, drowning out the raging bellows of the Minotaur.

Lykou snarls beside me, skidding to a halt so suddenly I almost leave him behind.

He's stopped us at another pair of archways, his jowls pulled back so high I could count every single one of his pearly fangs.

I hold the Phaistos Disc up, struggling to read the symbols in the darkness. A *meander*. Atop the left archway is a bird, and the other a *meander*. I stride for the right archway, but Lykou catches the hem of my uniform between his teeth.

I jerk away from his grasp. "We've got to hurry, Lykou. The Mino-taur will be on us again in a moment."

Sure enough, the Minotaur's roars are growing louder, and he is likely barreling toward us.

I step toward the archway again and Lykou leaps in front of me, snarling. But not at me—at the shadows lurking down the stone hallway. The back of my neck itches, my hair rising. I brush my fear away with an impatient snort. Lykou shoves me roughly, still growling and pressing his coarse shoulder against my legs, trying to herd me beneath the wrong archway.

"No, Lykou. A son afraid of the dark is no son of Sparta at all." I stride beneath the *meander*.

And step into a void. The darkness is impenetrable. I can't even see my hands before me. I reach for a wall but find none. I can't even hear the Minotaur's roar anymore. My heart pounds in my ears, a hollow pulsing that rises with each unsteady breath.

"Where are we, Lykou?" I reach for his familiar presence at my hip, but my hand only finds air. "Lykou?"

My heart thuds to a stop.

He's no longer beside me, his panting gone. Silence stretches around me, broken only by my own heartbeat. I pull free a dagger, brandishing it before me.

Bright, cerulean eyes pierce the void, floating in the air. I swing beneath them. My dagger cleaves only gloom and she chuckles.

"Now is that any way to treat the Muses' savior?"

"Pasiphae." Her name passes my lips like a sigh. "I thought you were no longer living on Crete."

"I thought to return and see what foolish nonsense my husband was up to now." Her husky voice hovers in the air. "And it's a good thing I did, or else these Muses would be dead, and my powers completely gone."

"How did you know they would be in trouble *here*?" My grip on the hilt of my dagger tightens. Apollo said that Pasiphae and her siblings were on the opposing side of some Olympian squabble.

"When Hermes called us all to Olympus and told Zeus that he found you and Apollo in Heraklion, I knew the Muses must be near." When Pasiphae steps close, I can see the resemblance to her daughter. Ariadne shares her creamy skin, raven tresses, and pert nose. "Your distrust toward me is misplaced, *kataigída*. To kill the Muses would leave me bereft of power. I've kept them safe from my son's insatiable appetite." She smirks, pale pink lips curling to the side. "Though I'm in no rush to return them to Olympus, either. Let Zeus fret a moment longer."

"Return them now." I raise my dagger between us. "Or else."

She cackles, not giving the blade even a cursory glance. "If you insist."

The ground drops beneath my feet. Screaming, I tumble through the air. My dagger clatters on a ledge above me. My hand catches on a rock outcropping and nearly jerks my arm from its socket. I slam into a stone wall, stealing the breath from my lungs.

Moonlight shining from a fissure in the ceiling illuminates the cavern around me, the gaping maw over which I hang. The world opens beneath my feet like a great mouth waiting to swallow me whole.

"Don't look down. Don't look down," I mutter under my breath. With gritted teeth, I pull myself up, handhold over foothold, eventually pulling myself over the ledge.

Amid a ruin of rubble and rotting bodies, a cage sits in the center of the landing. Bones make the bars, the locks and corners held together by circles of stone thicker than my arms.

Three tattered women huddle inside it.

"Please," one Muse screams. "Free us before it comes back."

I search for a lock to try to pick but find none.

"Stand back," I command, rushing to the cage. The Muses cluster in the back as I begin sawing away at the cage with my sword. The bones don't budge beneath my onslaught.

"The bones are impervious to weapons and our magic," one Muse says.

If only I'd known that before I'd ruined my dagger against it. The moonlight reflects off my blade, revealing a newly bent edge. "How did Pasiphae even get this thing open?"

"With blood." One of the Muses reaches an arm through, pointing. Carvings I hadn't noticed before are etched down the bones and flaked with dried blood. "This is the work of magic only a few Olympians can wield."

I wrack my memory for stories about the goddess and her siblings. Another roar echoes through the labyrinth. "What about Pasiphae's brother Aeëtes? Didn't his own daughter come up with a foil to his magic?"

"With blood sacrifice." The Muse's face is solemn. "She killed and dismembered her own brother."

"Well my brothers aren't here for me to sacrifice and you to resurrect." My lips press into a firm line. "But I've got plenty of blood to spare."

Before I can second-guess myself, I draw my blade across my palm. Blood pours from my hand and I slap it against the carvings.

My blood runs freely, too quickly, and my vision begins to spin. The bone crumbles beneath my hand, and I nearly tumble into the cage when it snaps in my grasp.

The Muses immediately climb through the opening. I stumble backward, delirious from blood loss. But I only need enough blood to get the Muses out of here.

"Thank you, thank you, thank you," the tallest says, again and again.

The shortest of the three has dark tan skin and a pinched face covered with grime. "You may call me Melpomene." She waves to her two sisters, both much taller than herself. "Urania and Terpsikhore."

I give them a cursory nod of greeting and look around for a way to escape. On the other side of the ledge, too far for a mortal to jump, is another archway and our way to freedom.

I search the crevice for a way to cross. A chunk of rock tumbles free and forces me to leap back. Along the far wall, a narrow lip, hardly large enough for my feet, stretches across the abyss.

A lonely howl pierces the air, quickly followed by a furious roar. Lykou must be lost, the Minotaur on his tail.

I can't worry about him now, though.

The Muses take their sweet time inching across despite the constant threat of the Minotaur's return. Nervous sweat drips down my spine, putrid waves of hot air licking the back of my neck. More than once, I swear I feel the beast's eyes on me. The Muses are taking too long, too assured in their immortality to truly fear the Minotaur's claws.

Melpomene shuffles across with quiet sobs. Her fingers scramble for any handhold possible. With a burst of Olympian power, Terpsikhore dashes across the infinitesimal ledge with the grace of a dancer in three bounding steps.

Urania goes last. I bite my lip as she inches across. Just when she's an arm's length away from the opposite side, her foot slips.

Urania tumbles with a short scream, barely catching herself on the opposite ledge. My heart takes a moment to start again as her sisters drag her over the ledge.

I press my body against the wall and inch across, my hands searching for any kind of hold. Shutting out all noise and balancing on the edge of my toes, my fingers stretch for their next hold. My palm is bloody, making my already tenuous grip slick. I lift my feet and press my toes flat against the rough wall.

One breath. Two breaths.

And I shove away toward the opposite landing.

A sickly sensation fills my stomach. I fly for what feels like an eternity.

I hit the opposite side and slide across the cold stone floor, a gasp of pain stealing past my lips. The skin on my arms and legs tears on the rough stone leaving a trail of my blood.

We don't have time to assess injuries. Fueled by adrenaline and following the Phaistos Disc, Ariadne's map of symbols is a beacon of hope in the darkness. Terpsikhore and Urania lope behind me. Their long legs are much more expedient than Melpomene's short ones. None of them protest. I have no idea whether fear or godlike strength fuels them on and on.

We burst from the depths of the labyrinth, rounding a corner and emerging in the flooded room.

A towering mass of muscle and death stands in the center, dangling Theseus from its claws.

CHAPTER

19

ts dark eyes turn on me. My ruined dagger is already in my unwounded fist.

Lykou leaps from behind me, issuing a bloodcurdling snarl of warning, and a rush of relief floods through me. We stand, side by side, in front of the Muses.

The Minotaur takes deep, shuddering breaths. Black saliva drips from the gaping, fanged maw of its mouth to pool on the ground at its hooved feet. Cracks split his horns, blood dripping from their tips.

"An unpredictable enemy is the most dangerous of all." Alkaios's lectures ring in my ears as I stare down the beast. *"Find a weakness, then find a second. Let the enemy assume you're focused on the first weakness, then steal beneath their defenses and aim for the second."*

A brilliant tactic—if my enemy wasn't impervious to pain and grafted of impenetrable skin.

It likewise studies me, probably debating which parts of my body will be the most delectable. My mouth hardens into a grim line. Poor bastard—I'm a tough one to chew.

The Minotaur releases his claws, and the Athenian falls to the ground in a heap. A deep moan from Theseus fills me with temporary relief—at least he's still alive, but like everything else in this bloody maze, the feeling is short-lived.

"I'll distract it long enough for you to escape," I command without turning to face the Muses. "Lykou, lead them to the surface. My sword can't break his skin, so I don't know how long I'll be able to hold him off. Run fast."

Spinning on his haunches, the Minotaur charges after the women with a wild roar. They run directionless and screaming. The beast gives chase on all fours, barreling through the water and crashing into walls. Its massive body crashes through the fountain, sculptures flying. It roars again, drool splattering in all directions as it beats its chest and stamps its hooves.

I run toward the Minotaur, leaping and landing on its back. I struggle to wrap my arms around its massive neck. The Minotaur is too broad to reach me and his arms flail above my head, horns stabbing the air. Shifting my grip on my dagger, I stab at the beast's jugular. The blade shatters.

The beast snatches my cuff and, as easily as if I were a gnat, yanks me from his back. He tosses me across the room. I don't even have time to cry out and cradle my head before I crash to the watery ground. Pain lances up my arm like a bolt of lightning, my elbow clipping something in the dark, just as my head cracks on a piece of debris. I splash into the black water.

The Minotaur charges Terpsikhore. Her screams echo around the room in dizzying heights. He lashes out at her, but she spins away with inhuman grace. Lykou leaps in the beast's path. He clamps his teeth on the Minotaur's fist.

My mind spins, stars dancing in my eyes. Dripping and aching, I struggle to my knees just as the Minotaur grabs Terpsikhore. His claws dig into her arms. A choked scream escapes her. Lykou snarls, jaws clamping down on the beast's other arm. He only holds on for a moment before the beast flings him across the room.

I struggle to stand, but my vision blackens and I collapse forward once more. My mind screams at me to stand, but my legs and arms refuse to work.

I should be dead.

My right arm hangs uselessly at my side. Blood pours from my shredded palm. Every breath sends a fresh wave of pain from my shoulder and into the tips of my fingers. My vision is still dizzy, the world refusing to right itself. But the water, that sweet, dark water, is somehow invigorating. With each breath, my strength returns, drawing life from the water.

On my hands and knees, the water is up to my chest. Apollo was right. There is more to my strength than I thought. But I'm not going to die before I find out exactly what that is.

I stagger forward, searching for a weapon. The one Theseus was sent to retrieve. A rock or piece of fallen rubble. Something. Anything.

I spy a piece of the Hermes statue protruding from the dark water. The *kerykeion* dangles from the statue's broken hand. Sliding across the slick floor, I scoop up the alabaster staff. My sudden movement draws the Minotaur away from Lykou and Terpsikhore.

"Come and get me, you ugly bastard." My challenge ricochets across the chamber.

It takes the bait. I dodge out of the way at the last minute, and it charges into the wall behind me. I spin around before it can retaliate and take one last flying leap.

I land on the Minotaur's back again. My legs wrap around the broad torso. My thighs burn with the effort, my battered arm barely keeping its grip. I grit my teeth and ignore the pain, like hoarfrost shredding through my muscles and tendons. I jerk my good wrist with the *kerykeion*, praying to Olympus that my aim is true.

With a single stab, the wing of the *kerykeion* pierces the Minotaur's eye and pushes deep into his skull. A last shuddering exhalation shakes its entire mass. It collapses and I rocket across the floor.

Silence settles across the chamber. I lay on my chest a moment longer, testing each limb and taking deep, gulping breaths. A motley assortment of pains makes themselves known throughout my body as I climb to my feet and creep toward the Minotaur's still mass.

Clutching my wounded arm, I jab the Minotaur with a toe. The piece of statue poking out the back of its skull tells me the beast is indeed dead. I should be cheering, giddy and jubilant. But I can't relish this moment of victory. There are still six more Muses, and only Olympus knows what horrible thing I must vanquish next.

I'm jolted from my thoughts by a warm wetness pressing into my wounded arm. Lykou sniffs me with concerned whimpers, ascertaining for himself that I'm not suffering from any life-threatening injuries.

Waving my friend away, I turn to Theseus. He's alive, if barely. Kneeling by his side, I lay a palm to his cheek, flinching at the deathly cold of his skin. His thigh's a mess of shredded skin beyond mortal repair; his chest is a mass of contusions, and his nose is broken, as well.

The Muses inch forward but still keep a wary distance, eyeing Theseus.

"Can you help him?" I ask, the words a rough croak. "Do any of your gifts extend to healing?"

Taking a deep breath, Urania steps forward. She drags one long, slender finger across Theseus's face, and the bruising begins to fade and his nose reassembles itself. Her finger continues down Theseus's broken body, and the slashes across his legs and chest begin to knit together. Her face turns ashen, weariness slumping her shoulders when she's finished the healing. Melpomene envelops her sister in a warm hug.

When his breathing returns to a healthy cadence, Terpsikhore and I drag Theseus from the room, Melpomene and Urania following closely behind as they cling to Lykou's shaggy fur.

The Phaistos Disk and the light of the rising dawn, filtering into the depths of the labyrinth, guides us to freedom.

CHAPTER 20

Apollo paces the length of the throne room, muttering under his breath. He stops when he sees us, though, and rushes to the Muses. After giving each a quick hug, he throws Theseus over his shoulders with a grunt.

Before we leave, one of his warm hands rests on my hip, for the merest of moments.

"I should be dead," I whisper, for only him to hear.

He nods, bronze curls catching the firelight. He knows what I mean. That he was right, and that he has so much to tell me about who and what I am.

For now, though, he ushers us from the gaping pit. "Quick, before the palace awakens and Minos calls for our heads."

The pale golden light of dawn spills across the floors of the palace. Lykou leads the way as we dart around corners and slink down corridors, careful to avoid soldiers. Though we make it undetected, I don't want to linger in Knossos long enough for Minos to discover his dead son *or* the trail of blood and grime leading to our rooms.

"Urania?" Apollo places a gentle hand on the Muse's shoulder. "Time is of the essence. We only have so many moments before Minos realizes that his son is much too quiet beneath the palace. Care to steal us some time?"

Urania nods wearily. She closes her eyes, wincing slightly as a whisper steals past her lips, indiscernible to my human ears.

I don't feel the change at first, but then there it is. A tickle at the nape of my neck, the hairs on my arms rising. Urania, Muse of the Earth, the cosmos, and astrology, has stalled time for us.

When she opens her eyes again, her pallor is deathly pale and sheened with sweat. "My time away from Olympus has drained me considerably. We only have a few moments more."

Apollo looks to me and I nod. Ignoring the assortment of pains lancing throughout my battered body, I retrieve Hermes's pipes.

Exhaling into the *auloi*, a soft trill spirals through the air, rising from the cadence of a small bird to the shrill cry of a rooster. A soft flutter of wings heralds his entrance—a flurry of sand and cool breeze sweeping into the room as the messenger god struts from the balcony.

"You've found them?" he demands, dark curls unkempt and his dark-blue chiton creased, skin flushed with excitement.

In answer to his question, the Muses flock to Hermes, sobbing and throwing themselves into his arms. He squeezes them tight, then winks at me over their shoulders.

Lykou worriedly licks my hands and sniffs my legs.

"I'm fine, Lykou," I say, though I feel far from it. I crouch and give his chin a gentle scratch, searching for any wounds. He seems to be the least wounded of all of us to emerge from the labyrinth.

Apollo presses close to my other side, his elbow brushing my shoulder. Weary yet relieved, he flashes me a grim smile. More disheveled than I've ever seen him, his bronze curls press flat against his sweaty brow, his lips are chapped, and the barest hint of dark circles linger beneath his eyes.

Perhaps a result of diminishing Olympian powers, or of fretting over the Muses in the labyrinth.

Without thinking, I rest a hand on his folded arms. Apollo's eyes widen at my touch before he envelops my hand in both of his. The simple movement is a welcome comfort, and I let myself lean into his warmth. I don't miss the narrowing of Lykou's eyes as he looks between us.

A soft sigh escapes my lips as a solitary cold finger, stroking up and down, from head to tailbone, makes my body convulse in shivers. Melpomene, having disentangled herself from Hermes, draws her finger along my body, erasing all my pains. The bones in my arm tingle as they repair.

"Thank you," I murmur, giving my arm a testing shake. No pain, not even a hint of tenderness, lingers in my skin. I look Melpomene deep in her dark eyes. "What can you tell me about your captor? Of the traitor to Olympus."

Apollo and Hermes hover behind me, hoping to hear what she has to say. But the Muse shakes her head. "We cannot remember anything of the person who stole us away. One moment we were tending the Tree, the boughs trembling on a sudden breeze. I remember a single apple falling into my hands before everything went black." She looks to her sisters, tears on her face. "We woke up in his dungeon a few weeks ago."

Apollo mutters a curse under his breath. "How is that possible? How could anyone even get into the Garden?"

"Because you weren't there, Apollo," Terpsikhore says, her chin raised high and trembling. Hermes wraps a comforting arm around her shoulder. "You should have been there."

My thoughts are wild, but I have one more question for the women. "Was... was there a strange smell?"

Melpomene blinks. "What?"

"Was there a strange smell? Before it all went black, do you remember smelling anything unusual?" I've found that, when the gods use their gifts, often a certain smell lingers in their wake.

"We were in the Garden." Terpsikhore shakes her head. "There are so many different flowers and smells, it would be almost impossible to distinguish one from the other."

"Perhaps if we tried harder we could." Melpomene's lower lip trembles.

Hermes wraps his other arm around her. "We won't make you relive that. Thank you, Daphne." He offers me a low bow, whipping the *kerykeion* through the air. The golden staff flashes in the sun. "What can Olympus ever do to repay you?"

I eye the *kerykeion,* chewing my lip. "You could let me borrow that." At Hermes's dumbstruck expression I hastily add, "But only for a little while."

He clutches the staff to his chest as though I might try to steal it from him. The indigo rooster tattoos strut and the snakes hiss in my direction.

"Your toy will be fine," Apollo says, words irritating his brother more than appeasing him. "You asked how you could repay her, and she answered."

"But with my staff?" Hermes looks aghast.

"Time has resumed," Urania warns. She and her sisters cast worried glances toward the doorway. "Minos will awaken at any moment."

I purse my lips and rest my fists on my hips. "Theseus told me that he was seeking a weapon to destroy the plague of Thebes in the depths of the Labyrinth. We found nothing. After the Minotaur destroyed all my weapons, the only thing left to defeat it was a marble *kerykeion* I collected from a statue of you. Call it fate or foolish luck, but I think I'm meant to use your *kerykeion* to destroy whatever plagues Thebes."

Hermes eyes me as though I've spouted horns. "You expect me to just hand over the herald's staff, the source of my power, based on a hunch? Are you delusional?"

"You asked me how you could repay me, and that is my answer." I tap my foot impatiently on the stone floor, though the effect is ruined by the squelching noise my drenched sandal makes.

"Do it, Hermes," Melpomene says, resting a calming hand on his shoulder. "She speaks true."

The messenger god shifts his grip on his beloved staff, looking between the Muses he so obviously loves and respects, before suddenly shoving the staff into my chest. "You have to earn the right to hold this."

The warm gold thrums in my hands; my grip tightens around the staff's intertwined snakes. "Haven't I done enough to earn it?"

"I should take it back because you asked such an imprudent question," Hermes says, reaching out to snatch it away.

Lykou snarls a warning, and Apollo steps in front of me. "Excuse her ignorance, brother. I'll make sure your toy is returned to you safe and sound." I can't see his face, but I know well enough that it's lit with a crooked smirk.

"Keep her alive then," Hermes mutters to Apollo. "Another fiasco like the one with Princess Koronis and there will be nothing in the world to save you from Father's wrath...or mine."

"Princess Koronis?" I turn to Apollo. The name echoes at the periphery of my memory.

His eyes dart to my necklace for a split second before he turns back to Hermes. "Take the Muses home and stir no more trouble."

With one last regretful glance at his precious *kerykeion,* Hermes herds the flock of Muses to the balcony where they vanish in a flutter of feathers.

A warm breeze sweeps up in their wake. Apollo places a reassuring hand on my shoulder. His grip is scalding, as if yards of leather don't lie between his touch and my skin. "Don't worry about my brother. You still have an ally in him. Well...at least as much of an ally as *anyone* can have in the messenger. Just make sure to return the *kerykeion* to him unbroken."

Like the pipes, the *kerykeion* becomes unbearably heavy in my hands. I set it gently on the bed next to the still-unconscious Theseus, though he breathes evenly. I push a lock of dark, wet hair back from his brow. "Should we wake him?"

I don't entirely trust the Athenian, nor am I sure that we even need his help.

"Not yet. Waking him will stall the healing. And I am enjoying the blessed quiet." Apollo rushes about the room, gathering our things and I follow suit.

I pause, gripping my bag, and ask, "Do you regret it now?"

He turns slowly. "Regret what?"

"Not believing in me." I raise my chin. "For thinking that I would only get in the way. For trying to leave me outside the palace."

He sets aside his bag and strides over to me. Brushing aside my curtain of dirty hair, he cups my chin. "I always believed in you, Daphne. This was my mistake to fix, not yours."

"So you wanted the glory for yourself?" I pull his hand away and step back.

"Not glory," he says, shaking his head. "Penance. I deserved whatever pain you went through beneath the palace."

My mouth opens slightly. "Why?"

"With so many revelations unfolding between us, I'm sure you'll learn in due time." A moment of silence passes before he, almost tentatively, asks, "Will you share with me the entirety of Prometheus's next clue?"

I hesitate, torn between throwing his own words in his face and thinking back to my meeting with the titan on Mount Kazbek. It feels as though an eternity has passed.

A traitor to Olympus stole the Muses, so surely that same traitor wouldn't also work to return them. Unless he learned the error of his ways, I suppose.

"He said that three have been sold to the plague of Thebes, behind doors opened using wit and words. He also said that an army stands between us and Thebes, and something about hooves and howls."

"Thank you for trusting me, Daphne." He straightens. "The road to Thebes is not for the weary. We will take great care to rest and heal on a ship to Argos, and from there we will ride to Thebes."

"What of the hooves and howls, though?" I ask. "Will the *kerykeion* be enough to stop them and the plague of Thebes?"

Apollo takes a step forward, so close that his hands brush my own. "Whatever Prometheus's words meant, there is nothing we can do to prevent them. But together"—he takes my hands—"we can conquer anything."

Throwing his bag over his shoulders, Apollo looks over the unconscious Athenian. "Best to wake him now. We will have to be ready to leave with the horde of fleeing nobles. Lykou, care to do the honors?"

Lykou jumps on the bed and barks in the Athenian's face. Theseus leaps up, sputtering and howling. Apollo drops a bulging bag at his feet. "No more time to rest. Let's go."

CHAPTER
21

The sea breeze is bitter, kicking up spray that lashes my face and tugs my hair. The moon, high and unforgivingly full above our ship, is a taunting reminder of how little time is left before summer's end.

Escaping Knossos without drawing suspicion was remarkably easy. The morning following Minos's sacrilegious announcements, nobles fled by the masses. We moved with the pack of absconding nobles, blending in easily amid the chaos. After collecting my things from the olive tree outside the city where I had hidden them, we rode hard to Heraklion, using Theseus's title to buy our passage to the port city of Argos.

My thoughts are dark as I chew on a piece of dried meat, mulling in the welcome silence of night. If it hadn't been for Ariadne's medallion and for Theseus's sacrifice, the Muses wouldn't have escaped the labyrinth and I wouldn't be alive. What were those feelings I gathered from the water, and how could I have gained such strength from it? The meat is suddenly sour in my mouth. I spit out the remainder into the waves below.

Lykou rumbles from beside me. He's pressed firmly against my legs and glaring at the men bickering from the prow.

"Your impatience will be the death knell upon all our necks," Theseus says, voice cutting above the waves.

Having recovered—physically at least—from our adventure beneath the city, he agreed to our help in completing his final labor. He doesn't have to know that I have my own reasons for traveling to Thebes.

Apollo crosses his arms, hands curled into tight fists.

"Argos is too close to Athens," Theseus continues, dark circles rimming his eyes. We're already well on our way to the port city, with ten days of sea between us and Crete; there's no point in demanding the captain turn us around. His voice hushes to a fervid whisper, "And much too crowded. Minos will have already sent men after us."

"Minos will be unable to follow us once we leave Argos. If we stick to the less-traveled roads, there will be nobody to mark our passing." Exasperation colors Apollo's words. The rapidly approaching summer's end weighs much more heavily in his mind than the need for stealth. For once, I agree with him.

"Once Minos discovered his dead progeny and the mess we left behind, he probably sent out a legion of his best warriors to hunt us across Greece. Nothing will stop him." Theseus stares across the dark ocean lapping the sides of our ship, gripping the railing so tight the skin across his knuckles stretches white. He has shifted from the open, amiable man who invited us to the banquet, becoming moody and reflective. "The Mad King will undoubtedly learn of his daughter's involvement, and what's to stop him from killing her when he does? We should have at least stayed to help Ariadne escape the palace, if not brought her with us."

In the moonlight, Apollo's skin is deathly pale as he pinches his brow between a thumb and forefinger. "Ariadne is in no danger. Dionysus watches and protects her."

Apollo told me of his brother Dionysus's fascination with Ariadne, how he had long intended to court the princess once freed from her father's curse. Ariadne is now far safer than we are.

"Can you not hasten our journey?" Theseus waves an arm to the sea. "At this pace, it will be time for the harvest by the time we reach Argos."

"My gifts are slower, weaker." Apollo clenches his teeth for a moment. "It will be a few more days before I am returned to my former strength, and even then it will only be temporary."

I harken back to when he compared his gifts to a tide. It must be receding right now.

Theseus asks the question that lingers on my tongue. "Shouldn't the return of at least a few Muses help?"

Apollo shakes his head. "Would a few drops of water quench your thirst or only make you hunger for more?"

Theseus kneads the railing of the ship beneath a white-knuckled fist. "Since you're so all-knowing, how do you propose we travel to Thebes once we land in Argos? There are only so many roads not commonly traveled, some dangerous, and deserted with very good reason. And now we have not only the enemies of Olympus on our tails, but also the Mad Anax of Crete."

Apollo's face is impassive. "It is worth the risk. We won't be followed on such roads."

Theseus understands what Apollo implies before I do. "*Foloi?* We're making for the Forsaken Forest? Are you insane?"

"It is worth the risk," Apollo repeats, dismissing the Athenian's concerns with an impatient wave of his hand.

"Be it your life taken by such brazen stupidity," Theseus says, venom lacing each word. "Not mine."

I've heard enough.

"Either you two call a truce until we reach Argos"—I storm over to them, my voice sharp and biting on the winds—"or you can both travel to Thebes on your own. I have no qualms about leaving either of you behind."

The two monarchs—one of Olympus and one of Athens—regard each other with dark glares that promise only a temporary truce. I don't understand where their sudden animosity arose from, but I don't have the time to care. Be it male rivalry or royal insecurity, I have no patience for it. Despite my warning, Theseus and Apollo begin to bicker like an elderly couple—*again*—at the prow, their voices loud enough to wake Poseidon, my threats forgotten.

"Pox on both of you." I turn and stomp below deck. My shadow, Lykou, follows at my heels.

Giving him a gentle scratch behind his ears, I pull myself into my hammock. My muscles protest the simple movement. Despite the healing ministrations of the Muses, my body is still sore and weary from the events beneath Knossos, and the rumble of an imagined Minotaur haunts my nights.

"You don't have to follow me everywhere," I tell Lykou.

He rests his haunches firmly next to my hammock, glaring in a way that says he won't leave my side.

"Please, Lykou." I give him a pleading glance. "I think I've proven twice over that I don't need your protection."

His glare is immovable.

With a soft sigh, I wrap my arms around myself and roll away from his penetrating gaze. "Give me just a moment alone."

Reluctantly, he pads into the shadows, leaving me alone to wallow.

The *kerykeion* strapped to my back, hidden under my chiton, is a scorching reminder of my growing anchors—no, shackles—to the gods. Hermes's pipes, my mother's necklace, and Ariadne's Phaistos medallion all jostle for space between my breasts.

Ignoring pains both real and imaginary, I focus on the snores of the sailors and the swing of my hammock, letting them both lull me into an uneasy sleep.

The hand slapping over my mouth is a rude awakening. Almost as disturbing as the other pawing beneath my cloak.

My first reaction is to free the dagger strapped to my thigh and press it against my assailant's throat. It's effective. He gives a sharp hiss. I punch his abdomen and a familiar grunt echoes in the darkness.

Theseus collapses to the ground, clutching his stomach. I leap from the hammock. The swing of the ship threatens to buckle my legs. I open my mouth to scream for Lykou when Theseus springs on me. We tumble to the deck in a tangle of limbs. My knife clatters across the boards.

The sailors continue to snore. I try to scream again, but Theseus snuffs the sound with a slap of his palm over my mouth. He pins me down, his forearm shoved across my chest. Panic rises as his knees dig into my thighs. My elbow finds his ribs.

Theseus makes not a single sound. He redoubles his attack, leaping across the space between us.

I use his momentum to flip him over, pinning him to the deck. A thud echoes in the dark, a shimmer of gold in the corner of my eyes. The *kerykeion* flung away. He'd taken it. Pulling another knife from a sheath on my thigh and leveling it above his chest. A wild, insatiable rage courses through my veins, begging for me to shove the blade into his heart.

Sweat beads and slides down Theseus's temples, the whites of his eyes gleaming even in the shadows. "The weapon, I need it."

"Then why not just ask for it?" I snarl, barely restraining myself from stabbing him.

Not a single sailor shifts in their sleep, their snores continuing through the night. Lykou and Apollo appear beside me. The wolf's fangs shine in the dim torchlight, and he snaps them above Theseus's throat.

"Give me the weapon, Daphne." Theseus's lower lip trembles. "Or she'll kill us all."

My rage stutters, stopping in time with my heart. Her pale face, haloed by dark hair, and her piercing ruby eyes fill my vision. "She?"

"She's here," he hisses. A cold sweat slides down my spine. "Right behind you."

Unthinking, I spin around, knife aloft.

Apollo catches my wrist. "Stop your nonsense, Theseus. Daphne is the only woman aboard this ship."

"No," I say, acutely aware of my heart thundering in my chest. "He means the woman from my dreams. The one who made me kill... you."

Apollo's nostrils flare. He glares iron pokers at Theseus. "You serve her?"

"Serve her?" Theseus bares his teeth. "She is all I see, all I feel on this damned ship. She will kill me if I don't give her that weapon."

My fingers curl tighter around the dagger's hilt. "You swore an oath not to betray me!"

"I cannot help myself, Daphne." Theseus's voice is pleading. "She's here, whenever I close my eyes."

I take another step forward. "And you're only telling us this now?"

Apollo's voice cuts through the air, stilling me. "The would-be king speaks true. He has no control once she invades his mind. And who are you to judge when you nearly murdered me through her scheming?"

Grimacing, I slowly lower the dagger.

"But—" Hands clenched at his sides, Apollo steps between my

blade and Theseus, staring down at the Athenian. For the first time on the journey, he is truly intimidating. His easygoing manner and flirtatious smile, the careless noble facade, have all faded away. In the bowels of the ship, his face is the implacable mask of a vengeful god. "If you ever touch Daphne again, I will curse your house into oblivion."

Theseus gulps. Sweat beads at his brow and his mouth pops open.

Apollo continues, "Your children, your grandchildren, and even your grandchildren's children, until men no longer walk the earth, your family will experience no love or joy. They will have neither victory nor power, and they will find no relief...even in death. They will all waste away, and even the harpies won't be inclined to pick your miserable bones. Nobody will care what becomes of the Royal House of Athens."

My dagger falls to the deck with a dull thud; Lykou backs away from Apollo, from the rage emanating from him in palpable waves. His skin glows with an ethereal light, a fire bursting to life inside him, the flames licking the inside of his skin.

Theseus looks to me, his eyes beseeching. "I will be your ally," he promises me. "In all ways for as long as I live, from now until eternity."

"If she doesn't trick you into driving a dagger into the base of my spine," I say, my words chill and biting like ice.

Apollo's voice is like the lash of a whip. "I can take care of that."

Horror drains the color from Theseus's face. "What will you do to me?"

"We still have need of you. It seems that your fate is intertwined with Daphne's," Apollo says. "Meet me on deck before I let Lykou here rip out your throat. The Nereids will no doubt be waiting for us."

Scrambling up from the floor, Theseus flees, not sparing us a second glance. Apollo turns to me, the fire only slightly dimmed behind his eyes and beneath his skin.

"What was that for?" I demand. "Why did you curse him?"

Apollo takes a step back. "I did that to protect you."

"I don't need your protection," I say, the words clawing through my bared teeth. "And neither do I want you to spell everyone in my life." I wave a hand in Lykou's direction. "Haven't you learned yet? Humans won't love the gods forever if they continue cursing them whenever they so please."

I shake my head, the words sticking to the back of my throat like a cloying, bittersweet tonic, but I say them nonetheless, "Our love must be earned, not bought with magic and curses."

The light beneath his skin dies. He takes a step back, then forward again. He grasps my hand between his own and I jump. His hands, for the first time since our journey began, are cold. Apollo's lips are a feather-light touch against my scarred knuckles, a shock of frost coursing up my arm.

"A threat to you is a threat to me, my *kataigída*," he says, voice cracking, before turning and disappearing into the shadows.

Lykou gathers my possessions, scooping them gently in his jaws and dropping them in my bag before climbing awkwardly into the hammock with me. This time, I readily accept his company, rubbing my face deep in his dark pelt. A breeze sweeps aboard the ship, peeling back my cloak and baring my legs. I wrap my arms tighter around my friend. Lykou rumbles happily.

"Do you think we will ever make it home?" I murmur into his coarse fur, inhaling his scent as deeply as I can. Did he always smell of pine?

Lykou rests his head on my arm with a huff, wriggling his shoulders until they press back firmly against my chest.

"Yeah, I don't know, either."

I rest my chin on his fluffy shoulder, lost in thoughts of Sparta, Theseus and Apollo, and the Muses. I fight sleep for as long as I can, my mind playing Apollo's words again and again.

"A threat to you is a threat to me."

The Midas Curse spins in lazy circles around the spot Apollo kissed. His words can mean many things. If a threat to me is also a threat to him, Apollo must have meant I can't be spared because of my importance to this journey, and consequently to his family. He couldn't have spoken those words out of affection toward me.

Apollo is a god. He cares not one whit for me or my affection— only that I remain alive to ensure the return of the other Muses. And, most important, his power.

CHAPTER 22

The edges of my vision blur as if looking at a reflection in burnished metal. Acrid smoke fills my nose and stings my eyes, screams rattling my brain.

Sighs echo down long corridors of white marble and polished gold. I'm no longer wearing my chiton, but instead my leather uniform still dripping with the Minotaur's blood.

Definitely a dream.

The largest man I've ever seen storms down the corridors toward me. I press deep into the shadows behind a marble pillar. Tall enough to fill an entire doorway, the jagged lines of sleek muscles under his blood-red chiton single him out as an agile fighter and force to be reckoned with on the battlefield. Skin deeply tan and face clean-shaven, his eyes are dark like obsidian, hair long and the red of spilled blood, shorn close to the scalp on a single side.

A vulture is emblazoned across his broad chest in blood-red ink, a living twin to the roosters on Hermes's skin. The wings unfurl and flap with each pounding step the man takes.

Ares. My eyes widen as I take him in, a mere few feet away from me.

I have no doubt that he could make even the most hardened soldiers wet themselves at the sight of him. A slight tremor even wracks my frame as he prowls closer to my hiding spot. He marches right past me, not even looking my way. But the vulture's face turns toward me, beady eyes monitoring my every movement.

With a deep breath, I shove away from the shadows and follow the god of war—even as my instincts scream that it's suicide.

Can Ares sense me trailing him down the corridor? Can he smell the stench of my fear?

If he does, he shows no indication of it, continuing his brisk pace down corridor after deserted corridor of pristine marble. He stalks forward, blowing out each torch we pass with a flick of his wrist.

At last, Ares turns a sharp corner and halts at the head of a dark stairwell. Shadows lick up the walls while he shifts from foot to foot, staring down into the gloom. After a long moment, he scrubs a hand over his face and stomps down the stairs.

I follow him into a small room, cramped and filled with a glittering assortment of weaponry. A hundred daggers hang on a wall, in a meticulous line organized by size, above a stand bearing fifty bows. The other wall, likewise organized, bears swords and spears, shields and axes.

A woman taps a long, jagged nail on the arm of a wooden throne. Her dark, voluminous hair hovers above her pale shoulders, and her ruby gaze skewers the man.

I know that face. The woman from my nightmares, the haunting specter waiting at the periphery of my dreams.

I can only guess that Ares isn't accustomed to such a cold, indifferent reception. He glares down at her, his body stretched taut like a bowstring. The tattoo vulture's dark feathers ruffle uneasily.

"I don't like to be kept waiting," she says, voice like nectar laced with poison. She is smaller than my nightmares led me to believe.

Ares gnashes his teeth. "Zeus bade me to stay behind. All of his favorite children have abandoned him, so he's resorted to me for company."

Neither god pays me any heed, but the Midas Curse pulses erratically above my navel.

She turns her attention to her nails. "If Olympus is so desolate, then I can only assume he fears the failings of the Olympian powers. How much longer until Zeus himself withers away to nothing but dust and memory?"

"The Tree will soon wither and die, and so will the faith of men," Ares says, his voice a rich baritone. The commanding voice of a practiced battlefield general.

"That isn't an answer to my question." She leans forward, claws clicking across the arms of her throne. Ares takes a precautionary step backward. "How much longer until Olympus falls?"

He sucks in a deep breath, eyes still locked on her claws. His hesitation is damning.

"Explain," she says.

"We made a mistake in trusting the Anax of Crete."

"We?" She gives a humorless laugh. "The fault is entirely yours. But please, continue."

Ares takes a deep breath before elaborating, "Minos has garnered enough distrust and animosity in his people toward Zeus to remain useful to us, but he has also managed to lose the Muses. They disappeared the night he made the announcement." He hesitates, nostrils flaring. "I think Apollo's meddling has something to do with it. You should have let me kill them and be done with it."

"I've always despised that little sunspot. I can smell his rat sister protecting him and that mortal every night. I managed to follow them across the Aegean, but that insufferable brat has shielded the Athenian's mind, somehow." Her claws dig into the armrests of her chair, gouging holes in the dark mahogany. The Midas Curse spasms at her words. "We needed Minos to dispose of the Muses because we *needed* the humans to witness the beginnings of Olympus's downfall, and in that he's succeeded. The humans saw him sacrifice the Muses, but have no knowledge of their rescue. What are gods without worship? Nothing."

Ares nods curtly, eyes betraying no emotion, no thought to the loss of his own powers. I wrack my memory of stories about the god of war, for any kind of hint as to what he could gain from all of this.

She pries her claws from the armrests. "Where are the Muses now?"

A long moment of silence passes. "Hermes has returned them to their garden. They are carefully guarded now."

The woman rises leisurely to her feet. I press back against a stand of swords, my hand curling around a cool hilt. Despite her being half the size of him, the god takes a step back.

"You don't want to leave any marks on me," he says slowly, watching her claws.

"I could always make it look like an accident," she replies, sauntering closer. Lips the color of fresh-spilled blood curve in a malicious smile; her claws elongate and sharpen into narrow daggers on each fingertip. Though I am not the focus of her attention, my heartbeat trips anyway.

Ares shudders as she draws a nail along his midriff, piercing his tan skin until a river of red, to match his long hair, begins to flow down his abdomen. He hisses between clenched teeth, glaring down at her. "You wouldn't dare."

"I'm going to destroy Olympus." She inclines her head. "What makes you think I won't bring down the god of war with it, if he displeases me?"

Ares takes her words with unflinching composure. "What will you have me do?"

"Find Apollo and make sure they don't recover the other Muses." The woman's claws retract, and she laughs so softly it might be a sigh. "Do not fail me again, Ares, or your fate will be mine to bargain." She points a long, pale finger behind him. "You've been followed."

My stomach hits the floor, my grip on the sword tightening.

Ares spins around. A distant thudding of bare feet on the stone floor echoes in the stairwell. I follow as he sprints up four stairs at a time. No match for the war god's impossible speed, Ares catches up to the spy instantly.

"Ganymede," Ares says, the words passing his lips in a slow hiss. He turns, baring his teeth in a feral grin that send fear skittering up my spine. "Hermes."

The herald's arms are like bands of iron, keeping Ganymede from fleeing. My hand clutches at the pipes hanging from my neck. There's no surprise on Hermes's face, no hint of mirth or fear. His face is impassive stone as he thrusts Zeus's attendant to Ares. "You should watch your back more closely, Ares."

"Is that a threat, brother?" Ares's hand lashes out, catching Ganymede by the throat. Without a tremble of muscle, he holds the choking attendant in the air before throwing him back against the wall.

Zeus's attendant curls in on himself, shivering and weeping. Like all of Zeus's playthings, Ganymede is absurdly beautiful, despite the sheen of nervous sweat across his golden forehead. Ares doesn't care about his beauty, though, and gives the spy a sharp kick in the ribs. The god's ribs crack audibly, and my breath catches in my throat, the sound so distinct that a phantom ache fills my chest.

I scream, "Stop! You'll kill him!" I turn to Hermes. "Stop him! What is wrong with you?"

Neither god acknowledges my presence, Ares continuing his ruthless onslaught, a wicked grin splitting his thin lips. Ganymede cries out, head snapping back as his nose crunches under Ares's heel. My breath escapes me in ragged gasps, dread holding me immobile.

"Please." Ganymede coughs, choking on his own ichor. "I promise not to tell Zeus anything."

Ares inclines his head, narrow lips pursed as though considering Ganymede's claim. After a long moment, the god of war sighs. "I'm afraid I can't trust you to keep that promise."

Ares's fist flies. Hermes catches his brother's arm before he can crack Ganymede's skull.

"Careful, brother," the herald says. "Kill him, and he will prattle everything to Hades."

A low growl escapes Ares's lips. "So what do you suggest we do with him? Zeus has allies in all corners of Greece."

Hermes throws his hands up in the air. "I don't know. Chain him up with Prometheus? Nobody visits that poor old bastard, anyway."

I fall to my knees at Ganymede's side and gently brush his sweaty curls from his forehead. Stars shimmer in his amethyst eyes for the barest of heartbeats, pupils dilating. He whispers, "Run."

Ares spins toward me, dark brows furrowing together in a frown as he searches for whom Ganymede speaks to—but he looks right through me. The shadow woman has reached us. She wafts over to Ares's side like a cloud of smoke. I don't miss the shudder of revulsion that slips down Hermes's spine when he looks her over.

But he still lowers his chin reverentially in her direction. "Your lapdog should take better care the next time he leaves to meet with you. Ganymede would have told Zeus everything."

"That is nothing compared to unraveling all the work we've done by returning the Muses to Zeus." Ares raises a bloody fist and points it at Hermes.

Hermes doesn't betray a lick of emotion. "Artemis knows her brother was successful in retrieving the Muses from Knossos, and that he passed their care unto me. She can see everything he does through her curse upon the mortal girl." I reach a shaking hand for the cool gold pooled atop my navel. A gift as much as a curse. "If I didn't return the Muses to our father, she would have declared me a traitor before Zeus."

I want to scream and throttle the *suagroi*, kick his shins and ram my knife into his gut, but I'm frozen with horror. I can feel his pipes still hanging from my throat.

"How could Zeus ever believe his favorite offspring betrayed him?" Ares asks with a sneer, his gaze raking Hermes from winged sandals to the snake slithering across his brow. "It was you who betrayed the Muses' presence on Crete. You led Pasiphae right to them. You even gave that mortal your favorite weapon."

"All a part of the ruse, I assure you," Hermes says. "Pasiphae, ever fond of her magic but never of our father, would ensure the Muses remained alive. And Daphne having the *kerykeion* is of little consequence. She couldn't hope to wield it, and their enemies still outnumber their allies."

"Dionysus is one of their allies," Ares says. "I could smell his power all over Knossos."

The goddess's pert nose scrunches. She angles it high and sniffs the air. "Just as I smell a god's power now."

My heartbeat stumbles to a standstill. She turns to face me, Hermes and Ares doing the same. I step back.

"I smell Artemis," she continues, curling her lips back in revulsion. "That gamey, horseshit stench." She sniffs again and takes another step toward me. I can't retreat any farther, my back pressed firmly against the cold stone wall. "And something else. Someone I haven't smelled in a thousand years."

Her eyes meet mine. Cold sweeps over me.

Faster than I can blink, she spins me around, slamming my face against the wall. A short scream escapes me. I struggle against her grip, but she is a battering ram, stronger than her size suggests. She slams an arm into the back of my shoulders, digging my chest into the wall and holding me immobile. I throw my head back to knock her own, but she dodges the blow with a cackle.

"Daphne?" Hermes steps into my periphery. His blanched face holds a mixture of panic and confusion. His eyes are impossibly wide. "How did you get here?"

I don't have the breath to answer him. The goddess presses me even harder against the wall. Tremors overwhelm me. I'm helpless, so completely vulnerable in that moment and entirely at her mercy. My panic chases away any Spartan training that could have prepared me for this.

"Daphne." Her voice, now deep and husky like smoke, echoes in the shadows.

"You know my name," I say between clenched teeth, and it is an effort to keep from stuttering. "It's only fair for you to tell me yours."

She spins me around, resting a claw above the hollow of my throat.

"You'll find out soon enough." She steps closer, assessing me, reaching for the white crow. Tremors overwhelm me as a single claw lifts the necklace higher. Her dark brows draw together in a perplexed frown. "Curious trinket. Apollo must hate to see it around your neck."

A long moment passes before I have enough control over my shivers to ask, "Why?"

"Ask him yourself." She drops the necklace, her claws traveling to my neck. I can barely feel their touch, so gentle upon my skin. "Or are you afraid that you might not like his answer?"

With her free hand, she takes mine, lifting it high before slamming it against the wall. She splays it against the rough wall and drags a talon along my quivering palm. A scream erupts from my lips as the veins shred beneath my skin. Blood pours from my hand, my entire arm like living flame. Pain arches my spine.

"Stop this." Hermes reaches for the goddess, only to be held back by the inexorable arms of Ares.

Somehow, I find enough strength to spit at the herald's sandaled feet. "I would rather die than take your pity or help, *prodótis*."

"Don't fret, my sweet Hermes. I won't kill her yet." The goddess licks the hand, searing the wound closed with her plush lips. Another scream erupts from the depths of my throat. Sweat beads and drips from my brow. She continues, "Who is helping you? Who brought you here to spy on us? What allies on Olympus could Apollo have left?"

I have no strength left, and all flight has fled from my body. I go limp against the goddess's grip. "I don't know."

Ares steps again into my line of sight. "Tell us now or my children will flay the skin from your bones."

"I don't know. I don't know. I don't know." I shake my head, sweaty curls falling about my burning face, voice nothing more than a pain-filled whisper.

"Let her go. You'll get nothing from her in this state," Hermes says.

"Why so protective of the little mortal, dear Hermes?" The goddess cocks her head. "No matter."

Her hands move to the sides of my face and grip my head tight. I scream again as the skin beneath my scalp threatens to erupt in flames. "I see Prometheus's clues. I see your path and the secrets you've kept from Apollo. I see your mother, your father. You cannot hide anything from me, *kataigída*. Your allies, Artemis, Dionysus, Theseus, and Prometheus, and whichever god brought you here to Olympus will be hunted down and slaughtered like the fools they are."

"The gods do not deserve your allegiance, my sweet. They do not deserve the powers of Olympus." She lets go and I crumple to the floor with a sob. She drops to a knee, her face pressed so close to mine that I can feel her breath across my cheeks. Ever so gently, she brushes a curl from my brow with a curved claw. Its tip grazes my skin. "You think you can stop me? I will stalk your every step, stall your every turn. The powers of Olympus have set like the sun, and I intend for them to never rise again."

The goddess reaches her hand back, talons glinting in the firelight of the torches. I close my eyes to await their strike. I'm shuddering, sweat drenching my clothes, my hand still burning with the fires of Tartarus. Hermes cries out a warning and I open my eyes.

CHAPTER 23

I awake with a short scream, startling the sailors around me. My chiton clings to my trembling frame, soaked through with sweat.

It felt too real, the smells too sharp, the pain too intense, to simply be a figment of my imagination. A tingle in my left hand forces me to look down. There, across my palm, shines a silver crescent scar where the goddess sliced me open.

My mouth opens and closes, my throat clenched around a silent scream.

Ares stole the Muses, and Hermes has betrayed us. They will be hunting down Prometheus, Dionysus, and Artemis. They know where we're headed next.

I have to tell Apollo. I force my body to roll from the hammock. Knees like jelly send me sprawling across the sodden deck floor. Lykou sniffs, pressing his wet nose into my stomach and chest. He whines when my terror-laced scent reaches his nose.

A sharp yell from above snaps my gaze toward the ceiling. I cannot help the wave of alarm that rushes through me at the sound.

We sprint to the top deck. A sailor points toward the sun on the horizon. I push through the crowd of frenzied sailors, overwhelmed by their tangle of curiosity, confusion, and fear.

"I'm telling you," the pointing sailor insists, "the star is in the wrong place." His finger rises, jabbing at the few remaining stars in the growing dawn. "The Morning Star is not *above* the sun, but instead to the west."

The soldier speaks true: the last glimmering star in the sky, the Morning Star, taunts us all as it hangs opposite the rising sun. I turn to Apollo for answers, but he also stares at the star, his lips pressed in a firm line and brows furrowed. Shoving through the crowd, curious dream forgotten, I press close to his side.

My words are a whisper. "What does it mean?"

He gives a barely perceptible shake of his head. He doesn't know.

"What do you *think* it means?" I press.

"It means something is wrong with Eosphorus." One of the celestial gods who control the sun, moon and stars' voyage across the sky. My mind whirls at the implications, the lives disrupted by the simple fact that the stars are not in their correct places. Our histories will vanish. The ships out to sea will be lost until they're lucky enough to find shore.

Apollo continues, "Luckily, we are just outside of Argos, and so we won't be needing the stars' guidance any further."

Beyond a fleet of ships, the shores of Argos glint on the horizon, a mere hour's distance away. But I don't care about Argos right now. I'm more concerned about Eosphorus. "Does this mean Eosphorus lost his powers? Could…could something have happened to him?"

I think of Ganymede and his bones snapping under Ares's onslaught. Did the god of war capture and torture Eosphorus just as he did Zeus's attendant? A chill sweeps over me, and I hug my arms around my chest.

"We can only hope this is a mistake and Eosphorus is just temporarily incapacitated." The doubt on Apollo's face belies his words.

"Apollo," I start, struggling to find the words. I tug him away from the crowd to the back of the ship. "I think Eosphorus is in danger."

Apollo is silent, waiting for me to continue. I would have almost preferred him to argue with me. I turn over my hand. He sees the scar on my palm, but still says nothing. A barely perceptible glimmer of worry shifts beneath his familiar, cocky mouth.

"I had a dream last night. Of Olympus. Hermes was there, and Ares. They betrayed your father." I don't know how else to say it, and the words tumble from my mouth like torrential rain. "The shadow woman was back, and she commanded them to kill us. She knows we're after the Muses and where we'll go next." I raise my palm until the scar is pressed before Apollo's eyes. "She gave me this as a warning."

The breeze cuts between us, stirring my hair and his. Apollo's face is unreadable. A long moment passes before he finally speaks. He takes my hand and pushes it into my chest. "It was a nightmare, Daphne. Nothing more. This scar is merely another littering your body after a life in Sparta."

I must have misheard him. "Do you not understand? Ares and Hermes will be after us. They will kill us before we have a chance to save the Muses."

Something akin to anger alights behind Apollo's gaze. "Your wet nurse may have filled your head with tales otherwise, but Ares would never betray our father. He loves Olympus, loves the power beholden to him as a god. An attack on our father is an attack on him. Hermes, too. Though there is no love lost between the herald and me, he would never betray our father."

"Ares is a psychopath," I snap.

"Ares is my brother," Apollo repeats, his lips curling back from his teeth. "Watch what you say about him. He may have done terrible things, but that does not make him a terrible person."

"Actually, that is *exactly* what it makes him," I say, my snarl matching his own. "Why don't you believe me?"

Apollo's face goes blank, his eyes suddenly so very cold. "Ares, as cruel as he can be, is only spurred by his desire for war. And I've done far worse, spurred by the taunts of my heart."

I take a step back, his voice like a pail of water tossed over her. "But you're the one who told me not to trust Hermes, or any of the gods."

"As I would tell a guileless girl entranced by a rake who means to steal her virtue," Apollo says cuttingly. "Hermes gave you his most treasured weapon, a sign of faith in our cause. Neither of my brothers would ever betray Zeus."

Hurt lances through me. My lip wobbles despite myself. "But they did, and even your blind faith in them isn't going to change that."

"Leave it be, Daphne."

Undaunted by the warning in his eyes, I continue, "Do you not believe me because you don't want to ask yourself why they would betray your father? That maybe they are right, and that you don't deserve the powers of Olympus?"

Apollo jerks back as if slapped. We glare at each other, fire matching fire, threatening to rise until it consumes us both. When he finally speaks again, his voice is raw. "If you truly believe that, Daphne, then return to Sparta and leave me to save my family on my own."

"I will see this journey complete." My nails dig into my palms. "But whether you deserve my help remains to be seen."

Wordlessly, he turns and shoves through the crowd of sailors.

*　　*　　*

We arrive on shore less than an hour later, the docks teeming with morning activity. Sailors move along the docks with speedy determination. Vendors crack timid smiles at our entourage despite the early hour. Many gawk at the strange position of the Morning Star, but most are focused on the distribution of their wares.

Eager to be on our way, we spare only enough time and money to purchase food and horses for the next leg of our journey. While I strap my bridle onto my horse, a familiar lyre sings above the dockside din.

Realization hits me like a slap across the cheek. Hermes watches us, and is undoubtedly how the woman was able to find her way into Theseus's dreams.

Ripping them from my neck, I throw his pipes into the harbor. The waves swallow them whole. The *kerykeion* hangs from Apollo's hip, keeping me from doing the same with the legendary staff.

I lead the way out of the city on the least-traveled roads, taking to the arid, rocky stretches of land leading to Thebes, far from the prying eyes of Hermes and reach of Minos. On the open road, I tuck away my *kalyptra* and let my hair fall, no braid, no veil. My curls relish their freedom, catching on the breeze to flow behind me.

True to Apollo's word, the roads are largely barren of travelers. We see a single man two days from Argos; his clothes hang limp from his malnourished frame, more skeleton than skin. His pale hair is wispy, eyes sunken deep in their sockets as he staggers forward. On reflex, my hand falls to the hilt of my dagger.

"Please," he says, voice rough and hollow. "I didn't have time to grab anything before I left. I have no money. No food. There are no animals to hunt."

He doesn't lie. There are no trees as far as I can see, and the game for dinner has been nonexistent since we left Argos. My stomach rumbles, resenting the rationing we've been doing with our own food.

"Where are you from, stranger?" Apollo asks, reaching into his bag and giving the man what remains of his dried meat.

"Nisaea," he says around a mouthful. He accepts my offered water jerkin eagerly, chugging down every last drop.

"And why have you left the protection of your home?" Apollo's hand inches toward a dagger he borrowed from me.

The man looks up, startled. "The great Poseidon has forsaken the city, my lord. It was swept into the sea fifteen days ago."

Apollo's face is suddenly ashen. His hand drops to his side. "What?"

The man nods and takes another bite of dried meat. "There was a storm. My people moved to the shores to watch the great waves. They were out of season, you see, and nobody considered the omen they might bear. Great clouds and lightning covered the horizon so few noticed the water as it receded. By the time the people saw the great wall of water sweeping toward them, it was too late. The temples, the homes, the palace of Anax Megareus. They're all gone."

"Wasn't Megareus an enemy of Minos?" I whisper to Apollo.

He silences me with a stern look. "How did you survive?"

"I was herding sheep in the hillside. I saw it all." The man sobs, his entire chest heaving with the movement. Tears have tracked trails down his dirt-stained face. "The waves dragged the entire city out to sea."

Ice races up my spine, gripping me. Theseus is deathly pale. Lykou is the only one of us not apparently shocked, too busy sniffing at rabbit holes in the distance.

Apollo touches the man's head. A golden light fills his cupped palm. "You have the protection of Apollo now. Two days from here is Argos." From the air, Apollo plucks a golden coin. An engraved peacock shimmers on its surface. "Bring this to the Heraion Temple as payment to the goddess Hera. She will protect you."

"And my sons?" The man looks up, blinking away tears. "Can she bring them back to me?"

Apollo hangs his head. Theseus dismounts, pulling a token from his bags and handing it to the man.

"After you visit Heraion, bring this to the Athenian palace," he instructs. "Anax Augeus will see you fed and clothed, and find you a place in his household."

Pride, despite my earlier misgivings with both men, swells inside me. When the man leaves us, with more lightness in his steps, Apollo turns to me.

With a wink, he says, "Don't look so surprised."

It is a two-week ride to Foloi; Apollo can spare no more of his power to hasten our pace, so we're left with nothing but our own endurance. We push our horses hard, galloping across the rough terrain as often as we can with Lykou loping by my horse's hooves. The days become warmer, dryer, and, overall, more miserable. I long for my own bed, my soft furs, and clean clothes, not the sweat-sodden chiton I wear day in and day out.

Despite the blistering sun, there is little warmth in our entourage. Apollo still treats Theseus with cold animosity and Lykou roams farther and farther away with each day, scampering across the hills and out of sight.

The circles still linger beneath Theseus's eyes, and I can no longer count on him for a ready joke, but he makes an effort to reconcile with me. When my bridle snaps, he mends it without question. He takes the lead on gathering wood for our fires, food for our suppers, and even gave me one of his swords to replace the one I shattered beneath

Knossos. I can forgive him, at least, for making the same mistake I did—allowing that woman to get in my head.

Clouds smother the sun above, painting the dusty road with smatterings of gray. While Theseus focuses on the road ahead, I draw my mare alongside Apollo. He quirks an eyebrow expectantly.

"What if she's there, in Foloi Forest? The woman from my nightmares? Or even..." I stumble over Hermes's name; all I can see are Ares's bloody knuckles. My stomach churns, and I shift uncomfortably on my horse. I haven't brought up my dream again with Apollo, but I know he is still angry with me for even voicing it.

"I don't know," Apollo admits, the weight of uncertainty beginning to bow his shoulders. "This...woman of the shadows is no Olympian, but the traitor who kidnapped the Muses for her, on the other hand..." He hesitates. "Whoever it is could be waiting for us where we least expect it. I wished to keep our journey as discreet as possible."

I open my mouth to remind him that I believe our plans have already been revealed, but bite my tongue. His sharp rejection of what I told him on the ship still stings.

He clears his throat. "Unless you want to sleep beneath the rain when that storm hits tonight, I suggest we pick up the pace."

Obligingly, we put our heels to our horses' sides.

Within the hour, Foloi rises on the horizon and our horses rear to a halt at the dreaded forest's edge. Theseus curses and even Apollo's jaw is clenched as they struggle to remain astride their horses.

The stories I've heard about Foloi, told by Ligeia, my brothers, and Spartans alike, are dark enough to make a lamb die of fright. I eye the line of towering oak trees, skepticism warring with my memories of the labyrinth beneath Knossos. After being thrown around by the Minotaur, I'm ready to believe that anything could be prowling these dark woods.

"Lykou," I call out to my friend. I have no intention of letting either him or me fall prey to Foloi's threats.

Lykou saves me the trouble of having to hunt him down, barreling toward us with a dead rabbit hanging from his mouth. I dismount, stooping to greet him, but he trots past me and into the forest.

Apollo studies the trees. One of his hands clenches his horse's reins, his knuckles white as doves.

"Should I be worried that *you* look so worried?" I ask, trying to keep my voice light, and nudge him with an elbow.

"We should be fine," Apollo says, though he doesn't sound so convincing. "The dryads of Foloi have always been...*unpredictable*, but Artemis has no doubt persuaded them to our cause."

My horse whinnies in protest, trying to pull the reins from my hands, but I wrap the thin leather tight around my wrist and continue after Lykou. As the dark trees envelop us, I keep a wary hand on Praxidikai.

Though Artemis's gifts may still protect us in the woods, Ligeia told me many stories about the half-man beasts, taking women as their concubines and men for food, of the dryads that lure men to their deaths atop Foloi mountain, and of the pools that can ensnare your soul for eternity with a single glance into their depths.

Following Lykou, I keep my ears tuned for any signs of followers. He leads us along a narrow, downhill deer trail. My weary knees jam with each step. I don't like the idea of traveling into an unprotected wooded valley, but there are no other paths.

Birds swoop and dive above our heads, singing a raucous melody. Despite my attentiveness to the forest around us, I smirk when Theseus curses colorfully behind me.

"Damned birds keep dropping their filthy business on my cloak!"

Smile still lingering on my face, I slow to walk beside him. "There are worse things than bird shit."

"I suppose." He meets my eyes. "I could be skewered by a Minotaur again, or have my mind invaded by a madwoman."

I take his words to mean the nightmares no longer plague his sleep.

"My point exactly, Athenian." I tilt my head, puckering my lips as though considering. "Though, I was thinking of something far worse. Imagine having to waste your years in a dreadful place like Athens?"

"Do Spartans just genuinely not understand empathy or the feelings of others?" He grins, the light from before the labyrinth flickering in the gray depths of his eyes.

"Oh, we understand perfectly." I punch his shoulder, making him hiss. "We just haven't the patience for either."

Midday sunlight filters between the branches, illuminating the forest in a hundred shades of green, dizzying compared to the golden plains we've traveled for days. We move quickly, soon sweating from the exertion and the midmorning heat. So intent am I on following Lykou and listening for any odd sound, I don't notice as our descent leads us to a quiet valley, thick with wide-spaced trees. Theseus announces the space is perfect for our midday meal and his sore legs demand he take a break.

I pull some dried meat from my satchel, handing a piece to Lykou and chewing distractedly on mine. Hermes could be following us, waiting with Ares to slit my throat while we sleep. The herald found us once before. He would have no trouble doing so again, especially after the shadow woman's forced intrusion into my mind. They know our path, goals, and allies.

The Athenian pulls a water jerkin from his satchel; I can smell the bitter tang of wine pouring into his mouth. He sees me watching and extends it in my direction. "Care for a taste?"

"No, thanks."

Apollo, acknowledging Theseus for the first time in days, snatches the wine and takes a long draft. He smacks his lips once before returning it. "Decent stuff. Did you steal it from Minos's cellars?"

Theseus shrugs a shoulder. "Perhaps."

"Have you not tired of games?" I roll my eyes to the heavens. "Why is it so impossible for either of you to just give straight answers?"

"Speaking of games—" Theseus turns to me. "Perhaps one is needed. I know nothing of your quest other than that it is tightly interwoven with mine. I know nothing about you, other than your home is in Sparta, and his is on Mount Olympus. I don't yet understand your kinship to the wolf"—he waves in Lykou's direction, and my friend bares his fangs—"nor do I know how you escaped the Minotaur with your life."

"And your point is?" I ask, wrapping my arms around my chest. I don't like where this is going.

He spreads his arms wide. "Let's play a round of *kottabos*."

"We should continue on and make camp somewhere more secure. Besides, we don't have any goblets to throw."

A *kylix* filled to the brim materializes before my eyes, as does another in front of Apollo, which he raises in a mocking toast.

"The mood is much too dark between us three," Apollo says. "Though there is no love lost between Theseus and I, if we continue on in this manner, our grievances will hinder our chances of triumph."

Kottabos is definitely one of the most flirtatious games in Greece; a favorite among the Spartans who already excel at showing off, especially in demonstrations of physical prowess. One takes a *kylix*, fills it with wine, and flings the contents at a specified target, naming the object of their affection.

If the body of wine meets the target, then the person named would spend some illicit time with the person who threw the contents of their cup. I've even lost once to Lykou, last year during *Hyacinthia*.

The memory of his pillowy lips pressed against mine, his firm body leaning into me, makes me swallow. I refuse to meet Lykou's gaze.

A blush rises in my cheeks when Apollo turns hungry eyes on me and says, "Because I know you would balk at the usual rules of the game, let's make our own variation of *kottabos*. With each successful throw, you may ask a question of whoever you choose."

I snatch the jerkin from Theseus and take a long draft. When I finally come up for air, I say, "This seems like a waste of your already deteriorating gifts."

Apollo winks. "I will take that to mean you acquiesce."

The idea of a game is tempting. I could use a distraction from the tempest of my thoughts, Hermes, Ares, and Pyrrhus's faces all swirling at the forefront. In answer, I walk over to a fallen tree and drop a small stone atop it for a target. Theseus whoops, and Apollo procures a *kylix* for him.

"It was my idea, so I'll go first." With an easy flick of his wrist, Theseus's aim is true, a fountain of wine splashing the small rock.

"Now, Apollo, let us start with the less personal questions." Theseus turns to the god, whose smile disappears quick as a blink. He must have been expecting Theseus to focus his questions on me. "Why are you accompanying us? Surely, as a god, you don't have other important matters to attend to?"

Because that's not a personal question at all. I'm about to snap at Theseus that it's none of his business, but Apollo cuts me off. "Because I'm cursed."

My mouth hangs open, Lykou gapes, and Theseus nearly drops his *kylix*.

Apollo releases a sigh as bitter as the northerly wind. "I was the protector of the Muses, and I have long been the subject of my family's ire, but the folly of my ego was the final straw."

He avoids my gaze. "On the day of the Muses' capture, my father, ever the hypocrite, chastised me for my womanizing ways. Like a spoiled child, I disguised myself as Zeus and sought the company of one of his lovers, Theodora, the princess of Aetolia. I left my charges for one night—a night I will regret for my entire life. The next morning Theodora was found dead and the Muses gone from the Garden of the Hesperides."

I force my face into a calm mask. "Continue."

"That's the true reason none of my family join us on our journey. It is my task alone."

"But Artemis—"

"My sister would do anything for me, and I for her. She is disobeying our father by helping me." He takes a deep gulp of wine before flinging the rest at the stone. "By dragging you into this mess."

He turns to me. "What is it you expect will happen should Sparta ever accept you as a true citizen? Do you think that they'll suddenly give you a spot in the army? That the Spartan court will embrace you with open arms?"

His words, though a truth as harsh as winter's frost, ring with understanding. It's as plain as the softness upon his face, the concern behind his eyes. Though I itch to tell him where he can shove his concern, I answer honestly.

"I don't know. Perhaps someday I will leave Sparta and adopt a life as a mercenary, or simply join the household of one of my brothers and have them pay me to act as a guard. It would be impossible to leave either of them behind."

Apollo's gaze bores into me with such a sudden, bald intensity that I'm forced to turn away, and I notice Lykou's gaze boring into me, too, his wolf-face unreadable.

Thinking of what those looks may mean makes my heart tighten in my chest, threatening to suffocate me. Brushing these uncomfortable feelings aside as I roll my shoulders, I easily splash the stone and pass the *kylix* to Lykou. "Are you hoping to follow your father's foot-steps and become a politician, or will you continue on in the army? Paw the ground for politician, bark for army."

Lykou both paws the ground and barks, choosing both. It's fairly common among Spartan sons to do some, even many, years of service in the army before moving to a political career. Alkaios would likely do the same, following in the footsteps of our father, if being a *Moth-akes* had not held him back.

Lykou's first attempt to play *kottabos* in the body of a wolf goes as horribly as you'd expect, with the wine kicking back to splash atop his long snout. Theseus and Apollo roar with laughter; I cover my urge to laugh by coughing into my hands. Lykou pulls his teeth back in a silent snarl, daring me to tease him.

"We know where Apollo gets his gifts." Theseus's wine splashes the stone before he turns to me. "But where do you get yours? What god imbued you with such strength to take down the Minotaur?"

"I am nothing more than the unwanted get of the islands, forced to become *Mothakes* in Sparta when I was rejected by my parents." I take a sip of wine. "I have no gifts or powers."

"You lie."

I scoff. "Please, save your breath, Theseus. You'll probably need it the next time I'm forced to save your life and have to listen to your rambling profession of gratitude."

"That's a lot of big words for a Spartan," Theseus says.

I bark a laugh. "Oh, I'm sorry. Does the Athenian need me to repeat them in simpler words? Let's see if you can understand this: you would be dead without me."

My wine glances off the target before Theseus can retort. I turn to Apollo. "Tell us about your bow."

He rolls the golden weapon in his palms, the sunlight reflecting off the shimmering carvings. "As I said before, this was a gift given to me in my earliest days, before I could even walk. My sister has its twin, the crescent moon. One must be willing to sacrifice their body and soul for a single shot of her bow, putting aside any selfish intent. And be a god, of course."

"So no archery for me, then."

"We can only hope that neither bow will ever have to be used."

Apollo's wine splashes the stone and he asks Theseus, "Why has Athena commanded you to complete these labors? Are you not entitled to the throne because of your birth?"

Theseus gazes into the depths of his *kylix*. "Much like you, I am a bane to my father. He questions my mother's love of him and believes me to be a bastard. He sought the advice of Athena, most sacred goddess of Athens, and she told my father to have me complete these six labors to prove my right to the throne. Only a true hero may sit on the throne of Athens."

"Do heroes typically loot the belongings of sleeping women?" I pin the Athenian with my gaze.

"Loath as I am to say it"—Apollo raises his *kylix* toward me—"you're not one to talk about the things one does in their sleep."

I don't let him see my embarrassment. Clearing my throat, I ask, "And have you learned anything from your curse? Or will your ego be our doom?"

All mirth is gone from Apollo's face. "You think we're so different? That you, a mortal, always striving to be accepted, to prove yourself, are any better than I." He sets down his *kylix* and shakes his head. "We are both on this quest to prove the same thing. That we're worthy."

I have no waiting retort, no snappy comeback. Shame burns my cheeks. I sip my wine, refusing to meet his gaze.

Theseus coughs, raising his wine to throw again, when Lykou barks, startling all of us. I spin around, hand on a dagger, but he is only digging through my bags, likely searching for food.

"Be patient," I snap. "Let me get it for you."

He growls, continuing his search of my bags.

"Lykou!" I shove him away as he pulls his snout out with a mouthful of dried meat. I try to yank it free. "That's supposed to be for all of us."

I'm rewarded with a firm snap of his fangs on my forearm.

The forest stills. My gut ices over like the first frost of autumn. Lykou's teeth dig into my skin, feral and inhuman. Apollo and Theseus stop what they are doing. Lykou's eyes widen with realization and he starts to lick my arm with little mewling noises. When my forgiveness isn't forthcoming—I'm too aghast to say anything—he bolts, breaking for the trees with his tail tucked between his legs. Numb, I sit for a moment, my mind spinning with the implications.

Apollo kneels at my side, thigh brushing mine. He's close enough that his inhuman warmth radiates over me. Despite the pain in my arm, my eyes trace the line of his jaw. My throat is suddenly dry.

He's right, though I am loath to admit it. We're the same. Two individuals with more curses than sense, chasing dreams of acceptance.

Theseus, after glancing between the two of us, coughs. "I'll try to catch your wolf."

After he's left, sword in hand, I hold my arm out for Apollo to see. The skin is unbroken, thankfully, the Midas Curse having taken the brunt of the bite. Apollo frowns, rubbing a hand up and down my arm, as if he can erase the pain as the Muses had. He is unsuccessful, the little twinges of pain from Lykou's bite still itching away under my skin.

"Lykou isn't just a wolf physically anymore. He's giving in to his feral side, slowly losing his humanity. I saw it in the Heraklion Market, but thought that returning some of the Muses would abate his transformation." My hands tighten into fists and begin to tremble. "He's learned his lesson, Apollo. Can you return him to his human body?"

"My powers are fading." Wildness lights Apollo's eyes. "I wanted to return Lykou back to his human form before we arrived at Knossos. It would have been much simpler to sneak another human inside the palace than a wolf. But when I reached for that well of power, it wasn't deep enough. Even with the return of some, I don't have the kind of strength to pull off the transformation. He might end up with a tail, or fangs. Some wolf might linger in his head."

"Then why waste your powers on these frivolities?" I yell, flinging my *kylix* at a tree. It shatters, pieces of clay flying through the air. "Save it up and give me my friend back."

"And then what, Daphne?" An angry tic forms in Apollo's jaw. "You'll have Lykou back, but what if we're injured? Would you rather I be able to heal him or be able to hold his human hand?"

Apollo watches me warily, waiting for the outburst, the outrage waiting on the tip of my tongue.

I whisper, "What will happen to him if we can't find the Muses?"

"My powers will be lost, and Lykou will live as a wolf for the remainder of his days." Apollo raises his chin, though regret pulls at the corner of his eyes. "Until we return the Muses to Olympus, his humanity will ebb and flow just as my powers are. Soon, there will be nothing left of the Spartan boy you loved."

I should be angry with him. If I was still that naïve girl, the one who underestimated Artemis's fury, I might have lashed out at him. But all I can think of is Pyrrhus. If Apollo's gifts are failing, then his sister's are, as well.

If my brother loses his humanity, as Lykou is, will Artemis still be able to control him? Or will he be wandering Taygetus forest like a wild animal, haplessly waiting for a hunter to claim him as a prize? My breathing grows shallow, a tightness filling my chest and squeezing my heart.

No. It might have started out that way, but now it is about more than my brothers. It is about Olympus, and the crumbling world around us.

"We will get the Muses back," I say, more for myself than him. "Artemis will give me my brother back—and Lykou. Olympus will be returned to normal, and we can go back to our lives." Part of me aches at that thought, the idea of going back to Sparta and the people who so openly despise me. I shove that ache deep inside.

Apollo's eyes widen slightly. He springs to his feet. Our horses nicker, ears twitching as the birds cease their song and the wind stills.

"What is it?" I ease toward the daggers still in my horse's bags, my eyes likewise glued to the forest.

Apollo continues searching the edges of our camp. A cold shiver ripples down my spine as he turns to me. "We are being watched."

"Yes."

A deep laughter follows the solitary word. I snatch up Praxidikai.

"We've been waiting for you, son of Zeus." From out of the shadows, centaurs emerge, surrounding us, each with a bow and arrow of their own.

The Kentauroi are lethal and beautiful, Ligeia once told me. *They share the body of both man and beast, they must also share the heart and soul of both. Notorious thieves of women and cattle, the Kentauroi are said to be savage and vengeful.*

The one who spoke is a burly beast, large enough to challenge even the Minotaur. He has the large body of an auburn stallion, and his massive pale chest ripples with muscles and scars, arms with biceps large enough to crush my skull.

I don't move, gaze trained on the twenty arrowheads pointed at my throat.

"Eurytion." Apollo gives a slight bow. "To what do we owe the pleasure?"

A sharp prick on the base of my spine makes me stumble to my knees, spear sliding across the dusty ground before me. I reach around to find a dart in my back. A thin shard of metal, red feathers blurring. Apollo falls forward at my feet. I'm too shocked to say a word as darkness seeps into my vision.

"We should kill them now," one says, a hiss singing across the camp as he unsheathes a sword.

"No." The one named Eurytion moves forward to tower over Apollo's unconscious body. "The Anassa of Darkness wants them alive."

CHAPTER
24

I'm standing hip-deep in a shallow pool. The sharp, comforting smell of sea fills my nose. Teal light blossoms and dances upon the walls and water, revealing a cave of barnacles and stalagmites; tiny green and blue facets glow between each fissure, flickering with each beat of my heart. The slightest ripple across the surface of the water draws my attention from the shimmering, phosphorescent walls.

Standing an arm's length away from me is a man, dressed in a shimmering black cloak and chiton. His long hair is an ebony sheet falling down his back. I don't recognize him.

"Ah, Daphne, if only I had enough time to explain things." He grimaces. "My powers wane with those of Olympus, and I cannot steal you away for much longer. You must know that the world is already irrevocably changed in the Muses' absence. The crops are failing, the seasons changing at a rate beyond mortal comprehension. Your

Spartan kin fight tooth and nail to ensure a harvest enough to feed them through the winter."

"Why did Hermes and Ares betray their family?" I ask, getting straight to the point and ignoring the dread creeping up my spine. "Are you the god that brought me atop Mount Olympus to witness their treachery?"

"I am indeed, but my name is not for you to know. Not yet." The man inclines his head. "Bringing you to Olympus nearly drained me entirely, but you needed to know who betrayed Zeus.

"I will be punished for even bringing you here," he continues. "She may have already learned of my betrayal, and I fear I may not survive her wrath. I cannot hold her nightmares at bay any longer."

I shake away the fatigue clouding my mind. His voice is hypnotic, and despite already being in the throes of sleep, my eyelids start to droop with exhaustion.

His face is old and wrinkled and he shares with me a small smile. He spreads his arms wide, onyx wings on his back unfurling with the movement. "The history of Olympus is one fraught with lies and betrayal, but do not succumb to her words. She will twist your fears, spin truth into lies, and use your own heart against you."

The stalagmites dim, snuffing the light from the cave. I can no longer see the man, but his presence still lingers.

The water starts to drag me back, sweeping me from my feet and pulling me deeper into the darkness.

"Who is she?" I shout, coughing as water fills my mouth with the effort.

"The most dangerous woman you'll ever meet." His voice is a mere echo in the darkness now. I struggle futilely against the current, arms pumping as I try to fight my way back to him. "Trust in the god of prophecy, Daphne. He will not desert you."

"Just tell me her name." I struggle to hear my own voice above the roar building in my ears.

He shouts a name, the single syllable unintelligible as a crash of water drags me below the surface. My head cracks against the cave wall. Light bursts behind my eyes and nothingness finds me.

CHAPTER
25

I jerk awake just as I first entered this world—fighting and screaming. Sweat drenches my skin, and my limbs ache, but when I sniff, my clothes smell of the sea.

I shudder, the movement pulling my limbs taut. My wrists are pinioned above my aching head. Strapped to a wooden pole, the feeling of rough wood against my back makes me scream and rage against my binds.

The centaurs have left me in a tent, growing ever darker as the sun begins its descent beyond the canvas walls. Likewise strapped to two different poles are Apollo and Theseus; my screams haven't succeeded in rousing either of them. Apollo sleeps soundly, bronze curls veiling his eyes. Theseus isn't so charming in his unconscious state, snoring a little bit with dribble at the corner of his mouth.

Another prisoner is strapped to a pole beside me, her head limp, chin pressed against her chest. Her cheeks are covered with mud and a deep gash splits her right brow. She still wears the leather chiton and bronze breastplate, though now flecked with dried blood.

"Lyta?"

Rage and horror escape me in a screech, and I wrench again on the binds. I dig my index finger into the bonds, feeling along the loop of tough leather.

"Lyta! Wake up!" Her only response is a low moan.

Twisting my wrists back and forth, I spin the knot around to my fingers. It is tedious, and the strap is so tight that it chafes my wrists. With the knot in reach, I fight with the first set of ties until they fall away. I will thank Pyrrhus for teaching me that trick should I ever return to Sparta.

Once freed from the pole, I go first to my friend, the most conscious of the three. Despite the almighty powers of an Olympian, they are hardly helpful when said Olympian is unconscious and drooling on his shoulder. Another moan escapes Lyta's lips and her head lolls to the side.

I undo her binds and she falls into my arms. I brush her bangs away, assessing the gash on her brow. "Lyta, what are you doing here?"

"The heirloom," she says, her eyelids fluttering, still struggling against consciousness. "The one my sister sent me to find."

I still. "What?"

"The heirloom was stolen by the centaurs." Her voice is hardly more than a whisper. "A gift from our father. I escaped with it, but the centaurs caught me fleeing toward Thebes. I must get it back."

Someone is bound to check in on us soon, and I would rather not be caught. They might resort to something less malleable to contain us—like shackles.

After gently setting Lyta down, I stride to Apollo and Theseus, slapping both their cheeks. Stubborn even in his sleep, Apollo remains unconscious, while Theseus comes to with a jerk. I slap a hand over the Athenian's mouth before he can yell and bring an army of centaurs into the tent. Once freed from his binds, he falls to the dirt.

Tearing free Apollo's bonds next, I catch him before he hits the ground. I press my lips to his wrist, cold as death. A pulse still flutters. I breathe a sigh through my nose. With gentle fingers, I peel the curls from his sweaty brow, my thumb passing over his lips. "Thank Tyche. I couldn't have done this without you."

"The ache in your heart would have been too painful." His eyes flutter open, then close again as he fights with consciousness. He's dragged back under but not before he says, "Someone will be in here to check in on us soon."

Lyta towers over Theseus, hands on her hips. A grin splits her lips. "You keep the most curious company. I'm sad to see that you traded your four-legged companion for this useless piece of vermin. The wolf would have been much more useful in present circumstances."

"Lyta? Is that what you're calling yourself these days?" Theseus spits out some dirt and glares defiantly at my friend. He climbs to his feet, brushing the dirt from his clothes. "Any brilliant plans to get us out of here or shall I resign myself to be tied up and drugged again by the centaurs?"

"We're not leaving without the *kerykeion*." I peel back the tent's flap.

A fist catches me in the abdomen. I double over, clutching my stomach. The burly centaur, Eurytion, storms inside the tent, his nostrils flared. Theseus doesn't have time to react before one of Eurytion's hooves catches him in the stomach. He crashes into a pile of crates.

With a wild scream, Lyta leaps onto the centaur's back. She punches the back of the beast's neck. She hardly gets a scratch on him before she's pulled from his back and flung into Theseus.

It's the Minotaur all over again. My panic doesn't have even a moment to register before he's yanking me by my hair. A strangled scream escapes me. I'm dangling in the air.

Lyta and Theseus climb tentatively from the ruined crates. Their gazes are locked on the centaur's hold on me. Their eyes widen when he takes my neck between his fingers, so long they wrap around it completely.

"Another move," he says, grip tightening, "and I snap her pathetic neck."

I claw at his hold. My legs kick futilely as wave after wave of panic sweeps over me. His grip is steadfast, fingers tightening with my every breath. Dark spots seep into my vision.

"We'll go with you, Lord Eurytion, without a fight." Apollo has climbed to his feet behind the centaur. "But if you kill her, Olympus will rain such a fury upon Foloi that not a single centaur will survive."

Eurytion sneers. "This one mean something special to you?"

Apollo nods, his brow furrowed.

Lyta raises her arms slowly before dropping to the earth. She presses her nose to the earth and Theseus does the same.

"Bring the ropes," Eurytion yells.

More centaurs walk into the tent. When Theseus and Lyta are bound, Apollo between them, I'm finally thrown to the ground. My lungs gasp for air, my eyes watering with each wheeze. Eurytion doesn't let me catch my breath, though, jerking me to my feet and binding my hands in the same movement.

"I expected more of a fight from you." He cocks his head. "Shame. I would have loved an excuse to brand that insolent human face."

We're dragged from the tent. My lips tremble, shame and dread warring inside me.

The centaur was right. I hadn't put up a fight, and now I will likely have to watch my friends die because of it.

CHAPTER 26

The sun sets beyond Foloi, filling the centaur camp with evening glow. Eurytion leads us to the center of a wide glen. The clop of a thousand hooves fills the camp, centaurs stomping or clapping their bare chests as they greet each other, tails swishing to brush away the flies clinging to their horse bodies. Many stop to watch us with hooded eyes and grim mouths. My feet drag in protest—until my wrists are given a painful jerk.

"Where is my friend, the good Chiron?" Apollo demands, pulling against his binds. "He would never betray Olympus like this."

"That old git hasn't been seen in these parts for fifty years, banished to the mountains," Eurytion growls. He jerks on Apollo's binds, forcing the god to keep marching. "His love of humans has made him weak. The Kentauroi of Foloi no longer follow his incoherent ramblings."

Lyta's keen gaze travels over each centaur. Her dark chin is thrust ahead and her sheet of ebony hair falls unplaited down her back. "I will stain the forest floor with your blood, beast."

"You humans are such worthless creatures," Eurytion says. "Our queen will slaughter each of you."

We stop before a great forge. Arrowheads glint in the corner of my vision, our hearts their target. The beasts surround us; their dark-green vests and vast array of weaponry single them out as soldiers, in contrast to the more simply dressed centaurs milling about the camp. Oak bows hang across their chests and daggers are strapped on their forearms. From each of their human hips hangs a single sword, deco-rated with a single red tassel atop the hilt, all weapons engraved with the insignia of a rearing stallion before rolling clouds.

Our captor rubs his hands together and calls, "Nessus. Bring the brand."

"Zeus and Hera will seek retribution for this, Eurytion." Sweat glistens across Apollo's brow, his jaw so tight a tic forms at his temple.

Eurytion's fist snaps out, catching Apollo across the jaw. The god crumples to the ground. A roll of thunder echoes across the glen.

"Why should I fear powerless gods?" The centaur's face cracks in a lecherous smile, unafraid. "Yes, we know of Olympus's folly. Our *anassa* was instrumental in the Muses' disappearance."

Apollo spits, ichor flecking Eurytion's hooves. "And who do the Kentauroi make the mistake of serving?"

"The only goddess your father fears." Eurytion drops to a knee, jerking Apollo's head back by his curly hair. "The mother of fate, sleep, and pain, the creator of light and goddess of the night."

Apollo bares his teeth, stained red with his Olympian blood. "Nyx."

Frost crackles up my spine. Our faces must be ashen. And if I didn't feel like a fool before, I definitely do now. Of course the specter plaguing my nightmares, the one who haunts me across Greece, is the goddess who controls shadows and gave birth to the Moirai.

Eurytion stands, dragging Apollo to his feet and over to the forge. Another centaur emerges from the smoke. In his hands he balances an iron poker, on one end the Foloi centaurs' insignia. He tips it into the forge and it emerges bright as flame. The Midas Curse stirs on my abdomen, thrumming in time with my rapidly beating heart.

One soldier jerks my arms back painfully. Eurytion points to me. "Our *anassa* commands you tell us which gods have betrayed her cause."

"I will tell you nothing," I say, raising my chin high. "You think I fear pain? Sparta has forged me into a weapon, and weapons feel no pain."

Eurytion shrugs. "That may be so, but can you say the same for your friends?"

I command my face to betray no emotion, even as my throat tightens. "They are no friends of mine."

He nods, and the centaur named Nessus slams the heated brand against Apollo's collarbone. The god's roars fill the glen. He rips away from Eurytion's grasp and crumples. Another centaur moves forward, throwing a pail of water over Apollo, and he yells again.

The memory of Apollo bleeding out beneath the moon will never leave me. If he is stabbed with the poker end of that brand, he will not survive.

He's jerked back to his feet, and Eurytion turns to me. Nessus rests the brand in the flames again. The air fills with the smell of smoke and burnt flesh.

"Shall I brand the others next?" Nessus asks, eyeing Lyta eagerly.

She raises her chin. "Bring that thing near me and I will shove it down your throat."

The centaur has the good sense to pale.

Eurytion shakes his head, gaze still on me. "No, focus on the Olympian. His pain will break her yet."

I cannot tell them of the god who brought me the vision atop Olympus, of Prometheus and his clues. I bite my tongue and say nothing to cease my friend's suffering.

My friend. Tears threaten to spill down my cheeks, the realization hitting me as keenly as a slap across the cheek. Despite myself, I've truly come to care for Apollo.

Eurytion shakes his head, disappointment pinching his brows together. "Again."

Apollo's chiton is ripped across the abdomen and Nessus stalks forward with the brand. The Midas Curse lurches to the base of my throat. Its movement across my skin is scalding.

"No, wait," I beg. Nessus stops, the brand inches from Apollo's skin. "We've had help from two gods."

Eurytion waves his hand and the brand slowly lowers.

"No, Daphne," Apollo growls. He pulls weakly against his binds.

I swallow painfully, my throat dry, and make a silent prayer to Olympus for forgiveness. "Ares armed us with weapons and told us where to find the Muses. And the other"—I hesitate, swallowing again—"was Hermes. He spirited the Muses away from Knossos and back to Olympus."

"You lie." Eurytion jerks me by my hair to face him and I gasp, scalp burning. "Ares and Hermes are the allies of our *anassa*."

Apollo's pale, sweaty face blanches impossibly further.

"I can prove it," I say between clenched teeth. "Ares gave Apollo a bow that never misses its shot, and Hermes bequeathed to us his *kerykeion*."

After a long tense moment, Eurytion turns back to Nessus. "Again."

This time, Apollo's screams are hollow, carved out from pain and defeat. I fight futilely against my binds.

"*Ánandros!*" I scream. "I'm telling the truth."

Nessus jerks the brand away. Apollo falls to the ground, unmoving.

Somewhere, somehow, I've offended the Moirai, and I—and consequently my friends and allies—will pay penance.

Eurytion walks over and nudges Apollo with a hoof. I breathe a sigh of relief when he groans.

Lyta steps forward. "I have also been aided by the gods. In my possessions is the Helm of Hades. If, and only if, you free us, I will bestow it upon the centaurs of Foloi forest."

Eurytion snaps his fingers and two more centaurs step forward. "And what is to stop me from just taking the helm for myself?" He nods, and the pair turn to leave.

"Wait." Lyta tugs against her binds. "To touch the helm without the blessing of Hades's ichor would kill a mortal, even a beast like yourself."

The centaur sneers. "Then what good would this helm be to me?"

Her back straightens. "Because I am Princess Hippolyta of the Amazons, the daughter of Ares, with the ichor of Olympus in my veins, and I have the power to give the helm to whomever I choose."

"You're Hippolyta?" I feel faint. "Sister of Penthesilea, Queen of the Amazons? Daughter of Ares?"

The daughter of my enemy.

I take a step back, mind suddenly blank. Apollo has climbed to his knees and inclines his head to Hippolyta.

"Niece," he says.

We're led to a tent at the far end of the camp. Four soldiers wait in front of the entrance after Eurytion shoves us inside. When two move to follow, he waves them away and snaps the entrance shut in their faces. Hunger lingers in his eyes, crackling like a flame. His gaze searches the shelves lining the tent, lingering on our belongings stacked atop them, and I suddenly understand why he turned the soldiers away.

Greed.

The Helm of Hades is said to bestow upon the wearer invisibility.

"Bring me the helm, *kerykeion*, and bow," he snaps.

Hippolyta lifts her bound hands. "Free me first."

Eurytion's hand hesitates above his dagger, and his gaze darts to our belongings. He cuts her binds with a single swipe. "Get on with it or I'll kill you."

"You inspire me." She tosses her long hair over a shoulder before turning to the shelves. She runs a narrow finger along the worn wood, smirking at the centaur, daring him to do something, anything. The centaur ignores the bait.

Hippolyta pulls her pack from a bottom shelf, dragging it across the dirt to where Eurytion waits, digging his hooves into the earth. She rifles through it, and Eurytion leans over her shoulder to examine her movements.

"Do you mind?" the Amazonian snaps.

His face darkens a furious crimson. He's about ready to spit fire when Hippolyta turns back to her bag and exclaims, "There it is."

Eurytion snaps forward again, ready to grab the helm from Hippolyta's hands, but not before she jabs a sharp elbow into his throat. The centaur rears back, front hooves punching the air as he gasps and grabs at his neck. Silver glints in Hippolyta's hands. Eurytion doesn't have the time to regain his breath before she jams a small dagger into his shoulder.

He blinks once, twice, then collapses amid a flurry of dust.

"What did you do?" I cough as dirt fills my lungs.

The dust doesn't even have time to settle before a soldier demands from outside the tent, "Dioikitís Eurytion?"

My heart stutters. Apollo strides to the entrance. "Everything is fine."

The inflections are perfect, his voice an exact imitation of the unconscious centaur's. Apollo runs his bound hands along the tent flap edges as he speaks, and the fabric sews itself shut with red and green threads.

The soldiers outside are oblivious. "Hail us if you need anything."

"Oh, I will." Apollo steps over the fallen centaur's trunk-like legs. He stumbles slightly, and I reach out to steady him.

Sweat dripping from his brow, he gives me a smile meant to reassure. I reach for his wounds, but he brushes my hands away. "I'll be fine, Daphne."

I turn to Hippolyta. "Do you really have the Helm of Hades?"

"If I did, do you really think I would have been caught by these brutes?" She shakes her head. "Besides, the helm's been lost for hundreds of years."

The unconscious centaur's chest rises and falls, steady as the tide. "You didn't kill him?"

"You really think I'm that ruthless?" Hippolyta flashes me a grin, her white teeth glinting despite the shadows inside the tent. She slices my binds.

"Don't let her pretty face fool you," Theseus calls from behind a shelf laden with great black axes. "She's the most ruthless person in this tent."

"Okay, maybe I let my fury get away with me from time to time." Hippolyta shrugs and holds up the dagger. "A curious sleeping draft the goddess Achlys made for me," Hippolyta explains, dark eyes traveling the blade's length before flicking back to the unconscious centaur. "There's only one cure in all of Greece. That *suagroi* won't wake up until all the powers of Olympus are gone."

"I still can't believe it," I whisper.

"That I would poison this bastard?" Hippolyta kicks the centaur and he doesn't even budge. "He deserves far worse."

"No." I shake my head, mouth hanging open. "That you're the famous Hippolyta. Ligeia told me so many stories about you."

I'm a captive of the centaurs with my idol—the princess of the Amazons—one of the best warriors the world has ever known. She and Penthesilea are said to have slain a titan with their bare hands. Conquered kingdoms with no less than their wits.

I spin around and give Apollo my fiercest glare. "Did you know this entire time and not tell me?"

He holds up his still-bound hands. "No, but I should have. Ares doesn't exactly make a habit of announcing his offspring to the entire family. In fact, I think he rather despises them."

"That's true." Lyta—Hippolyta—grimaces. "I apologize for the subterfuge, Daphne. A princess traveling without escort draws far more attention than... what did you think I was? A mercenary?"

"A mercenary?" Theseus scoffs. "I wouldn't pay for your services could I help it."

Before Theseus can blink, Hippolyta's heel rams into his gut. "Bold words from the worm I can crush as easily as I breathe."

"As much as I would love dearly to witness that, my niece, I'm afraid the magic of your potion is dwindling much sooner than it should." He nods to Eurytion, whose fingers and hooves are twitching. Apollo lifts his hands. "Cut my binds. It's time to leave this cursed place behind."

CHAPTER 27

Thunder peals behind us, from above and below, heralding both the arrival of the summer's first storm and the army of centaurs bearing down on our heels. Hugging my bag to my chest, I fling myself down the rough terrain. Rolling down the hill, sharp branches rip my skin and tear the ragged remains of my chiton. Praxidikai groans beneath my weight.

Before my vision even has a chance to spin, I'm on my feet again and sprinting deeper into the labyrinthine forest.

We've run for so long that night has fallen. Without the stars to guide my flight, I have nothing but instinct and adrenaline pushing me on. My eyes adjust poorly to the dark. The forests outside Sparta may be my domain, but we're in centaur territory and we've pissed them off. Hippolyta, Theseus, and Apollo struggle to keep pace with me, tripping over logs and rolling ankles, the mossy ground beneath us grabbing onto our feet as if to hinder our escape.

The oncoming storm threatens to smother the moon's limited light filtering down between the leaves. I leap over a stream and surge on. Someone behind me isn't so quick, a splash giving away our position.

"To the north!" A centaur roars from behind us.

Panic propels me faster. My heart thunders in my chest.

I push my feet harder and farther. I barely recognize the dark abyss in time, skidding to a halt before I can tumble headfirst over the cliff. Theseus bulls into me. I anchor my arm around the nearest tree to keep us both from tumbling down the cliff. Rough bark rips my skin. Hippolyta and Apollo skid to a halt beside us. A rock skips over the ledge and smacks on every outcropping along the way down.

"Quick! They're headed toward the cliffs!" The shouts of the centaurs herd us as we flee deeper into the forest.

My ankle rolls, a distant ache as I run blindly on. A branch slashes my cheek and yanks my hair, jerking my neck, but I don't falter. An arrow sings past my temple. I stumble again, exhaustion wearing down my bones.

Apollo's searing hand catches mine, yanking me upright into his hard chest. I don't have time to thank him before we're barreling down another hill and deeper into the forest. His chest heaves with every step. His power is its weakest yet.

The dark trees are dangerous and unforgiving as we fly past. Hippolyta hurtles ahead, but a log rises from nowhere. It catches her feet and she crashes to the ground. Theseus also stumbles, his howl a beacon to guide the centaurs in our direction.

Apollo yanks Theseus upright and I fling Hippolyta's arm over my shoulder. The trees close in tighter around us. Before we know it, we limp across a clearing, a murky swamp that grips our feet tight and cuts off our escape.

A choked scream claws from my throat as half a hundred centaurs step from the trees. They line the fringes of the swamp, forming a solid, unbreakable ring around us. We press our backs together, bracing for the attack. A distant peal of thunder heralds the arrival of a sudden deluge, soaking us in seconds, blinding in its intensity.

I struggle to blink away the rain from my eyes. Arrowheads gleam in a flash of lightning. Swords are unsheathed and the centaurs' snorts mist in the cool night air.

I reach slowly for the sword at my hip, stolen from the centaur armory. I don't have time to cry out before Apollo shoves me aside, taking an arrow through his bicep. He roars, crumpling at my feet. I reach down for him, then gasp as a searing pain blossoms across my forearm. Blood drips from the fresh arrow wound across the back of my wrist. Silence falls between my friends and the centaurs surrounding us, broken only by the steady rainfall.

"The *anassa* wants you alive," one soldier announces, stepping forward but careful not to enter the water. Rain pours from his bronze helm and armor, from the nocked arrow. "Surrender peacefully and no further harm will come to you."

"And what has Nyx promised the Kentauroi of Foloi?" Apollo demands. He curls a fist around the wound on his arm, dark ichor streaming between his fingers. "Who has enough power to turn you against Olympus?"

"She has promised us retribution. We will no longer bend the knee before the powerless gods of Olympus." As the centaur speaks, all arrows focus now on Apollo. "The goddess of darkness will—"

A cacophony of howls rip through the night, cutting the centaur short. Everyone snaps their focus toward the sound, all arrows pointing to the trees.

It begins with a slow rumble, a tremor beneath our feet that sends ripples across the water. The night grows sharply colder, the wind stolen from my chest. The centaurs shuffle.

The trees begin to move, surging toward the centaurs. Chaos erupts and lightning cracks across the clouded sky, illuminating the terrified faces of the centaurs as they struggle to make sense of the impending danger, of the trees moving of their own volition against the laws of nature.

Trees thrash and flail, black limbs flinging centaurs across the swamp and into the grasp of more waiting trees, who crush them beneath their roots. A pack of wolves leap between the trees, snapping and ripping at the centaurs attempting to flee.

Hippolyta and I move as one. In a flash of moonlit steel and limbs, we cut our way through the remaining centaurs. I whirl, she rolls across my back as my blade, a silver arc of deadly steel, cleaves my nearest assailant. The metallic tang of blood fills the air.

A wolf's squeal of pain distracts me, cutting through the chaos. Hippolyta surges ahead.

"Lykou," I scream. The familiar black wolf spins on his haunches to face me. My back unprotected, a centaur yanks on my bag and flings me into the water.

Another bolt of lightning streaks across the sky. I catch sight of Lykou leaping for the neck of the centaur. White teeth flash with dark-red blood before my bag weighs me down. I'm pulled into the deep water of the swamp. Even beneath the murky water, the screams and shouts, the rumble of angry thunder and Apollo shouting my name echo dimly in my ears.

My wounded hand snatches uselessly at the water around my sinking body, searching for anything to hold on to. Gritting my teeth and clenching my eyes, I will the water to give me strength. Nothing happens.

My back brushes against the swamp's floor and, against all odds, my hand catches a firm leg, warm and hard. I pray that it's not the leg of a centaur as I use it as leverage to pull above the surface of the water. Rain and swamp water flood my vision, but not before a familiar auburn stag with white antlers leaps beneath the flailing trees. I catch a glimpse of a solitary figure, a tall woman with a crescent moon brooch on her shoulder.

"Pyrrhus?" I cough up a lungful of water. "Artemis?"

The goddess has come to our aid, likely using the last of her gifts. Theseus pulls me to my feet. Apollo, Hippolyta, and Lykou following, we hurtle through a break in the thrashing trees and into the darkness beyond.

It isn't until I fall again and cough up dirt, many miles later, that Apollo allows us to stop for the night. All that remains of the storm's passing is the damp earth and steady drip of water on leaves. My wrist won't stop bleeding and dark spots blur my vision.

Theseus collapses beside me, clutching his side, blood dripping down his tan skin.

My hands flutter uselessly over the wound. I don't know anything about healing.

"We've got to stop the bleeding," he says between gritted teeth. "Get some cloth."

I tear the hem of my chiton and reach for the Athenian's side. Apollo takes the cloth from my hands with a firm shake of his head.

"You'll only make his wound worse with that filthy cloth," he says, unsheathing a dagger. His fingers wrap around the blade. It begins to steam and spit sparks. When he pulls his fingers away, the metal is bright red. Before Theseus can protest, he slaps the blade against the wound.

Theseus roars again, his skin hissing upon impact. His eyes roll into the back of his head and, before I can catch him, he collapses backward.

I ease over him, searching his face. "Theseus?"

He's unconscious.

Cloth in one hand, I turn to Apollo and ask, "What possessed you to take that arrow?"

"I took the arrow because"—a strangled growl cuts him off, and he shakes his head—"it doesn't matter. What's done is done."

Speechless, I hold up the still-steaming blade. "We need to seal your own wound, too."

"Just another burn to add to the many." The brands shine despite the dim light, healing much more slowly than they would at Apollo's full power.

"Thank you for saving my life," I say softly before pressing the blade against his arm. A strangled howl claws between his clenched teeth. Sweat forms on his brow. When I pull the blade away, a gasp of relief exits his chest.

Lykou licks the arrow wound on the back of my hand. He presses up against my side with little whines, as if begging for forgiveness.

"You don't even have to ask," I murmur, pressing my face deep within the folds of his dark fur. He smells of pine trees and dirt and blood. "Is that my blood or one of those centaur bastards?"

He rumbles a soft growl in answer, and I'm too tired to press.

Fatigue threatens to pull me under. I lean slowly back into the dirt and my eyelids slide shut. Before my mind can pass from this world to one of dreams, the familiar smell of cedarwood cuts through the blood and pine, waking me as Apollo jostles my shoulder.

"I need to bandage your wound." Apollo cradles my wrist, and I'm further pulled from sleep. I struggle to keep my eyes open as he examines the slash on my hand, then moves on to the assortment of bruises and cuts littering my entire body.

Hippolyta's right arm still hangs limp at her side, bones in her shoulder jutting out. I shove Apollo toward our wounded friend.

"Take care of her first," I insist, curling up against Lykou. "My wounds are nothing serious."

The throbbing in one of my ankles suggests otherwise, but exhaustion weighs me down. I fight it no longer. The last thing I see before sleep overtakes me is Apollo looking down on me with a mixture of regret and pain.

CHAPTER 28

I wake with a great gasp, flinging myself up and pawing the ground for any weapon I can reach. Centaurs must watch us now. They couldn't have given up their chase already. Whining, Lykou rolls over and forces his entire body onto my lap.

"I'm sorry, Lykou." Sweat slicks my skin, making my dress cling to my back.

When no centaurs step from the trees, I force myself to focus on Lykou in my arms, willing my trembling hands to still. He licks the sweat from my arms and shoulders. I dig my fingers deep into his fur and the tremors start to slow.

Everyone else awakes much more slowly, still weary from the night's events. Nursing a variety of wounds, we stagger the remainder of the way through Foloi Forest. After what feels like hours of painful limping, we finally come to a gap in the trees and step out into a wide field of tall, golden grass.

With Hermes's *kerykeion* strapped again to its hiding spot at the small of my back, I begin to regain optimism. The plague of Thebes can't be as traumatic as the terrors we've left behind, but I won't be underestimating it, either.

Hippolyta's limp is hardly noticeable as she walks beside me, Apollo's healing having largely taken care of her shoulder and leg. Theseus is likewise patched up and makes small talk with the god. Apollo's own wounds have healed, hastened by whatever remains of his Olympic gifts, but the brands remain, shining, pale scars against his tan skin. Lykou trots close to my side, brushing my legs. I make a mental promise to make more efforts to talk to him, connect with him, and appreciate his presence before his feral nature wins out again.

Her true identity revealed, Hippolyta has no need for secrecy. She chatters amiably about her sister and friends, soldiers so formidable that even a Spartan would think twice before engaging them in battle. I would love nothing more than to meet them all, train and battle with them. I likewise share my stories, telling her of the bowels of Knossos and my bargain with Artemis.

"Where do the Moirai send you next?" Hippolyta asks.

"To Thebes. I've got a plague to fell." My friend raises her eyebrows and I tighten the straps around my waist that hold the *kerykeion* in place. "Still unsure as to how. And from there I have to find my way to the edge of the Okeanos and the Underworld."

Hippolyta purses her lips. "I'm not sure how you will manage to vanquish a plague, either, but to venture to the Underworld, I suggest you seek the advice of the goddess Persephone. There is a temple dedicated to her mother, Demeter, in Eleusis. Perhaps you can find your path there."

"Can I ask you a question?" I rub the back of my neck.

Hippolyta cocks an eyebrow. "Go ahead. Whether I'll answer is to be decided."

"What was your real reason for not telling me who you are?" Reaching out, I hold up the hem of her cloak. The golden thread of the *meander* shimmers in the midday sun. "Why were you so upset when I realized?"

Her dark eyes are unreadable. We walk in silence for so long, I assume she has simply chosen not to answer my questions.

When she speaks again, my head snaps in her direction. "Because only someone with ichor, Olympian blood, can see the pattern woven by this thread."

My heart stutters. Hippolyta continues, "And I, just as much as you, have reason to distrust the gods."

"Why?" I ask, the word a croak.

"Ares may be my father—" Hippolyta's voice is resigned. She bends and rips up a clump of grass, shredding it between her nimble fingers. "But there is no love in my heart for the bastard."

Another moment of silence passes before I nudge her with an elbow. "I'll make sure to pass your sentiments along when Zeus punishes him for his betrayal."

"Penthe will be delighted. She hates him just as much as I."

I don't say as much, but I wish she would stay with us before returning to her sister.

As if reading my mind, she wraps a warm arm around my shoulders, the other strapped across her chest in a makeshift sling. "The stars have prophesied that we will meet again. Let that thought warm you for the remainder of your journey."

I flash the Amazon princess a crooked grin. "Didn't figure you for a star-reader."

"Only when their prophecies are in my favor," she admits with a short laugh. Hippolyta pats the girdle hanging over her uninjured shoulder. "And I have to return this to Penthe before she grows impatient and declares war on Foloi. My sister's temper is legendary for a good reason."

I can't help but laugh. "I am jealous of you."

Hippolyta blinks. "Of me?"

"Of your relationship with your sister."

She scoffs. "Now you've completely lost me. Why would you be jealous of a sister with no qualms about sending me to the far reaches of the world, at the mercy of monsters unimaginable, all for a girdle that belongs to a father she doesn't even like?"

"Because she trusts you enough to get the job done," I say with a lopsided shrug. "Alkaios would sooner make a deal with Ares than entrust anything to me."

"Alkaios," Hippolyta says, murmuring the name. "He is your eldest brother, yes?"

I nod.

She inclines her head, her gaze far away as her fingers trail over the tall grass, a sea of green stretching between us and the Cithaeron mountains. When she speaks again, her words catch me completely off-guard. "Perhaps he trusts you more than you give him credit for." When I bark a laugh, she continues, "He trusted you enough to train among the soldiers of Sparta, enough to race for your family's honor during *Carneia*."

"Because he had no choice." I yank on a piece of tall grass, ripping it into a dozen pieces before tossing it aside. Alkaios doesn't think I'm fit enough to marry, let alone carry our family's honor. "He couldn't race because he is married and the rules of *Carneia* dictate that only unmarried men compete."

"Unmarried *men*," Hippolyta says, rolling her eyes. "Not unmarried women? Typical Greeks. Ignoring the blatant stupidity of people who rest their fate on the shoulders of men and dismisses the capable strength of women, have you considered that, by letting you compete, the rules were compromised anyway? It seems that Alkaios had a choice: break the rules by competing himself, or break the rules by letting you compete. And he chose you. He trusted *you* to win the race, more than even himself."

"Could the same not be said of Penthesilea? She entrusted this mission to you and you alone."

"There is a truth to your words that I cannot deny. It's strange" —she hesitates a moment, weighing her words—"how we came into each other's lives at such precise moments. Upon the sea, when I needed assurance that I could find my father's girdle using my own wits and not the blind impulses of my sister. In Foloi, when we became one in order to survive and elude an army of centaurs. Without you, I would have never escaped with my prize, let alone with my life.

"I am in your debt." She looks me over, assessing my face as a small smile tugs at her narrow lips. "Should you ever tire of the oppressive rule of men, when you finally realize that you owe nothing to Sparta, know that you will always have a place at my side among the Amazons."

"Are you sure I cannot change your mind about continuing on with us?"

"There's no room for me in this part of your journey." Leaves and twigs cling to her sleek dark hair. She dips her face close, kissing me lightly on the cheek. "Until we meet again. Fate has her eyes on you, Daphne."

Hippolyta turns and strides toward the rising sun. Flushing, I touch my cheek with a shaking hand. When I glance to Theseus, he faces the mountains in the distance.

"What I would give for a kiss from a woman like that. Before Athena cursed me, I once considered her to be my future *anassa*. I traveled all the way to Themiscyra, a dozen carts of gold, livestock, and delicacies from the southern continent," Theseus muses, his eyes taking on a gleam. "She told me where to shove the gifts I brought, and that a true husband of an Amazon would instead gift her with weaponry.

"My friend Alcides never let me hear the end of it the entire journey back to Athens." He turns, considering me. "I'd say her charms weren't entirely lost on you, either. You're positively glowing."

I drop my hand to my sword to cease its trembling. "Must be the sunlight now that we're out of Foloi."

Theseus looks straight through me. "Never been kissed before, young spitfire?"

"Of course I have. I'm not going to get all moony over a chaste kiss or two." I blush, stammering despite myself. "Spartans have no time for such trivial things. What good are kisses compared to the bite of steel?"

Theseus roars with laughter, so hard that he nearly falls over. I wait for him to stop, fuming and blushing furiously. I can almost feel the steam coming out of my ears.

Theseus wipes a tear from his eye, still chortling. "You've got much to learn if you don't know that a kiss can be just as deadly as a sword."

With a grumble, I jog ahead. Apollo crests a ridge on the edge of the field and turns to look back once, his gaze unreadable from this distance.

"How did we get stuck with these jerks?" I ask Lykou.

He huffs and trots ahead to catch up with the god.

"Don't blame me. Blame Pyrrhus for getting caught and setting us on this damnable journey!" Grumbling, I ignore the pained protests in my ankle and speed up.

I won't let Apollo beat me to Thebes.

We arrive at the Cithaeron mountains after a week of hobbling across the rolling green and gold hills between Foloi and Thebes.

"This is the only road to and from the Theban kingdom for hundreds of miles," Theseus says. "And this is where we will find the mysterious plague."

"Will we have the protection of the Ourea as we travel through?" I ask Apollo, thinking of the gods that lurk atop the mountains.

"The god Cithaeron, who used to oversee this range, hasn't been heard from for nearly a hundred years," Apollo says. He takes a drink of water and brushes the corner of his mouth. His hand leaves a smear of dirt across his cheek.

I blink, reaching out to brush the dirt away with my thumb. He stills beneath my touch. "And Zeus didn't think it odd for a god to disappear?"

"Does a king know where all of his subjects are at all times?" Apollo shrugs. "The last I saw of Cithaeron was his hide fleeing for the eastern continents before Zeus could catch and kill him."

I search Apollo's face, but no hint of mirth lingers there. "But they're family."

"When you've spent thousands of years together, familial lines tend to get blurred." Apollo shrugs. "I'm sure you've heard the stories."

I sniff. "I thought you said I shouldn't believe all of them."

He steps close enough that our shoulders brush and smiles crookedly at me. "So you *do* listen to my advice. I thought some god had charmed your ears to ignore my sage wisdom."

"That would imply you had any wisdom." I return his smile, feeling a traitorous burn rise in my cheeks.

"If you two are finished flirting," Theseus says, shoving between us. "Shouldn't we worry more over what evil waits for us in these mountains and less about Apollo's dysfunctional family?"

"You'll need a proper weapon of course, Athenian." I tug the *kerykeion* from its spot on my spine and toss it to Theseus. He catches it easily.

We trudge on, the sun beating down relentlessly above our heads, burning my shoulders. I cover my eyes with a hand to see through the hazy light. The bottoms of my feet ache, the soles of my sandals so worn down that every piece of sand pains each step. What I would give for a nice, cool stream.

I keep Praxidikai drawn as we press deeper into the darkening mountainside. The sand beneath our feet hushes our footsteps, making it easier to sneak through the mountain pass, but it can also mask a predator's footsteps.

We arrive at a dead end, the canyon walls narrowing to a single point where a solitary cave entrance cleaves the junction.

I don't know what I expected from the "plague of Thebes," but this is not it.

A smiling Sphinx sits before the mouth of the cave.

I near with measured steps, attuned to her every breath. She ruffles wide, golden wings before pouncing forward. Lykou snarls a warning, but the Sphinx laughs at the threat.

"Have you come here to try to kill me?" She paws even closer. Reflexively, I heft Praxidikai higher, trained on the bridge of her nose. Her large yellow eyes swivel toward Theseus and Apollo behind me. "I know *they* have, but I had hoped for some civility from you, at least, *kataigída.*"

A shiver slips up my spine.

Theseus, brandishing the *kerykeion,* takes a step forward. Though his wide eyes betray his fear, he has enough courage to strike her down then and there—if he can move quick enough.

Apollo stands behind Theseus, arms crossed over his chest. He holds no weapon and betrays no hint of fear. The Sphinx points a long, dark claw toward him.

"I have come to expect such ignorance from mortals, but from you, Son of Zeus? What a pity. You truly are just a pretty face." Apollo has the grace to look properly affronted as the Sphinx turns back to Theseus and smiles. An unsettling purr escapes her lips, and I can see the blood staining her elongated canines.

"No weapons made by men, mortal or immortal, can strike me

down. Ligeia shared with you few stories of the magic of my kin, so I shall forgive your ignorance." She blinks slowly, turning back to me. "I expect you had a hard time slicing open the Minotaur. My skin is thrice as resilient, and you won't find any weaknesses."

Quick as a snake, she leaps above me. I don't have time to cry out before she lands on Theseus's shoulders and they collapse into the sand. Her claws are at his throat. Lykou howls and Apollo has an arrow trained on the back of her neck. With a roar, Theseus rams the wings of the staff into her chest.

And she does nothing but laugh. Nimbly, she climbs off of him. We gape. The *kerykeion* didn't even leave a mark.

She examines her claws. "The Athenian won't be getting the herald's staff into my heart, at least not while I still have magic coursing through my veins."

Despite my instincts screaming at me, calling me a fool, I lower Praxidikai; its bronze butt thumps in the sand.

She sits, wrapping her long tail around her forepaws. "I could kill you here and now, especially you two, for your obvious incompetence." A long claw points at Apollo and Theseus, who climbs to his feet, glaring. With a soft sigh, she says, "I hope your precious Ligeia had the competence to teach you how to battle a Sphinx, but that might be giving her too much credit."

I don't ask how she knows so much about me. I keep my mouth clamped shut instead of asking the million questions that tickle the back of my throat.

"I like games, and since I'm feeling particularly bored today, let's play the most reckless one of all. Appease me by playing a game of riddles."

There must be a catch.

"We can pass unscathed if I answer correctly," I continue for her, and she grins. "But if I answer incorrectly..."

"I will have a feast tonight," she finishes for me. She languidly licks her lips, her tongue black and forked at the tip.

Raising my gaze to the cloudless sky, I sigh through my nose. I still hate riddles.

And though plays with words vex me to no end, I have an uncanny knack at solving problems. Perhaps Tyche does indeed favor me. No time like the present, I suppose, to test this theory. Theseus's fate with the Sphinx notwithstanding, I still need to reclaim the Muses.

The Sphinx saunters back to her dais, indicating I should follow with an impatient flick of her tail. Lykou moves to follow, but after a stern shake of my head he sits on his haunches in the dirt with an exaggerated whine. I bring Praxidikai with me as a precaution. Even if I fail her test, I won't go down without a fight.

"Did they teach you how to read and write in Sparta?" the Sphinx asks, looking me over with unveiled curiosity.

"If you know about Ligeia, you already know the answer to that question." Like most Spartan girls, I know the basics of reading and writing. Though I don't have an impressive aptitude for either, I still can trade barbs as well as the next literate person. I don't add that this conversation is meaningless if one of us is going to die anyway.

"I'm only being polite," she says, eyes narrowing to slits. "I like to know the humans I play with, and you are something of a mystery."

"Oh?" I kick aside a wayward pebble.

"I see through the layers of time. I stole the gift from an Oracle who challenged me to a battle of wits," the Sphinx explains, waving a paw through the air. "But you challenge my gift. I only see snippets. A beast below a palace. An oracle. Two brothers. A deer with a garland around its neck." Her smile turns wicked, baring those fangs again. "A dead mother. *Mothakes.*"

"Of you"—her critical gaze turns to Theseus—"I see curses, an insurmountable quest, and a sow with flames reaching from its lips. Black sails, and a bloated corpse among the waves."

The Athenian's shoulders hunch, pain and fury warring in his gaze. But the Sphinx's gaze has moved on to Lykou.

"There's not much man left in you," she says. "It's a shame that your father will never understand why you deserted Sparta. It must pain you to watch the love of your life fall for the god that transformed you into a beast."

Before she can enrage Lykou into attacking, I interrupt, "If you know so much about us, then you must know who we're hunting. What can you tell me about Nyx?"

"That you will need to embrace the power stirring in your veins if you ever hope to defeat her. That she and Zeus have been enemies for longer than a millennia, before the god of lightning even ascended his throne." The Sphinx's gaze darts to Apollo before returning to me. "That their battles spawned the founding of Olympus and a pact among all the gods loyal to Zeus."

"Is she more powerful than him? What are her goals?"

Her tail twitches. "She wants to restore power to the rightful gods."

Trepidation stirs in me. I swallow. "What does that mean?"

Apollo steps forward before the Sphinx can answer. "Daphne is still waiting for your riddle, or are you stalling?"

The Sphinx hisses, her molten gold eyes flashing. "Don't you dare patronize me, boy. Your fate balances in my palm. Or shall I share your history with your new traveling companions? Do they know about the kingdoms you've brought to ruin?"

The god crosses his arms. "You're still stalling."

"Fine," she snaps, giving us all a last appraising glance before turning her full attention on me. "Now we play."

CHAPTER
29

I square my shoulders, ready for whatever tangle of words the creature can throw at me.

Behind me, Theseus slaps his palm with the *kerykeion*. Lykou's
legs are bunched, ready to launch at the Sphinx at the slightest provocation. Apollo's arms are crossed over his chest, trusting me to best
this next challenge on my own.

Finally, the Sphinx asks, "What swallows what is before it and
what is behind it?"

A wave of relief sweeps through me. Pyrrhus told me this one
before. "Time. The answer is time."

The Sphinx's pointed smile vanishes. Her feathers ruffle in annoyance, some falling into the sand at my feet. "Correct, but that was just
a test. Your turn."

My mind whirs and thrums as I wrack my memory for anything
resembling a riddle. Pyrrhus was always the one with a way with

words, Alkaios lacking the patience and proclaiming them to be the province of children. I decide on Pyrrhus's favorite. "What has one voice and yet becomes four-footed and two-footed and three-footed?"

"How droll." The Sphinx yawns. "The answer is man. My turn. There are two doors. One of solid gold, the other of unforgiving iron. One leads to Olympus, and the other to Tartarus. Each door has a single guard for protection. One guard always tells the truth, and the other always lies. What single question would you ask of one guard to find the door to Olympus?"

My head begins to spin. I want to ask her to repeat it all for me, but that won't help. "How long do I get to find an answer?"

The Sphinx's tail swishes. "Until I'm bored."

I withdraw into myself, taking a deep breath, and put it all together like some gods-damned equation in my head.

Two doors. Iron and gold. Two guards. Truth and lies. Olympus and Tartarus. One question. I could ask one guard a question I know to be true, to determine which guard is the liar and which spoke the truth, but that won't help me determine which guards the way to Olympus and would waste my single question.

I glance to Apollo and Theseus, but both of their faces are blank. My mind whirls faster, my palms are suddenly clammy, and the Sphinx begins counting down the time in a singsong voice, grinning at the prospect of a fresh, juicy meal.

What if I simply ask a guard which door he protects? No, he could be the liar and lead me to my death. So many different variables. I need to ask the guards together with my single question, but I can only ask one question of a single guard. The answer hits me like a slap in the face.

It doesn't matter which guard I ask first. They will both tell me the same answer.

It is my turn to smile. The Sphinx scrutinizes me with wary disbelief.

"I would ask one guard, 'If I asked the other guard what door led to Olympus, would he point to the door of gold or the door of iron'?"

It doesn't matter which guard I ask, because the answer is always the same: both guards would answer with a lie, I must take the door not pointed to. The liar would point me to the door leading to the Underworld, and the other would answer as the liar and also point to the door leading to the Underworld. No matter which guard I ask, I would always be pointed to the Underworld's door, and should take the other.

The Sphinx's face slips from shock to fury. Before I can react, she leaps. I duck and her claws miss my face by a scant few inches. Lykou yelps and Apollo roars. I spin around, Praxidikai held high.

Lykou lies in the dirt. The Sphinx stands atop him, claws digging into the scruff of his neck and above his eyes.

"You gave your word," I say, incredulity filling my voice. My stomach clenches, limbs suddenly numb. "Let him go."

"I made no promises to *his* fate," the Sphinx says, grinning so that I can see the jagged fangs mere inches above Lykou's helpless throat. "Perhaps a snack would urge this game along."

Theseus yells, rushing forward. Both Apollo and I cry out warnings, but they have no effect on the Athenian. Shimmering gold arcs in the air, the *kerykeion* flying at her face.

She easily bats it aside.

Hermes's staff flies, end over end, and embeds itself into a wall of sandstone. Theseus's mouth gapes.

"Let Lykou go," I command, pointing Praxidikai directly at her heart.

"Make me," the Sphinx says. Her claws dig deeper into the wolf's scruff. He yelps, bucking, but she presses him harder into the dirt. Water pools in the corner of his eyes, blood dripping from the wound on his neck.

"One last chance," the Sphinx hisses, licking the blood from

Lykou's neck. Her fangs come back stained red. Apollo moves forward, arrow aimed at her heart. She only laughs. "I am impervious to your weapons. Use your words. I can only be defeated by wit."

Her fur, once a luscious gold, is now dull and her feathers fall quickly; her eyes are bloodshot, and I swear she broke a talon when she leaped. As though each riddle foiled has weakened her.

But I don't know any more riddles. My mind scrambles, searching memories for anything to throw the Sphinx's way.

Lykou's eyes have glazed over. Time is running out, escaping my grasp like a runaway spool of silk thread.

I'm pacing, my eyes locked on the blood steadily dripping from Lykou's neck. I'm not clever like Alkaios. I don't talk my way out of trouble, I barrel through with swords and fists. The difference between the two of us has always been as stark as night and day . . .

That's it.

It takes me a moment to find my voice again. "There are two siblings. One gives birth to the other and she, in turn, gives birth to the first. Who are they?"

Her eyes widen. Hope fills me.

"War . . . and peace? No, that's not it. Stupid, stupid Phix, always disappointing your kin." She moves away from Lykou and paces across the sand.

I hold Praxidikai aloft, ready to fling.

"Wait!" she demands, holding up a single onyx talon. "I need more time."

My smile is cold as ice. "I'm bored."

She turns to me, her eyes wild. "Fine. But my true riddle has yet to be sung."

Her haunches bunch and she leaps, fangs flashing and claws stretching toward my throat.

Praxidikai soars before she is even airborne.

CHAPTER 30

The spearhead embeds deep in the Sphinx's heart.

I vaguely recall the sound of Theseus whooping behind me, of her body falling to the dirt.

I'm by Lykou's side in an instant. He whines as I check the puncture wounds in his neck, peeling apart the blood-sodden fur. Shallow, but deep enough to leave a scar. Apollo kneels beside me, pouring water over the cuts. When he's finished, I tear the hem of my chiton and wrap the fabric around my friend's neck to stanch the bleeding. It's not much, but for now it will do.

Lykou climbs gingerly to his paws, swaying a bit. I want to tell him to lie down, but he huffs and pads past me into the cave.

"You're welcome for saving your life," I mutter, accepting a hand from Theseus to help me to my feet.

"I'll admit," Theseus says, having the decency to look at least partly mollified, "I didn't believe you had the wits to take on that Sphinx."

I thump his unwounded arm. "Liar."

We follow Lykou inside the cave, Praxidikai strapped across my back once more. My mouth drops open and I gasp.

Cages, made from bars of gold and bone, crammed to bursting with creatures and humans and objects too extraordinary to believe, fill the cave. Sunlight shines down through gaping crevices, illuminating the cages and mountains of treasure. A beautiful woman, with flames for hair and legs made of bronze, reaches through the bars of her cage. Lykou snarls a warning as I step past, and the woman bares extended yellow canines with a feral hiss.

From the cage next to her, a manticore watches me from the shadows. His face is that of an old man, crow's feet reaching across his temples; his tail has been removed of all its spikes, and his cobalt fur is matted and dull. His black eyes bore into mine until I'm forced to break his gaze.

Inside the next cage sits the cause of so many of my nightmares as a child. The lamia, an immortal demon with the upper body of an adolescent and a serpent's tail in place of legs. Her eyes are cold onyx stones.

I hurry past this cage and the next, and then the next, all with creatures from my dreams and nightmares. Some horrible, others gentle. Some are corpses, left the rest of their days to rot behind unforgiving bars.

I halt in front of a caged centaur. She studies me with haunted, sunken eyes. Her body is frail and malnourished, and her black hair hangs limp and tangled around her gaunt face.

"Please," she croaks, pressing against the iron bars of the cage. "Free us."

I turn to Theseus, ready to demand the *kerykeion*. He takes a step back from my outstretched hand and surveys the cages with growing horror.

"We can't set them free, Daphne," he says, and a cold furor overwhelms me. "We can't inflict these terrors upon the human race. These are monsters, and they deserve to be locked away."

The manticore hisses from the shadows of his cage and the lamia stands high on her serpent tail with a screech.

Outsiders, monsters, and murderers. I am no different from any of them.

Theseus sighs when he recognizes the frown of resolve on my face.

"Who are we to decide which creatures deserve to be set free or locked up?" I ask. "If we don't free them then *we* are the monsters. Give me the *kerykeion*."

"Not a single creature was created to live its life in a cage," Apollo says, his voice the dark rumble of a storm. A quiet fury lingers in the taut panes of his face. He expected the Muses to be here.

"No more tarrying." I wrest the *kerykeion* from the reluctant Athenian and swing. A lock falls to the ground in a burst of sparks and the door swings open of its own accord.

The centaur accepts my offered hand with a grateful smile, her fingers like ice as she grips me tight.

"Thank you," she says, her voice a rough croak. Tears spilling down her face, she dips into a wobbly bow. "I cannot describe the despair of believing you will spend the remainder of your days a prisoner."

I offer her my water jerkin, and she accepts it gratefully. After a hearty gulp, she bows again. "I must return home. It has been many long decades since I've seen my husband."

I smile as warmly as I can, thinking of her kin we've left behind.

"My name is Chariclo." The centaur bends her forelegs in a semi-bow, inclining her head slightly. "The centaurs of Foloi are eternally in your debt."

I raise my eyebrows. "I guess I can't complain about a few more friends. We passed through Foloi on our way here, and I suspect that your kin may not share your gratitude."

Chariclo assesses the scab on the back of my hand, the rope burns around my wrists and the bruises dotting my arms and legs—the remnants of my escape.

"It's good to know that my family is still alive. I haven't heard any whispers of them since my capture." Without a word to my companions, she turns and begins her slow journey home, each step dragging across the sand. Apollo drapes his own water skin around her neck, and she nods before exiting the cave.

"We're all prisoners here." The woman with flaming hair grips the bars of her cage, the metal hissing beneath her claws, burning scarlet and spitting steam. "Cages, physical or imaginary, we are all prisoners to our destiny."

"I make my own destiny," I say.

Next, I free a pair of women made of gold. Their gilded bodies step lithely from the cage, even their hair and blank eyes resonant with the brilliant metal. With curt nods to us, they flee as well.

I let the *kerykeion* swing to unlock the cages of dozens of satyrs, nymphs, humans, and even chimeras. They all promise me the same thing as the others, to owe me a debt that I never expect to actually be paid. I release them all nonetheless, watching as some fly to the ceiling and others run to the crevice and rush to freedom.

I heft the *kerykeion* in my hands, unmarred despite the beating it's taking, and stand before the lamia's cage.

She cackles. "I guess it was too much to hope for you to share your family's idiocy."

"Glad to see that you still have reason and that you didn't let your victory with the Sphinx go to your head." Theseus crosses his arms over his chest and glares at the remaining cages. "It would be simpler to kill ourselves rather than set these beasts free. Let that lamia loose and all our heads will be off."

I shift from foot to foot. Apollo offers no advice. He stares at the creatures. His lips press in a firm line, dark brows drawn together in a frown.

"I am not a fool, but neither am I cruel. Let's find the Muses first."

A deafening roar from the corner of the cavern makes us all jump. I spin around, *kerykeion* raised high. Not bound to a cage but instead clapped to the unforgiving iron of shackles and chains, crouches a gryphon.

The chains wrap all over its body, hooking onto its wings and legs tight enough for the gryphon to flinch with each breath, corners of its eyes tightening with the simple movement. Any attempt to unfurl its wings tightens the collar around its neck. Despite its apparent pain, the gryphon focuses a defiant gaze solely on me. Daring me to set it free.

"I will give you your freedom," I say, stepping over its claws. "But not yet. Let me ensure the Muses are set free before I possibly lose my life to those talons."

I turn away from it, searching the cavern for clues. Aside from the cages, I skirt around mounds of treasure and weapons, scattered about the cavern like mountains that dazzle in the sunlight filtering down from the ceiling.

The sandstone walls along the cavern are beautiful, rolling and rippling like waves in warm colors of red, orange, and tan, reminiscent of a summer sunset. Following the nearest wall, it leads me to a corner where two waves collide in a splash of dark crimson sand. The deepest part of the corner is pitch black, and I squint to see deeper into its depths. "Lykou, come here for a moment."

Lykou huffs, padding over. The irritation on his face at being beckoned like a pet vanishes immediately once he joins me, though, nostrils flaring at some scent too infinitesimal for my human nose to discern. Padding inside the dark corner, Lykou disappears. I crawl after him and hear the shuffle of Apollo doing the same behind me.

I'm only in the darkness for a moment longer before blinding sunlight greets me. I shield my eyes with the back of my dirty hand. We emerge in another chamber filled with mountains of gold and precious gems. My mouth drops open as I stagger to my feet, ignoring the sand sticking to my sweaty legs and palms.

The Muses aren't here.

A cold rumble of laughter spins us around. As one, Apollo and I draw our weapons.

With a sword point pressed against Lykou's neck, Ares grins at both of us. "Miss me, brother?"

CHAPTER
31

I brandish the *kerykeion* before me. Ares's full lips split in a wide smile, digging the tip of his sword against Lykou's neck. My throat constricts.

"What is this, Ares?" Apollo holds both hands out in front of him in a placating gesture.

Before either of us can blink, Ares tosses Lykou aside. In the same movement, he crosses the distance to Apollo, his brother's throat in his grip. He lifts Apollo off his feet and slams him into the sandstone wall. I swing the *kerykeion*.

The golden staff digs deep into the skin of his back. Ares roars and the entire cavern trembles. The walls crack and stone rains down around us. I don't have time to cry out before Ares's free hand catches my head and slams me into the wall.

"Daphne!" Apollo chokes out, clawing at Ares's hand around his throat.

Stars litter my vision. The world won't stop spinning. I stumble and reach a hand to my brow. My fingers come back covered with blood before I fall to my knees. My other hand reaches for the *kerykeion*.

Ares rips the staff from his back before I can reach it. "You won't need this." It disappears in a puff of smoke and sand. A strangled cry bursts from my throat.

I can only watch as Lykou springs for the malevolent immortal, but is flung backward by an invisible surge of power. He flies through the air, the piles of gold blown around us.

Apollo's face is beet-red, veins popping in his temples as he struggles for air. He can only choke out a single word. "Wh-why?"

"I do as my *anassa* commands." The vulture painted in blood-like ink atop Ares's chest beats its wings. "With Olympus in turmoil, humanity will likely fall as well, and the wars that will be incited will stretch well beyond Greece. They will stretch to the ends of the Earth. What could a god of war possibly love more than that?"

"We trusted you," Apollo spits out. "How could you do this to Father? To Aphrodite? To your family?"

I try and fail to climb to my feet. My vision has yet to stop spinning, the world turning on its axis. I cannot even grab Praxidikai or daggers, my fingers fumbling uselessly in the sand.

Ares grins when he notices me blundering about. "I will never understand how you managed to escape my *anassa*'s grip."

"For such a big man, your hands are unenviably small." I cannot stop the words before they tumble from my mouth, nor do I want to. I spit sand and blood at his feet. "Is that why you betrayed Aphrodite? Did she leave you to find her satisfaction with someone else? Someone with hands larger than a toddler's?"

I am a fool, but I don't care. Not when my life's blood pools around me.

The stories of Ares's temper are true. He flings Apollo aside and the god crashes through mountains of gold. Ares plucks a sword from the air. He spins it, and before I have time to draw a last breath, slices down toward me.

The blade shatters on my abdomen.

Gaping, I look down. My chiton is cut cleanly across my stomach, revealing the shimmering Midas Curse.

"Artemis," Ares says the name like a curse. He grabs another sword from the air. "I'll kill her next, and your pathetic, mewling brother, too."

"No." Apollo has staggered to his feet. His face is stricken, tan skin leached of any color. "Leave my sister out of this."

"She was never *out of this*." Ares raises the sword again. This time, he won't miss.

His sword falls. Apollo yells at me to move. The blade is aimed directly at my neck. Lykou leaps between us.

He catches Ares's wrist between his teeth. The god of war roars. Lykou clamps down even harder, and then rips his hand clean from his arm.

Ichor pours from the stump of Ares's wrist. Lykou dashes away with the hand before the god can seek retaliation. Ares stumbles, reaching his only hand against the wall for balance. Apollo pulls a dagger from the air and flings it at his back. Ares spins around, grabbing the dagger midflight.

"I will make you pay," says the god of bloodlust. His eyes flicker, then turn black as smoldering coal. "You will all pay. Your allies, your families. I will kill them all."

He turns to me again, a cruel smile splitting his disturbingly beautiful face like a gaping wound. "Nyx has a message for you. Return to Sparta, mourn what remains of your family after I find them. Ignore her warning, continue on this quest, and we will kill the Muses. Their deaths will be upon all of you, and then nothing you could ever do will return the powers to Olympus."

Ares disappears in a flash of sunlight, and I turn to Apollo.

He looks as broken, in body and spirit, as I feel.

CHAPTER 32

Apollo crawls over to me. Lykou whines anxiously behind him, having discarded Ares's hand somewhere among the spilled gold.

I have no energy nor desire to resist the god's touch. Gently, as though I'm a newborn child, his lips rest atop the wound. I feel a sudden heat surge from his fingertips, and the pain recedes, but not before I brush his hand away.

"Save your powers," I say. "I will be fine. I've hit my head much harder than this before."

"You're delirious." He ignores me, hands rooting deep in my hair to massage my scalp. A warm tingling spreads across my skin, and the painful ache in my brow begins to recede.

"I'm so sorry, Daphne," Apollo says, pulling me close until I'm cradled in his lap. Tears spill down his cheeks. "I should have believed you when you told me of Ares and Hermes's betrayal. Had Ares not fallen victim to the weakening powers of Olympus, I would have lost you." He brushes a blood-soaked curl from my face. "And I don't know what I would have done with myself should that have happened."

A beam of sunlight halos his head, gilding his bronze hair. Apollo waits, his body tense, as I take in his face, his body, everything but those eyes I've seen melt even the fiercest will of steel.

After many long moments, I meet his gaze. My voice is hardly more than a whisper as I say, "I forgive you."

I don't blame him for the ways in which our lives are now inexplicably intertwined. He isn't entirely at fault for the capture of the Muses, or for my involvement. This journey, as much a quest for him to reclaim his father's pride and restore Olympus, is also about the rescue of my brother, and of the answers I have so mindlessly sought.

"Nyx will kill them, Daphne." A ragged sob bursts from his chest. "I can't let that happen. I can't lose my sisters."

"No," I say with a firm shake of my head. "She won't."

Lykou's cocks his head quizzically from behind Apollo. The movement is so puppy-ish that, despite my lingering pain, a sharp laugh bursts from my lips. Perhaps I hit my head harder than I thought.

Apollo seems to think so, too, and resumes healing my head despite my protests.

I stop him with a finger upon his lips before he can say any more. "Now you have to trust me when I say that she won't kill the Muses."

He's still tense, body hard as stone. He softens beneath my touch as my fingers move down his arm and grip his elbow.

"She won't kill them," I repeat. "She is a woman who thrives on power, mystical or otherwise. Without the Muses, she would be as powerless as a mortal, just as Ares is feeling the effects. They are doing this to take down Zeus, not Olympus."

Lykou nods behind Apollo, understanding my meaning.

I push from Apollo's arms and stagger to my feet. The world has stopped tilting, thankfully. "We have to kill her, and Ares, too, before they destroy our families."

"But first, we have to find the three Muses hidden here." I glance around the cavern. "Then we must return them to Olympus, rejoin Theseus, and go next to—" I hesitate, suddenly unsure.

"Eleusis," Apollo says, his mouth pulling into a grim line. "We'll have to reach Demeter's sacred temple before the first frost. Persephone only makes her pilgrimage once a year. If we miss them, our only other hope would be to seek Prometheus's advice again, though Ares may have taken care of him already."

"Do you think he and Hermes have done the same to Artemis?" A chill sweeps through me. "And my brother? They risked so much helping us in Foloi. Now Ares and the shadow woman will know where they are."

Apollo grimaces and shrugs. "My sister is a wily one. She will, no doubt, lead Hermes on a merry chase until the dawn no longer stirs. If anyone can outwit Hermes, it's Artemis. Mortals don't give her enough credit."

In a field of war, where our enemies are ripping the earth from our feet before we have a chance to stand, removing our allies, weapons, and resources from around us, I have little choice but to go straight for the enemy itself. My own words to Hippolyta harken back to me.

"A well-matched army may battle for years, even decades, numbers diminished by foolish actions, battles won by wise men. But even the most powerful army can fall from a single misstep," I say again. "She will think us cornered and wounded. We will have to be quick, go straight for the kill."

Lykou sits at my side, pressed against my legs. His tail thumps, kicking up sand when I reach down and stroke his ears. My fingers and his fur are coated with sticky blood. Even with Apollo's magic and Lykou's feral senses, the three Muses waiting here elude us. They are hidden too well.

I had thought that the test of wit Prometheus spoke of was my battle of words with the Sphinx, but there seems to be more than that. This entire gold-littered room is a mystery waiting to be solved. The Sphinx's last riddle.

Apollo stalks between mountains of gold, having already done a thorough search of the cavern walls, as well. Among the gold are jewels and weapons, pottery and tapestries. A kingdom of wealth, with nobody to loot it.

I stride over to the god when my foot hits a plate. It bounces across the sand, sliding to Apollo's feet. He picks it up, miraculously unbroken, and when I peer over his shoulder, a painting in black darkens the clay surface.

Laurel leaves adorn the edges, spiraling toward the center of the plate where an *auloi*, lyre, and cithara dance.

"Whoever owned this plate before must have loved music," I murmur. I drag a finger over the cithara's strings, and the plate suddenly releases a hum. Gasping, I snap my hand back.

"This is no mere plate." Apollo's eyes light up and the first smile since Foloi threatens to alight on his face. He points to the instruments. "The Muses love nothing more than poetry and music. Calliope loved the lyre, Erato the cithara, and Polyhymnia the *auloi*. This plate"—he holds it higher, angling it toward the sunlight filtering down into the cave—"is the answer to finding them."

Apollo sets the plate down reverentially, as if afraid it might shatter in his hands. I haven't the heart to tell him that, if it was going to break, me kicking it across the room would have surely done it. After ensuring its safety, though, he begins storming around the room faster than if Cerberus were on his heels. He kicks aside a mountain of treasure. The gold sings as it clinks together in a small waterfall and thuds to the sand, spreading across the cavern floor like a gilded carpet.

There, in the mountain's center, is a lyre. Apollo snatches the instrument. "We find their instruments, we find the Muses."

Understanding dawns on me like the rising sun. Lykou and I join Apollo in his search; the cave is large, the hoard of treasure endless, but together we pillage and plunder until all three instruments sit together in Apollo's hands.

"Now what?"

Apollo's mouth opens, then he hesitates, snapping it closed. Lykou whines, pawing at the god's legs. He grabs the lyre between his teeth and presses it into my chest before taking up the *auloi*.

"Perhaps," I start, the idea sounding insane even to me, "we need to play all the instruments at once?"

"Prometheus said that the Muses would be revealed through a test of wit and words, correct?" Apollo asks. When I nod, he continues, "Maybe the two refer to different tests. You bested the Sphinx using wit, and now we must recover the Muses using words. Calliope, Erato, and Polyhymnia are goddesses of poetry."

"So, I recite a poem while we all play these instruments?" I take up the lyre and sit, cross-legged, in the sand across from Apollo.

"No." Apollo takes up the cithara. "I will recite a poem."

"Well, then you better have a good poem ready, because I can assure you that I'm about to make every musician in Greece weep, and not in a good way."

Apollo points a thumb at Lykou. "Surely you can't be any worse than a wolf with a flute."

Lykou's eyes narrow.

My thumb passes the strings, and the noise the poor instrument makes is hardly musical. Grimacing, Apollo sets his own instrument aside and takes up my hands. My cheeks are burning as he rights the instrument in my lap, and places my hands in the correct position.

"You Spartans have always been terrible musicians," he says, though the crooked tilt of his lips softens the words.

"I don't have the excuse of being Spartan." I drop my chin into my chest, letting a curtain of curls cover my blush. "I'm a *Mothakes*, remember?"

"No." He tucks the curls behind my ear and takes my chin in his hand, forcing me to meet his gaze. His thumb passes gently over my bottom lip and my heart skips a beat. "You are neither."

I can't breathe. His face starts to slowly lower itself toward mine, eyes dropping to my lips. His lips are mere inches from my own when Lykou snarls beside us.

"Let's just get this over with." Coughing, I pull away with a tentative thrum across the strings. I'm still hopelessly out of tune. Apollo merely inclines his head and picks up a tune of his own with the cithara, Lykou following with occasional blows from the *auloi*. Once a tentative rhythm is established, Apollo's eyes meet mine again and he begins to sing.

His voice, more beautiful than the melody of a bird, trickles through the air. If I thought his deep timbre intoxicating before, it was nothing compared to this.

The plate begins to glow at our feet, light pulsing in time to Apollo's song.

I stumble over the strings. The plate's glow dims. I pick up the melody once more, cheeks burning, and the light of the plate is suddenly blinding. The glow reflects off of the gold, creating shimmering facets throughout the cave. Lykou dutifully blows into the flute, I pluck the strings.

The plate is now brighter than the sun. My eyes water and Lykou's blowing falters, but Apollo still sings. And, just as his song reaches its crescendo, the plate shatters.

CHAPTER 33

The music cuts off raggedly. Apollo tosses aside the cithara and reaches out with trembling hands to cradle the broken pieces. He looks up at me, anguish burgeoning in his eyes, when a tentative voice cuts through the silence.

"Apollo?"

We all stagger to our feet, spinning around.

"Apollo!" The three Muses clutch the bars of their cage, jumping with joy and faces shining with ecstatic tears. Apollo runs to them, hugging them through the bars with a choked sob.

Two have red hair, one a deep maroon and the other the color of a bright poppy flower. The third has dazzling blond hair, and they all share long, narrow faces. And all three completely ignore me.

It isn't until I pick up a bejeweled sword from the piles of gold, using it to break open the lock of the cage, that they turn to me with undivided attention. Their meticulous gazes travel over my dirty clothes and the curved sword in my clenched fist, lingering on my light curls and gray eyes.

The blond Muse breaks the silence first, covering her heart with a graceful hand. "Our thanks. Without your help, we would have been bound to the servitude of the Sphinx for many millennia. I am Calliope and these are my sisters, Erato and Polyhymnia, Muses of poetry."

Polyhymnia, with the poppy hair, speaks next. "We are eternally grateful."

Lykou rumbles and rolls his eyes, as if to say, "Get in line."

Apollo says as much, "Your gratitude is nice, and I am so unbelievably elated to see you alive and well, but do you have any ideas about how to get yourselves home?"

The Muses exchange glances. "You mean that *you* don't have a plan?"

"Not a plan." I turn to the sandstone wall, and a certain beast beyond it. "But certainly an idea."

When we begin our climb through the tunnel between caverns, the air is close, the journey seemingly infinite. I understand why when my head collides suddenly with a wall in the dark. Ares must have closed off the tunnel so that my newfound allies couldn't come to our aid, which explains why we haven't heard a peep from Theseus. Apollo crowds beside me, his body so inhumanly warm, and punches a fist clean through the wall. The magic of Ares's cage shatters easily, the sandstone wall crumbling to nothing but sand.

I gasp, the wave of fresh air hitting me in the face, before tumbling through the broken opening and into the cavern beyond. Theseus pulls me to my feet; his hands are as bloody and bruised as mine.

"What happened?" We both ask at the same time.

Theseus's eyes are wide, and he points to the wall. "I heard you scream from the other side, and Lykou's howl, but when I tried to follow, the wall sealed itself. I tried breaking through, but nothing worked."

"We were ambushed," I say, throat clenching. "Ares tried to kill us. If Lykou hadn't wounded him, he would have succeeded. We found the Muses, but we must return them to Olympus."

The Muses in question have emerged from the tunnel behind me. Theseus's mouth pops open as he looks them over. But my attention is focused on the gryphon.

It returns my stare with perceptive amber eyes and paws the ground; an iron choker clings to its neck, and the skin beneath is rubbed raw and devoid of the soft, downy feathers on its head, wings, and forelegs. Despite the golden sheen to its feathers, the dark-brown lion coat of the gryphon's body is dull and matted.

Lykou leaps in my path with a bark of warning. The gryphon roars again. I keep my eyes locked with his, ignoring Lykou and the bright claws that can slice me in half.

Taking another step forward, I run a trembling hand down his muscled spine. Despite its extended stay as a captive, bound to the earth and immobile, it still maintains impressive strength, tangible in the muscles covering its entire body.

I turn to the Muses. "Climb on its back."

"Are you insane?" Calliope squeaks. Apollo says nothing, his face unreadable.

Erato takes a step backward into his chest. "That thing will kill us."

I look in the gryphon's eyes, amber meeting my gray, and am filled with an unconditional knowing. "He will take you home in return for his freedom."

The gryphon's head nods. The chains rattle as it drops to its knees. Polyhymnia steps forward first.

"If Apollo trusts you, so do I." Her chin is raised, poppy hair a tangled mess down her back and yet more regal than a queen. She runs a hand along the gryphon's side before swinging a leg over its back.

When the gryphon doesn't immediately throw her off, Calliope and Erato join their sister. Apollo gives them encouraging nods and they climb aboard the gryphon's back. With no time to waste on farewells, I spin the sword in my hand and swing. The chain breaks in a flurry of ruby sparks.

I'm flung away when it unfurls its wings. The gryphon's eyes focus on me as it sheathes and unsheathes its claws, kneading the floor. Mesmerized, I am at its mercy. The gryphon bows and dips its head, taking a careful step toward me, and releases a huff of hot, putrid breath across my face and into my hair. The Muses grip its neck and one another, holding on for dear life. I pray to the Moirai that I didn't just exchange their death for another.

With a deep inhale, the gryphon rises above me on its hind legs. It launches, sending another flurry of sand and dust over us, and vanishes amid a shimmer of vibrant, golden air.

"You're welcome." I cough, choking on sand, and glance quickly back to the others, all coughing and hacking from the settling dust.

A shower of golden feathers flutters down around me. I catch one and the feather dwarfs my entire hand.

The manticore is the first to speak. "There are few gifts greater than a gryphon's feather. You will dream of gryphons for as long as you live," he says. "The beat of its wings will follow you everywhere."

Apollo walks over to help me to my feet. As I brush the sand from my chiton, a useless thing to do—my clothes are primarily sand and dirt by now—he collects the dozens of feathers littering the ground and rips the hem of his *peplos*, placing the feathers in a makeshift sack from the ruined cloth. He hands them to me with a warm smile.

"You will have your freedom, too." I turn to the final creatures.

Theseus curses colorfully from behind me but makes no move to interfere. "But only under three conditions."

"First, you must swear on Olympus to not harm me or my traveling companions. Not in this lifetime or the next. We are taking great risks to set you free, and to take advantage of our kindness will incur the wrath of Olympus."

"Secondly," I continue, "You must not hurt an innocent human, animal, or creature. I understand the nature of your abilities and curses, so I know that this will be an especially difficult condition to follow."

"We might as well just die in here," hisses the fiery-haired demon. "The conditions of our livelihood demand the sacrifice of human life."

"Okay, fine," I say, my grip on the sword tightening reflexively. "Forget that condition. It's obviously asking too much of you to be decent."

"Who is to decide what decency is?" the lamia hisses. "Who is to decide what sacrifices are acceptable for everyone in order to live?"

I hold the sword high in one hand, and a single finger up on the other. "My final condition is that you not align yourselves with the goddess Nyx. A war is brewing on the horizon—I can feel it, and the fewer enemies the better."

I open the manticore's cage first. Despite a warning snarl from Lykou, the beast walks toward me, sniffing the air.

"I will remember your scent for as long as I shall live," he says. His unsettling voice sends a ripple of shivers down my spine. "I am too old to needlessly take some lives like my fellow captives. You do not need to fear the death of innocents because of me. It is simply a gift to be able to die free from captivity. I owe you a debt, young one. Look for me when you are abandoned of all hope."

Without time to second-guess myself, I break the lock of the lamia's cage, giving the beast the freedom she might not deserve.

"When your allies have dwindled, and the roar of battle is too strong, for this act know you can count on my kin," she says and slithers to freedom, her serpentine tail cutting a jagged line through the sand.

I turn to the fire-haired demon. The silver tips of her talons glint as she waves them through the air. "I guess I should be flattered that you fear me above all the others." She grips the bars of her cage, lips pulled back to reveal a hundred sharpened silver teeth. "I'm one of the least dangerous creatures you will face before your journey has ended."

She nods to Apollo. "Some of which are already in your company."

I ignore the blatant warning, swinging the sword for the last time and setting her free. Once she leaves, I turn at last to my waiting allies.

Theseus, face pained, looks to Lykou, then me and Apollo. "I cannot apologize enough for what I did to you, for searching your things, for searching you at that woman's behest. For violating your trust on our voyage. You've helped me defeat the Sphinx, the plague of Thebes, and regain my kingdom. I will be eternally in your debt. Athens will be in your debt. But now your quest needs my aid. I will help you complete your journey," he says all in a rush, words trailing together like a length of braided rope. He takes a deep breath. "What I am trying to say is that I would be honored if you allow me to accompany you and see your mission to its end."

I'm partly inclined to refuse his offer and insist he return to Athens. But now, as I study the sun-painted lines of his face, I finally find myself understanding the Athenian prince. He is led by the words of the gods, shoved through the world by their guiding hands. Everything he's done is to see their will completed.

Just like me.

"What makes you think I need your help," I ask, a small smile pulling at my lips.

His mouth hangs open for a moment. "Well, if I do say so myself, I make a wonderful distraction while someone else does the rescuing."

I take his hand in mine and squeeze tight. "We would be grateful for your distractions."

Now, I want nothing more than to put the entire mountain pass behind me. Ignoring my maelstrom of thoughts and assortment of pains, I take off quickly, not even looking back to see if the others follow.

CHAPTER
34

After buying horses in Thebes, we ride hard across the desolate Grecian countryside, galloping toward the Aegean, over craggy foothills and through dreary mountain passes. Few travelers share our road; our weapons bounce uselessly on our backs. The rise and fall of the sun, day after day, taunts and reminds me of how little time we have left.

So focused are we all on the road, that I nearly don't notice the glaring darkness settling around us, blotting the nighttime landscape despite the rising moon.

Gaping, I jerk my horse to a halt. Apollo and Theseus do the same, following my aghast expression. Our horses whinny in protest but I barely notice above the roaring in my ears.

"Apollo." I turn to the god. "Some of the stars are missing." I point upward where Aquila should be.

"The Eagle is gone, and Ikhthyes." I search the sky in vain for the constellation. One after another, stars begin to blink out of the sky, filling the night with inky darkness. "And Auriga. Where's your chariot? What does it mean?"

"The celestial gods are losing control of the sky." Apollo's face is severe, lips pressed in a firm line. "It means we're out of time."

Theseus looks from the rising moon to the god, and Lykou sniffs the air, jowls pulling back.

"We will rest here," Apollo announces, dismounting without argument. With no trees for cover, we're completely at the mercy of the elements, but our options for camp are limited on this desolate road.

Lykou's trot is slow, and I notice a slight limp in his gait, favoring one of his front paws. Despite his pain, he trudges along without even a whimper.

As Apollo and Theseus tend to the horses, I walk to the small creek running beside our campsite. Hints of silvery fish reflect the moonlight beneath the surface, darting away as I wade into the water.

My thoughts are awhirl as the water laps hungrily upon my dry skin. A sigh escapes me as days of dust and grime wash from my body to float away with the current. Careful not to irritate the tender sunburnt skin of my shoulders and neck, I scrub away the dust of the past days of riding.

First the stars, and now possibly the entire sky. Entire cities swept into the sea, the waves no longer controlled by Poseidon. Olympus is nearly beyond my rescue.

I dunk myself below the surface to clear my clamoring thoughts. Beams of faint moonlight pierce the water, plucking the light from the length of the Midas Curse atop my clavicle. The gold now encases my abdomen almost entirely, stretching from my stomach with gilded vines that reach down my arms and legs.

Lykou belly flops into the water beside me. Lying on his side, the water rolls over him, and he rests his head on a rock above the current.

When I reach over to pet him, his lips pull back in a faint growl that makes me snap my hand back.

I nearly leap from the water when Apollo appears on the bank, the ghost of a smile on his lips. Echoes of the pain that poured from him in the Sphinx's cavern still linger in his face. His hesitation to smile, the lack of cutting jokes, and the way his eyes follow every shadow.

"See anything you like?" I ask in an effort to lift his mood. I carefully force my face into an awkward, crooked smile.

He barks a startled laugh, tipping his head back, eyes squeezed shut. I jump to my feet and kick him with a spray of water that stops his sniggers. Before he can retaliate, I spring from the water and storm over to my horse.

I should have known that my awkward attempt at flirting would only amuse a god with a trail of broken hearts left over thousands of years. Cheeks burning furiously, I hide behind my horse's bulky frame, muttering the entire time about twice-damned flirtatious gods and their thrice-damned perfect smiles. I tear off my drenched chiton and change into my single spare. It's just as dirty and will have to be washed in the morning.

As I finish pulling my chiton over my head, Apollo saunters over with that cocky, infuriating, cheek-burning strut.

"Would you like me to dry those off for you?" He points to my drenched chiton, draped unceremoniously across the back of my horse, and steps closer, pressing me firmly between him and the horse.

His body is an unyielding mass, scorching against my chilled skin. His hips press against mine. My knees tremble despite my best efforts as he reaches behind my head, fingers running gently through my soaked curls. "I can dry these, too, if you like."

His eyes sear me, every inch of his expansive chest burning into my own. My lips part, my breath catches. I'm feeling too much at once. I could kiss him, right now, with a simple rise on my toes and soft press of my lips. I could explore his chest with my hands, feeling his smooth skin that I've admired from afar. I could enjoy his hands as they roam my body...

If I only let them.

The wings of the metal crow dig into my skin, dragging me back to reality. A nagging voice itches at the back of my subconscious, reminding me, warning me that many women have been in the same position as I, and have suffered for it.

I scoff, the sound hardly believable, and pry myself from the immovable wall of his body. "Wouldn't that be a waste of your already dwindling powers?"

Apollo blinks, the fire dying in his eyes instantly, and then shrugs. I try to ignore the disappointment that fills me at his casual dismissal. His heat leaves me when he steps away, striding toward his horse.

Ignoring the ache blossoming in my chest, I briskly rub my arms and ask, "Perhaps a fire instead?"

Apollo shakes his head, turned away so that I cannot read his face. "We should do without a fire tonight. I'd rather not wake up with a dagger at my throat because our fire led a band of brigands to us like a beacon."

"Fine," I snap. After struggling with the ties of my chiton, I throw my bedroll on the ground and collapse.

While I pry apart my tangled curls, Apollo sets up his own sleeping space.

He rests on his side, chin cupped in his palm, and watches me untangle my hair. The otherworldliness of his appearance slides away beneath the moon's gaze, as if rinsed from his skin by a midnight storm. The goose bumps of a chill prickle his arms. Seeing him feel the effects of mortality fills me with sickly dread. The man lying across from me is entirely different from the one who woos women at royal banquets and saunters with the grace of Olympus.

His curls don't shine, and lines from a thousand years of laughter stretch from the corner of his eyes. If I stare closely, light freckles on the bridge of his nose and high on his shoulders stand out against his fair skin, his cheekbones and chin kissed with light-brown stubble.

This human Apollo, this façade drawn up by his dwindling powers, is the one that pulls me in and clouds my feelings. Against my better judgment, and despite knowing all the stories, I want nothing more in that moment than to run my lips across his own.

"See anything you like?" he asks, mimicking me.

I blush, realizing that I've been staring. I pray the moonlight doesn't betray my scarlet face.

His perceptive eyes catch everything, though. "What were you thinking?"

I open my mouth to lie, but instead say, "That I've never seen you look so human."

Something unreadable shifts on Apollo's face. He's rigid, gaze averted, before his shoulders suddenly slump forward and a heavy sigh escapes his chest. "That means that my family's power is nearly gone."

"I still don't understand." I shake my head. "Why, with each return of the Muses, does your power only seem to dwindle more?"

"Because we haven't stopped anything. The powers of Olympus still leave us all the same. All the Muses need to be returned to the Garden of the Hesperides for that river of magic to truly be dammed." He shifts closer to me, stretching his long legs so that they brush mine.

"Then I definitely won't ask of what dwindling power remains to dry my clothes," I say with a short laugh.

He returns my laughter, chuckling softly and drawing his fingers in the dirt.

I roll onto my side to face him, knee jostling his. "Have you ever wanted it?"

"Wanted what?"

"To be human." My voice is so soft, I'm surprised he can hear me, but he nods.

"Once. I asked my father for mortality and he gave me a single day." Apollo holds up a finger between us. He touches the white crow hanging from my neck, brushing the base of my throat.

He's close enough now that I can make out the edge of one of the brands peeking from under his chiton. In the moonlight, it shines like silver, matching the one on his arm, and the tiniest scar on his chin that I hadn't noticed before.

I reach out, touching it gently. "Was it when you got this?"

His breath catches. My eyes lock with his and my lips part.

Lykou climbs from the river and shakes wildly. He sprays both me and Apollo with a deluge of water. Despite my drenched hair and clothes, Lykou is still dripping as he plops onto my bedroll.

I shove him off it, but the damage is done; my chiton and blanket are completely soaked. He ignores my protests, pressing close and drenching me further. "Please make a fire, Apollo," I beg. "I won't be able to sleep if I'm shivering all night."

He rolls his eyes, ignoring the water now dripping from his brow. "Only a small one. The protection of Olympus should be enough."

I wave a hand irritably to the darkness stretching around us. "Protection from whom? Nobody uses these roads but tinkers and oracles."

He doesn't argue, climbing to his feet and calling Lykou with him to collect wood.

"When did you two become best friends?" I mutter, laying my head down. Sleep comes easily to me, despite the rough ground beneath me and the damp of my clothes and bedroll.

I dream of my brothers. We wander Taygetus forest, searching for an elusive stag. I smile and laugh, enjoying this precious moment of camaraderie.

Pyrrhus and Alkaios press forward, disappearing in the brush. My ears follow the sounds of their laughter, the jokes they share. In the waking world, they would never make such noises as we hunt, which would scare the game away.

Pyrrhus moves into my sight, his head bedecked with tall antlers. He waves a hooved hand in my direction, and Alkaios laughs. They turn black eyes in my direction, their jokes and smiles malicious.

I move past dream-painted trees, their weathered gray limbs and jade leaves far too realistic to be the product of my crude imagination, fleeing my brother's taunts. The sound follows me, mocks me, turns far darker the deeper I travel into the forest. The trees twist and warp, spindly arms reaching out to grab my hair and clothes, stealing the weapons from my waist and back before I can react.

When all my weapons are gone, I pass beyond the line of dark trees, emerging into a chamber of glistening stone. Not unlike my last curious dream, this chamber smells of sea. In the surrounding blackness, a steady rumble of waves grows. I expect the man with wings to step from the shadows and share more words of prophecy, but the figure sauntering from the shadows steals the breath from my lungs.

Nyx's eyes glint like rubies in the shadows. She saunters close, grinning wide to reveal elongated canines. She beckons, claws lashing across the distance between us.

Coward, coward, coward, the shadows seem to hiss as I dance from the woman's reach.

I open my eyes, passing from the world of sleep as a cold knife digs deep into my neck.

CHAPTER
35

M ake a single move," a voice hisses against my hair. "And this dagger goes straight through your pretty little neck."

Panic grips me tight, my limbs suddenly numb. My eyes adjust too slowly in the dusk. A slight scuffle on the other side of the camp echoes in the dark, followed by a short grunt.

The fire. That thrice-damned fire led the only bandits for miles and miles to our camp. The remaining embers mock my stupidity as I'm dragged to my feet with the blade at my neck.

My eyes finally adjust in time to watch Apollo stagger forward, a blade pressed against his spine. Even in the darkness I can see the fire burning his cheeks as he flushes with fury. Theseus is likewise dragged to his feet, yelling obscenities at the men who hold them. There is no sign of Lykou.

A summer under the protection of a god and I forgot the most basic principles of travel. Maybe it is best that I can never be drafted into the Spartan army. Neither of my brothers would have done anything as irresponsible as fall asleep without a weapon within reach. Even my sword and Praxidikai are tucked uselessly away in my bags.

"We have nothing of value to you." I want to kick myself for my stupidity.

"We're not after your coin."

Ice coils in my stomach. I know that voice.

"Did you truly think I wouldn't hunt you down for what you did?" King Minos and a contingent of soldiers step into my line of sight, their swords drawn. The man holding the blade to my neck jerks me closer. I try to yank my arm away. His hands are sweaty, but his grip tightens, nails digging deep into my skin.

"Tie up the prisoners," Minos commands, ignoring me. "Toss their belongings in the river and let's go."

My captor's grip eases just enough. I yank free. The soldiers close in. Twenty-five in all. Minos jumps from his horse. His limp is more pronounced, but his movements are still assured as he strides toward me, stopping just out of my reach. "I knew you were no noblewoman. Never in my life have I ever met a woman so unmannered."

"Your methods of deduction are astounding—absolutely brilliant." I force a laugh as Minos's face blossoms a morbid red.

"Let us go, Anax Minos," Theseus says. "You do not want a quarrel with both the gods and Athens."

Minos points to the Athenian. "You, I will ensure a slow, painful death as recompense for your treachery."

"Not if we kill you first," I say, voice low with menace.

Minos moves to slap me. Before his hand can connect with my cheek, I catch his wrist. I hold it suspended in the air, his fingers stretching for my face like daggers.

A choked scream makes us all spin around. A low-pitched howl echoes outside the ring of assailants.

With the distraction, I slam my fist into the nearest soldier's throat. He collapses, dropping his sword. I bend to collect the fallen weapon. Theseus breaks free of his captors and rolls beneath their reach. Apollo paces just outside of the soldiers' reach, twirling a dagger with expert skill. Still watching me from the corner of their eyes, half of Minos's men turn to Apollo and Theseus, weighing the danger they pose.

Focused on them, they don't have time to react before Lykou leaps among them. He snatches one and drags him screaming beyond the camp. White teeth flash, the sharp tang of blood hangs heavy on the air. A moment later, Lykou returns to tear another soldier into the dark, his screams snatched from the air by a terrifying snarl.

I flash the remaining soldiers a grim smile. "Still eager to defend your *anax*?"

Apollo tears through the line of soldiers, as if they are mere stalks of grass and he the farmer's scythe. Blood arcs through the air and screams erupt around me. Ares may be the god of war and bloodshed, but there is a reason Spartans worship Apollo above all other Olympians. The god of prophecy and music moves through the line of soldiers with deadly efficiency and precision, a warrior when threatened. The sharp song of metal meeting metal echoes into the night around us, Apollo and Lykou focused on the soldiers.

Theseus prowls toward Minos with a short sword. He twirls the blade. "You should have stayed on your gods damned island, Minos."

"You killed my son." His face flushes an ugly scarlet, the color spreading down his neck. He draws a dagger slowly from the sheath at his hip. "You killed my son, stole the Muses—my prizes—and I will make you suffer for it. I'll make you wish the Minotaur took your worthless life in that damn labyrinth."

"Says the king who fed the citizens who displeased him to his monstrous son. You are as much a beast as he ever was." Theseus rushes forward. "Let the gods decide who deserves to be punished."

They dodge each other's swings before leaping away. Minos lunges forward and Theseus parries his swing. Again and again, they attack then flee. A grin splits Minos's face and his teeth shine in the moonlight.

Theseus towers above the Cretan king, but Minos excels in speed. For each of my friend's attacks, Minos gets in two or three more punches. They collide and then part. But this time Theseus stumbles away. He struggles to remain upright, his hand pressed over his abdomen.

Blood rushes in my ears, louder than the roar of a furious sea. Theseus drops his dagger and staggers backward. My heart flings itself against my rib cage. Time seems to slow.

Pick up your dagger, I want to scream. *You can't give up, Theseus. Not now, when we are so close to our journey's end.*

But the words are stolen from me when Minos rushes forward. He easily bats aside Theseus's sluggish punch and rams a dagger into my friend's gut.

CHAPTER 36

Theseus collapses in the dirt, eyes locked on mine. His blood pours into the earth. I need to sear the wound before he bleeds out.

I roll across the sand and kneel by my friend's side. I flip him onto his back, ready to stanch the wound. Theseus's eyes bore into mine. His mouth opens and closes, blood beading in the corner.

"You," he croaks out. He raises a shaking hand and presses it atop my heart.

"I'm here, Theseus." A choked sob escapes me. "Apollo will heal you soon."

"You," he says again. He chokes slightly, his eyes desperate, begging me to reverse this. The warm pool of blood beneath him stains my knees. A whisper escapes him, too low for me to hear.

Tears streaming down my cheeks, I lean forward. His bloody lips press against my cheek.

"You were the weapon all along," he says. "The weapon I was meant to find to save my kingdom."

The light shutters out behind his eyes and his hand falls from my breast.

I can't meet his vacant gaze any longer, turning my eyes up to the skies.

And scream. I scream like one of the Erinyes, my fury and guilt and despair leaching into the sound. It's all at once somehow hollow and wrathful. Tears burn down my cheeks, my fingers curling like talons as I grip the front of Theseus's chiton. If the gods can hear me now up in Olympus, they would fear me.

I'm cut short by a demoniac laugh. I turn, my nostrils flared.

"I did say that you could try." Minos cackles a few feet behind me. "The gods saw fit to punish him, not me."

I climb to my feet with Theseus's dagger clenched in my hand. My legs tremble, begging me to leap at Minos. A storm grows in my chest, daring me to release it. I would unleash a tempest upon this man, without any hesitation. *Kataigída*, Ligeia calls me. The name has never been more fitting than now, when a calamitous typhoon threatens to burst from inside me.

In my periphery, Apollo struggles against a trio of captors, while seven of Minos's guards hold Lykou at sword point. A rope tightens around my friend's neck, the whites of his eyes shine in the moonlight.

I cannot lose any more friends tonight.

I toss aside the dagger, baring my arms wide. "Then let us see if the gods will punish me just as they have the King of Athens."

Minos grins wide in acceptance of my challenge. He begins to circle me, searching for a gap in my defense. I follow his every move. His stride is careful, predatory, even. His left leg trails ever so slightly, the knee scarred from an old wound. His breathing is rough from too many nights sitting before a fire.

"Do you know how I managed to garner so much power?" Minos asks. I can almost feel his beady eyes trailing over my body, like the grip of leeches up my arms and legs.

"Rumor is you killed your own brothers for it," I say. His left foot is angled slightly in my direction—ready to leap. Paidonomos Leonidas once told me that my movements were unthinking, reckless, and that I needed to read my own movements as much as others. My feet shift in the sand with his every movement. My fighting stance is level, prepared for anything.

He goes in for the hit, swinging his dagger toward my abdomen. I leap backward. Minos swings again, this time for my face. I avoid his fist and swing out my own. When I clip him across the chin, he snarls with rage.

"Ares told me all about you." Minos kicks, hoping to take me by surprise. *"Mothakes."*

I stumble, and he immediately steals the advantage. His leg swipes my feet from under me. Before he can kick me, I spring to my feet.

"He told me of your precious handmaid, Ligeia." He drags his tongue over his lips and swipes toward my midriff with the dagger. "Of your brothers. How disappointed in you they will be when I bring you before Anax Menelaus and proclaim you for the murderous thief you are."

My heart thunders in my chest. I wrack my memory for the techniques taught to me in Sparta. How to disarm a foe flashes in my mind.

I swing for his unprotected midriff. When he moves to block me, I drop. I swing a foot. And he leaps right over it. I barely raise my arms in time to block his dagger aimed directly between my eyes.

"I've lived so long not through blood sacrifice," Minos says, grunting as he stabs again and I barely roll away in time, "but because of my fighting prowess. You think I don't know every single fighting move known to Trojans? Mycenaeans, Athenians, and Cretans? Even your pathetic Spartan techniques."

His fist catches me across the jaw and my head snaps to the side. I don't have time to cry out before dropping like a stone. Darkness flutters across my spinning vision. I've bitten my tongue and blood floods my mouth.

Minos yanks me back by my hair. I yelp, the sound muffled by the blood in my throat. With a dagger pressed against my neck, he hisses in my ear, "I've killed every Spartan foolish enough to challenge me."

Theseus's blood on the dagger clings to my skin. More tears seep from my eyes. I can see Lykou struggling wildly against his captors. Apollo roars something unintelligible.

"I'll kill you just as I killed Theseus." Minos's knife pricks my throat. "Just as I've killed all Spartans."

But I'm not a Spartan. Not truly.

I grab his arm holding the knife. Using every ounce of my strength, I bring it up to my mouth and bite hard.

His skin shreds between my teeth. Minos roars and releases me. I roll away and jump to my feet. He lashes out with the dagger again. I duck beneath his swing and slam my elbow into his throat.

Minos gasps. Clutching at his neck, his drops his dagger.

"My brothers won't be disappointed in me." I ram my fist into his abdomen before he has a chance to catch his breath. "They will be proud of me."

Minos leaps at me with a wild roar. I dodge all his punches and knee him in the groin. He doubles over, wheezing. Without hesitation, I break his nose.

Blood streams down his face. His teeth are stained red when he bares them at me.

"How did you find us?" I demand. I grab him by the collar of his *peplos*, my fist raised high and ready to knock out his teeth.

The darkness behind Minos's eyes hardens. "You're not the only one with friends atop Mount Olympus."

"Who…" I spin around, the question dying on my lips. Two of the men holding Apollo rip free of their clothes in a flurry of blue and orange sparks. They shift in a burst of shredded skin and hair, transforming into demons with translucent skin and forked tails.

Before charging straight for me.

CHAPTER
37

The horses rear and whiny, bucking their tethers, breaking free to stampede across the camp. The soldiers holding Lykou flee but they don't make it far. The demons leap on their shoulders, one by one, and bite down. I can only look on with horror as each of their throats are ripped out.

Apollo yells at me to run. With eyes black as pitch, the monsters leap at me next, snapping pointed red teeth and unfurling jagged talons. I roll clear of their reach to grab a fallen sword and swing wildly. Blade meets clawed hand with an inhuman screech.

More cautious than its brother, the second beast bares its sharpened teeth. I take another step back, almost tripping over my bedroll in my haste. The beast steps closer, its steps jerky.

Apollo and Lykou circle the first demon. It snarls, searching for an opening. Its mouth rips open in a disgusting gleeful smile, teeth stained red from blood. They meet in a tangle of fangs and claws.

I struggle with my own demon. It lunges for my arm, teeth snapping. I spin free from its reach and slash my dagger across its throat. Steaming black liquid spurts from the gaping line on its throat but the demon doesn't hesitate.

There's a roar to my left. I barely see the blade swinging for my neck in time.

I roll across the dirt. Minos's sword cuts through the air above me, but talons rip through the ragged hem of my chiton.

Without hesitating, I throw a backhanded swing in Minos's direction. He dodges me easily. I spring to my feet just as the demon launches at me. I shriek as nails like the sharpest knives drag down my spine. Blood streams like a river down my back.

I fall backward beside the fire, dislodging the demon. The Midas Curse jumps to my hand, forming a golden glove. Without thinking, I reach into the fire and grab the nearest stick. Flame licks my face as I thrust it at the demon. The beast screeches, clawing at where I ram the fiery branch into its chest.

Alkaios's lessons echo and rattle throughout my skull, telling me to move faster than my enemy. If I could only get behind the beast, like I had the Minotaur. Keeping my eyes on its encroaching claws, I wrack my mind for ways to distract it.

I take my bedroll into both hands and chuck it at the demon's face. I hit my target, giving me just enough time to slam my knife into its heart. The creature falls to the ground. It shrieks and writhes beneath the bedroll, then rattles a final gasp.

Minos doesn't hesitate. With bloodstained teeth, he leaps across the flames, sword raised high. It bites the earth where I just laid. Rolling, I yank my dagger free from the demon's corpse. I jump to my feet and block his next swing.

"Take me by surprise," Apollo once commanded me.

I raise my sword high and Minos raises his to meet mine. My ankle hooks around his bad knee and tugs.

He tumbles backward, falling directly into the fire. His roar pierces my ears. Without thinking, I bring my dagger down and stab right through his throat.

Minos coughs blood. My chest heaves with a ragged gasp. I still grip the dagger's hilt with my golden hand. His dark eyes meet mine, imploring as his mouth opens and closes with short, wordless gasps.

"May you burn in Tartarus," I hiss, ripping the dagger free and splattering the earth with his blood.

A thump and pained whine from behind makes me spin. Apollo rams his own dagger into the second demon's heart, and Lykou lies on the ground.

Without looking to Apollo or the multiple dead men at my feet, I run to Lykou, skidding to my knees at his side.

"No. No. No," I gasp. The Midas Curse releases my hand as I stroke his fur.

His eyes won't open. Hugging his limp form to my chest, I let my tears roll down my cheeks, sobs wracking my chest.

I can't lose Lykou, too. It's my fault he's here. I've dragged him across Greece only to almost get him killed because of my stupid mistake. That gods damned fire. I should have listened to Apollo. I should have let him use his gifts to dry my clothes, should not have let my pride cost me my friend's life and almost Lykou's.

"You were my first love, Lykou," I say, sobbing lightly and petting the blood-soaked fur of his chest. "Did you know that?"

Lykou whimpers, his eyes fluttering open. I kiss his temple tenderly and my tears wet his fur.

Apollo wordlessly strides over to the lifeless demons. He flips over the one I daggered. Its empty eyes watch the setting moon. A sharp hiss from Apollo spins me around, cheeks still glistening.

The bodies of the demons are shriveling, forked tails twitching. They're turning in on themselves, steaming and emitting horrible popping noises as their souls leave this world.

"Ares's sons, Phobos and Deimos." Apollo kicks aside the bodies. "Likely sent by their father to lead Minos to us and make sure we don't reach Eleusis."

I cradle Lykou's head against my chest, and gasp when the wound on my back makes itself known with a vengeance.

Seeing my mangled back for the first time, Apollo strides over. I hiss as his fingers trip up my spine across the deep gashes. The pain immediately fades, and despite the relief, I jerk away.

"There will be scars," Apollo says, sweat beading on his brow. "I cannot heal them completely." Because his power is too weak, he doesn't add.

I thrust Lykou's limp form into Apollo's arms.

"Then use what little you have left to heal him. Not me." My voice is halting and low, the words bitter in my too-tight throat. Theseus's lifeless eyes still weigh heavy in my mind. Another choked sob escapes me. "You don't have enough power left for the both of us."

He relieves me of my friend's wolfish weight and I stagger forward. A haze clouds my mind. I collect my bloodstained bedroll and limp to the creek. Submerging the blanket below the surface, my body follows. My knees slam into the water, weariness and blood seeping from my body to flow down the current. I scrub the blanket with a rough rock, my hands trembling with the effort.

Theseus, Minos, the soldiers, the demons, and the Minotaur. All their faces reflect in the water, their deaths searing my skin more deeply than any claws could. The centaurs who died because of our desperate escape from Foloi, the dead animals in the Sphinx's cages, the Sphinx herself, they all judge me, and they all hate me.

I almost cost Lykou his life. I did cost Theseus his. Tears pour down my cheeks and drop into the water around me. I should have insisted he return to Athens, but instead I let him come with us. And die because of me.

My mind spins in circles, always returning to two words.

My fault. My fault. My fault.

I scrub and scrub, forgetting all about the blood and gore on my blanket, the water around me.

This is more than a mission to return my brother to his human form. This is more than returning to Sparta. Olympus balances upon the precipice, so close to crumbling, and my slightest discomfort cost Theseus his life and nearly cost the world.

I thought the gods invincible for too long. I assumed their protection would never waver. I've killed two mythical beasts, faced the demons of the underworld and demanded a bargain. But the regret inside my stomach still coils like a cornered snake, even as I remind myself of these things.

Strong hands pluck the rock from my grasp. I meet Apollo's gaze as he kneels in the water before me, hands cupping my cheeks. "You're in shock."

It isn't a question, just a statement of fact, and I can't even find the words to deny it. I've rubbed the cloth thin, the stone piercing through the fabric. The sun has risen during my struggle against my blood-stained blanket, and the orange glow of the sunrise lights Apollo's face as he presses it close to mine, his warm breath tickling my cheek.

"I killed him." Each word is a thorn, digging deeper into my heart. "I killed Theseus. It's my fault he's dead."

"You couldn't have known," Apollo says. "All you can do now is continue on so that Theseus didn't die in vain."

"But Lykou could also die." I shake my head. "And you."

"Yes, I can."

I meet Apollo's eyes. "Are you not afraid of death?"

"I would be lying if I said no," Apollo says, gaze earnest. "But I have faith in a girl born by the sea, a girl not restrained by the conventions of men. I have faith that she will save me, that she would pull me from the River Styx if she needed to. Especially if I die before returning Lykou to his human body."

My lower lip trembles, but a small smile tugs at the corners of my mouth. "Truly?"

"You are a gift to this world, my *kataigída*," he says. "A storm, calamitous and powerful. You take root where you want to, listen to no voice of command but your own."

"A storm can kill," I say, voice barely a whisper.

"And it can also give life." His hand cups my head, fingers rooted in my hair.

The blanket slides from my lap, floating down the creek on the irrepressible current. Staring into each other's eyes, we fall into a moment of understanding. I let him rub my palm with a gentle thumb. His hands are littered with calluses, and they are comforting, reminding me of my brothers. When I peer close enough, I can see the barest hints of golden lights in his sea-blue eyes. The scent of cedarwood that follows him wherever he goes is fainter now that his powers are ebbing, but I take comfort from the traces that remain.

Focusing on these trivial pieces of Apollo, I detach from the shock and grief gripping me, drifting back to the world and falling back into my body like the last leaf of autumn.

I return to myself with a ragged sob. Apollo pulls me close, his warm arms wrapping around my shuddering frame as I weep into his chest. We sit there in the creek, letting the cold water run over our legs as the sun inches its way above the horizon.

CHAPTER
38

Buzzards soar above our heads, eagerly awaiting our departure. The air reeks of blood. I avoid looking at the bodies littering the ground while I pack up what remains of our camp. Lykou digs through the soldiers' belongings for anything that might be of importance.

"What will we do with the bodies?" I ask. The skin Apollo partially healed on my back is still tender. I roll my neck to loosen the tightness, but an itch still persists.

"What do you suggest?" Apollo kicks Minos's corpse over. The king's lifeless eyes make me shiver.

"Leave them. Scavenger birds will pick them clean," I say. Apollo looks up at the hollowness in my voice, brows pulled together in a questioning frown. "Except for Theseus. He deserves an *anax*'s funeral."

Lykou barks his agreement and Apollo wordlessly leaves to collect more wood. On a dais of scavenged wood, we lay Theseus's body.

I clean the wounds on his abdomen and braid back his hair before tucking one of the gryphon's feathers in his fist.

"I forgive you," I say to the body. Apollo lights the pyre. The wood quickly goes up in flames, writhing tendrils of smoke reaching into the sky. "I can only hope that you will forgive me, too."

We reach Eleusis nine days later. The temple isn't particularly large or ostentatious, a large chamber surrounded by stone walls and ivory columns. It stands on a hill overlooking the Aegean. The city below is packed with worshippers, though the palace of Eleusis is hardly noteworthy.

I crane my neck to look at Demeter's temple, squinting my eyes against the sun's glare. I can feel her presence here, as tangible as a guiding hand on the base of my spine. The trees lining the road up to the temple are plump with fruit, the city flush with hundreds of different flower bushes and lined with fields of shimmering golden wheat.

Apollo guides us, weary and bedraggled, up the hill along a serpentine path overlooking windswept Eleusis. But, the deeper into the city we traverse, I see the waning of her powers. The fruit on the trees is rotten, sagging and falling to the ground from even the slightest breeze. Gray forms at the edges of flower petals, and the scent of rot hovers in the air.

We make way for many worshippers during our ascent, each flashing curious looks to the wolf at my hip. Cresting the hill, the wind whips around us, urging us quickly and unceremoniously inside the temple.

Inside, high-sloped garnet ceilings are supported by carved, sun-bleached columns, behind which stand walls of midnight-blue stone. In the center is a magnificent white marble statue of Demeter, beautiful and ethereal, rising on the toes of a single foot while she stretches a hand high, reaching for something unseen above her.

Apollo waits on the other side of the statue with his arms crossed.

He smirks when he notices me ogling the statue. "It's a spectacular likeness. Demeter must have had quite a bit to say in the making."

Demeter. I'm here to meet her, not ogle at statues. I turn around, searching the temple for any kind of hint.

A handful of worshipers murmur around the temple. Many bend to the floor in front of the statue in prayer, others shuffle around aimlessly, eyes vacant. Priestesses dressed in brown *peplos* move among them, placing hands on shoulders and kissing foreheads.

Apollo steps up behind me, placing a warm hand at the base of my spine. Tingles course through my body at the slight touch.

"Follow the gryphons," he says, his breath warm in my hair. He points a finger to the paintings above us.

My mouth drops open. Bister paintings of gryphons amid a field of flowers frolic and dance across the ruby-colored ceiling. The rows of gryphons turn in a spiral, starting from the center of the ceiling and arcing out to curve toward a column in the back corner of the room where Lykou sniffs the floor.

Stepping away from Apollo, I move toward the column and place a shaking hand on the cold stone. A fleeting moment of comfort and warmth courses through my body at the connection, and I peer around the corner. In the tiniest of spaces between the wall and the column is a sliver of impenetrable darkness.

I reach for the darkness and a grasping warmth envelops my fingers, a soft hand gently grabbing mine. I let it pull me from the temple and into another world.

My bare feet alight on soft, cool moss, making my toes curl delightedly. I'm in an impossibly beautiful garden. The walls of vines, flowers, and trees I've never seen stretch high above me; birds twist and dive as golden lyres float in the air, playing a soothing melody.

In the center of the garden stands a woman with her back to me. She is tall and thin, her birdlike frame enveloped in a warm yellow *peplos*. She turns around, dropping her *kalyptra* around her shoulders, leaving me speechless.

Ligeia worships the goddess of the harvest above all others, venerating her at an altar in the corner of our kitchen. She always ensured that my brothers and I made offerings to her altar each night and would likely burst from happiness if she stood where I am right now.

Demeter's long, ebony hair falls down her spine in a river of curls, her dark-brown skin is impossibly smooth. Stepping around Demeter, Persephone breezes toward me. Their resemblance is striking. Demeter's appearance suggests she is hardly a decade older than her daughter, the laugh lines in the corners of her eyes and the furrowed line in the middle of her brow the only signs of her age. The lines every mother has.

"You have come a long way, Daphne, for a girl with little knowledge of where you're going or where you've come from." Demeter waves to the garden surrounding us. "Take respite. You have endured much and will endure even more before this journey's end."

Persephone rests a gentle hand on my shoulder. "My mother and I are bonded to all humans through the earth. The human race survives upon the gifts we give them each harvest. You, though, are much more closely bonded to us than most humans."

I don't have to ask what she means. My mysterious heritage still follows me. Just as death does. Theseus's face flashes behind my eyes.

Suddenly overwhelmed, I fall to the ground. Tears stream down my cheeks when I look up at the goddesses. Fingers curled in the moss, I ask, "How many more lives will be taken from me?"

Demeter kneels beside me and brushes the curls from my face. "The Athenian's death was no fault of yours, nor was it in vain. There will be many more necessary sacrifices before your journey reaches its end."

Not exactly the words of encouragement that I wanted to hear.

"My daughter and I will aid you as best we can. Have you learned the identity yet of the traitors to Olympus?"

I hold out my hand, laying bare the crescent moon scar, curving from the base of my thumb to the base of my pinky, for both of them to see. Persephone leaps back with a short scream.

The goddess of harvest takes my hand, her fingers warm as they trace the tender skin. "This particular scar," she says, tracing the faint silver line, "comes from a dangerous creature, one even my brother fears."

"Nyx." My heart thunders in my chest, so loud I'm sure even the goddesses can hear.

"She was condemned long ago to the depths of Tartarus. The consequences of incurring her wrath are always deadly. She does not know justice or compassion, only revenge and death."

"How can a mortal hope to kill someone so powerful?"

"If she could, she would have stormed Olympus and killed my brother long ago," Demeter says. "But her power matches Zeus's. Only a weapon forged by Olympus can hope to fell her."

I pull Praxidikai from my back and hand it to her. "Can Olympian powers be used to forge this into something able to destroy her?"

Demeter, lips pursed, rolls the spear in her hands. "We will do what we can. But you must understand, there is only so much that we can do, and only so far that we can take you."

Panic stirs inside me, fluttering in my chest like a caged starling.

"Apollo cannot make the journey to Tartarus with you," Demeter continues, inclining her head. A dove swoops low and settles on her shoulder. "There is a price to pay for crossing the River Styx."

"A price even a god cannot pay?" I ask, my voice quavering.

"Not until the Muses are returned to Olympus. Apollo is now nearly mortal."

"Do not despair," Persephone says, gripping my quivering shoulders. "We will prepare you for the journey, equip you as best we can. But first, let's see to that hair and get you out of that disgusting chiton."

Songbirds sweep down to strip the dirty fabric from my body as Demeter plaits my hair and Persephone wraps a golden chiton around my frame. The cloth slides across my skin like morning mist. Cut short to float around my knees like a cloud, the folds cling to my chest while held in place by a gold-painted leather breastplate.

"This chiton is made from the strongest fleece in the world," Persephone says, tucking my mother's necklace—alongside the small pouch of feathers and Ariadne's Phaistos Disc—beneath the breastplate. "The golden fleece of Colchis is impenetrable. No weapon made by man can pierce its weave.

"The gold suits you," she continues, rubbing a cooling salve on the various scratches and bruises dotting my weary body. "I'm sure Apollo will feel the same. He seems quite taken with you."

"That is neither here nor there, you little busybody," her mother scolds, softening the words with a warm smile. Demeter tips my blushing face toward hers with a cool hand beneath my chin. A dark-green gecko reflects on the skin of her temple, watching me as carefully as the goddess. "I was right to send Ligeia to you."

My mouth pops open and Demeter nods. "Yes, Ligeia was once an oracle in this very temple, personally gifted by me with future sight, revered and sought by many."

"She still worships you above all Olympians," I tell her, smiling warmly at the memory of Ligeia's *kepos* shrine to Demeter. I feel my smile suddenly disappear at the thought of home.

"Use that sadness, daughter." Demeter angles my face again toward her. "You will always be a *Mothakes*. No amount of won races and fights will ever change that, will ever make you a Spartan. But, if you turn this sadness into strength, you could be even *more*."

"More what?"

"You were born amid tempest and destruction, Daphne. An omen before you entered this world." She stands, eyes locked on mine. "Be the hero my brother needs, *kataigída*. The Storm of Olympus."

Persephone hands me Praxidikai. The wood thrums in my hands, spearhead imbued with an unearthly glow. "This spear is now a conduit for mine and my mother's powers. It might not be enough, nor will it last long. You must hurry."

Girding myself for this last leg of my journey, and possibly the last few days of my life, I take a deep breath. Ligeia told me stories of mortals who dared to enter the realm of the dead. Very few returned with their souls, let alone their lives.

I will arrive in the Underworld like a platter of gold and the darkness will eat me whole like I'm a banquet.

CHAPTER 39

Persephone insists on spending her last moments alone with her mother—should I fail, she will be stuck in the Underworld, the world trapped in eternal winter, with no way to reach her mother ever again—and assures me that she will meet us that night. Apollo and I ride our horses a safe distance from Eleusis, making camp along the beach. Lykou scouts, opting to keep watch duty. Like me, he's restless, eager for this damnable journey to finally be over, and ready to be human once again.

Nervous trepidation licks the back of my legs and arms, itching my skin and urging me to go. Where to, I haven't the slightest. Back to Sparta, and the relative safety of my family's home, or to the depths of the Underworld to finish this once and for all.

Apollo sets about building a fire and avoids meeting my eyes; he fumbles with the wood, trips across the sand, and struggles to make even the smallest flame. When I first emerged from Demeter's garden, his eyes had grown impossibly wide. Lykou had strode over to me, rumbling happily and rubbing my legs, but Apollo had stood there a long moment before remembering that we were in the middle of a crowded temple. I grin, realizing he is still nervous, and take great pleasure in seeing the god unbalanced for once.

The gentle swell of the ocean waves rises closer and closer to my outstretched feet, pushing and tugging the sand as the sun sets. The sea lights with a glorious fire that shifts from blinding orange to warm maroon. I want to rip off my chiton and run into the waves, glorying in the feel of the cool water as it envelops my body.

Fire crackling behind us, Apollo eases down on the sand beside me. "Before you jump into the sea," he says, laughter dancing in his eyes, "know that Demeter is likely to take it personally if you ruin that new dress."

"How'd you know what I was planning?"

"I can see it in your face." Apollo's thigh brushes mine. "You've been itching to escape into the sea ever since we arrived."

He stares across the water, and warm hues of sunset that highlight strands of copper from his hair and fan across his cheeks leave me staring for far too long.

"Can I ask you a question?" My heartbeat quickens, fluttering like the wings of a hummingbird.

"Anything."

"Who is my father?"

Apollo reaches out to take my hand. "You are a child of prophecy, Daphne."

"That's not answering my question."

"I said that you could ask, not that I'd answer."

"So we're back to playing that game again." I turn to him, searching his face. "Why won't you tell me?"

"Would you believe me if I said that I don't know?"

"No." I turn again toward the water.

With a long finger, he tips my chin to face him. "Your father is even more powerful than I am."

I scoff. "If I am no mere mortal, then why am I not immune to disease, or blades? I'm not even gifted with extraordinary senses or strength. What good could the inheritance of a god be if I'll die saving his home, anyway?"

Apollo is silent for a moment, and I frown when he drops my hand. "Those are only the gifts and curses of gods. Your gifts are something more."

I open my mouth, about to protest, when he pushes away the curtain of curls that have escaped their braid. I hold my breath.

His eyes dart to my lips, hunger brewing in his gaze.

I catch his hand as it travels down my neck, placing it firmly between my own. The cool necklace hanging around my neck tells me not to do this. Nyx's words stoke the fire of doubt raging inside me. Loss still fills me with a lingering ache, but I don't give myself a moment to second-guess my actions before I lean in.

Warm and sweet, our lips fold together in a warm embrace. A fire erupts inside me, turning my fears and doubts to ashes. And from the ashes rises a wanting so intense my entire body aches. Our lips meet and then meet again, turning and diving into each other.

I barely resist running my hands along his chest. I moan against his mouth. His hands wind themselves deep within my curls, pulling my hair free so that it falls about our faces. Lykou, the beach, the Muses, my destiny... it all fades away to nothing. I surrender as my carefully built walls fall away with each pass of his tongue across my lips, like a forest beneath the calamitous rage of a wildfire.

But I can't let him burn me whole.

I force myself to pull away. Apollo's eyes are frenzied, filled with an insatiable wanting, his hands still rooted in my hair. His lips part, and I resist the urge to swoop down and claim them again. With a deep sigh, I gently extricate myself from his arms before I do anything I might regret.

"That was...I don't know what that was," I admit, shivering once bereft of his warmth.

"I don't know, either." Apollo says, reaching for the folds of my chiton and grasping the fabric with desperate fingers. I clench his hands, partly to ensure that they wander no further, and partly because I want to feel his fingers tangled with my own.

I glance down at our intertwined hands, my lips trembling. Apollo drops my hands and cups my face. I should stop him, but desire still fogs my senses. His lips move toward mine again.

A deep, feral sound cuts through the air, stilling us both.

I turn slowly, dread rising inside me. Lykou watches us from the other side of the fire. His eyes are lit with fury. His jowls pull back, revealing pearly fangs.

"I'm sorry, Lykou," I say, at a loss for any kind of explanation. "I—"

He cuts me off with a snarl, making me jump. Apollo climbs slowly to his feet, eyes locked on my friend's. The rage inside Lykou narrows, thoughtless and dire, singling in on one person. They watch each other, the wolf's gaze growing steadily more feral until there is nothing left of my friend inside him.

All fury and wolf, he leaps across the flames.

Apollo barely lifts his arm in time. Lykou latches on, fangs digging in deep enough to make Apollo roar. The tang of Olympian blood fills the air.

"Lykou, no!" I bolt to my feet and grab my friend around the furry scruff of his neck.

He lets go of Apollo's arm, twisting in my hold. I drop him before he can bite my face, vaulting back and tripping in the sand.

His fangs shine in the moonlight, red with Apollo's ichor. My breath catches. A war fights in his eyes, humanity and feral nature battling over whether to rip out my throat.

Apollo draws a knife. I stop him with a raised hand.

Lykou blinks. Recognition dawns in his gaze, whites of his eyes growing. His humanity wins that fight for the final time. He spins and vanishes into the night with a howl.

"No!" I yell, climbing to my feet to run after him. "I need you, Lykou."

A cold hand catches my arm. Persephone materializes in the shadows and holds me firmly to her side.

"Let me go. I've got to go after him." A sob bubbles up inside me. "I can't lose him, too."

Persephone shakes her head. "Soon, he will no longer be the Lykou you knew from Sparta."

"But I can't just let him go." I yank from her grasp and grab my weapons, strapping them around my waist. I pull at the collar of my chiton, suddenly too tight. This is my fault.

"You will not find him tonight." Persephone blocks my path. "Even if you wait until morning, there is no time to waste looking for your friend. Who knows how much time we have left until the power of Olympus is gone?"

I look to Apollo to back me up, but he says, "My cousin speaks true, Daphne. We cannot waste more time."

My hearts rages at me to argue, to search for Lykou anyway, Olympus be damned. Despair and frustration war within me, and I scream into the darkness. I scream until my throat aches, a fire filling my lungs. I fall to my knees. Apollo catches me. I curl into his side, my screams tapering into sobs that leave me exhausted and clinging to the god.

As the sun completes its descent beyond the horizon, stars pierce the night sky, one by one. I've never paid much heed to the stories the stars share before, but now I wonder if one of those stories is the tragic story of the Daughter of Sparta, and the friends felled and lost due to her selfish whims.

CHAPTER 40

The absence of Lykou is as tangible as a knife wound, digging deeper with each step. The weight of Apollo's gaze follows my every heavy, determined step. His tension grows the closer we get to the Underworld, a sun rising only to be eclipsed by a cold moon. Together, we walk across the sand, our footsteps muffled by the steady roll of waves and the songs of seabirds.

Persephone walks ahead of us, moving with the gentle grace of a deer across the silver sand. The night is clear and crisp, and the moon, despite being the barest crescent, lights our passage like a beacon.

We carry our belongings on our backs. Praxidikai bounces between my shoulder blades, my remaining daggers strapped to the tops of my thighs and a sword from Foloi swinging from my hip.

A small inlet cuts off the sandy terrain to strike the wall of cliffs to our right. Persephone strides straight into the water. A gust of wind rips past us, diving into the water in a flurry of moonlit sand

and spray. The water begins to ripple and churn, fizzing and spurting around Persephone's body before parting in two crashing waves to reveal a stone path at her feet.

She flits across the stones, dancing like a silver wraith to the end of the path and disappearing into a cave at the edge of the cliffs. Careful not to slip on the sea-slick stones, I follow, wary of being swept away by the roaring waves, and step tentatively into the black abyss.

The water swells and crashes, sealing us inside. A row of orange torches flicker to life, spiraling down the walls of a narrow, curving stairwell.

Persephone moves on, dropping down the stairs that smell of sea brine and smoke, covered with barnacles and fish scales that reflect in the torchlight. Reminiscent of my downward journey to the bowels of Knossos, the shadows climb the walls. I take a steadying breath. Now isn't the time to let my fears control me.

We reach a level of onyx sand that fills an enormous cavern; a river of ethereal black flows before our feet, eating the sand hungrily and stretching far across the dark cavern, red and green lights bobbing up and down within the waves. I take a step back to avoid touching the ghostly waters. These waters would steal my soul and wither away my body before I could even paddle an arm's length across—this is the River Styx.

We don't have to wait long on the river's edge. Silent as the rising moon, a small ship emerges from the mist. No sails, no flags, and not even an oar to guide its passage, the ship cuts through the water toward us. My knees are suddenly weak, and I instinctively grab one of my daggers.

The ship collides heavily with the bank, and the ancient wood groans as it slides across the black sand. Charon's glare measures us from the prow. He's a sunken old man, with weathered, papery skin stretching over his bones and black eyes deep in their sockets.

A gangplank is thrown to the ground by invisible arms; it balances precariously from the railing as Persephone darts up to the deck. We follow tentatively, our arms outstretched for balance. The wooden ship's deck sways beneath my feet in time to the hypnotic rock of the Styx's waves.

Charon lurches over from the prow. One foot drags behind him as he crosses the ship, his eyes focused on my own. Once an arm's length away, he stops and tilts his head.

"What does he want?" I ask Persephone.

Apollo answers for her, his voice a scratchy rasp. "The ferryman for the River Styx always demands a toll." He coughs. "He demands something of value, something unusual. Something worthy of crossing the river of death."

I have nothing of immediate value but the coins I stole from the Sphinx's lair. Withdrawing the pouch of feathers and coins from around my neck, I dump the coins into my hands, offering them to the ferryman. With a look of profound boredom, Charon collects the coins.

"No, wait!" Before I can stop him, he throws them all over his shoulder. They rain into the Styx with a hiss. I want to growl and throttle him, but I won't get to Nyx that way. Carefully reining in my temper, I pull the remaining gryphon feathers from the pouch. They glimmer, despite the dim light, gold and lovely in my callused palms.

This time, Charon smiles and curls his hands in a beckoning gesture. I drop the feathers in his hands, grimacing as I part with their magic. I will worry about my return journey only when I have the last Muse in my custody.

With a nod, he drops them into a satchel at his hip—I've earned my seat on this ship.

But something still eats at me inside, telling me there is more to this ship. Words once spoken, reminding me of sacrifice and oceans.

"The edge of Okeanos," I say, my voice rough and raspy. "This is the edge of the ocean, of the world."

Persephone turns sharply toward me. Apollo's face shares her confusion, their brows so similarly scrunched it is impossible to ever think of them as unrelated.

Charon is likewise staring at me, obsidian eyes filled with a knowing light.

"Two of the Muses are here." I turn to the dark water lapping the side of the ship. "To be revealed through sacrifice."

Apollo sucks in a sharp breath and steps forward. "A sacrifice of what?"

The ferryman cocks his head in answer, considering us.

"Nothing you can buy," Persephone interprets.

"What of my seat upon this ship," Apollo says. He steps forward, hand over his heart. "I will stay on this side of the River Styx if you return the Muses to me."

I open my mouth to protest, but the floor of the ship suddenly opens, a gaping maw from which a shaking hand reaches up. Emerging from the bowels, two Muses step onto the deck, wary and battered, but their faces split into wide grins at the sight of us.

"Thalia," Apollo says, swooping both women into his arms. "Euterpe."

Both women weep, grabbing on to any part of Apollo that they can, clenching his worn chiton and burying their heads in his arms and chest. They likely never expected to see their brother again, believing they would die lonely deaths in the bowels of Charon's ship.

I turn back to the ferryman. He watches me expectantly.

"You knew we would come looking for them," I say, more accusation than question. "Have you no allegiance to Hades? To Olympus?"

Charon shakes his head and, already bored with me, he turns to the front of the ship.

"There must be something else I can barter for Apollo's passage." Unshouldering Praxidikai, the gift from King Menelaus, earned through my sweat and blood, I offer it to Charon, thrusting it forward. Charon shakes his head, waving away my offering with a pinched face like it disgusts him. I pat down my body, searching futilely for another offering as Apollo stands behind me in stunned, unhelpful silence.

"Daphne, stop." I ignore Apollo and yank at Ligeia's necklace.

With trembling fingers, I unclasp it, letting the warm metal pool in my palm. Without a second thought, before I can regret it, I shove it at the ferryman. He takes the necklace in his skeletal fingers, the crow spinning in the air. The necklace stops spinning, and as I'm about to release a sigh of relief, Charon pushes the necklace back with a firm shake of his head.

"For Thalia and Euterpe, Apollo has bartered his passage across the River Styx," Persephone says. Her words echo across the water. "The god of prophecy can now only travel between the lands of living and dead when the last Muse is returned to Olympus."

Lip trembling like a leaf in the wind, I turn to the god that has been with me since the beginning.

"You said I would need you," I remind him, my voice laced with the barest hints of bitterness. "That night in the forest, you said I would need you more than I could know. You were wrong."

"I've never been so happy to be wrong." Before I can protest, Apollo steps forward, gentle hands turning my face upward as he leans down and claims my lips.

With no reservation, I pour every ounce of my burgeoning feelings into our kiss. Desperation, fear, and longing, each feeling stirs inside me with each pass of his tongue across my lips. He is the sun, and I am the Earth, unfurling beneath his lips. The sparks between us threaten to be rekindled, setting my world aflame, and I tear myself away with a gasp.

Apollo presses his forehead firmly, painfully, against my own. "I've never been so happy to be wrong," he repeats, his voice a harsh whisper against my cheek.

"Get those Muses to Olympus," I whisper against his lips. "And I will bring the final one to you."

Before he can respond, I shove away from Apollo. With a last nod of encouragement, he descends the gangplank, Euterpe and Thalia following.

Turning away from shore, I face Charon and Persephone. "Shall we?"

CHAPTER
41

Once, when my brothers and I were exploring a cave in Taygetus forest, we got lost among the winding dark paths. For hours, we followed fragmented lights on cavern walls under the assumption they would lead us outside, but instead they led us deeper and deeper into the mountain. It wasn't until the next day that we emerged again, bedraggled and weary, using the currents of air to guide us out of the caverns.

I always thought of the Underworld, thousands upon thousands of leagues below the earth, to be a similar maze of dread and death, of eternal darkness waiting to devour happiness and light.

To think I had been wrong. It isn't the darkness one should fear, nor what lurks within, but instead the deceitful light.

The Styx reflects with colors, red and blue, green and yellow, all rippling like ribbons in the breeze and, instead of a lonely cavern ceiling, the night sky stretches above. Stars shimmer across the inky expanse, the barest glimpse of the moon reflecting upon the water lapping up the sides of our ship.

Alkaios used to share stories with me he'd heard from the fishermen that visited Sparta, from all the way across the *Mesogeios*, others only from neighboring villages, and some from even thousands of leagues away, from the lands dark and cold. Alkaios told me of magical lights that color the nighttime sky in such places, reflected across the snow-crusted earth. The people living there believe that those colors are the passing souls of their loved ones. The waving colors are exactly how I imagine the white land's lights to be. An ache grows in my chest at the thought. I clutch a fist over my heart.

Persephone's nervous energy is palpable, hands fluttering at her sides and toes wiggling in her *kothornoi*. I remember then that she isn't here by choice, as I am. Swallowing the lump in my throat, I move to her side.

"Are you frightened?" I ask, at a loss for anything else to say.

"Frightened?" Persephone peers at me, her face lit with the smallest of smiles. She looks so much more like her mother when she smiles. "I'm excited. I haven't seen my husband in many months."

I raise my eyebrows. "You're excited to be stuck down here for months, possibly eternity if I fail?"

"Did Ligeia ever tell you that I was once called Kore, and that Hades never stole me away? I came here of my own free will." She looks at me askance. "The stories about him aren't entirely truthful. He never stole me from my mother. Hades is a kind man, and a loving husband."

I tightly grip the railing of the ship. "Apollo has made it very clear to me that the stories about you and your family have it all wrong."

"Well, not all of them." She sighs, inclining her head. "As you've no doubt discovered, there is nothing good in Ares."

"He's waiting there for me, isn't he?" His face flashes in my mind and my knees threaten to buckle. "With Nyx."

Persephone nods. "I believe so. He must have been the one to free her." A grimace sours her lovely face. "I should have been more suspicious of the extra time he was spending down here, but I only thought he was trying to get away from Aphrodite following one of their many quarrels."

I swallow. My throat is painfully dry.

"Perhaps I'm not being entirely truthful when I say that I'm not frightened. I will miss my mother and the living, should you fail." She returns her gaze to the water. "But I can wander the Elysian Fields if I am feeling particularly bereft of sunlight and things that grow. I always have Cerberus to keep me company, and despite what you may think, Charon is a wonderful conversationalist."

My eyebrows rise as I flash the ferryman a doubtful look. He resolutely ignores us, gaze fixed ahead.

"Do you love Hades?" I ask hesitantly, and my cheeks burn as Persephone turns to me with a coy smile.

"Do you love Apollo?" Her smile widens as my cheeks flush further.

When I open my mouth to answer, Persephone's smile drops suddenly. She shoves me to my knees, pressing my face against the deck of the ship.

"Hey!" I struggle against her grip, to no avail. The woman kneeling beside me is as strong as a hundred horses.

Her voice is a fervent hiss against the back of my neck as she shoves me harder against the deck. "Don't look above. The Elm Tree carries false dreams and foolish hopes. To see will lead your soul astray."

Although my eyes are fixed on the deck, I can hear the whispering of the Elm Tree, the cries of my loved ones, and even the unborn children I might never know. They hurl insults and whisper taunts, making promises and offering me bargains. I quit fighting against her grip and let the words of the tree lash over me.

"The god doesn't love you. You're his human plaything to toy with," one whispers.

"Pyrrhus and Alkaios are dead, this mission futile!" another screams. "You killed your mother, and now you've killed your brothers, too."

I breathe slowly, in and out, and clench my eyes shut. My nails dig into the deck, but I refuse to turn.

"You'll never be a Spartan. You're an outsider, always and forever," one taunts. "You spell disaster for the people of Sparta, will incite wars and leave behind a river of blood."

The branches of the Elm swoop down to trail along my spine. Eyes still squeezed tight, I wait until Persephone's warm hand leaves the back of my neck and the whispers dissipate.

"You've passed the Elm's test." Her dark hair fans out behind her on a sudden breeze. "We're here."

My legs are unsteady as I climb to my feet, my knees trembling. The great mouth of the Underworld looms before us. On either side are towering gates of onyx topped with black metal wolves. Through the gates, Hades waits with the ever-faithful Cerberus in tow.

The king of the Underworld is unremarkable by Olympian standards. Hades stands only an inch or so taller than me, and his skin is pale. His face, though appealing, doesn't hold any of that ridiculous, unearthly beauty the other gods are gifted with.

His eyes are all for Persephone, and the face that instills dread in millions of mortals is lit by a welcoming smile. He wraps her in a warm embrace. "My love."

"Daphne," he says, turning in my direction. His face is narrow, framed by long white hair and his eyes an intense, icy blue. "I've been expecting you."

The three heads of Cerberus pull back their jowls to reveal teeth longer than my arms and thicker than my entire torso. The center head watches me, eyes perusing the weapons adorning my body, assessing my threat to his beloved master. Sweat slides down my spine, my fingers itching to reach for the sword at my hip.

Before I can decide, one of Cerberus's head dips, quick as lightning, and licks me from head to toe.

"He smells wolf on you," Hades says, cocking his head. "He thinks you are his kin."

Thinking of Lykou stirs a new wave of sadness inside me. I scratch behind one of the overgrown dog's floppy ears. With a smile and one last pat on his head, I follow Hades and Persephone. A forlorn howl follows us, and I quicken my steps.

Cries, both exultant and despondent, ricochet around the massive cavern as I stand high on a mountain overlooking a valley of death. This is the Underworld, and it is everything my fevered nightmares and imaginings conjured, and so much more.

There is no dark cavernous ceiling above my head, only a sky of blue and ethereal light. If I hadn't taken the steps myself, I would have never known that I was currently far below the earth. Far to my right stretches the River Kokytos, a silver streak across the Fields of Asphodel, with stalks of golden hay and trees with autumn-turned leaves. Beyond the reach of my mortal eyes, on the shimmering azure horizon, would be Elysium and the Isles of the Blessed.

Reaching toward the sky is a cold basalt palace, with tall, spindly towers that reflect the gold, blue, and green of the land surrounding. The giant oak doors of Persephone and Hades's home open to a spacious entryway, filled with sweeping staircases in all directions.

I follow a wide staircase to another massive chamber, this time filled with a dozen hearths and a long table made of jet-black wood. There, directly in front of me, is a towering plate of feta. An insatiable hunger twists my stomach, filling me with the overwhelming desire leap on it and stuff my mouth. A twinge in the recesses of my memory keeps me from devouring everything in sight.

"Never eat the food or drink in the Underworld," Ligeia whispers in the back of my mind. *"Or you will never see the light of the mortal sun again."*

Stomach grumbling, I force myself to turn away from the food. Persephone nods approvingly before moving past the tables lined with thousands of different varieties of food and drink.

Hades turns to the only window in the room, one that reveals the expanse of the Underworld. Whispers trill through, as tangible as curtains billowing in a faint breeze. Voices familiar and not tease the curls circling my ears. I swear Theseus lingers on my shoulder.

I open my mouth to ask Hades about the voices, but Persephone silences me with a sharp shake of her head.

"He isn't *here*." From the way she says "here" it is obvious Hades's mind has wandered away from us, roving the fields and rivers below. "He does his duty. He will return to us in a moment."

I nod my understanding. "And what is his duty?"

"My duty is not to judge these souls." Hades comes back to himself with a weary sigh. His shoulders are heavily sloped as he says, "My duty is not to decide their fate. I only ensure the fallen continue on to where they need to go."

He surveys the fields, shoulders curled inward. "When the Muses went missing, the Underworld was thrown into upheaval. The Elysian now brims with unworthy souls and the River Kokytos runs dry. Even with the other Muses back on Olympus, the powers in the Underworld are unreliable." He turns, his eyes sunken deep and ringed with shadows. "Nyx must be killed and all nine must be returned to the Garden of the Hesperides before the land of the dead overcomes the living."

I hold my sword aloft. "Then let me kill the *kuna*."

*　　*　　*

Descending ever deeper into the Underworld, we follow spiraling stairwells and long, shadowed hallways, the whispers of the dead dogging our steps. Torches of red and green flame light our path, winking out behind us when we pass. The whispers suddenly hush when we reach a final torch, and the green light swells, revealing a hinged iron door. Silence fills the chamber, and my gaze narrows on the blackened iron handle of the door to Tartarus.

Doubts suddenly assail me. My body is a mess of scars and still-healing wounds. I couldn't save Theseus, and even lost Lykou. What if I can't kill Nyx? What if I can't save the final Muse? I am the last person Olympus should entrust with this task.

As if reading my thoughts, Hades says, "What you find beyond this door will test you, Daphne. Nyx knows you are coming for her, and she will try your courage, test your resolve, and all of your loyalties."

"May Olympus guide and protect you. I cannot pass into Tartarus," Persephone says, giving my hand a tight squeeze. "For beyond that door is only death, and my gifts are life."

Persephone and Hades turn and ascend the stairway, hand in hand. The torch begins to die in their absence, so I reach a shaking hand for the door's handle. My arms strain with the effort to turn it. The door shudders open and the stench of death and decay pours from the doorway, sticking to my face and arms like a coat of cold sweat.

I hold my sword high and step into the darkness.

CHAPTER

42

The shadows embrace me hungrily. The Midas Curse wakes suddenly atop my breast, trembling with each step I take. As though it knows what awaits me in the dark.

Thousands of minuscule eyes, glimmering like onyx gems, suddenly open. They're everywhere, clicking and snapping, at my heels and above my face. They follow me on thousands of tiny legs. The air is suddenly too thin.

Nyx has sent her welcoming committee to greet me.

Infinitesimally small spiders, their eyes glittering in the darkness, herd me toward Nyx's next challenge reclining on a throne of glistening silver webs. She waits for me with a coy smile, her long, velvet legs resting on the arms of her throne. Egg-shaped, onyx eyes inspect me, unblinking and calculating.

Arachne, the greatest weaver in Greece and condemned Queen of

Spiders, hops to her feet, stepping toward me. "She told me you would arrive."

Not even a flicker of surprise registers through me at the sight of her. It's no doubt that, having been cursed for eternity by Athena, the Queen of Spiders would have a vendetta against Olympus, too, and would ally herself with Nyx. She and her children wouldn't be the gatekeepers to the land of the most deplorable dead if they couldn't easily kill me.

Torches of silver fire hang from the walls, illuminating her children clicking hungrily around me. Arachne's arms and legs, though spindly, are covered with lavender velvet that ripples with each movement. Her face, also lavender and oval-shaped with large onyx eyes, cocks to the side. She stands and takes a couple sauntering steps closer. Her feet click on the stone floor, claws extending from her fingers and toes.

I brandish my sword in warning.

"Nyx has been waiting for you for a very long time." Arachne takes yet another step. Her spider children do the same. "It's a shame that you'll never meet her. My children will devour you, peeling every piece of skin from your bones before you leave this room."

I resist looking at her face for fear of being held captive by her hypnotic eyes, instead admiring the silver dress that sheathes her lithe body. The spiders circle and Arachne mimics them. My heart thumps wildly in my chest, like the wings of a hummingbird. If I kill the queen, will her children fall, too, or will that only infuriate them?

I take a measured step toward the nearest tapestry, letting my sword drop to my side; I feign a cursory examination. Arachne's silver silk, the same as her dress, is woven into an ocean scene, complete with a ship and leaping dolphins. It is astonishingly beautiful, but I'll never tell her that. I must tease her famous ego to find my way out of this mess. I cannot outrun her children, and I have no idea where to go even if I do.

"You'll have to forgive me. I've never been a fan of tapestries. But is that supposed to be…a porpoise? And is that supposed to be a ship?" I press my face as close to the tapestry as I dare. "My eyesight must be failing me. At first glance I thought this to be a dancing troupe. I must have confused it with a fresco of better quality in Knossos."

Arachne gasps and her spiders skitter frenziedly around my feet.

"Forgive me, I've never been a good judge of…*art.*" I grimace and, pretending to be blissfully ignorant to her rising fury, examine the careful webs suspending the tapestry from the ceiling.

"These are the finest tapestries in all the world," Arachne says, looking upon her handiwork with a fond smile. "Completely flawless works of art. The only thing capable of breaking one of these strands are the claws that weave them."

She clicks said claws in my face. They have a black, oily sheen on their tips.

Noticing my attention to them, Arachne waves the claws close enough to my nose for me to notice their sickly-sweet smell. "The most painful venom in the world. A slow, agonizing death awaits the fool who crosses my path."

She gives them another click, just an inch from my nose. "There is no antidote."

I ignore the goose bumps prickling the back of my neck. The next tapestry is the largest in the room, held aloft by the barest of spider threads. Hanging before a darkened archway—and possibly the only exit in the room—it depicts the gods surrounded by a giant wall of flames. I recognize Athena by the owl resting atop her beheaded corpse. My mouth is suddenly dry.

The warm, cloying air of a sigh presses against the back of my neck. Arachne hovers behind me. The still-healing scars on my back stretch painfully as I shiver and resist shoving her away. Her claws linger above my head.

"What lovely hair you have. Like a field of wheat beneath a setting sun," she muses. Sweat beads on my brow. "I once knew a princess with hair like yours. As lovely as the dawn, and as stubborn as an ox. My children tell me she died an excruciating death."

I spin around, putting my sword between us. "Why ally yourself with Nyx? What do you stand to benefit if Olympus falls? Is your grudge against Athena worth the ruin of mankind?"

"What do you stand to benefit if you succeed? Do you really think that Zeus would just let a weapon such as yourself go once the Muses are returned?" She smiles, revealing a thousand silver teeth, like a row of diamonds.

"You and I, we're of the same thread," Arachne continues, brushing aside my sword like it's nothing more than a wisp of smoke. "We are victims of the gods, forced to take part in their wicked games."

"I am no pawn," I say, the words a growl between my clenched teeth. I am tired of being told otherwise, as though I have had no choice. I chose to save the Muses and seal my part in this journey.

Her face is so close to mine. I can see hints of blue in the lavender fur on her cheeks, a red sheen in her dark eyes when they meet the torchlight. I wonder what she looked like before Athena cursed her to this misery. Was she a beauty of great renown, or homely? Either way, it was enough. Her skill with thread may be legendary, but she is famous above all for her arrogance.

Turning, I reach for the largest tapestry. "This one is lovely. Is this truly spider silk?"

Her hand lashes out. My sword parts it from her arm in a spray of blood. I catch the falling hand and Arachne's spiders leap forward, the room filling with their furious screeching. She collapses to the ground, screaming and clutching her bleeding stump of a wrist.

I fling myself toward the tapestry and cut its feeble binds with Arachne's clawed hand. It falls, enveloping the still-screaming body of Arachne. Her spider kin screech and rush to separate their queen from her woven prison. Victory surges through me. I leap toward the archway.

But something snatches my feet back. I slam to the ground with a gasp. My head snaps back. My feet are glued to the sticky fibers.

I swing my sword at the tapestry, only for it to cling to the fabric. The spiders reach me then, their teeth like a thousand needles digging into me. A scream pierces my lips, fire shooting beneath my skin. I writhe in agony as their venom fills my veins.

Arachne begins to cackle, the sound echoing about the chamber. The thread falls apart like a silver wave beneath a swish of her hand. She emerges slowly, clutching the stump where her other hand used to be. Black blood pours from the wound. "You will regret that, mortal. The next threads I weave will be made from your skin and hair. That venom is my final gift to you, human. Pray it takes your life before Nyx does."

I climb to my knees and the lair tilts, the floor spinning away. Using Arachne's hand, I slice away the binds holding my sandals to my legs and kick the shoes free.

Throwing my aching and bleeding body through the black archway with a ragged gasp, I tumble into impenetrable darkness.

CHAPTER
43

I fall, thrashing and spinning, deeper into the Underworld. The darkness comes rushing up to meet me, singing in my ears as it flies by, and I meet the bottom of the abyss with a giant splash.

I gasp upon impact, swallowing a lungful of the black water that surrounds me. The cool water eases the burning pain coursing through my arms; the bites are already inflamed and swollen. Aching, I swim toward shore and drag myself across the sand. My entire body turns in on itself, head spinning as I heave an impossible amount of water from my lungs.

I flop onto my back, spread-eagled across the sand. The ceiling stretches above me in an endless, black expanse. I can't see where I leaped from or where to go next. I've fallen into a tomb with no escape, to die slowly and painfully, the venom overcoming my body as Nyx succeeds in destroying Olympus.

A choked sob escapes me. "Damn Artemis and damn all of Olympus.

Damn Tartarus and whatever *suagroi* thought it would be a good idea to leave Apollo in charge of the Muses," I scream, pounding the sand.

The only weapons I have left are Praxidikai and a single dagger. My sword is with Arachne, and I lost her clawed hand in the fall. The venom will kill me whether or not I escape this hole and slay Nyx. Even if I save Olympus, I'll never see my brothers again. Because of yet another careless mistake.

"I'm going to die here," I say to nobody in particular. Tears stream down my face now, and a hysterical laugh bursts from my lips. It echoes around the cave, rising into a piteous screech. It isn't until my throat burns that I stop, coughing and gasping for breath. I brusquely rub the tears away with the back of my hand.

A shimmer of red light sparks to life on the far side of the water. It bobs up and down, a ball of flame dancing midair. My instincts scream at me to turn away, to find another way from this black abyss. But my options are few.

Staggering around the lake, I let the light guide me. When it disappears, I run a hand along the edge of the cave until I reach an opening in the stone wall at my feet. When I crawl through, a dozen red torches burst to life to reveal a long tunnel.

Who waits for me at the end is hardly surprising and not in the least bit welcome.

Ares's arms are crossed, his feet firmly planted apart in the sand. The crimson lights of fire make his face all the more menacing, a collection of sharp angles and panes half hidden in shadow. The vulture blazoned across his chest is midflight, wings stretching from shoulder to shoulder.

"*Prodótis,*" I say, my voice a tired croak.

"You killed my children," he says, his voice a haggard rasp, hardly the commanding man from the Sphinx's cave. Though he had no love for his children, they were still *his*, and I took them away from him.

"They threatened my life and almost killed my friend," I say. "What excuses do you have for the crimes you've committed?"

Ares grins chillingly, and saunters closer. "This has nothing to do with Nyx." He waves an arm, revealing the stump where his hand used to be. "The gods, your dearest Apollo, my kin and I, are not so different from mortals. We play games, we drink, we make love, we create civilizations, and we play with powers that are greater than most could ever comprehend. We pretend we are worthy of these powers, but inside of us is a weakness. We crave love and admiration, but, unlike you, we also need it to survive. Without your love and admiration, we are worthless. This has everything to do with the powers my family so carelessly wields. They don't deserve the gifts of Olympus."

"And you believe you do?" I scoff. "You think this won't affect you? Your powers will abandon you just as they have your family. Otherwise you'd have your hand back by now."

Something unreadable wars in Ares's dark eyes. Doubt, perhaps, or even insecurity—I cannot place it. But then it's gone, vanishing in a blink. "There was a war, long before even I was born. My father was the victor, his prize, Olympus."

I blink. Words escape me.

Ares sneers, and I half-wonder if his face is permanently set in such a disagreeable expression. "But he doesn't deserve either the power or throne of Olympus. I will see both to their rightful heir."

"And who is that?" I cough, my mouth suddenly sharp with the taste of blood. I haven't got much longer.

"I'm sure you're hoping that your death will still benefit those traitors that call themselves gods." Ares's nostrils flare. "You hope that I will divulge all my secrets for you to take to your grave, and promptly to Hades's eager ears. I'm no fool, mortal."

"Pity."

He leans forward, taking a deep sniff from the curve of my neck. I shudder as his eyes spear through me, lit with the flames of a thousand fires.

"I can release you from your mortal toil, spare you the agony of venom's slow demise. Nyx would be so angry with me." He smiles, as though the idea of her wrath excites him. Revulsion churns my stomach as he drags a hand down the side of my face, brushing the curls from my eyes before gripping me. He is much bigger than she is. Inhumanly so. She was also trying to goad him before so I will stet this one. "You would look far prettier surrounded by your own blood."

His grip on my throat constricts with my every ragged breath. My lungs burn and stars litter my vision.

"Save the dramatics for your next play, Ares."

Ares spins around, releasing his hold on my throat. Coughing, I stagger to the nearest wall, torn between panic and relief as Hermes saunters toward us. His dark, wiry curls are dull and his tan skin flushed with a sickly sheen. He's wearing his famed winged sandals and carries his *kerykeion* again, but the animals on his skin are still, lifeless even.

"Your unwelcome presence is as repulsive as ever, brother," Ares says between gritted teeth, looking over his brother with barely concealed disgust.

"Do any of your siblings like you, Hermes?" I ask, the words rough and rasping in my bruised throat. "The tales of your games don't exaggerate too much, it seems."

He tilts in my vision as the spider venom takes hold. I brace a hand against the wall. "Don't you think you're taking this game a bit too far, though?"

Hermes considers me, and I search desperately in his gaze for some hint that this is a ruse, that he did not truly ally himself with them. Any lingering hope I have sputters out like a dying flame when he turns to Ares and says, "Nyx would have been very cross had you stolen her chance to torture the girl."

"She can consider it payment," Ares says, meaningfully waving the stump where his hand used to be.

I pull my last dagger from its sheath on my thigh. "Get out of my way, both of you."

"Did Apollo ever tell you how the Muses went missing in the first place? Or why exactly he felt compelled to join you on this foolish quest?" Ares turns toward me.

"Yes." I should ignore him. I should take what is left of my strength and storm past them both. "He's shared everything with me."

"Not everything," Hermes says, arching an eyebrow and having the audacity to look almost bored.

Ares swaggers around me, like a child enraptured by butterfly, only to pluck its wings. He trails a callused finger down the delicate length of chain around my neck, stopping just above the white crow. "This was a gift to Apollo's greatest love.

"As I'm sure you've heard and maybe even experienced for yourself, he is quite the romantic. Judging from the pathetic, lovesick look in your eyes, you are no less immune to his charms. You are not the first to fall prey to them," Ares continues. "Centuries ago, there was a princess named Koronis."

The name stirs a vague memory in the back of my mind, nothing more, but still a sickly feeling sweeps over me.

"Apollo loved her more than life itself. More than Greece and more than his family. He was willing to sacrifice being a god for her. Until his spy, a certain white crow"—Ares hooks a finger under my necklace, jerking me forward—"told him Koronis didn't share his feelings. The princess had fallen in love with another. In a fit of jealous rage, Apollo and his sister, that vengeful little minx Artemis, stole her throne and left Koronis stranded in the middle of the sea with her lover."

The cold in my stomach spreads like a blizzard, freezing my veins like arms of hoarfrost. "You're lying."

Ares makes a noise in his throat, looking me over with something akin to pity. "I *never* lie. Hermes, on the other hand—" He looks to the herald. "His motives are always questionable. But that is beside the point. The kingdom of Phlegyantis fell without its princess, forgotten by the world, and with it a mighty sum of Olympus's power. Zeus fell into a rage the likes of which the world hasn't seen since.

"He and Apollo fought for a hundred years, blows between the god of prophecy and the Olympian *anax* leveling mountains and turning continents to ash. Zeus beat his son within an inch of his life. Apollo's ichor flowed freely on the final day, and the earth smelled most divine." Ares's face is suddenly blissful, a smile pulling at his lips. "I will never forget that smell, nor the stirring of hunger inside me. Regretfully, the storm and prophecy gods came to an accord. For a millennium, Apollo has kept watch over the Muses as punishment."

Apollo's eyes were cold as he once told me, *"Ares, as cruel as he can be, is spurred by his desire for war. And I've done far worse, spurred by the taunts of my heart."*

My knees threaten to buckle beneath me. I tell myself it's the venom, but my heart knows that for the lie it is.

"I'm sure you've heard many times now how much you look like her."

I don't—can't—meet his eyes. "Koronis?"

Ares nods. "You would have loved Phlegyantis. Their women were strong, fighters like yourself, and independent."

Ares drops the necklace. It hits my chest with a dull thud, as though it is hollow and abandoned by my heart. "Have no doubt that Apollo loves nobody so much as he does himself. Especially not you."

I swallow, but my lungs can't seem to get enough air. Notching my chin high, I refuse to let the god of war see the tempest of agony he has stirred inside me.

"Why, Hermes?" Tears of defeat prick the corners of my eyes. "Why betray your own family? I thought you loved the Muses."

"Our father doesn't deserve that throne." Hermes steps between us. His body is an impassive wall. "That is why I'm doing what is best for them. What Apollo is too selfish to do."

"Is that the lie you're telling yourself, brother?" Ares sneers.

Hermes dismisses him. "You can stop this, Daphne."

"Hermes," I say, a pleading edge rising in my voice. "Just tell me why."

"This is beyond the Muses." He takes another step toward me. "My family's history is drenched with blood, and more betrayal than you could imagine."

"Try me." I sneer. "I've lived through quite enough of both just this summer."

"It's true. Betrayal and Olympus seem to go hand in hand." He brushes a sweat-soaked curl from my face. "But I can change that."

My heart thuds. I whisper, "You want the throne for yourself."

Hermes's hand freezes in the air between us, his eyes slowly narrowing.

"Perhaps the mortal is wiser than I gave her credit for," Ares says with a chuckle.

"Daphne." Hermes's face is suddenly pleading. "I can heal and return you to Sparta, wipe your memory clean."

"But you can't bring me my brother back." I raise my chin. "And no amount of power on the Olympian throne can raise the Muses from the dead."

Hermes stills, azure eyes widening. "What did you say?"

I bare my teeth, pressing my face close enough to his that he could smell the hatred on my breath. "I said that you could never bring the

Muses back. Ares threatened to kill them, and he'll succeed if your father is powerless to protect them."

He steps back as though slapped, his body beginning to shake. "You're lying."

"I don't lie," I snarl. "He wants to steal their power for someone else."

We turn as one to Ares, who has stilled behind his brother, nostrils flared and shoulders tense.

"Brother." He raises his two arms, one hand, between them. "Don't do anything rash."

Hermes holds his *kerykeion* aloft. "You would murder our sisters? The Muses are our family, siphons to the power of Olympus."

"We don't deserve their power, Hermes," Ares yells, waving his stump through the air between them. "I will do whatever it takes to keep it from falling into the wrong hands."

"Even murdering our family," the messenger says, each word rising to a roar. The walls of the cavern begin to shake, red lights waving around us.

"When did you become so sanctimonious?" Ares sneers. "Suddenly concerned only when your own powers come into question."

I could walk past them, and they would never notice.

Instead, while his back is turned, I take my last dagger and slam it into Hermes's back.

With a yelp, Hermes falls to his knees. The shaking stops and the lanterns still. I wrench the blade from his back, and he convulses before falling face-first into the dirt. I level the ichor-stained dagger at Ares's heart.

He doesn't betray even a sliver of fear. "Wise to pit us against each other.

"But he's not dead yet, and neither am I." Ares steps over his brother's body, smiling crookedly. "Perhaps the wiser choice would have been to stab me first?"

He's so close now. Near enough for our chests to brush with my every ragged breath. "Perhaps *you* should have stabbed *me* first?"

He pulls back a fist, lightning quick. I don't have time to flinch before he punches my stomach.

And howls in pain. "What treachery is this?"

He cradles his hand, the knuckles already bruising. My golden chiton isn't even wrinkled.

"With that pretty dress or not, I can still kill you," he says with a snarl.

He's right. Even with my magic dress, with my power-imbued *dory*, and even if I was at my full strength, Ares could overpower me. No amount of skill could help me best the god with a thousand years of war beneath his belt. He knows that, too.

"I can snap this as easily as I would a branch." He brushes his callused knuckles up and down my bare arm.

I look anywhere but at his eyes boring into my face. I fix my gaze on his bare chest. The vulture on his chest still hasn't moved, wings still stretched wide. Its eyes are locked on mine, unblinking and utterly still. His unmaimed left hand still rubs my arm, the other hanging uselessly at his side. My fingers tighten on the hilt of my dagger.

He notices the movement and sneers. "Toss the dagger aside, mortal, before I break the wrist that holds it."

"I have a better place for it."

I slash the space between us. Ares reaches out to block my swing with his good arm. I toss the dagger between my hands, catching it neatly in my left. I jab past his right arm, reaching handless to stop me, and ram my dagger into his side.

It clips a rib before sliding to the hilt, jarring my arm. Tears of rage and agony shine in Ares's eyes. He falls to his knees, clutching the dagger with a gaping mouth. Black ichor beads in the corners of his mouth. His dark hair falls before his face in wisps, a shaded mask of fury.

"Without the power of the Muses, you are mortal, the same as I." I drag a finger along the wings of the vulture, its stillness betraying Ares's burgeoning mortality. The god of war collapses to the ground. Stepping over him, I stride into Tartarus.

CHAPTER
44

In the center of Tartarus is a pit in which the most damned of souls wait, crying and moaning, tortured for all eternity. And there, staring at me amid the chaos of flailing souls, is a woman. In the bedlam of fighting prisoners, it takes me a moment to realize I've found her. She stands out as the single calm soul, sitting in the middle of the pit and watching me with dead eyes.

"And the last, the most pure, joins Tantalus in his endless suffering, demanding a sacrifice of body and soul."

Elation fills me. I'm buoyant, an inkling of hope slipping through the weariness and defeat. I could actually succeed and still save the last Muse. But first, I need to find a way to free her from the pit.

I stride around the edge of the pit as close as I dare. Many of the prisoners spot me, watching from the depths of their prison and rouse themselves from their collective stupor, fighting one another in a desperate bid for freedom. I'm helpless to do anything for them. I turn around to look for anything useful and find the tree that taunts the prisoners. From the tree's branches dangle fruit, barely out of reach of the souls' grasping hands. Along the length of dark-brown wood climbs a stretch of vine.

With a grim smile, I begin up the tree. I push and pull my exhausted body. My hands are sweaty, making my grip on the tree tenuous at best, and my arms are growing steadily numb from the venom. Every muscle in my body trembles and my temples throb from clenching my teeth so hard. I strain against the pain and pull myself onto the branch.

A couple of short jerks affirm the vine's sturdiness and strength after I rip it away from the tree. Fruit drops among the prisoners below and chaos erupts. The prisoners fight and screech over the prizes, but none notice when I drop the vine down to the Muse.

She ignores the fallen food and wraps the length of vine around her hips twice. Straining against the pain and her weight, I heave the Muse higher and higher, inch by inch. She watches me, holding on so tight her knuckles are white. A prisoner notices her ascent and emits a horrible, inhuman screech. The Muse kicks at the prisoners' flailing, grasping hands as they climb atop one another to grab at her.

Just as she is even with the edge of the pit, the world begins to shift beneath me, and Tartarus begins to swim in my vision. Whether by the failing powers of Olympus, or by the venom winning its fight for my body, my time is up. And with trembling hands, I give the vine one last mighty pull before my eyes slide shut and darkness overtakes me.

My broken and battered body is being dragged across the length of Tartarus like a corpse to its grave. Violent convulsions course through my frame as the venom takes complete hold. A cool hand circles my ankle, a relief against the venom's fire, pulling me across the rough ground.

I groan. The hand drops my ankle and a pained cry escapes my lips. A voice calls out to me through the haze of pain. The sound is muffled, but grows louder and louder, drawing me inexorably from the delirium.

"Please wake up," a girl begs. "We haven't much longer before she finds us."

It feels as if the entire Aegean crushes my body. I must have fallen from the tree when I blacked out. My head aches something fierce, and careful twitches of my fingers let me know that none of the bones in my hands and arms have broken, by the grace of Olympus. But there's a suspicious lack of feeling in the toes of my right foot.

Lifting my head, my eyes find the mangled mess that used to be my right leg.

Something between a gasp and sob chokes itself from my lungs. Distracting myself from the horror of my body, I look to the Muse, and I can't stop the plea spreading pitifully across my face.

"My name is Kleio." She lays a hand over her heart, offering a small smile that warms me despite the pain. She hovers over my leg, and I'm grateful to see that she collected Praxidikai, which is slung across her shoulders. It might be nearly impossible to throw with only one leg to balance on, but it will still be easier than with a broken arm.

"You are lucky that you wear the dress of Chrysomallos. It saved your ribs from shattering in the fall. As for your leg, I tried to heal you," she says, fingers fluttering over my mangled limb. "But my powers have left me."

"It would have been a waste," I say, accepting her hand to pull me unsteadily onto my good leg. In a voice too low for her hear, I add, "I'm going to die soon anyway."

To see how much weight I can bear, I take a hesitant step on my bad leg. A bolt of blinding pain rips through my body. I collapse to the ground with a short scream. It's a long moment of agony before I can climb to my feet again. Kleio flutters around me.

"With you as a guardian, I know we will escape," she says with forced confidence, her voice too high pitched, too sharp to fool anyone.

My mind spins in a maelstrom. Will the pain never cease? Will the tests never end? Through the pain and rage is a resignation that rises with my every agonized step. The pain in my leg matters nothing in the grand scheme because I will likely die before even seeing this journey to its end. All that's left to me now is to return the final Muse to Olympus and hope that it is enough to restore power to Olympus.

"We must hurry. Something dark and dangerous hunts us." Kleio glances to the shadows, pressing close.

A cold draft settles around us. I sense it, too, whatever waits for us, watching from the shadows. Rivulets of sweat trail down my spine.

Nyx.

My weight sags on Kleio's poor shoulders and my broken leg drags behind us. Tears spring into my eyes with each step. Little pitiful, humiliating mewls of pain escape my mouth with every pebble my leg bounces over. It is all I can do not to stumble back into unconsciousness when the heel of my broken leg collides with a stone in our path.

"Do you know where we're going?" I whisper, though I don't know why. Whatever lurks in the dark clearly already knows that we've arrived.

Kleio shakes her head emphatically. "There are only two ways to leave Tartarus, and I choose to avoid an angry Ares and Hermes. They are, by the way, very much alive." One of her hands latches firmly on one of my upper arms, a cool balm against the burn of venom. "Couldn't you have just killed the traitors when you had the chance?"

I shrug apologetically. "I thought I did."

We move deeper into the impenetrable darkness. Praxidikai's spearhead still glows, though the light is faint and sputters the deeper we go. A cloud of cold mist wafts the briny, salty smell of sea over us, at once both a relief, and troubling. With the mist comes a low rumble, building louder and louder.

We limp into an enormous cavern. In the center is a raging pool. The water heaves from side to side like storm-tossed waves. Above us is a cavernous ceiling that mirrors the one above the pit, covered with glowing stalagmites and gaping crevices to reveal the starry sky above. We collapse at the impossibility of it all, Kleio to her knees and me to my side, mouths agape and breath ragged.

We stare despondently up at those taunting holes, and her eyes brim with tears. I feel the beginning of tears in my own eyes, though mine are the result of the searing pain coursing through my body.

It is in that moment, when our hope has fled, that the darkness chooses to speak to us.

"You've come far, Daphne of Sparta." The voice is sickly sweet, wrapping about us like a spider's web. "But you are weak. You are failing. Who will save you now that you cannot save yourself?"

Born from chaos and darkness, Nyx stands before us. The living personification of night, prepared to spill any blood keeping her from shrouding the world in darkness.

The Midas Curse trembles on my belly, flaring across my skin to encase my chest and arms. Either Artemis's last gift to me, or the final tightening of her leash.

Kleio gasps and ducks behind me. I let her cower, pulling the last weapon in my diminished arsenal from her shoulders. The white wood of Praxidikai slides to my waiting fingers. I balance on my good knee, aiming directly into the heart of the Queen of Darkness.

Nyx doesn't even spare the *dory* a cursory glance, her throaty cackle rocketing around the cavern. "My powers are not tied to the Muses. Your mortal weapons are useless."

She saunters close enough for me to see the soulless darkness behind her eyes, the malevolent twist to the smile pulling her lips back. Her teeth are a shocking white, just as I remember, framed by dark, plump lips, and from her fingers extend long, ruby talons that click together with each step. Grimacing against the pain, I heave the spear back, poised to throw. The spearhead's unnatural light flickers.

She takes another step forward. I let my spear fly.

My aim is true. The bronze butt protrudes from the goddess's heart, the *dory* sliding clean through her body. The barest twinges of victory flutter in my heart. Ichor begins to drip from the wound.

Nyx gives an exaggerated sigh, sliding the spear from her chest without even a grimace. Both my heart and soul crumble as she snaps it cleanly across a knee.

"Silly girl," she says, flashing a disappointed smile. She strides toward me, her eyes oblong ruby disks in a face of terrifying beauty. The shadows leap from behind her, dark tendrils reaching across the distance between us. "Nothing can save you now."

CHAPTER
45

The stench of death hangs in the air, a warning that waits on the wings for the goddess of night to break me.

I raise my fists and ignore the throbbing, incessant pain in my leg. I will go down fighting to my last breath. Nyx takes another step closer, her hips undulating as the shadows rise around her, reaching across the distance between us.

I must buy us time to figure out a way to escape. I cannot kill Nyx on my own, but if I can get Kleio to Olympus in time, the gods might be able to reclaim enough power to help me.

"Why now? Why destroy Olympus and your kin?"

"There's more to Olympus than your dear Apollo has shared with you. This is no mere revenge scheme." Nyx waves a hand toward me. A shadow leaps from her palm, and I stumble backward to avoid its reach.

A piercing scream escapes my lips as I make the mistake of stepping onto my broken leg, but Kleio keeps me from falling to the ground. My vision spins, fixing on the rough walls, slick with sea mist. I shuffle backward, herding Kleio away from Nyx.

"There's no way out," she sobs. Her small fingers squeeze the tops of my arms.

We stand dangerously close to the edge of the pool. The water laps at the edge, drenching our legs with its spray. I glance quickly down at the water, now a raging whirlpool with no bottom in sight. Could it be our last hope?

"You're going to have to jump," I yell over my shoulder, struggling to be heard over the water's roar.

"You can't be serious. I'll be killed."

"There's no other way out," I say over my shoulder. "What other choice do you have? You need to get back to Olympus and send help. I cannot defeat her on my own."

I glance quickly behind me. Kleio hovers at the edge of the water, biting her lip.

Nyx smiles again. "The Muse can try to escape. Nobody leaves Tartarus without the will of the gods."

"Then it's a good thing the gods demand her return." I turn once more to Kleio and yell, "Jump!"

She leaps into the water, disappearing among the waves. Nyx's smile turns predatory. I will buy Kleio time even if it is with my dying breath.

I swing my fist. It cracks against her chin and Nyx's face snaps to the side.

Then, with impossible strength, she tosses me through the air. I land on my bad leg and scream so loud it must be heard all the way in Sparta.

Nyx's smirking face fades in and out of my blurred vision. A painful shudder rips through me. With a clawed finger, she hooks my mother's necklace and rips it from my neck. Without even glancing at the white crow, Nyx tosses it among the waves. She slashes my breast then, claws screeching across the golden dress.

Nyx jerks her hand back, clutching her wrist. Her nails are dull as pebbles, stunted by the resolute gold encasing my body. I pat with my hands along the dark ground, searching for some sort of weapon. My grasping fingers find the handle of Praxidikai.

Nyx sneers and stomps on my arm. A short screech escapes me, my wrist threatening to snap between her heel and the cold stone floor. She snatches up my spear before I can grab it. She stabs both pieces into the earth on either side of my abdomen, caging me in. Tears leak from my eyes, betraying my agony. She bends close, foot still locking my wrist in place. I thrash helplessly beneath her.

She clamps my chin savagely and whispers, "Mortals are loveliest when they meet their demise. Their despair, the agony, the mourning. Like the falling of leaves in autumn, colors red and black, of blood and desolation. You will look just as lovely as you fall."

She lifts her foot and, with my one good arm and leg, I push myself away. I'm out of options and weapons, but I won't die on my back. I climb onto my good leg awkwardly, attempting to look as brave as possible.

"Without the Muses, your plan has failed." I spit, and my blood sprays the dirt at her feet. My death is near. Please let Persephone have spoken true. "The Olympians will be here any moment."

"For a mortal, you've proven remarkably resilient." Nyx studies me, lips puckered into a pout. "Maybe I will enslave your soul. I was a fool to let Ares take on the responsibility of destroying you. He was much too arrogant in thinking it was going to be an easy task."

"So glad I can oblige and be the nuisance you deserve."

She jerks forward. Unthinking, I try to step back. My broken leg betrays me and I fall to the ground with a pained gasp. Agony paralyzes me.

"I'm going to enjoy ripping you apart. And then, when I'm finished, I'm going to find your brothers and do the same to them." Nyx grabs me by the frayed remains of my chiton. She drags me to my feet and slams her forehead into mine. Stars flash behind my eyes before she flings me across the room again. My head cracks on the unforgiving stone ground, and the dark abyss of death flickers across my vision.

In that abyss, I'm presented with a choice. I can hold the flickering dying coals of my soul and breathe life back into them, or I can lose myself to the delicious cold of the encroaching darkness.

I sense the velvety sweetness of Hades. He strokes my cheek and tugs on my hand. Despite the overwhelming pain wracking my entire body, these simple nudges reverberate throughout my entire being.

"Let me die," I beg the god of death.

"Live," Hades whispers. "For Olympus still needs you."

"Daphne!"

Hope flickers inside me. Kleio must have made it safely to Olympus and sent help. I turn toward the sound and the hope immediately dies, snuffed out like a candle. Apollo sprints from the darkness with a bow aimed not at Nyx's heart, but at my own.

Nyx cackles, giddy as she wags a clawed finger at Apollo. "Oh, you vile little ray of sunshine, did you finally decide to abandon your father? Though, I must say, you're quite late to the party."

"Apollo," I choke out, his name escaping my lips.

He pulls the bowstring tighter.

I scan the cave for another weapon at my disposal, but all that the cavern offers are the broken pieces of my *dory*. I glance up toward the sky, desperate for guidance. The barest glimpse of the crescent moon flickers through the fissured ceiling.

I climb atop a trembling knee. My body burns like fire, my soul ignited in a last burst of flame. I cannot trust the gods who betrayed me, left my mother to die, and stole my brother from me. I won't trust the god who ruined a woman's life because she didn't love him back.

I look up again to the moon for answers, curved like the white antlers of a stag, and think of Pyrrhus stuck forever in the body of a deer. His face flickers at the edge of my vision, screaming at me to fight.

I reach high for that crescent moon, embracing the gods' ichor in my veins.

And take up Artemis's bow for myself. The moon becomes solid beneath my trembling fingers. A star elongates and burns in my other hand, transforming into a silver arrow.

The gods will not save me, but I can still save them.

Nyx's grin slips, replaced with a look of mute horror. Even as the loss of blood and venom steal the final moments of my life, I find my words.

"You found pleasure in my pain! You enjoyed watching me fall!" I roar, darkness flooding my vision. "Now watch me rise!"

Apollo fires his arrow just as I aim my own at Nyx's heart and let it soar.

CHAPTER 46

I'm suspended in darkness for a time, painless, bodiless, and lifeless, but not without the agony of a human soul. I struggle against the dark that overtakes me, my movements sluggish and not entirely my own. The bleak abyss drags me deeper still, as if guided by an unseen current.

Out of the oblivion, a flashing light blinds me and fills me with an incendiary heat that pierces what remains of my heart. The firm arms of Hades envelop and carry me, as if I am a child. The pains of my mortal body are gone, mere memories. I move closer into Hades's chest, seeking the warmth emanating from him, carrying me higher and higher.

"Bring Pyr home," I mumble into his hard chest. "I did my part."

"Yes, you have. That and so much more."

A silk rose canopy hangs above my head. A warm breeze tickles my legs, and I tuck them back under the white furs. With a grumble, I cover my face with my hands, willing the light to go away. Another tickle dances up my neck to my earlobe.

"It's time to get up, Daphne. You still owe me another match."

I cannot contain my grin. "Even with half of my legs, I could soundly beat you. Go away, Lykou. I think I've earned about a century's worth of sleep."

He sprawls languidly next to me, legs tangling with mine. I reach a tentative hand out, running a hand up his tan arm to assess for myself that he's real, he's alive—that he's no longer a wolf. With a grin, he pulls me forward, crushing me in a tight embrace.

"Please tell me this isn't a dream," I say into his chest. Tears stream down my cheeks.

"Hugs in bed? Hardly a memorable dream." Persephone grins from the foot of the bed, with Hades's arms wrapped firmly around her shoulders. Demeter stands behind them, smiling down on us.

I push myself up onto stiff elbows before patting my legs with frantic hands, pieced back together with immaculate care. My leg is no longer broken, my ribs no longer hitch and protest with each breath, and the Midas Curse no longer encases my entire body. "How...how am I alive?"

A small smile graces Hades's narrow lips. "I told you before, Daphne. My job is to ensure the fallen continue on to where they need to go. And you needed to come to Olympus."

I look beyond my crowded room to the terrace overlooking a mountainous city filled with pillared palaces. I throw the furs from my body, ready to leap to the terrace and see more. But Lykou presses a firm hand on my chest, keeping me confined to the bed.

"Just as my brother and I are twins, so are our bows." Artemis appears beside Demeter, a vision in a silk, emerald-colored *peplos*. In her hands rests the crescent moon bow, made of blinding silver and thinner than any normal bow. "Mine has the gift to take any life, while Apollo's can give life. When you fell, Apollo struck you with an arrow from his own bow, and so Hades guided your soul to Olympus."

"And Nyx? Is she dead?"

"You destroyed her body." Hades's eyes pass over my face. "But there was no soul to guide."

"A pity," Artemis says. "That witch deserves to rot in Tartarus for all eternity."

"Your father felt the same way," Hades says, turning to his niece with a stern look. "And she managed to escape her prison."

"What of Ares?" I don't want to have the god of war breathing down my neck with thoughts of vengeance. "Hermes?"

"My brothers have fled." A tall goddess steps up to the bedside, bedecked in shining blue armor. She shares her brother's long raven hair, and a small owl is tattooed on her bare left shoulder. Its wings flap, stretching from her ear to her nose, and its head swivels from side to side. Athena continues, head bowed, "You needn't worry yourself over Ares, nor Hermes. I can always find my brothers, and I will." Without any further words, Athena gives the room a sweeping bow before storming away, sword already unsheathed.

"So melodramatic." A mahogany curl dangles in front of Artemis's eyes as she watches Athena's departing back.

"She's never been one to simply stop and enjoy the moment," Persephone adds.

"She gets that from her father." An unfamiliar woman sweeps into my room, dressed in a purple silk chiton, with gold and peacock feathers adorning her long black hair. Hera's narrow, deeply tanned face shows no hint of gratitude nor warmth.

"If you're finished wasting my family's time," she snaps, her deep-set amethyst eyes cold, "You'll find my husband waiting for you in the pantheon." I don't miss Hades's grimace or the infinitesimal worried glance between Artemis and Persephone. Hera sweeps from the room in a flurry of lavender silk and streaming black hair.

Demeter shakes her head at the Queen of Olympus's turned back. "Don't take the slights of Hera to heart, Daphne." She reaches across the furs, cupping my face in one of her warm hands. "She is a proud woman, and though relieved to be free, she is still a mother before all else. Despite the sins of Ares, Hera will continue to love him."

I crawl from the wide bed, finding myself dressed in a shimmery ivory chiton. With Lykou striding at my side and an assortment of gods behind me, I stride through the halls of Olympus, looking for the one god who was by my side even to the end.

Apollo waits for me in the pantheon, sitting atop a white marble throne and pulling distractedly at the gold filigree hem of his ruby-colored chiton. Thrones for fourteen gods and goddesses surround him, high pillars to house their heated discussions, and enclosed by towering oaks.

Lykou steps up beside me, and I take his reassuring hand. The gods and goddesses flow like a current past us to take up their seats. Zeus, the monarch of the gods, a bigger and burlier replica of his son, watches me with hooded eyes from the center throne. On Zeus's right is the empty seat of his brother Poseidon, and to his left is his wife Hera, resting her chin on a clenched fist. Athena and Demeter confer together in hushed tones next to Hera, and beside them sits the stunning Aphrodite. Opposite, Artemis and Apollo flash me smiles and nods of encouragement, the empty seat of Hermes between them. Rounding out the seats are Dionysus and Hephaestus. Persephone and Hades stand to the side, while Zeus's sister Hestia stokes the hearth in the center of the pantheon.

I saved these gods and goddesses, protected and reclaimed the source of their power, but I also committed a number of sins on this path. Though the gods are great, they are also righteous. I promised to help a sworn enemy of Zeus, the titan Prometheus, on his path to freedom. I stabbed two gods, and killed the sons of Ares, and possibly have not been as discreet or respectful in my comments about the gods as I could have been.

And I died.

But will my life be payment enough to free me from their servitude?

CHAPTER 47

I command myself to betray no fear. Squaring my shoulders and clenching my fists, I look down my nose at the gods and goddesses who appraise and judge me. Lykou likewise stands to attention, back rigid.

Zeus shares the same unreadable gaze of his son, and like his wife, he rests his chin on a fist. When he speaks, his words roll across the pantheon like an oncoming storm, low and dangerous like thunder. The flames of the hearth flicker in their wake.

"Time has his eyes on you, Daphne."

I blink once, twice, and then a third time. Those were hardly the words I was expecting from the king of Olympus. Hands clenched behind my back, I choke out, "What does that mean?"

"The goddess Nyx is far from destroyed. I have no doubt that her machinations against my family have only begun." Zeus leans back, rubbing a large thumb across his brow. "My father and Nyx were once allies, and since the day I smote Cronus, we have held a tentative truce. I have no idea why she decided to betray said truce and declare war on Olympus, but we will no doubt find out.

"With Ares and Hermes vanished, Nyx merely wounded"—he hesitates, gripping the arms of his throne hard enough to crack the marble—"the balance between men and gods is fragile. Their love and worship is waning.

"Olympus needs you, Daphne," Zeus continues, "Will you take up your birthright and become the Storm of Olympus?"

My hands clench and unclench behind my back; a drop of sweat slides down my spine. I throw back my shoulders. "Have I not sacrificed enough for the gods?"

"We will give you the means to become the greatest warrior Sparta will ever know." Zeus waves a hand in the air, swords, spears, helmets, and armor appearing and disappearing above the hearth.

"I am already a great warrior."

"You would be dead without the blood of my family," Zeus says, lips pulled back to bare his teeth. "The ichor running in your very veins."

"As would be the Garden of the Hesperides, and all of your powers lost." I wave an arm to all the gods, sitting atop their marble thrones.

The gods exchange uneasy glances. Zeus's eyes harden at my words. A rumble of thunder stirs in the distance, and the hair on my arms stands on end. I hold my chin higher.

"Nyx is still loose on the world." He points a finger at my heart. The sky darkens suddenly, angry black clouds swirling above to block out the sun's light. "And she will come for you before any of us. Accept my offer, and it will be an alliance of equal benefit to both of us. We will equip you, train you, and empower you to take on the goddess of night...but only if you agree to become our emissary to the realm of men."

Though I have gathered a newfound respect for the powers these gods wield, I cannot help but still doubt their intentions. I resist looking to Apollo and Artemis, my hand moving to where the crow necklace once hung on my neck.

I look to Lykou. He knows firsthand what it is to be punished by the gods. He meets my eyes and gives my hand a gentle squeeze.

For him and Pyrrhus and Ligeia and all of Sparta, I will continue to play their games. Because, whether I accept Zeus's offer, Nyx's war will come for them.

"Promise to no longer include my family and friends in your games—" I hesitate, the words caught in the back of my throat. "And I will agree to be your emissary."

Zeus smiles and the clouds dissipate.

"Daphne?"

I spin around at the sound of my name, tears immediately spilling down my cheeks.

Pyrrhus runs forward, sweeping me off my feet in a great hug. He is human, whole and unharmed. His fiery curls tickle my nose as he sets me down, eyes wet with unshed tears. "I knew you could do it."

"I've missed you," I say, choking back more tears. "I can't believe you're alive."

When Pyrrhus releases me, Persephone and Hades are the first to step forward. With warm smiles, they hold out their clasped hands in front of me. My eyes widen as they each drop stones in my palms, one a dark onyx and the other the color of a golden sunflower; both are warm and comforting to the touch.

"They are tokens," Hades explains. "Reminders of the debt that we owe you, and should you ever need that debt fulfilled, all you have to do is blow on the stones."

"Thank you," I whisper.

I receive Athena next. She towers over me. She bends at the waist, allowing me to meet eye to eye with the blue owl on her shoulder. "You may ask anything of the owl, a single question. This is the greatest gift I can ever bestow, a gift of infinite knowledge."

Before I can think of anything to ask, Athena straightens. "But not now. Wait until you have absolute need for a question answered, otherwise you would waste such an opportunity."

Demeter gives me a stone much like Persephone and Hades's, this one the color of the brightest poppy. "I know how much you love your people, so take this stone and bury it deep in the fields of Sparta. This will ensure plentiful harvests for many years to come."

Aphrodite stands next, dainty nose pinched in a disdainful sniff. She tosses her long, ebony hair over a shoulder, eyes scathing as they strip me bare, right down to my soul. The withering glare the goddess of sexuality bequeaths me is hardly amorous.

"I owe you nothing," she hisses, trouncing from the pantheon. Hera shares much of the same sentiment, following without any acknowledgment of my existence.

Dionysus saunters forward next, sloshing a bejeweled *kylix* of wine before my nose. "Take a sip, Daphne, and forgive their behavior. Their love of Ares and Hermes clouds their judgment."

A deep gulp of wine passes the back of my throat and warmth radiates throughout my core.

Hephaestus promises to forge weapons and armor tailored specifically to me. Artemis makes no promises and bestows no gifts. But with a small smile, I know that she will always be my ally.

Then, wings tucked close to his side, a familiar face drifts between the gods to stand before me. I don't miss the distrustful glares Artemis and her father throw his way, or the baleful glance Aphrodite spares him.

Small bats flutter around his head in a spiraling crown. One will occasionally land on his brow, becoming one with his skin like the tattoos of Ares and Hermes. His long dark hair is parted down the middle, hanging over his shoulders. Crow's feet still edge at the corners of his eyes, and he still smells of the sea cave in which we first met. He smiles widely, placing a wrinkled hand over one of my own. "We haven't had a chance to meet yet. You may call me Hypnos." He tilts his head, considering me. "My mother will be cross when she learns of my betrayal, but it was necessary."

"You're Nyx's son." Shock roots me to the ground. "You would betray your own mother to help me?"

"To help Olympus." Hypnos waves an arm to the gathered gods, ruffling his feathers with the movement. "You had to know of Hermes's betrayal, and Ares's wrath. Otherwise you would have handed those Muses straight to the god of war."

"Why not show Zeus?" I ask. "Why not tell Hera, Hades, or Poseidon? Why not stop your mother?"

"My power is nothing compared to hers, and do you really think they would believe the son of their greatest enemy?" Hypnos shakes his head. "No, they would have been just as unlikely to believe me as Apollo was that morning on the Aegean."

Apollo has the good sense to look ashamed.

"It had to be you," he says, pointing a long, wizened finger.

"If you can control my dreams, why didn't you stop Nyx from entering mine? Or Theseus's?" Saying my ally's name sparks a sharp pain in my chest.

Hypnos laughs. "Who do you think taught the naiades that magic?"

I blink. "I...thank you."

"You're very welcome, *kataigída*," Hypnos says. "I will leave you to your other admirers now, but expect me to come to you again to return the favor."

He turns, disappearing among the crowd of Olympians and, before

I have even a moment to process his words, nine Muses descend upon me. Happy, giddy, and very much alive.

They crowd me, cooing and hugging, kissing my cheek and exclaiming, showering me with thanks and affections, all home and unharmed. I tell myself to make Apollo promise to teach these women how to protect themselves.

Kleio places in my cradling hands their expression of gratitude: an apple, gold and unblemished. The hair on the back of my neck stands high as a ripple of nervous energy courses through me.

Ligeia told me many things about the golden apples of the Hesperides. Not only do they grant immortality, but they can also bring much devastation. Chaos likely bides her time, waiting to stir trouble anew. Having an apple in my possession, I would be in control of the fate of the entire world. Again.

I want to shove the apple back at Kleio, but with the gods and Muses watching me so closely, I can do nothing but give her a forced smile of gratitude. Meeting Apollo's eyes over the heads of the Muses, the wariness in them tells me he feels my plight.

This is a gift not to be taken for granted.

I am weighed down with gifts and praises as Zeus leads me to the gates. We walk slowly down the marble-paved path, lined with myriad different trees. Some are as tall as the clouds and reach long, spindly branches toward the sun. Others are short and softer than the fur of a fox. Beyond the line of trees, I pass next through the curved golden gates of Olympus. Lykou and Pyr begin their descent from Mount Olympus ahead of us, chatting amiably.

"Wait!" I spin to face the ruler of Olympus. "Have I not earned some honesty from you?"

Zeus gives me a look of mock disappointment. "I have been nothing but honest with you."

"Then tell me who my father is." I stand with him, toe to toe, daring him to refuse. "At which Olympian's feet can I place the death of my mother?"

"Your father"—Zeus looks back through the golden gates, to the towering palaces beyond—"is not of Olympus."

I blink, taking a step back. "What?"

"But that doesn't mean that you don't belong here," Zeus says, waving a hand toward his home. "I may not be able to tell you who your father is, but I can tell you that you come from a considerable power, and my family will have need of you in the coming years."

He turns to leave and I dare the fates by grabbing his *peplos*. "You must tell me more. A place, a name, anything."

"I cannot." He pries my hand from his clothes. "You must learn that for yourself, which you will. Sooner than you think, I'm sure."

I can only nod, biting my tongue to hold back the arguments waiting there.

"I will see you again, Daphne." With a small wink, Zeus leaves me at the gate with Apollo.

He and I stare at each other for much longer than we should. I want to hug him close, inhaling that cedarwood scent deep enough to sear into my soul as my lips crush his. I force another smile, barely restraining myself from leaping into his arms.

"Apollo..." After everything, I still cannot believe that we've made it, that we've survived with body and soul intact.

He brushes a thumb along my jaw. My heart flutters in my chest. His eyes close and face dips toward mine.

There are still so many questions left unanswered, about my heritage, about Princess Koronis, about what he wants from me.

"I cannot let you destroy me," I whisper.

Apollo jerks back as if stung. "I thought we were past this, Daphne."

"Not like Koronis." My lips tremble. "Why didn't you tell me about her?"

His hands drop to his sides. "Koronis died hundreds of years ago."

"You brought an entire kingdom to its ruin because that woman had the audacity to not return your love." I shake my head. "What would you do to Sparta should I do the same?"

"But you do." Apollo closes the space between us, cupping my face between my hands. "You do love me."

Tears stream down my cheeks. "No, Apollo. I fell in love with you as a human, not as this. Not as the god that can bring my world to its knees should I refuse you."

I place my hands on his chest, warm, hard, and smelling deeply of cedarwood, and push him away. What trust we spent the summer building with each other is now lost.

"I can't ignore your history." A sob wrenches from my chest. "And I can't trust you."

"What can I do?" His eyes, so unbelievably blue, are beseeching. "Tell me what I need to do in order to earn your trust again."

I shake my head. My voice is barely even a whisper when I say, "I don't know."

"Well, until you know"—he brushes my curls from my face—"I will be waiting."

"And until then, I will see you when the gods decide to use me again." Without a second glance, I turn around, following Lykou and Pyrrhus down the mountain.

I could betray myself and take a bite of that golden apple, granting myself an eternity to live, fight, love, and rebuild that trust beside Apollo. Through this journey I have learned that the fire is inside me, and that the fire he stokes in me is too dangerous for my mortal soul.

I have no need for more charred bones and scorched hearts.

EPILOGUE

Autumn arrives with bitter winds and golden leaves.

I kneel in the center of Sparta's withered crops, indifferent to the mud staining my knees. Ligeia will make me clean my muddied clothes later, but it can't be anything like scrubbing the blood of Ares's son.

Ligeia was beside herself upon my return to Sparta. Lykou, Pyrrhus, and I snuck into the city in the dark of night like guilty thieves. As if awaiting our return, Ligeia met us at the city gates, dismissing our pathetic excuses.

When I left Sparta, she had excused Lykou's and Pyrrhus's extended absences on a matter of importance with King Menelaus, and mine on a pilgrimage to give thanks for winning *Carneia*. Too low to be missed by the monarchy, but with an excuse that demanded secrecy, our absence had gone unquestioned by our family and few friends.

Alkaios had also been suspicious upon our return, though he tried to hide it behind wide smiles. In his dark eyes many questions remain unasked and unanswered, but he remains silent on the curious matter of our absence. Though grateful for his unusual tact and reticence, it doesn't escape my notice the ways in which he congratulates Pyrrhus for completing a matter of such importance for the king and only rewards me with a look of begrudging respect. Once this would have stoked my temper, and I may have even snapped at him for it, but now I understand his reluctance to show me affection.

Not only had he been forced to step into the father figure role for both Pyrrhus and me, at the tender age of six, but he had also been forced to embrace the fact that we do not share a father. We will never share the familial camaraderie that Pyrrhus shares with us both, and I've finally come to accept that.

After a restless first night back in my own bed—much too comfortable compared to the rough roads of Greece—I wake up early. The golden light of dawn lights my path, the rising sun alighting upon the gold line stretched taut across my abdomen from hip to opposite shoulder. The remnant of the Midas Curse is a permanent reminder that I have yet to leave the service of the gods. Though still and lifeless now, I'm not foolish enough to believe that it can't be reanimated once again.

Sparta's fields are desolate and dry, my feet cracking the parched earth with each step. Kneeling with Demeter's stone cradled in my palm, I still have no energy nor desire to curse the gods that firmly hold my life in their hands. Ligeia told Pyr and me last night that most of Greece's crops suffered this summer, and I wish I had more than one of Demeter's stones to share. But for now, before I make any demands of Olympus, I resign myself to being content with Sparta's illustrious future harvest.

I dig deep beneath the earth as the sun inches its way across the horizon along its correct trajectory, clawing into the dirt and tearing away the roots and muck. With earthen clay beneath my nails and dust up to my elbows, I drop to my knees into a hole reaching my high waist, making quick work before the harvesters come out to see the damage I've done. Once I am assured that I've dug deep enough for the stone to never be unearthed, I gently press it into the soil with a thumb.

The earth beneath my knees begins to stir and awaken, the powers of Demeter stretching beneath the surface with gentle hands to prod her plants to life. With a soft smile, I climb to my feet. It is useless to brush off the muck from my chiton; I am covered in dirt, caking my skin and clothes from chin to toes.

With a sigh, I turn to climb out of the hole. "I should have known you would follow me."

A tan hand awaits me, outstretched and offering to help pull me out. My smile widens as I peer into Alkaios's face, his smile matching my own. I accept the hand gratefully, reflecting upon the smooth curves of his brow, the smile he and I share. "I'm sure you have lots of questions."

"None that cannot wait until you're ready to answer them honestly," he says.

I return to my work, not protesting when he bends to help me. We push the dirt into the hole, burying Demeter's stone and all traces of my activity as the early morning mist rises around us.

When finished, I lead Alkaios through the fields toward the Taygetus forest. As we pass through the first line of trees, I remember vividly the last time I pushed aside these branches. The screams and cheers of *Carneia* will forever echo in my memory.

If asked, I would take Pyrrhus's place again. No matter the cost. I clutch at the space above my heart, mouth upturned in a hopeful smile.

I would still do it all again.

AUTHOR'S NOTE

Stories take on a different meaning depending on who is turning the pages. When I first started writing Daphne's story, my goal was to bring to light the often-underappreciated women of Greek myth and history—I wanted to give these women the stories they deserved. Gone are the jealous wives and damsels—here are strong, nuanced women who tell their own stories. Women in ancient Greece were allowed very few, if any liberties; places like Sparta, where they were allowed many more privileges and rights, were the exception, and make for some exciting storytelling, both in historic and contemporary writing.

In my effort to bring these stories to light, I have had to adopt a bit of creative license with the mythological timelines. Theseus did not die by Minos's hand, but instead by the king of Scyros, Lycomedes. Oedipus, not Daphne, outwitted the Sphinx of Thebes. Nisaea was never swept into the sea and *Carneia* is believed to actually take place in the late summer or early fall. But that is the beauty of myths, stories that are ever changing—we can take from them what is most relevant to us personally, and revel in the fantasy. Students and scholars of ancient Greece will likely do much hand-wringing, some sighing, and possibly a bit of eye-rolling as they follow Daphne's journey. For that, though, I offer no apology except to say that history is often said to be written by the victors, usually men, and Daphne has won this particular battle.

My own personal Greek mythology journey began as a child with the timeless *D'Aulaire's Book of Greek Myths* by Ingri and Edgar Parin d'Aulaire. However, many books, essays, and articles have supplemented my research for Daphne's story. Endless thanks to *Ancient Greek Civilization* by David Sansone, *The History and Culture of Ancient Sparta* from Charles River Editors, *Soldiers and Ghosts* by J. E. Lendon, *The Greek Myths* by Robert Graves, *The Spartans* by Paul Cartledge, *The Archaeology of Greece* by William R. Biers, "Ideology and 'the Status of Women' in Ancient Greece" by Marilyn Katz, "The Rise of Women in Ancient Greece" by Michael Scott, *The Rise of the Greeks* by Michael Grant, and *The Landmark Xenophon's Hellenika* and *The Landmark Thucydides*, both edited by Robert B. Strassler.

GREEK GLOSSARY

aeráki—breeze

agon—competition

agora—designated part of the city where merchants could sell wares and civic announcements were made

ánandros—Greek insult. One who is craven or cowardly

anassa—queen

anax—king/emperor/tribal leader

auloi—double-reed flute

Carneia—festival in Sparta held in honor of Apollo

chiton—a single rectangle of woolen or linen fabric that is either wrapped or tied around the body

chlamys—a short cloak that was draped over the tops of one's arms and pinned at the right shoulder. Most commonly worn by men

cithara—a professional version of the two-stringed lyre

dioikitís—general

dory—a three-meter-long spear used by the infantry of Spartan soldiers. Commonly made with wood, it often had an iron spearhead and a bronze butt-spike

ephor—an elected Spartan politician

gymnasion—the gymnastic school in which Grecians practiced a number of physical activities and trained. Mostly found in Sparta

himation—a heavier, much larger cloak than the *chlamys*. Worn by both sexes. Could be used as both a cloak, or in the absence of a chiton, wrapped around the body and over shoulders

Hyacinthia—three-day festival in Sparta celebrating Spartan heroes, particularly in war

kakos—coward

kalyptra—a thin headdress worn as a veil

kataigída—storm

kepos—cultivated bit of land between houses, much like a garden or yard. Often sacred to the household

kerykeion—a caduceus/staff

kline—couch, much like a lounge chair.

koprophage—insult; a person who eats dung.

kosmetikos—makeup/cosmetics

kothornoi/kothornos—high-laced sandal/boot with thick soles that often went as high as the knee

kottabos—ancient Greek drinking game

kuna—an explicit curse word

kylix—a wine-drinking cup

lambda—the letter lambda (Λ), standing for Laconia or Lacedaemon, which was painted on the Spartans' shields

lyre—a small U-shaped harp with strings fixed to a crossbar.

meander—also known as the "Greek key." A pattern typically found among frescoes, jewelry, or along the hemlines of clothes worn by royalty

Mesogeios—Mediterranean Sea

Mothakes—social class of people in Greece; "Non-Spartan." Not allowed many of the same civil rights as full Spartans, but still allowed many liberties

ochre—powder makeup for the eyelids and cheeks

paidonomos—the headmaster of Spartan military training

pantheon—domed, circular temple

peplos—full-length dress that hangs loosely around the shoulders and is tied loosely around the waist

petteia—game similar to checkers, chess, and backgammon

pithos—large jar often used as a storage container

prodótis—traitor

pyxis—a cylindrical box with a separate lid

rhomphaia—falchion

salphinx—trumpet

Spartiates—males of Sparta with full citizenship

suagroi—person with a romantic attachment to pigs

symmachos—ally

ACKNOWLEDGMENTS

This book was born in the pages of my childhood. It wouldn't be here without my ingrained love of reading and Greek mythology.

For that, I have to thank my mum, Sheila, for handing me my first book of Greek mythology so many years ago. Thank you for encouraging my love of stories, and for guiding and holding my hand on this seemingly endless journey. More than anyone, this novel is thanks to you.

Thank you to Scott, who brought me to Greece for the first time. I loved bringing our time as a family in the ruins of Knossos to these pages. I hope we can all return to Crete soon. Thank you to Charlotte, the best sister in the world, for indulging my love of walking. All my best plotting for this story was done on our *very long* walks around the Highlands.

To my Alaskan family, for your love and unerring faith in me and this journey, especially my wonderful, supportive Nana and Grandma. I would still be a wild child without you amazing ladies.

To Bunny, for your infinite wisdom and encouragement. To Amy, for your laughter and friendship, and for letting me spend months parked in Barristers eating all your chocolate and drinking all your coffee while I wrote the first draft of Daphne's story. To my favorite yogi, Molly, the first person I told when I got the call and who I can always count on for words of wisdom. To Autumn, cousin through thick and thin, and my greatest cheerleader. To Elliott, who always had sage advice when I needed it the most.

To the brilliant Professor Erica Hill, for indulging me in my love of Greek archaeology, and for encouraging me to follow my passion and dreams. The world needs more teachers like you.

Boundless thanks to my critique partners, early readers, and fellow authors. This would not have been possible without all of you: Ellie M., Carly H., Diana U., Katy P., Mike C., Rosiee T., Laura N., Rose D., Katie M., Hershey, Wendy G., Carol H., and Rifka. Your invaluable advice and support is what brought this book to life.

Endless gratitude to my wonderful editor, T.S., for your unerring faith in Daphne's story. Your brilliant insights really made this story shine brighter than the dawn of Eos. To the Jimmy Team—Jenny Bak, Laura Schreiber, Caitlyn Averett, Erinn McGrath, Josh Johns, Daniel Denning, Charlotte LaMontagne, Flo Yue, Jordan Mondell, Liam Donnelly, Scott Bryan Wilson, Tracy Shaw, Blue Guess and Alexis Lassiter, Shawn Foster, Danielle Cantarella, Ned Rust, Linda Arends, Janelle DeLuise, and, finally, Jimmy Patterson—thank you from the bottom of my heart for taking a chance on Daphne and me, and bringing this story into the hands of readers.

A million thanks to my magical agent, Amy Elizabeth Bishop. I truly could not have asked for a better champion. Thank you for your wisdom, patience, and excitement for this book. To Lauren Abramo, for bringing this book around the world.

To Nizhoni and Mazel Tuff, who deserve all the salmon and cuddles.

Finally, to Zach, the love of my life, a bajillion thanks for your unfailing support and wisdom. I wouldn't trade anything in the world for the priceless laughter, joy, and warmth you bring to every day of my life.